More praise for
How Will I Know You?

"A set of complex character sketches revealing deep flaws and human weaknesses but also examining how people live with their most devastating mistakes...Nuanced, probing, and honest. Well worth a read." —Kirkus

"Sometimes a book pulls you in so deep that it's hard to let go. HOW WILL I KNOW YOU? is such a book. A mystery story, yes, but more than that, a compassionate, wise study of humans under pressure. I read furiously to find out the truth about the central crime, and I read slowly to savor Treadway's many stunning insights. A wondrous book!" —Robin Black, author of *Life Drawing* and *If I Loved You, I Would Tell You This*

"An amazingly written and intense novel, an outstanding thriller with a wonderful plot and memorable characters." —*BookReporter*

"In this exceptional novel by Treadway, no one is safe from the secrets and lies that prevail in the small town where Joy's body is found...[Treadway's] ability to define meaningful characters stands out, and the ending is a shock." —*RT Book Reviews*

Praise for *Lacy Eye*

"Deftly plotted...Treadway paints a devastating portrait of a family torn apart from both the outside and within." —*Publishers Weekly*

"It's been a long time since I've read a novel at once this gripping, and this wise, and psychologically complex. As a portrait of motherhood, and an exploration of the limits of knowledge—of others, of one's self—LACY EYE probes, devastates, and informs."

—Elizabeth Graver, author of *The End of the Point*

"An intricately plotted psychological thriller."

—*The Chicago Tribune*

"Perhaps there's always something inexplicable about evil but at the heart of Jessica Treadway's new novel is a woman who is determined not to explain it at almost any cost. I defy anyone to read these beautifully written, brilliantly observed pages without becoming deeply involved in Hanna's life and her choices. LACY EYE is a wonderful, and deeply suspenseful novel."

—Margot Livesey, author of *The Flight of Gemma Hardy*

"Since her debut story collection *Absent Without Leave*, came out in 1992, Jessica Treadway has wowed critics with resonant depictions of flawed, all-too-human characters."

—*The Boston Globe*

"Quietly disturbing...nail-bitingly suspenseful."

—*The Columbus Dispatch*

"Complex and nuanced...an author to watch."

—*Reviewing the Evidence*

"Treadway is a deft hand at crafting complex mysteries...asks provocative questions."   —The Reading Nook

How Will I Know You?

ALSO BY JESSICA TREADWAY

Lacy Eye
Please Come Back to Me
And Give You Peace
Absent Without Leave and Other Stories

HOW WILL I KNOW YOU?

A *novel*

Jessica Treadway

GRAND CENTRAL
PUBLISHING

NEW YORK   BOSTON

This book is a work of fiction. Names, characters, places, and incidents are the product of the author's imagination or are used fictitiously. Any resemblance to actual events, locales, or persons, living or dead, is coincidental.

Copyright © 2016 by Jessica Treadway
Cover design by Claire Brown
Photography by Todd Hido
Cover copyright © 2016 by Hachette Book Group, Inc.

Hachette Book Group supports the right to free expression and the value of copyright. The purpose of copyright is to encourage writers and artists to produce the creative works that enrich our culture.

The scanning, uploading, and distribution of this book without permission is a theft of the author's intellectual property. If you would like permission to use material from the book (other than for review purposes), please contact permissions@hbgusa.com. Thank you for your support of the author's rights.

Grand Central Publishing
Hachette Book Group
1290 Avenue of the Americas
New York, NY 10104
grandcentralpublishing.com
twitter.com/grandcentralpub

Originally published in hardcover and ebook by Grand Central Publishing December 2016

First Trade Paperback Edition: August 2017

Grand Central Publishing is a division of Hachette Book Group, Inc.
The Grand Central Publishing name and logo is a trademark of Hachette Book Group, Inc.

The publisher is not responsible for websites (or their content) that are not owned by the publisher.

The Hachette Speakers Bureau provides a wide range of authors for speaking events. To find out more, go to www.hachettespeakersbureau.com or call (866) 376-6591.

Library of Congress Cataloging-in-Publication Data
Names: Treadway, Jessica, 1961- author.
Title: How will I know you? : a novel / Jessica Treadway.
Description: First edition. | New York : Grand Central Publishing, 2016.
Identifiers: LCCN 2016022956 | ISBN 9781455554119 (hardcover) | ISBN
    9781478927198 (audio download) | ISBN 9781455554102 (ebook)
Subjects: LCSH: Teenage girls—Crimes against—Fiction. |
    Murder—Investigation—Fiction. | City and town life—Fiction. | BISAC:
    FICTION / Family Life. | GSAFD: Mystery fiction.
Classification: LCC PS3620.R43 H69 2016 | DDC 813/.6—dc23 LC record available at
https://lccn.loc.gov/2016022956

ISBN: 978-1-4555-5409-6 (trade paperback)

Printed in the United States of America

LSC-C

10 9 8 7 6 5 4 3 2 1

To Sadie Johnson,
beloved niece since 22:22, 02/02/02—
Sadie Sue, this one's for you

*Truth, that lasting joy, fills in all that
is missing.*

—*Auguste Rodin*

After

Black, Maybe?

Two days after a snowshoeing couple literally stumbled across Joy's body in the woods at the edge of the pond, the police came to ask Harper questions. It was the first Sunday in December, and her father had gone to work as he often did on the weekends—"to catch up," he always told them, but Harper believed it was just an excuse to get himself out of the house. There was nothing to catch up on. He supervised production at a jigsaw puzzle plant.

The officers rang the doorbell just before noon. "Get that, will you?" her mother called from her bedroom. "I'm in the middle of a thought." Harper waited for her brother to go to the door, because he was closer, but he muttered "You do it" and she knew he was afraid to leave his game, so she went to answer the bell herself. When she called back upstairs that it was the police, her mother said to wait a minute, then came down in jeans and a misbuttoned cardigan, her face streaked with makeup she'd obviously rubbed on without looking.

"I'm not sure I want you to talk to my daughter when my husband isn't here," she told the interim chief, who had been on the news so often in the past month, since the night they'd conducted the first dive to search for Joy under the ice at Elbow Pond.

"She's not in trouble, Mrs. Grove." The chief was standing closer to Harper than to her mother, and his eyes were so blue that Harper thought he must have worn tinted contacts. Armstrong, Harper remembered his name was. The eyes made her just as nervous today as they had the first time, when he came to interview her about Joy's disappearance. "We're just trying to piece together what happened that day."

"I thought you already talked to her about that."

"Some new information has come to light," said the other officer, whom Harper remembered from the day they came to arrest Zach Tully at school. He was even older than the chief, and he offered her a lemon drop as he took one out for himself.

Harper declined the candy and told her mother it was fine, she wanted to help, and she sat down on one end of the couch, gesturing for the men and her mother to take seats, too. She could tell that Truman was listening from the dining room—he slapped the cards down on the table more softly than usual—and she could tell that the officers noticed the condition of the tree in the corner, which had been up since before Thanksgiving. Their mother always got what she called an early dose of the Christmas spirit, and every year she managed to persuade Harper's father to find a tree lot that would sell to them before it officially opened. She spent the whole afternoon decorating, and by the next morning she seemed to have forgotten all about it. The tree was always ready to go out the door in the middle of December, but they kept it around until after New Year's, when her mother would finally allow the rest of them to undecorate, and her father and Truman carried it to the curb.

Before the questioning could begin, a sudden, random piano chord made them all turn toward the sound in the corner across from the tree, where an old upright sat against the wall. Her mother sucked her breath in and put a hand to her heart. "Get off," Harper said sharply to the cat, who'd caused the disturbance by jumping onto the keys. Chip leapt down and scrabbled out of the room.

In some ways Harper was sorry the cat cooperated; she would have liked to stall further, if she could. The chief began asking Harper the questions she remembered from the day after Joy disappeared. She grew confused, unsure as to why he wanted her to repeat what she'd told him then. The familiar flush of embarrassment—from not knowing the right thing to say, or from saying the right thing the wrong way—began at her temples, spread down her cheeks to her neck and beyond, to the point that she imagined her lungs and legs bloomed as hot and red as her face. It made her look as if she were lying, she knew. Or at least holding something back.

They asked what she'd seen. She pulled her favorite afghan around herself and watched another needle fall from the dark and dying tree. "I already told you." Saying this gave her an unfamiliar thrill of defiance and she waited for a rebuke, but the chief only shifted in his seat. Harper elaborated, "Kids skating, mothers standing around."

They weren't writing anything down, as Armstrong had the first time. "We're talking about what you saw at the *shack*," the officer sucking the lemon drop said, and though she sensed he was trying to hide his impatience, she heard it come out in a little cluck of his tongue.

She wanted to say *Why are you treating me this way?* But instead she just blushed some more and said she was sorry.

Armstrong waved at his partner to shut up. He leaned closer to Harper on the couch, and in a tone they all recognized as self-consciously casual, he asked if she had noticed a man with a mask.

"A mask?" All she could think of was Eric Feinbloom trying to pull off the Joker costume at the Halloween party. He'd tried so hard it made Harper's heart hurt.

"You know, a ski mask. Black, maybe?"

She hesitated. "Black mask or black man?"

He hesitated back. "Both."

Why that moment before he answered? she wondered. Were they trying to trick her somehow?

But then she saw Lemon Drop touch the gun at his hip (was it a habit, or did he really think he might need to use it, here in their living room?) and pull back in his seat a little. A meek signal to his superior, she thought—they're not supposed to feed people clues. She had watched enough police shows to understand that.

"There was a black man," she said.

"Was it this guy?" The chief reached into his pocket and pulled out a photograph.

"Yes," she answered. "That's him."

Armstrong asked, "Where was he?" and she saw that they were both trying not to act too excited, which caused the confusion to swell around her like a steadily rising sound. "In the crook? Where we found her?" Everyone who'd grown up around there would know what he was talking about—the crook of the elbow that gave the pond its name.

"No. He was outside the shack, in his car."

"Just sitting there?"

She nodded.

"And he had a mask on?"

She sensed her mother's eyes on her, fresh with a focus Harper hadn't felt in a long time. She nodded again, understanding that she'd just crossed a line she had not seen coming. Before now she'd never known how good recklessness could feel.

"What did the mask look like?"

Harper's mother leaned forward and said, "You already said it was a ski mask. Is this really necessary?"

The chief ignored her, not even turning her way. "Did he stay there?" he asked Harper. "Or did he drive off?"

"Drove off." She felt relieved to say it; this part was true.

In a louder voice Harper's mother said, "Are you almost finished? She just found out her best friend was murdered. Hasn't she been through enough?"

Again the little electric thrill to Harper's heart. And again Armstrong persisting as if he hadn't heard her. "We understand there was an argument," he said to Harper. "Before you went up to the shack to use the pay phone. Can you tell us what it was about?"

She shook her head. "No," she said in the small voice she hated but couldn't seem to grow. This was where she would fail them, she knew. This was where they would get mad. She knew the answer all too well—the argument she remembered better than she wished to—but something (loyalty to Joy? Did it matter if you were disloyal to someone who was dead?) kept her from telling them what she'd seen and heard.

"Really? Why not?" It was a new line of questioning. The first day, when he believed along with everyone else that Joy had drowned, the chief had asked just a few things, acting as if Harper's answers weren't important. Now that they knew she'd been murdered, he paid more attention. "Was it about drugs?"

When she looked down at her lap and shook her head again, he sighed. "We were hoping you might do your best to come up with something to help us. If you don't mind my saying, you don't seem all that sad about this. I thought she was your best friend."

Was. *Was your best friend.* Of course he used the past tense because she was dead, but he didn't know that the past tense had begun before that.

"Did anyone threaten her? Maybe one of the other girls?"

In her memory, Harper heard *Try again, you'll be sorry.* "No. Not threaten."

Her mother told the officers, "I think that's enough now."

They stood and said thank you. In the dining room, Harper heard the familiar sound of Truman scooping up his cards in frustration, because he'd lost again. She watched the officers from the window, grateful that they'd come in a regular car—"unmarked" was the word, she knew from TV. She hadn't helped at all, she was sure, except that they'd seemed to like it when she agreed with them that she'd seen the black man wearing a mask outside the shack that day.

"Do you want to go somewhere?" she said to her mother. "Maybe Christmas shopping?" *Since you're awake, and dressed, and upright?* She knew better, but asked anyway.

"Maybe later." Her mother gestured toward her bedroom. "I was just trying out a new idea. I should get back to it." *It*, Harper knew, was the notebook she kept on her nightstand, which she filled with scribbles before transferring them onto her laptop. In November she'd joined an online group of people who all wanted to write a novel in a month, and except for the night Joy disappeared, she spent most of her time working on what she called a literary thriller, only to throw the notebook away a few days after Thanksgiving and send Truman out for a new one.

"I think I might be on to something this time," her mother added, heading up the stairs. Truman had dealt himself another game. Alone in the living room, Harper began to straighten the star at the top of the tree, then gave up and let it droop back to its original crooked position. If no one else cared, why should she?

Condition White

Tom kept the sound on the TV muted because next to him Alison was asleep when the news came on. In the middle of the top story (BREAKING was all the crawl said, as if the item were so momentous it defied detail, which, as it turned out, it was), he made a sharp movement in the bed and Alison woke up murmuring, "What?"

She was already agitated because it was Sunday night, and though she'd been teaching for three years now—not to mention in the same classroom she and Tom had shared for homeroom all through high school—the beginning of a new week always made her nervous. She just wanted to stay home and bake holiday cookies, she said. ("What the hell is a holiday cookie?" her father had asked, and Alison told him it was more politically correct than *Christmas*. "Oh, for sweet Christ's sake," Doug groaned, giving her remark a dismissive wave, and Alison laughed with affection.)

"Hold on," Tom told her, turning up the volume.

"What is it?" She struggled to raise herself, her flannel nightgown bunching around her chest above the growing moonbump of her belly. Squinting at the screen, too lazy to grab her glasses from the nightstand, she said, "What is that?"

He shushed her, and they both listened to the end of the report. "That's not Joy they're talking about though, right?" Alison asked.

But it was. The girl everyone assumed drowned on Friday the 13th of last month had, in fact, been murdered. The victim of a homicide: autopsy results showed she'd actually died of strangulation, after which the killer dumped her body in the woods.

Tom had almost recovered from the first surprise—where she'd been found. If Joy Enright had never been under the ice, as they'd first thought, what was it that had grabbed him when he went diving for her that night? They'd called it a rescue mission, though on the boat, they all knew the goal was to bring up a body. The ambulance standing by was ready to pull out under Condition White (meaning no need to hurry), not toward the emergency room but the morgue.

But he'd failed at the job, panicking when he thought he felt a hand closing around his wrist. Abandoning the search and telling them all he'd found nothing down there.

By the time he got home that night after finishing all the paperwork, Alison had already heard. "I have her. She's one of mine," she whispered, as if she could somehow soften the truth by not giving full voice to the words.

Tom loved how much his wife cared about her students, referring to them as if they belonged to her. Her devotion extended beyond the classroom. Once a week during her lunch hour, she ran an informal discussion group for kids whose parents drank too much or in some other way were falling down on the job. She attended their pep rallies, their field hockey and soccer games. It was not lost on Tom that the compliment Alison seemed to value most was any variation on "I guess the apple doesn't fall far from the tree." How often had he heard her say that her own mother was her role model? He always did his best to look pleased rather than dismayed.

"She's the smartest kid in school," Alison added, the night they all thought Joy drowned.

Was she the type who would run away? Tom asked.

"Run away?" Though it was close to midnight, Alison had pulled ice cream from the freezer and started eating it straight out of the container as they turned on the little TV in the kitchen to watch the rerun of the late news. Ice cream was her treat to herself when she was pregnant, and it was sometimes hard for Tom to believe how fast she could go through a carton. "I thought they said she was in the water. And they found her scarf."

"That's what they thought, because of the ice break. But maybe she fell through and then managed to pull herself out. Maybe she's hiding somewhere—embarrassed, scared, I don't know. It's possible." How much he would have liked to believe this, that Joy had never actually been under the ice, and that what he'd felt gripping him around the wrist was a vine or a strong slug of mud.

"She didn't run away," Alison had said. "I get why her mother wants to think that, though." She nodded toward the screen, which showed Susanne Enright, her face contorted in tears, issuing an appeal to anyone who knew anything about what could have happened to Joy. "Let's face it—she's a floater." A cop's kid, Alison used the cop's term for a body that rose on its own gases or surfaced in a thaw. And as with a cop, Tom knew, something allowed her to separate the lingo she used from the person she was applying it to.

He'd thought Joy was a floater, too. But three weeks later, here were the news people, telling him that his wishful thinking might have been right: the police now believed that after being murdered, the girl had been in the woods the whole time, despite the fact that the ground had been searched. Instead of hidden under the surface, she'd been right in plain sight, or what should have been plain sight. It happened: sometimes what people were looking for was right in front of them, and they missed it because they were paying attention to something else. In this case, it could have been because the original reports put her under the water, and most people—even the searchers—assumed she was there.

"No." Alison was watching through her glasses now, her hand pressed to her heart as she spoke directly to the TV. "She wasn't murdered; she drowned."

He'd always loved this, too, about his wife: her knack for feeling what it was like to be inside other people. Sometimes she couldn't shake what took hold of her when she observed or heard about someone suffering, even if she didn't know the person and even if it was far away in the world.

Tom knew that as she listened to the news report, she did not want to have to imagine her student enduring an assault before dying. In the old days, she would have told him this; she would have wanted to talk about it. But with each miscarriage she'd begun saying less and less, and though he'd done his best to put off realizing it as long as he could, he'd understood for a while now (even before what she did to him at the end of October) that if something didn't change—and soon—they might never find their way out of the trouble they were in.

He decided not to correct her about the manner of Joy's death. What was the point? Watching the familiar footage of Susanne Enright begging the public for information about her missing daughter, he recalled the day he'd gone to the family's house, at Susanne's request, two days after Joy had last been seen. Susanne appeared not to have slept at all, and her speech came out slow and uncertain, as if she were trying to find the right words in a language she'd only just learned. How would she absorb the shocks she was suffering now? The first had been the discovery of the body two days ago—a blow in itself, of course, because it was obvious that she'd been trying her best to believe that her daughter was still alive. Now that she knew Joy was not only dead, but murdered, how would she react?

Beyond that, who could have done it? Who would have strangled a teenager in a random encounter, after she stalked away from her friends in a fit of fury? No one could have anticipated her behavior that day, or where she'd end up at the moment she encountered whoever killed her.

No, it was more likely that someone had been following her, watching. Waiting for the right moment to pounce and grab. Maybe he (it was always a he) hadn't meant for her to die. Maybe he just wanted to scare her for some reason. But why?

The anchorwoman reported that Interim Chief Douglas Armstrong had begun a preliminary investigation, and it showed him speaking at a news conference from the six o'clock broadcast. Even though Doug had been in the position for five months, Tom found himself still doing double takes when he saw his father-in-law on TV; the dark cloth of his uniform showed up his blue eyes brighter than in real life, even on the small screen. "Police are looking for a black man seen in the vicinity of Elbow Pond the day Joy Enright disappeared," the anchorwoman said, her face and voice containing that solemnly ominous tone they all used when they wanted to make it seem they felt personally affected by the stories they read from their scripts. "The man is not being sought as a suspect at this time but as a person of interest."

A black man seen in the vicinity of Elbow Pond. The words rose to jab Tom under the ribs, and he shoved the covers aside.

"What?" Alison murmured.

"Nothing. You should get some sleep."

"How can I do that?" She gestured at the TV.

"Just try." He came back toward the bed and tried to speak in as calm a tone as possible, with all the movement inside his chest.

His impulse was to call Doug right away, but he remembered the first rule he'd been taught in the rescue-dive class: *Stop, think, and breathe.* Everything he hadn't done the night the call came in and he was sent down to find the girl. Acting on instinct could lead to freezing, or "passive panic," if a diver fixated on a single, ineffective plan while overlooking the obvious better ones. He stood in the kitchen, gripping the counter, and after a few minutes, he realized his training had paid off. Instead of picking up the phone, he went out to the truck, where he'd left his notebook in the glove box. Then he headed to wake up his father-in-law, whom he knew would be happy to see him—for once—when he saw what Tom had to offer.

Monday, December 7

I know I shouldn't care, especially given where I'm sitting, but it matters to me. They keep calling it a *journal*, smirking as if I'm some teenage girl mooning over a crush. A *commonplace book* is what my notebook would have been called in the old days. A commonplace book is what I keep.

But it has been confiscated. They've given me this pad and a cheap, blunt-pointed pen (*Liberty Mutual/We've Got You Covered*) to use while I'm confined here. I am not technically allowed a writing instrument, the guard told me—I might use it as a weapon on him, my lawyer, or myself—but he is kinder than some of the others, and the fact that I'm an art student (which probably means to him that I am gay) seems to make me less of a threat, despite the reason I'm here.

In my own book, the one they took, I write something every day, even if it's as mundane as the words *Nothing to note*. I like the discipline of it, which I know can only help me in my work. Then there are the events I want to remember, and I might spend an hour recording those. *Don't skip the details*, Grandee told me when she gave me that first notebook right after my father died, containing my first homemade bookmark. *Don't just write this happened today, or that happened. You think you'll remember, but trust me, you won't.*

I also use the book to make notes about things I read and to copy down quotes from the great artists (my favorite being Alberti's assertion that painting makes the absent present and the dead almost alive). It contains the draft of my Artist's Statement for *Souls on Board*. I can't afford to lose anything in there; I want my own book back.

The pad they gave me is a poor substitute for the quality Leuchtturm notebooks I choose for myself. But since I have nothing to do but sit in this holding cell with the man introduced to me as Drunk Dave, who is using a coverless paperback copy of *The Clan of the Cave Bear* as a pillow, I might as well document the events of today. For all I know, these notes will be confiscated, too, but if they're not, I'll have them to look back on. Not that I can imagine wanting to anytime soon, but I might as well, in case.

This morning after my swim, I went up to my attic studio and tuned the radio to Rochester's classical station. Though we are a hundred miles northeast of the city here, I can usually get it to come in. Someone told me once that hearing a good performance of classical music should make you feel like the top of your head is coming off, and that is how I judge what I listen to. Sometimes I picture the woman who is my mother—Linda Martin—playing the piano at the Eastman School of Music, where my father met her, with the expression of intense absorption I feel in my own face when I'm painting. In front of my easel, I might look up and find that three hours have passed, without my being aware of the world. The space I occupy in that time is reflected in the canvas; my thoughts are shapes and colors, instead of words. I don't feel hunger, thirst, or any other biological needs; I don't, with my brush in hand, inhabit a body. Especially this past summer, in the days after Grandee died, I was so grateful to know I could achieve such a state that I almost wept.

In the past few months, since Susanne put an end to things for good, I've felt desperate to find that internal place again. But the desperation gets in the way of my simply being able to settle in. ("Desperation is the worst perfume," Grandee used to tell her single friends who were looking for husbands, and though I have heard the phrase many times in my life and recorded it in my commonplace book, only now do I understand from the inside what it means.)

This morning I had not even had a chance to open my paints when I heard the knock downstairs at the front door, which I mistook at first for the sound of my landlady's son loading lumber into his truck. When the knock turned into a bang, I went downstairs, pulling a sweatshirt around my GOT ART? tee-shirt, and saw two police officers standing on the stoop. I knew they were officers not because they wore uniforms but because of the smug set of the men's mouths, which caused my throat to clench. When I opened the door and the younger, Hispanic-looking one spoke my name, I felt the room close in.

"We have a warrant," added the older of the two, whom I recognized from his constant appearance on the news since Joy's disappearance and especially since her body was found over the weekend. *Cerulean* is the color of the chief's eyes; I identified it from the artist's color chart inside my mind. "To search the premises."

"For what?" I'd been expecting them to say I was under arrest, not that they were looking for something. Stalking is a crime, isn't it? (I'd never thought of it as *stalking* when I sat in Grandee's car outside Susanne's house trying to summon the courage to get out, go up to the house, and talk to her, but I knew what her neighbor, who'd "caught" me out there idling, must have thought, and must have reported to the police.)

"You can read it if you want." The chief held up the piece of paper like a challenge or a taunt, but I shook my head and told him that it was fine for them to come in, the way Grandee taught me to do if I ever got pulled over or stopped on the street by the police.

"You'll be careful, right?" I asked. "A lot of what's here are my grandmother's things."

Instead of answering, Armstrong told the Hispanic officer (who stood only as high as Armstrong's shoulder) to go upstairs and search. "Be careful of his *grandmother's things*," Armstrong called after him, giving a scornful snort.

The chief and I stood in the living room without speaking, listening to the partner as he clomped around upstairs. After a while he came back down carrying my commonplace book, saying that was all he'd turned up. I told him there was nothing in there they wanted, they were just notes to myself. The chief said, "What's the matter, afraid we'll read something in your diary you want to keep secret? Like when you got your first period?" He ordered the other officer to put it in a bag, then told us to wait there while he searched the kitchen.

We heard him yanking cupboards and cabinets in the next room. He said, "Jesus Christ, bring him in here," and the Hispanic one indicated that I should precede him. Armstrong held up a black ski mask by the eyeholes and said, "What the fuck is this?"

"That's not mine," I said, but when the chief whistled and said, "*Bingo*," my response was lost.

Armstrong slipped the mask into a bag and told his partner to finish the search. "Hey," the partner said, after unfolding a piece of paper from the junk drawer. When I remembered what was on it, I felt a punch from inside my chest.

"Who's this a sketch of?" Armstrong held the sheet up in front of him. Though I know it's a cliché, the only phrase I can think to describe what was on his face at that moment is *sheer delight*.

"Nobody," I said, recognizing even as I said it how stupid it was to lie. I am good at what I do, and I knew they recognized the face as Joy's.

"Holy Christ," Armstrong said. The sketch seemed to please him even more than the mask. "We *got* you."

They told me I was coming with them. I asked if I was being arrested, and the chief said, "What do you think, douchebag?" before putting on the cuffs and leading me outside. My landlady, Cass, was watching from behind her own door on the other side of the house, and she told me to call her if I needed anything. Armstrong muttered that there was nothing she or anybody else would be able to do for me, but this was likely only for my benefit; I don't think Cass heard him.

I waited for them to read me my rights, but they did not. I knew it would be wiser not to talk, but I couldn't resist asking during the short drive, "Aren't I supposed to know why you arrested me?" (Looking back, I see that I was still allowing myself the delusion that it was related to stalking, even though stalking was not what I'd done.)

"That's only on TV." The Hispanic officer didn't turn around in the passenger seat as he answered. "But hey, as long as you're wondering, let's see—how 'bout we call it murder? Does that work for you?" He gave an obnoxious laugh in search of the chief's approval and got a sideways smirk in return.

The word made my gut go cold, and I clenched my jaw thinking I might puke. The anger I'd felt being led to the car in handcuffs slid straight down to fear. I wanted desperately to say something—to defend myself—but I knew there was no point. Only in that moment did it penetrate, what I had been denying to myself because it was too much to comprehend: the officers' visit to my apartment, and my presence in this car, was related to Joy's death.

And if Susanne didn't know already that they suspected me,

she would find out any minute. Of course she knows by now. I can't even bring myself to imagine what she feels.

At the police station, which before today I've only ever seen from the outside, they fingerprinted me and took my picture. (*Mug shot*, I reminded myself as it was happening, feeling glad for the first time ever that Grandee is not still alive; she said to me more than once that she never wanted to see my face in a mug shot on her TV, and when I asked, *Why would I have a mug shot?* she saw that she'd insulted me, but instead of apologizing she said, *You know what I'm talking about.* And, of course, I did.)

After the processing, a woman sitting at a computer recited questions—my name, my date of birth, where I worked. "I'm an art student," I told her, and she said, "Well, la-di-da" before asking me which school. She was angry at me, I could tell. I could only imagine how she would have reacted if I'd said I was an *artist*. What I felt coming from her was my first real clue (it went buzzing through my blood) that I was in more trouble than I'd let myself believe. They took my keys, my wallet, and my pen.

I asked when I would get these items back; the pen was a gift from Grandee when I graduated from college. The woman at the computer only sneered and gave a signal to the chief that she was finished with her part.

Armstrong came over to the desk and told me to stand up. "We just need you to clarify some things, okay?" he said, and the counterfeit warmth in his voice grated me more than when he'd called me a douchebag.

"I think I'll wait till I have a lawyer." I tried to make my own tone sound pleasant in return, as if we were two guys just shooting the bull about which team had the better quarterback. I asked if I could make a call, and the chief swore as he turned to tell the woman at the desk to let "the ass-wipe" use the phone.

In that moment I was glad that instinct is not visible, because my instinct was to call Susanne. And how wrong, how offensive I knew that would be to these people, who saw in the hands I offered up to them for the cuffs not hands that worked so precisely and painstakingly to make art but hands that would strangle a teenager, choke the life out of a child. A girl I spent time with and liked, the daughter of someone I loved. Not past tense: *love*. Why would they suspect me? Even if they knew about the stalking, how did they get from that to murder?

But things had shifted out of the realm of logic and into a territory I know all too well, though I often pretend not to. The police brought that mask into my house. The joke Susanne and I shared—*It's because I'm black, isn't it?*—isn't funny now, not that it ever really was.

More than anything I want to talk to her, tell her myself what's happening. She knows I am innocent. Doesn't she? She herself sent me after Joy that day. *Make sure she's okay, okay?* The idea that she might see merit in my arrest, might consider even for an instant that I could be responsible, is too much for me to bear. When they handed me the phone, I dialed Violet, in Brooklyn, instead.

When I told her why I was calling, she was silent for a moment before uttering a long, drawn-out *Shit*. Then she told me to sit tight and said she would be there with a lawyer in the morning. "You don't have to do that," I told her, only then realizing that if she didn't, I'd have to get the court to appoint someone to defend me. Violet told me not to be an idiot, then asked how they were treating me.

"Okay." I could feel through the phone that she didn't believe me. "Well, you know."

"Shit," she said again. She told me to try to sleep, she would see me tomorrow, she had to make some calls.

So I came to this cell, a ten-by-twelve room with benches along the walls and a single stained toilet in one of the corners.

The guard from the front desk brought me dinner—the same microwave mac and cheese I nuke for myself a couple of nights a week—and, when I asked for it, this pad and the cheap pen, which will go dry long before I run out of things I want to write with it.

Until We Meet Again

I'm telling you, he's not the one," Susanne whispered to Gil, as he pulled to a stop at the light. As long as she'd known him he always just bombed through a yellow, but he was more careful now. Not taking any chances. "You need to listen to me."

"Ssh," he said, because the news report wasn't over yet.

"Don't *ssh* me."

"Shut up!" His own whisper was fierce, whipping at her across the space between them as he reached to turn up the volume. They were on their way to the funeral home, and when he asked her, "Radio?" she said "No," but he either hadn't heard her or hadn't comprehended, and he turned on the news despite the fact that they already knew what the voice would say.

A local man, Martin Willett, had been arrested for the murder of Joy Enright. Officers had taken him into custody after executing a search warrant at Willett's home and finding a ski mask, among other items police believed might be related to the crime. Willett had been held overnight in the Chilton jail and was scheduled to be arraigned the next morning.

The police chief had visited them three days in a row: Yesterday, to tell them about the arrest. The day before that, to tell them that Joy's death was a murder. Two days earlier, that her body had been found, though they were withholding this fact from reporters until they could determine a cause of death. The first time, Susanne went to the sink and vomited; afterward, there was nothing left to purge. "No, no, no," Gil had said each time, even going so far as to place his hand on the chief's chest and push him slowly toward the wall. The first time, the chief flinched. After that, he just let Gil do whatever he wanted.

When Armstrong named Martin as the man they'd arrested, Gil's fingers turned to fists. The sight made Susanne double over again, and clutching herself she thought of Martin's fingers—around a brush, on her body. When they were alone again, Gil placed his hands on her shoulders, and she thought he might shake her—she wished he would—but instead he just leaned in close and whispered, "Look what you did. He killed her. Look what you did." The whisper made it even worse than it might have been; she wished he had shouted instead. After he left without telling her where he was going, she ran to find her phone, then remembered she'd erased Martin's number. When she finally found it and dialed, it went to voicemail. She tried three more times, left no messages, thought of contacting Violet but realized she didn't know her last name. When Gil came home, Susanne was still slumped on the floor in the kitchen, and they both knew he would step over her without speaking.

Twenty hours later now (twenty hours neither of them could remember), Gil stabbed the car radio off only when the announcer moved on to something else. "Susanne." Gil hardly ever said her full name, the way Martin always did. For a moment she thought with a clutch of dismay that her husband must know this somehow, then realized it was impossible. "They found a *ski mask*."

"I know," she murmured, looking out at the gray sky, gray snow, gray street. Impossible to tell him that Martin had gone to the pond that day at her own request. "But there's some other explanation. It wasn't him."

When he took a turn too fast, she sucked in her breath and began rummaging through her purse. In the past three days she'd taken to carrying a plastic bag around with her because the nausea was constant. The only relief came when she slept, and that had been only a few hours. So far, even when her stomach pitched the worst, nothing had actually come up since the first time. But it made her feel better to be prepared in case.

"We should go to the arraignment," Gil said. He rubbed his chin on the collar of his coat, a gesture she'd come to think of as one he turned to for comfort, like a child with a blankie.

"No. I don't want to."

"Why not?"

"What's the point?"

He sucked in his own breath as he stared straight ahead, and she wondered if nausea on its own could be contagious. "We need to see him. We owe it to her." Neither of them had been able to speak Joy's name since she'd gone missing, nearly a month ago now.

"They're arraigning the wrong person. When they figure that out and arrest the right person, then I'll go."

Gil muttered something in reply that she couldn't hear. She could tell he'd forgotten the exchange they'd just had when he pulled into the funeral home parking lot, turned the car off, and sat there still looking straight ahead, still with his hands on the wheel. "You okay?" Susanne asked, understanding as they both did that *okay* was a relative measure now.

They got out of the car, and though the lot had been shoveled and sanded, Gil came around to take her arm as they began the walk across the ice to the entrance. Susanne couldn't tell whether her husband was holding her up, or vice versa; most likely it was a system of mutual support. *Team Us*, only minus the third member. Once they stepped in the door, they'd have to plan Joy's service.

Ever since Joy started kindergarten, Susanne had dreaded taking her off to college when the time came, having to leave her behind. Now there was nothing she wouldn't give to anticipate that pleasure.

GOOD-BYES ARE NOT FOREVER, said the sign on the funeral-home awning, followed by UNTIL WE MEET AGAIN.

Usually Gil moved at a faster pace than Susanne could keep up with. It was how he could fit so many jobs in a day, he used to say.

But now she felt his hesitation in every step they took together, and their progress across the ice was slow. No wonder, Susanne thought—there was no difference between this and walking up to the hangman's noose.

Families often like to write the appreciation themselves, the funeral director told them as they discussed the arrangements.

That's what it always said in the paper, that people were making arrangements for the ones they'd loved who'd died.

But what "arrangements" did Joy need now? Cremation or burial, that was it. Though Susanne and Gil had specified cremation for themselves when the time came, they couldn't bring themselves to order it for their child. At least with a burial, they would always be able to imagine she'd just faded into the earth.

When Susanne had spoken to him on the phone, the funeral director told her that he wouldn't recommend a viewing, and she kept herself from asking why. Gripping her husband's arm as they climbed the sanded steps, she faltered, hoping he would pause and give her the time they both needed before they went in. But if he noticed her stalling he ignored it, and pulled her like a punishment into the perfumed hall.

What's the appreciation? Susanne asked, and next to her Gil clarified: *Obituary.* Hearing him say it made her wince, and she understood why the mortician had used the other word.

Also—here the man hesitated again (and to Susanne it seemed less like genuine reticence than the practiced rhythm of giving the grieving those details they needed to know)—some people like to bring in objects to be buried, or placed in the crematory, with their loved ones.

An object? Like what? Susanne was the one who asked again, and again Gil was the one who gave the answer: *Like a stuffed animal or something. Right?* and the funeral director nodded and said it was, of course, up to them.

On the way home he said, "So what do you think about an object going into the—in with her?"

She shrugged. "I don't know. Nobody would see it, right?"

"Right. It would just be for us, to know it went with her. Whatever it was."

"I guess if we could find something, I wouldn't mind her having something she liked." She knew this was ridiculous; Joy could no longer *have* anything, the same way she couldn't *like* or *know*. She understood that it was only to make themselves feel better that she and Gil entertained the idea. And yet if it did so, even in the tiniest measure, what was the harm?

They divided up the job of searching for something they might put in the casket. Gil volunteered to look in Joy's bedroom; Susanne didn't think she could cross that threshold yet. She said she would walk through the rest of the house, and they'd meet in the living room with any of Joy's possessions they thought she might "want" as company through eternity.

In the kitchen, her eyes moved first (as they always did) to a charcoal drawing Joy had done four years earlier in a Saturday-afternoon class at Susanne's school. For an assignment on diminishing perspective, she'd painted the convenience store at one end of Elbow Pond, in the viewer's distance, a tapered triangle of water leading to the small, dilapidated building everybody in town called "the shack." Lucas Hannay, who taught the class, told Susanne he couldn't believe the drawing had been done by a thirteen-year-old: it was better than anything he'd seen by a master's student all year.

But now Susanne couldn't remember when she'd last seen Joy pick up her pencils. She'd asked a few times, but Joy always shrugged and said "Whatever," as if that were an answer.

Susanne left the drawing on the wall; there was no way she would sacrifice it to the ground. She moved into the hallway and began rummaging through the mail basket, picking out the envelope from the College Board. This was not something to put in the casket, but she wondered if it would do to mention—in the *appreciation*—that Joy had gotten a perfect score on her SATs.

No. The time for bragging was past. Besides, in the basket right next to the College Board envelope was the citation from the Chilton police, which Susanne had found in Joy's jacket after they brought her home following her arrest the week before she disappeared.

No, not disappeared. Before she *died*, Susanne reminded herself. For almost a month she'd allowed herself to think there was a possibility she would see her daughter again, but after the most recent visits from the police chief, there was no way to sustain that fantasy.

And not only had she died rather than having run or been taken off somewhere—still to return or be returned to them—she had been *murdered*. And Martin—*Martin!*—had been accused of doing it. In the day since Doug Armstrong notified them of his arrest, Susanne barely allowed the fact to penetrate the haze of shock she still felt from the first news that her daughter was dead. The chief had told them without elaborating that the police felt confident in their "good evidence" against the suspect they had in custody. "Locked up," Armstrong added, as if anticipating their need to be reassured on this point.

Susanne had never seen the actual jail at the Chilton police station, but she imagined it was not a place she would want anyone she cared about to spend any time in. She and Gil had been to the station with Joy the night she got processed after the nursing home raid. Joy's name had been kept out of the news because of her age, though because Chilton was such a small town, the arrest was almost general knowledge. Despite Joy's insistence that it was a mistake—or not a mistake, she corrected herself, but a setup—Susanne and Gil had grounded her and confiscated her cell phone.

That was another thing Susanne was forced, now, to live with; if Joy had had her cell phone with her that day, would she have been able to call for help? Susanne hadn't agreed with Gil that taking the phone away was the best way to punish her, but after their daughter disappeared, she did her husband the favor of not reminding him that it had been his idea to deny her that privilege.

She went to the door of Joy's bedroom empty-handed. "Anything?" she asked, seeing Gil just standing there in the middle of the room, looking as if he didn't know where or how to begin. When he shook his head, she took a breath and stepped in to join him. Immediately she felt the simultaneous sensations of comfort and longing (the air in here still smelled faintly of Joy, or did it? Was that possible?), nostalgia and grief. She could tell her husband felt it, too—it was what had stopped him in his search.

A year ago, Susanne and Joy had painted this room together (only a year! Before the bottom fell out of so many things; that expression recited on the news so often, *the bottom falling out*, making her think of a wet cardboard box and its contents spilling through the mushy floor that was supposed to hold it all—the economy, her marriage vows, the way her daughter felt about her). When the paint dried, Susanne helped her move the furniture back in, and within an hour Joy had restored the room to the sanctuary she'd always cultivated for herself there, everything neatly in its place, including the under-bed boxes where she stored her art supplies, old toys, keepsakes, and out-of-season clothes.

On Sunday, when they learned that the autopsy showed Joy had been strangled, the police had searched the bedroom, with Susanne's and Gil's permission. When Gil asked why they hadn't done so sooner, Armstrong said that since she'd been presumed drowned, there was no reason to believe a crime had been committed. They took her computer, where they found the messages leading up to her final meeting with Delaney Stowell at the pond. Gil asked when they could have the computer back, and Armstrong said after the trial, if they caught who did it. They were following up some leads, he told them, and though Gil demanded to know what they were, Armstrong put him off, saying they'd know soon enough. Martin was arrested the next day—yesterday, now.

"They did a good job," Susanne said, meaning that the officers had managed to set the room mostly back to rights after their search. The clothes in the drawers were not refolded quite as precisely as Joy herself would have liked, but someone had made an effort. The boxes under the bed looked to be in their usual uniform rows, and though the items on Joy's desk and bureau had been rearranged (and didn't it mean something—didn't it mean she was a good, attentive mother—that Susanne knew Joy kept her pens and pencils separate, her earring tree on the left side instead of the right?), they still looked like the belongings of a meticulous teenage girl.

"I suppose we could put Brown in with her," Gil said, nodding toward the rubbed-raw stuffed bear Joy had slept with since her days in the crib, but they both rejected this idea immediately without even having to say so. Not for anything would they give up Brown, even if they'd been able to believe in the idea that Joy could welcome him now.

"I'll keep looking," Susanne told him. "Do you want to pick out something for her to wear?" Again: the phrase she would have used if their daughter were alive, capable of actively doing anything: wearing, choosing, looking nice. Gil took in an audible breath, went to the closet, and began sliding hangers across the rod.

Susanne opened the top drawer of Joy's nightstand, rummaged among the various tangled cords and spare earbuds, and then gave out a cry as she felt her chest buckle. "What?" Gil said, turning. He was holding a blouse Susanne had bought for their daughter on her last birthday. "This is pretty, right?"

"I thought so, too. But she never wore it." She was barely aware of thinking the words before she said them, knowing she would have to look back down and return to the shock of what she'd just seen. As Gil placed the blouse back on the rod, she reached into the nightstand drawer and drew out the homemade bookmark, bright orange fabric sewn over a cardboard rectangle. She'd seen it before, of course—it belonged to Martin.

It belonged to Martin. It belonged to Martin. She had seen it in Martin's house; where, exactly? In which room? She could not remember.

But in Martin's house. For a moment, she forgot to breathe.

Gil was holding up another outfit: the dress Joy had worn for her induction into the National Honor Society. After the ceremony they'd taken her to the Inside Scoop, their family tradition to celebrate every good report card, which meant that they went out for ice cream every semester. "Good," Susanne murmured. "That's good."

"What?" He could tell she'd been distracted. "Did you find something?"

She dropped the bookmark back in the drawer and shut it

with a bang she had not intended. "I think maybe we should just put a few charcoal pencils in with her," she said. "You know?"

"Oh, I like that." Gil's face brightened the way it always did when he got excited about something; it was a moment before he remembered the context and looked sick again.

They laid the dress on her bed—they would take it to the funeral home later—and left the room. "Come on, Salsa," Gil tried to coax the cat, but Salsa refused and jumped onto the bed, where she proceeded to stretch across the dress. Gil moved to pick her up, then stopped himself. "I guess it doesn't really matter, right?" he said, and Susanne agreed. When she returned a half hour later to retrieve the bookmark, the cat had managed to lift one of the dress sleeves around her paw, covering that part of herself with the remnant of Joy.

Gil went into the garage to rearrange the cans of leftover paint and stain they had accumulated over the years. He'd rearranged them only two nights earlier, a few hours after the police chief came to tell them that Joy's disappearance, which had turned into Joy's death, had now turned into Joy's murder.

In a different circumstance, Susanne might have followed him out—after they closed the door to Joy's bedroom behind them—and asked, *Why are you doing that now? Why are you doing it again?* But instead she went into their own bedroom and closed *that* door, so she could only barely discern the sounds of him performing his pointless task. She laid the bookmark on the bureau and traced her fingers over its soft edges, the jolt of its discovery still ringing in her heart. Martin's grandmother had given him the first bookmark on his birthday a few days after his father's fatal airplane crash, when Martin was twelve. That meant he had twelve altogether, the last received earlier this year, just before his grandmother died. He kept them in a mesh spiral box next to his bed—an array of vibrant colors from her various sewing projects—but now Susanne remembered that he also had a similar collection up in the attic, his studio.

What did it mean that Joy had in her possession one of Martin's bookmarks? And that Susanne had not known this while her daughter was alive? She could barely articulate the question to herself, let alone imagine an answer. She reached for her cell phone before knowing whom it was she was moving to call.

Doug Armstrong had instructed them to notify him of anything that might help with the case—new information or new memories, no matter how small. They could never know what might be useful, he said, encouraging them to "reach out."

Yet something kept Susanne from dialing his number. Part of it (but only part) had to do with the fact that she hated the phrase "reach out"—reaching out was what babies did toward their mothers, and what Adam did toward God on the ceiling of the Sistine Chapel. It didn't mean calling someone to ask a question, or for help.

She flipped through her contacts to find Tom Carbone's number instead. She pressed the button before she could think any further, and left a message asking if he would meet her. Then she sat down on the bed and waited, listening to the faint noise of the paint cans being lifted and set down again, over and over, just outside the door.

Tuesday, December 8

I didn't sleep at all last night. Instead, after Drunk Dave started snoring, I pulled *The Clan of the Cave Bear* gently from beneath his head and read it until, after bringing me a breakfast I didn't eat, the guard came to tell me I had visitors.

It was Violet with a white woman lawyer, the daughter of the man Violet takes care of in Brooklyn. Her name is Ramona Frye: she's about forty and what Grandee would have insisted I call "big-boned" instead of "fat." She wore a white blouse with a black skirt, like an orchestra member. When she excused herself to use the bathroom an hour into our talk, Violet told me Ramona always wears black and white because she's color-blind and doesn't trust herself to match clothes. Because of this she's seen as a bit of an oddball in New York legal circles, but Violet told me Ramona uses this to her advantage. "They think just because she's a little quirky, she doesn't know anything. But she does. Trust me."

I have no choice but to trust her. Ramona's willing to represent me pro bono, which I hate because it feels like charity. It *is* charity. But I don't know any other lawyers, and I don't have enough in my bank account to pay for one.

Ramona told me the arraignment was scheduled for ten

o'clock in the town court. She sent Violet to my apartment to get some clothes so I wouldn't have to appear in my GOT ART? tee-shirt and sweats. "We'll know more about their case after this," Ramona said, having scribbled some notes from what I could tell her: that they'd taken a ski mask and a sketch of the dead girl from my house, along with my journal. (I told her it was a commonplace book, not a journal, but when she asked what the difference was, I gave up and said it didn't matter.) "Is there anything about her in there? The girl?" Ramona asked, and I had to answer yes, thinking she would ask me right then *What?* but she said that could wait till later.

I told her that the mask they found wasn't mine. They planted it, I said.

"I believe you," she said, but I couldn't tell if this was true.

"I mean, if I *had* committed a crime in a mask, why would I hang onto it?"

"I know. I hear you." She fiddled with her pen. "But they say they have a witness, maybe two of them."

"Witnesses? Who say what?"

"That they saw you wearing a mask that day. At the pond."

I stared at her. "That's not possible."

Ramona made a face I couldn't read—disgust, maybe? If so, at what or whom? "I hate to say it, but let's face it. You're black. Living in a place that isn't all that friendly to black people. Anything is possible."

The heat that rose inside me as she spoke made sweat break out on my face and arms, even as I recognized that the room itself was cooler than it should have been. "Look," I said, knowing I had to get it out of the way. "I *was* there. At the pond that day. But I wasn't wearing a mask."

Her eyes narrowed, and I tried not to read suspicion in them. Anticipating her next question, I saved her the trouble. "I went over to the house, and I heard Joy and Susanne arguing. Joy

took off in her mother's car, and Susanne asked me to go after her."

Ramona held a finger up. "Don't use phrases like 'go after her.'"

"Okay." I felt myself flush further.

"Why were you at the house in the first place?"

I hesitated before saying only that I had wanted to see
Susanne.

"Were you sleeping with her?" Ramona did not look up as
she asked me this but kept her eyes trained on the notepad in
front of her.

My face growing warmer, I told her, "We *had* been. But it was
over." I watched her write the word—*over*—and was shocked at
how much it stung.

"Okay, you can give me those details later—when it started,
for how long. So you go to the house why? You were planning
to do what, before you heard them arguing?"

Again, I paused before answering. I know you aren't supposed
to hide things from your lawyer. But I could almost hear her
follow-up if I told the truth. *Understand that I have to ask you
this, okay? Were you sleeping with the daughter, too?* and even
though I could honestly have answered *No*, I did not even want
to hear the question.

Besides, another perfectly reasonable response had presented
itself to me in that moment. One that no one would be able to
refute. Ramona was asking about my intentions, right? And no
one could see into those except me.

"I wanted to show her the sketch I made of Joy. The one they
found in my drawer, the one they think is evidence of something. Susanne had asked if I'd do a portrait."

Ramona pursed her lips as she wrote it down. "So what
happened after the girl took off? You and the mother have a
conversation?"

I told her that Susanne had been worried about Joy, because she'd been arrested the previous week. I told her that Susanne wasn't sure what was going on with her.

"She wasn't sure she could trust her?"

"I think that's fair to say. She thought Joy was in trouble, and she wasn't sure how much. Or what kind."

Another scribbled note. This time I couldn't make out the words upside down, and I hoped she'd be able to decipher her own handwriting when it came time. "So what happened then?" Ramona continued. "You get in your own car and drive to this pond?"

I nodded. "Why didn't the mother go with you?" she asked.

"I think she was afraid it would escalate things, if Joy saw her. If Joy knew her mother had followed her." Again, not precisely the truth. *I'd* been the one to suggest that Susanne stay behind, thinking that because of my conversation with Joy at my apartment a couple of weeks earlier, I might have some sway over her that her mother did not. How presumptuous I had been! Yet it hadn't come from a delusion of power; I think I wanted only to remind myself, and perhaps prove to Susanne, that I was still important to her life, whether she knew it or not.

"Only we're not sure what 'things' we're talking about—the things that might escalate," Ramona said. "Right?"

"Well, not at the time. She was out on the ice with some girls—on the news it said they were girls from her class—and then *they* had a fight. An argument, I mean."

"This girl was doing a lot of arguing," Ramona murmured. "And you saw her out there, arguing with her friends?"

"I didn't know they were her friends, but yes. I couldn't hear it, but it looked tense."

"So you do what?"

"I didn't necessarily think she was in trouble. I figured it was just teenage stuff. You know, high school drama. So I went into the store—there's a little store there, what the kids call the shack—and after a few minutes I came back out and went home."

She interrupted her scribbling to ask, "Did anybody see you inside this shack?"

I told her that I'd stared a little too long at the cashier behind the counter, and it seemed to make him angry. I told her about my short conversation with the man I took to be the owner of the place. "I'll talk to them," she said. "Maybe they can be useful. Did you notice anyone else?"

Not that I remembered, I said.

"Did you call Joy's mother at any point?"

This had not occurred to me, in all the ruminating I'd done since, about that day. "Oh. Yes. Yes! I called to let her know Joy was okay. They can check those records, can't they? Won't that help?" I tried not to let my voice get away from me, the way it wanted to.

Ramona made a *hmm* noise—ambiguous at best, I thought, but then maybe she was trying not to get her hopes up, too. "Yes, they can check the records. But it won't prove anything other than the fact that you called her, and what time. It won't prove what you might have done after the call. It's like what they could say about your notebook: a prosecutor could always argue you'd written certain things after the fact, to use precisely in a situation like this. As an alibi."

Only then did it sink in exactly how much my accusers must hate me—that they could think I would murder a girl, then go to such cold-blooded, deliberate lengths to conceal the act.

"You have to do something," I told her.

"I will." Ramona didn't elaborate *what* she would do, or how, and I forced myself not to ask, in case she couldn't answer.

"Can you prove he planted the mask?" I asked.

"I don't see how. Unless he confesses, or the other cop testifies. And I doubt he will. Even if he did see Armstrong plant it, cops tend to stick together. And after all, he's the chief." She looked back at her notes. "You and the other officer were in the living room when the chief entered the kitchen? So neither of you actually saw him open that particular drawer."

"Right." *He got me*, I thought, the same way I would if the chief had stood over me with a gun and fired into my belly.

Ramona, appearing to perceive my dismay, leaned forward and said, "Look. The mask is circumstantial. Assuming everything else they have is also circumstantial, then we have a better chance."

I told her that everything else *had* to be circumstantial. Then I worried that the force of my tone might have put her off. More quietly I asked, "Nobody will be at the arraignment, will they? I mean, would Susanne—the parents—be there?"

Ramona hesitated. "They might."

"Is it possible for me not to go, then? Can they do it in absentia?"

She rolled up the sleeves of her white blouse, and I sensed she was only making the gesture to buy time. "That would just make you look guilty. *Especially* if the family is there."

She told me not to worry, but I barely heard the words. My relief when I entered the courtroom and didn't see Susanne was so great that I forgot my fear. In the next moments the relief expanded when I saw that the judge was a black man. I sensed that Ramona felt the same, although of course I couldn't be sure.

But then Gil Enright stood from the back row. "You sleep with my wife and then you kill my daughter?" The words were not shouted. I could barely make them out. Absurdly, I remembered what Susanne had told me once: Gil doesn't swear, ever. He doesn't raise his voice. Now he did not resist or say anything further when the uniformed guard took him gently by one arm and led him out. I felt more shaken than if he had run at me with a knife. But Ramona told me to pay attention to the proceedings. Worry about him later, she said.

Standing up for the other side, an assistant district attorney told the judge why the prosecutor believed there was reasonable cause to charge me with the second-degree murder of Joy Enright: I had recently been rejected by the victim's mother, with whom I'd been having an affair. I'd been seen having an intense exchange with Susanne outside her house just before Joy went missing. On prior occasions, I had been observed by neighbors, sitting in a car outside her house with no reason to be there other than to stalk her. (Only twice, and not *stalking*! But by now I understood that they were allowed to get their licks in, say what they wanted to say.) Witnesses had seen me on the day of Joy's disappearance, at the scene of her disappearance, wearing a ski mask. (*Who is saying that?* I wanted to shout. But I did my best to obey Ramona's instructions and appear calm. I was taught to never show anger in front of white people, to the extent that when I'm with them, I sometimes don't even realize I'm feeling it. But I knew it now.)

The prosecutor continued to say that my own journal provided evidence that the victim and the accused had a personal relationship. At the word "relationship," the judge's head snapped up from the notes he was taking, and the prosecutor must have noticed because he was quick to amend it to "I mean, they were acquainted," and next to me I could feel Ramona wishing she'd followed up on this instead of leaving it for later.

"When police executed a search warrant for the mask," the prosecutor concluded, "they also discovered a sketch of the victim. And although we have not been able to question him yet, we do not believe the defendant has an alibi for his whereabouts after he was identified at the location Joy Enright was last seen."

I had driven straight back to my apartment after leaving the pond. Cass might have seen me from her window—she often moves the curtain to check out my comings and goings—but even if she could vouch that I'd been home directly after I admitted to being at the pond, I'd gone up to my attic to work and had no contact with anyone else for the rest of the day. There was no one to account for my actions, and according to what I learned from the news, the police couldn't be sure exactly when Joy was killed.

After the prosecutor described his case, he asked that the judge order me to remain in custody. Then it was Ramona's turn to make a case for bail; she cited my "pristine" record, with no prior arrests or any mental health issues; the fact that I had arranged for the care of my ailing grandmother in Rochester when I enrolled in graduate school; the fact that I owned her house now and planned to return to it when I received my degree; my current status as a student at the art college; and the fact that from what she'd just heard, the prosecutor had only a circumstantial case against her client. I made sure to meet the judge's eyes as he contemplated the bail amount. It couldn't hurt, right? Wouldn't this judge be able to see something in my face that a white judge could not? I was both surprised and not surprised to identify this thought in myself as I stood before the bench, looking up at this man who'd earned the right to determine my fate. But he looked not back at me but down at his papers as he announced a bail amount of seven hundred fifty thousand dollars.

I made a sound, and Ramona lifted a hand—whether toward the judge or me, I couldn't tell, nor could I read what the gesture meant. The bailiff led me out to the hallway and into a windowless room, and when Ramona came in she asked, "How much is the house in Rochester worth?" before she was even fully seated.

I said, "It's my grandmother's house, she raised me there, I'm not putting that up."

She slapped a pen hard against her yellow pad. "It's *your* house now, and your freedom is on the line," she told me. "This is not the time to get all sentimental. How much?"

Chastened, I told her probably two thirty, two fifty at the most. "Is there anybody who can help you out with the rest?" she asked. "Anybody you know with discretionary funds?"

I began to shake my head, then stopped when I remembered something I hadn't thought of in years. Ramona asked *What?* and I said, "My mother's family has money. Or they did, anyway, when my father knew her." I explained the circumstances of my birth: My parents had met at the Eastman School, where my mother was a piano student and my father the head piano tuner. Their relationship began with an argument over high C; she wanted him to keep refining the note, he told her it was perfect the way it was. A professor passing by in the hallway confirmed that my father was right, causing Linda to concede, and my father invited her out for coffee. *Why?* I asked when he told me the story, the night before sixth grade started and I couldn't fall asleep out of nerves. *Because I felt guilty*, my father said. *Why?* I asked again, and when he only shrugged, I knew it was one of those things that had to do with her being white and him being black that he could never quite find words for. When Linda got pregnant, she wanted an abortion (although that was not how he put it; he said, "She did not want to bring the baby to term," as if I might not realize that the baby was me), because they had no plans to marry, she was too young, and she wanted a music career. My father persuaded her that if she would just agree to carry out the pregnancy, he would take over from there; Linda could move back to Georgia and never have to hear from him again.

I abbreviated all of this in telling it to Ramona. "And you've never heard from *her*? Not even once?" She paused in her scribbling, and when I shook my head, she persisted, "Do you have any idea where in Georgia she was from?"

"No. I mean, outside Atlanta somewhere." The word "Atlanta" held a bitter taste for me; its airport was the origination of my father's fatal flight.

But this was not what my lawyer was interested in. "All I know is her name," I told Ramona.

"Which is?"

"Linda Martin. I'm named after her."

I watched her eyes flicker and imagined she was trying to decide whether to reveal that she assumed I'd been named after Martin Luther King, as most people do. Instead she only groaned slightly and said, "Common. And she's probably married now, so it will be harder to track her down."

"Track her down?" I'd forgotten that the questions about my mother had been prompted by my need to find bail money. "I don't want you to do that." The idea of Ramona locating Linda—after all this time, and in so dire a circumstance—stirred the nausea that lies constantly in my stomach under the word "mother," a silt base waiting to be kicked up.

"You mean you want to stay in jail? When there's possibly a way out?"

I considered. "How long are we talking about?"

"Through an indictment and a trial. That could be a year or more, easy."

"How would you find her?"

"I have some contacts down there. They'll recommend an investigator."

"And what would you tell her?" Ever since my father's death, whenever I'd imagined my mother finally letting go of whatever it was that had kept her from finding out about me, I relished the notion of her coming to understand that her son was an accomplished, admired artist. She'd regret having given me up, having let so much of my life pass without knowing me. Never had I even entertained the vision of her learning instead that

I'd been arrested, let alone for murder. The possibility that this might cause her to shudder with relief, realizing what she'd escaped, made my breath skip a beat.

"First things first, okay? Cross that bridge and all that." Ramona rubbed her hands over the lap of her black skirt, and I wondered if she were wiping off sweat. If so, was it hormonal? (I remember Grandee's trouble when she went through that time—sweater on, sweater off, on, off, laughing at herself as she did so and asking me did I know how lucky I was to be a boy.) Or did the sweating have to do with nervousness around me?

She told me to sit tight and said she'd be back tomorrow, and then they returned me to this cell, where I'm about to spend my second night listening to the snores of the drunk man and wishing I could sleep myself.

Ghostwriter

S o what is this, opposite day?" Harper only halfway hoped
that her mother, in the driver's seat next to her, would take
it as a lighthearted remark. "You're supposed to be teaching *me*."

She did not feel like giving her mother a driving lesson, especially at rush hour when the roads were slick. It was all she'd
been able to do to get through school that day, even though regular classes were canceled and it was just a bunch of counselors
coming into the rooms to ask if anyone had questions or wanted
to share, and to tell the students they should reach out if they
had issues concerning the tragedy, now or at any time in the future. None of them spoke Joy's name.

"You're not 'teaching' me." Her mother gripped the wheel so
tightly that Harper could feel the pressure in her own hands. "I
know how to do this; I just haven't practiced it in a while." There
was no benefit, Harper knew, in pointing out that her mother's
conception of "a while" was different from most people's; she
had not been behind the wheel of a car since the winter day
she'd skidded off Reservoir Road on the way to pick up Harper
and Joy from the season's first skate at Elbow Pond when they
were freshmen. That had been the start of her mother going
downhill, which was how Harper preferred to think of it. Her

brother called it *mental*. "You're helping reacquaint me with an old skill."

Her mother's going downhill had blunted Harper's motivation to get her own license. She still only had her permit, which was why Truman still had to drive her wherever she wanted to go. Though he always made a big fuss about it, she knew he didn't really mind; driving was the one activity he seemed to be able to do without feeling the need to engage in magical thinking. (That was what their mother called it; Harper found it hard not to refer to it in her own mind as OCD, which was Truman's nickname at school: OCD Boy.) So she imagined it was a relief to him, chauffeuring his mother and sister around instead of playing solitaire until he won, no matter how many hands it took. The rest of the family indulged him by pretending to believe that his objections to driving on demand were genuine. Truman told Harper that if she didn't bake him whatever he wanted, whenever he wanted it, he might "forget" to pick her up sometime when she really needed it.

She didn't mind. She liked to be in the kitchen anyway, and it made her feel good to know that somebody appreciated her baking enough to request it, even if it was only her brother. She considered it practice for the business she and Eric Feinbloom talked about opening someday.

She'd planned to come straight home from school and pick out something to read at Joy's funeral. She planned to pick out something to wear. But her father was at work, Truman had signed up for a shift at the dollar store, and it was so inconvenient for her mother not to be driving—the family had gone through such contortions, these past few years—that Harper knew she didn't have a choice when her mother announced at breakfast that she thought it might be time to get back on the road.

"Stop!" Harper cried. They had come to the crosswalk in

front of Hair Raising, and her mother stabbed at the brakes, causing both of them to be pushed a few inches toward the windshield. The blown-dry woman who'd just entered the street jumped at the screech of the sudden halt and glared at Harper's mother, shaking her head.

"Oh my God." Her mother clapped a hand to her chest. "Who is that woman?"

The car behind them beeped, and Harper's mother jumped. "That wasn't my fault," she added. "She stepped off the curb without even looking."

"You have to pull over, Mom. Either that or keep moving." She thought her mother might refuse and tell Harper to take the wheel. But after waving in the rearview at the beeping driver, she managed to inch ahead a few car lengths to the first open spot. "Awesome, Mom," Harper told her, when they were finally parked with the engine shut off. "You did it."

Her mother's expression told her that though she considered the congratulations pathetic, she relished her daughter's words nevertheless. "Let's take a break," she suggested, and Harper assumed she meant that they should sit in the car for a few minutes before pulling back into traffic toward home. But her mother was unclipping her seat belt, her hand on the door as she said she thought they should get a treat at the Inside Scoop.

"Are you sure?" Harper said. "Won't we ruin our appetites?"

"Appetites are meant to be ruined," her mother said, and Harper thought, *Who* are *you?*

They sat across from each other in a booth and ordered hot fudge sundaes. "I think I know who that was." Her mother gestured with her spoon behind them, toward the near miss on the street. "I think it was the police chief's wife. Something Armstrong." Harper watched her running names through her head until she came to it. "Helen."

"Really?" Harper wished she'd taken more notice; she would have been interested to see what her English teacher's mother looked like. From his questioning of her, she remembered Mrs. Carbone's *father* all too well.

"You don't recognize her? Her picture's always in the paper. She's always doing do-gooder things."

Her mother saying "doing do-gooder" made Harper smile, remembering the old days when she was learning to read and they took turns reciting pages to each other from Dr. Seuss. *Four fluffy feathers on a Fiffer-feffer-feff.*

"So is Mrs. Carbone," she told her mother. "I heard some of the other teachers call her Mother Teresa. But she doesn't seem like a saint to me."

She waited for her mother to ask her what she meant. Instead, her mother lifted a spoon of gooey fudge above her mouth and let it drizzle in slowly. "Why don't we do this more often? I miss this kind of thing."

Um, Harper wanted to say, *Mom? We don't do this because you hardly ever go out of the house.* The meaner, more injured part of her added, *Because you're mental.* Immediately she felt ashamed, disloyal, even though of course she knew her mother could not understand her thoughts.

Her mother sat back in the booth and said, "I wanted to talk to you about something." When Harper shifted nervously in her seat, she added, "Don't worry. I just wanted to say how proud I am of you for the way you're helping with this investigation."

"Oh." How had it all gotten away from her like this? She looked down at the table and remembered telling the policemen the lie about having seen the black man wearing a mask. (Though each time she thought about it, it took another moment before she remembered it was a lie.) It had only been two days ago, but it seemed like much longer. She'd told herself she would call the police station, before things got out of hand, to say she'd been confused. But it was probably too late now.

"What happened to Joy, anyway?" her mother asked. "She did seem to change, toward the end. What was she doing hanging out with Delaney Stowell? Isn't she kind of a troublemaker? I didn't know they were friends." She seemed surprised by the string of sentences she'd just uttered; she leaned back and caught her breath.

Harper felt tempted. Not only to tell her mother she'd lied to the police, but about the drugs she'd seen change hands at the Halloween party; about the police confronting Zach Tully at school, not long before Joy's own arrest; and about how things had really been between her and Joy, especially since Joy had told Harper about her mother's affair. She'd pulled away from Harper at school and said she was too busy to meet up after school or on weekends. Which wouldn't have been so bad— they all had a lot of homework—except that Joy seemed to have time, suddenly, to spend with Delaney.

Her mother waited for Harper to answer. She could have said all of these things, or only a part of them. Instead she just said, "I hate Delaney."

"It's not nice to hate," her mother said, then seemed to reconsider her own response. "Oh. I guess that's the kind of thing you say to a child, isn't it? I have to get used to thinking of you as an adult. I can tell you the truth about things." Harper blanched—she very much did not want to hear whatever truth was forthcoming—as her mother leaned closer. "You know I've always wanted to write a novel, right? Well, it hasn't worked out yet. I'm still trying, but in the meantime, I was thinking maybe we could do a different kind of book project. Together." She dropped her voice as if she didn't want anyone to hear her idea and steal it.

"'Book project'? What are you talking about?"

Despite her mother's shrug, Harper could tell that this was something she had given a good deal of thought. "A memoir, kind of. About the case." It took Harper a moment to realize that the "case" was what had happened to Joy. "Apparently, it's easier to get a contract for nonfiction. And people go for books like this. Murder in a small town, drugs and teenagers, that kind of thing." Her mother leaned closer, and Harper smelled chocolate on her breath. She wanted to pull back but was afraid her mother would feel offended. "I'd do the actual writing, but we could tell people the book was by you. I'd just be your ghostwriter."

"Why should it be by me?" Harper's voice was louder than she'd intended because what she really wanted to ask was *Why would you want to write a book about Joy being murdered?*

"It would make it stand out, a teenage author. And you're a witness. Not only were you best friends with the victim, you were one of the last people to see her alive. And you're going to testify in the case."

"We don't know that for sure." Harper felt her ice cream coming back up into her throat.

"Of course we do. You saw him there at the pond that day. With a mask! How likely do you think it is that he would be at the scene of the crime, and then the police find evidence at his house, if he isn't guilty?"

Her mother's conviction was contagious. Or was it just that Harper saw no choice other than to feel it sliding across the table, infecting her as well? What if Martin Willett *had* done it—killed Joy—and the lie was what they needed in order for him to be punished, to get what he deserved? Did it matter if Harper lied but the right outcome came from it?

"We'll do it together. I want you to know I'm here for you," her mother said. It was an expression Harper hated, because she knew it came from her therapy group. The counselors in school had said the same thing.

She was saved from having to respond when the waitress, a girl in Truman's class, brought the check over. "Aren't you the friend?" she asked Harper, not even appearing to try to hide the fascination in her face. Harper nodded as she slid out of the booth, pretending not to notice the look her mother gave her: *See?*

When they got home, her father was already there, working at the puzzle whose pieces were spread out across half of the dining room table. He looked up surprised when her mother followed Harper in, and Harper realized he'd forgotten about the driving lesson. She tried not to notice the excitement in his face. *Don't get your hopes up*, she wanted to tell him, as she was telling it to herself.

They never ate at the table anymore, sitting down instead to eat in the kitchen individually or in groups of two or three but very seldom all four of them, so her father and Truman had taken over the dining room and spent hours there on nights and weekends, playing solitaire or fitting jigsaw pieces together. But today Truman wasn't home from his job at the dollar store yet, so her father sat at the table alone. He'd brought the puzzle home from the factory, without the box it would have been sold in. He just dumped the pieces onto the table from a gallon-size ziplock bag and started searching for the edges. When Harper asked him once, he said he couldn't even be sure all the pieces were there. "Doesn't that drive you crazy?" she said, because she couldn't imagine beginning a puzzle if she didn't know she'd be able to finish it in the end.

Her father shrugged and said it didn't matter. "I just like sitting here and trying things, moving the pieces around," he said.

Though he was halfway done by now, it was still hard to tell what the picture would be.

Harper sat with him for a while. Sometimes she told herself she'd stay until she found something he could use, but this hardly ever happened; too often she believed she'd made a match, only to have her father point out that she was mistaken—the colors were off, or there was just the slightest gap of space between pieces, instead of a perfect fit. Mostly she just kept him company and watched as he ran his hands over the pieces, leaned over the table to peer at them, picked one up, and either locked it in somewhere or tossed it into the pile again. Today he seemed distracted when she sat down, and without looking at her he said, "I'm sorry about what happened to Joy. I'm sorry you have to go through this."

Why was the effect so different when her father said what he did from when her mother had? It was because her father did not want her help in writing a book; he was not getting anything out of what she was suffering. She thanked him and stuck her hand out to pick up a random piece, and miraculously, she managed to fit it into the middle of the puzzle. Her father reached out to high-five her, and not having the heart to tell him she didn't think people really did this anymore, she high-fived him back.

Then she wrapped herself in the afghan and went to sit in front of her mother's poetry shelf, where she began searching for something to read at the funeral. The task felt unreal; part of her wanted to laugh at the absurdity of it, and she pictured Joy across from her laughing, too, her legs stretched straight out in front of her as she leaned against the bookshelf tossing a doll's plastic head back and forth like a baseball or an orange. In life, she always caught it. But in Harper's conjuring now, the head fell through watery hands and vanished, followed by Joy herself, though her laughter lingered.

She spent an hour looking, and during that hour she only found a single line that felt right. *After the first death, there is no other*. It struck her so hard that she had to sit back on her heels. It was about virginity, she realized. It had never occurred to her that there might be more than one kind, and that she'd lose hers without even having been aware it existed.

The Undead Forest

When she called Tom after the discovery of Joy's body, Susanne asked him to meet her at the mall, but he requested that she pick a different place. He told her it was because it was too hard to find a parking space with all the Christmas shoppers, but really it had more to do with the fact that his mother-in-law spent so much time there during the holidays, picking out presents for migrant families or doing other work for charities she prided her association with. The last thing Tom needed was for Helen to spot him having a conversation with the mother of the dead teenager whose murder Doug was trying to solve—the case that could make or break his bid to move from interim to permanent chief.

So Susanne suggested they meet at Brewed Awakenings instead. When he arrived, she was the only customer sitting at a table; she was hunched over a cappuccino and wearing a Yankees cap with the bill pulled forward, and he realized it was her effort at a disguise. He tapped the stack of magazines on the table—*People, Entertainment Weekly, Real Simple*—and asked, "You were reading these?" What he meant, he realized, was *Can you read them?* With what's happening now?

"No. I just look at the pictures." She twisted her mouth in

what was probably an attempt at a smile, before it became a grotesque signal of her grief. She must have seen it reflected back in Tom's expression, because she pulled up and into herself like a turtle not liking what he sees when he sticks his head out. "Thanks for coming," she said. "I wasn't sure what to do. With—this." She reached into her pocket, and for a wild moment Tom expected her to pull out a gun and shoot him. Even though he understood now that he had not failed to recover her daughter in the water that night, as he'd originally feared, he still felt residual guilt from the weeks he spent assuming he had.

He tried not to flinch as her hand came out of the pocket. But she was only holding a strip of cardboard covered with orange cloth, which she handed to him as she told him where she'd found it and where she had seen it first. "I have no idea why she would have had this," she told him. "Where it came from. I mean, I know *where* it came from, but I have no idea *why*."

Tom tried not to let on how hard his mind was working. The homemade bookmark was evidence—of something. Surely Susanne understood that the proper course of action would be to call the police. "Don't take this the wrong way," he said, "but why are you telling *me*?"

She gave a smile now that appeared more genuine, less tortured, and said, "Don't *you* take this the wrong way, but I'm not sure I trust that guy. I know he's your father-in-law, but . . ." She trailed off, sounding uncertain as she searched Tom's face. "If you tell me to turn this over to him, I'll do it. But I wanted to ask you first."

He understood; they had a history together. Two days after her daughter was presumed drowned, she'd called and left Tom a message, saying she'd seen his ad in the Classified section of *The Chilton Free Press*, offering his services as a private investigator. It was something he'd done—mainly, surveilling people who'd filed insurance claims, to make sure their injuries or illnesses were legit—because he thought it might, like his willingness to join the first responder and rescue dive teams, improve his standing when it came to what his father-in-law thought of him. *Let me find out what you need to know,* the ad went. *Licensed/free initial consultation. No infidelity.* He'd added the last because the guy he replaced in the gig for the insurance people had advised him to do so. *Otherwise you'll mostly get women wanting to catch their husbands in the act, and it doesn't take long to lose your stomach for that shit.*

In her message that day, Susanne told Tom that she wanted to hire him to find her daughter. "I get that the police don't believe me," she said, "but I know she ran away. We had a fight. She was doing some things she shouldn't have—I'm sure you know she got arrested for selling drugs, but it wasn't what it sounds like." A pause made him think she'd hung up then, but then she'd ended the message by adding, "I know she wants to come home, but by now she's too embarrassed."

He did not want to call her back but couldn't allow himself to let it go. He reminded himself that she'd have had no reason to guess that he'd been the diver who went down looking for her daughter two nights before. And especially no way to know what had happened down there, because he'd told no one: the fingers gripping his wrist and his shaking the hand away in panic, thinking that the girl (still alive? Already dead?) had tried to grab him as he swam by.

"I wouldn't know where to start," he'd told Susanne. Her voice saying hello had sounded distant, as if she held the receiver away from her mouth. "It's not really the kind of thing I do."

"You could ask people. Her friends, teachers. Anyone. *Please.*"

It was the last word—the desperation in it—that persuaded him. He owed her, didn't he? Even if she didn't know it.

And what if, by some miracle, she was right? What if her daughter *was* out there somewhere, and not under the frozen pond as everyone had assumed? In addition to being a hero for bringing the girl home, he'd be off the hook of his own conscience, knowing that it had only been mud or weeds, and not fingers, that caught him down there. He sighed, and probably sensing from the sound that he would agree, she offered to pay him a deposit. "I won't take any money," he told her. "And I can't promise anything. But I'll see what I can do."

His attempts were halfhearted, because he didn't expect them to turn up anything. Why would they? Everyone in their right mind—which seemed to include everyone except Susanne Enright—believed that Joy had, after yelling at her friends and stomping off, almost made it to the shore near the woods on the other side of the elbow's crook when the ice cracked open and the pond sucked her under. A four-year-old boy, who'd skated out too far while his mother was distracted, claimed to have heard a cry from that direction, though he didn't mention it to anyone until that night when he overheard his parents talking about a missing girl and a diver being sent below the ice to search for her. Police had already made the assumption that she was down there based on the ten-foot-square hole they'd found thirty yards from the farther shore, and the discovery of Joy's scarf (made for her by her grandmother during Emilia's last round of lucid knitting), which lay on the ice between the hole and the woods. Nobody offered a theory for how the scarf got so far from the hole; wind made the most sense, but the wind had been mild that day. Some animal might have carried it, someone suggested, without further suggesting what kind. An off-leash dog? A coyote or rabbit? It didn't particularly make sense, but in this part of the country in winter, everyone was accustomed to nature being responsible for things they would never have guessed.

Nobody went so far (at least in public) as to suggest that Joy had fallen prey to the woods' phantoms. For years high school students had gathered in a clearing by the crook to drink beer and smoke pot, but the parties stopped when they began hearing howls around midnight and seeing ghosts in the mist. This was about the time the obsession with zombies really took off, and kids began calling it the Undead Forest, moving their parties to King's Hill.

After Joy's body was found in the woods, the police figured whoever strangled her had left the scarf on the ice precisely to throw them off and lead them to the wrong conclusion. "If that's the case, we're dealing with a pretty clever killer," Doug told reporters.

On his way to the shack the day Susanne enlisted his help, Tom had stopped by the Enrights' neighborhood—not all the way "uphill," where the best houses were, but decidedly not down-hill, either—and knocked on a few doors. Asked a few questions and wrote down a few things, before approaching Susanne's own house. "What are you doing?" she asked him, and he realized she'd been watching through the window. He explained that this was what PIs did, in a case like this—interviewed people who knew the subject. (He was proud of himself for switching to *subject* from *victim* a moment before it would have been too late.) He was tempted to ask her if she'd ever noticed, as some of her neighbors had, a black man in a parked car across from her house, or down the street on the same side. But he knew the wiser thing to do was wait. "You won't find out anything *here*," Susanne said, gesturing at the homes surrounding her own.

They talked about Joy then—who her friends were, where she went with them, what she liked to do. Tom took notes as if he believed any of it might matter. Susanne asked him not to let her husband know she'd called to ask for his help. After an hour, Tom excused himself (it seemed clear to him that Susanne could have talked all day about her daughter) and said he had to get to work, allowing Susanne to believe he was referring to the effort to locate Joy.

After stopping in at the shack to make sure the new guy had shown up for his shift, he swung by the art school where Susanne was a faculty member. Though he'd lived in Chilton all his life, Tom had never actually visited the campus before, and now he wished he'd done so sooner—it was a nice place, with contemporary buildings someone had put care into designing, and sculptures surrounding the quad: some he could understand and appreciate, even though they had snow on them (a man in a toga, reaching and gasping, looking as if he were parched or wounded or both), and some he could not (a stack of spray-painted milk crates secured to one another with bungee cords; this Tom assumed was a pile from the cafeteria, until he saw the plaque identifying the crates with a title: *After Delivery*). From the directory he found the sculpting department, and in Massey Hall he spoke to one of Susanne's colleagues, a snobby-looking guy with a blond goatee, named Bart, who said that while he didn't want to speak ill of another faculty member, he was pretty sure there was something not right going on between Susanne and her teaching assistant.

"Not right?" Tom asked, playing dumb.

"You know. *Inappropriate.*" Bart made a motion putting quotation marks around the word. "I know they're both adults, but still. There's the power thing." Tom asked for the assistant's name and wrote *Martin Willett* in his notebook. Later he would find the word *hyperrealist* next to the name and assume that Professor Richlieu had been describing Willett's temperament.

"He's black," Richlieu added, and almost immediately seemed to realize he'd made a mistake. But he blustered through it. "I mention that because it's unusual, you know, around here."

If there had been any reason to believe that Joy Enright had been murdered, Tom might have told his father-in-law back then that it appeared Joy's mother had had—might still be having?—an affair with one of her students, who showed more of an interest than he should have in the life she led separate from him.

But as far as he knew, everyone aside from Susanne believed that her daughter had drowned, so he kept the information to himself. Until this past weekend, when, after hearing on the late news that the autopsy showed Joy had been murdered (and that a black man was being sought), he'd gone to wake up Doug to show him his notes. Doug had answered the door with his Glock raised, peering out to the stoop, then asked anxiously "She okay?" as he let Tom in. Tom assured him that he hadn't come about Alison, struck for perhaps the hundredth time by how strange it felt to share a love of the same person with someone who so obviously hated him. Maybe *hated* was too strong, but maybe not. Doug had never forgiven Tom for the fact that Alison had gotten pregnant their senior year, or for that first miscarriage she suffered a month after their hasty wedding a week after graduation, though in fact this had made it possible for her to start college on time. Tom knew Doug had advised Alison to file for divorce back then, but she refused, and Tom welcomed this as his new wife's first step of independence from her parents. Instead, it was the *only* step; taking it seemed to have a more traumatic effect on her than the miscarriage. After the second one a year later, it became clear that Doug actively believed his daughter deserved someone better.

Wishing Doug had lowered the Glock faster when he saw who was at the door, Tom handed his notebook over and said, "I knew you'd want to see this."

After flipping through the pages, his father-in-law looked up, and Tom waited for thanks and congratulations. Instead, Doug said, "What the fuck? You wait until the body turns up to hand this over? An active investigation—we had a right to know."

"It was a private job." In the dimly lit kitchen, Tom had done his best to keep his fist from clenching, an automatic habit when he felt a situation slipping beyond his control. "And it was just a favor to the mother. I didn't expect to turn up anything relevant. We all thought she was a floater."

"'Relevant,'" Doug said, mocking the word as he pronounced it. "You've hung around my daughter too long." From anyone else, it would have sounded like the joke it was intended to be. From Doug Armstrong to Tom Carbone, it was a genuine message: *You've hung around my daughter too long.*

"You're not afraid he'll see it and run? The black guy?"

Doug reached for his phone and said, "He's going nowhere. I'll put Pancho on him, and we'll get a warrant in the morning."

His real name wasn't Pancho, but Tom knew Doug didn't give a shit. Raul Dominguez was the department's most recent hire. He'd been forced on Doug by the Town Board, but that wasn't the only reason Doug couldn't stand him. "He's got two strikes against him he can't help," he'd told Tom once. "Being the size of an eight-year-old and being a spic. But on top of that, third strike, he's a pussy. That kind of cop doesn't do anybody any good."

When Susanne asked Tom now if he could help find out how Joy had come to possess Martin's bookmark, he knew he should advise her to give it to the police. She was asking him to go behind Doug's back, as he had done the first time. Recognizing this, Tom felt not apprehension (which would have been more apt), but a charge of excitement. "Are you doing this because you think he's innocent?" Instinctively he knew better than to speak Martin Willett's name.

She pressed a fist to her lips, and for a moment he worried that she was trying not to be sick. "I don't know," she whispered. "I can't bring myself to even imagine he might have done this. I don't think I could survive. I was sure they got it wrong, but then—that." She nodded at the bookmark on the bench between them.

"Did you tell anyone about this? Besides your husband?"

"I didn't even tell him." Guilt glinted in her eyes as they darted away from his. Then she rushed to justify herself. "I mean, we don't know if it means anything, right? And if it doesn't, then why—why—" Again she left her sentence unfinished, and again he understood what she was saying, anyway.

"If I do this," Tom said slowly, knowing that as he spoke he was in the act of acknowledging that he would, "it stays between us. You can't mention it to anyone. Okay?"

She agreed by nodding, and it looked to Tom as if the movement took the last of her energy. But he was wrong; she rose from the table and said she was getting another coffee. Did he want anything? He shook his head and said, "It won't keep you up?" before realizing it was a stupid question—caffeine would not be the thing to interfere with her sleep.

The next day he waited until he knew school was over, then drove over to interview the best friend. He was surprised when Barbara Grove answered the door, because he knew this was the house with the mother who hardly ever left it. He introduced himself, and she said, "Carbone? As in the English teacher?"

"That's my wife."

"My daughter's in her class."

"Oh, really?" He'd assumed this would be the case, since he knew that Alison's students included Joy and Delaney and Delaney's posse. But he pretended it was news to him. "That's great. Maybe I won't seem like such a stranger to her."

"You want to see Harper?"

"Harper, yes." Susanne had given him her name, but he'd also seen it while scrolling urgently through the case notes, having accessed them on the computer at the police dispatch desk after telling Natalie he'd take over for an hour while she went Christmas shopping. Normally she just left the automated message on the phones when she took a lunch break, but she wanted to hit the stores at ten, before they got crowded, and she worried that Doug would discover she'd slipped out when she was supposed to be on duty. Tom told her no sweat, he had an hour to kill, she should stay out longer if she wanted. He felt guilty for taking advantage of her—they were partners from the rescue dive class, so when they were out there with the tether between them, their lives literally depended upon each other—but he told himself he wasn't hurting anyone with what he was doing. He wasn't interfering with the official investigation, merely conducting a parallel one of his own.

He watched Natalie pull out of the lot, leaving it empty except for his truck, then started searching for the key to the Property and Evidence room. He knew that in big-city departments these rooms had surveillance cameras and fancy access security, but in Chilton, Property and Evidence consisted of a utility closet they'd expanded by knocking a wall down and adding some shelves. The plan was to install a keypad code system, but it wasn't provided for until next year's budget. In the meantime, there was a simple lock on the door that opened with a key, which Tom found in an envelope marked "P&E" in Natalie's middle drawer. If he hadn't felt ashamed of what he was about to do, and for exploiting her trust, he would have smiled at how simple it was.

He put on gloves, and in bags labeled with Martin Willett's name and a case number he found the black ski mask, the sketch of the dead girl, and a fine-ruled, classy-looking notebook that turned out to be some kind of journal. The final entry, dated the day before Monday's arrest, was a reworked draft of something from the earlier pages of the book, called an Artist's Statement. Tom knew he should hurry or risk Hal Beemon or one of the other guys coming in, but what he saw made him want to read more, so he flipped through to scan random entries from the previous year, each time telling himself it was the last one, then finding something else that interested him.

Back at the dispatch computer, he went through all the notes Doug had entered, including those covering his two interviews with Harper Grove—one from the second week in November, after her best friend had disappeared, and the other from this past Sunday, the day of the rush autopsy report. He copied the pertinent information into his own notebook, and when Natalie came back, he shot the shit with her for a while before saying he had to get back to the shack, then drove to the Groves' instead.

Without offering any description of the capacity he came in, he told Harper's mother that he was just looking to confirm some facts. "The chief likes to cross all his t's so there's no discrepancies when the case goes to trial," he said, hoping she would assume Doug had sent him. It must have worked, because Barbara Grove pulled the door open further, invited him in, and called her daughter's name up the stairs. "I'm sure she'll be happy to cooperate in any way she can." She hesitated, and above him Tom heard a door opening. When Harper appeared, her expression made it clear that she was not as enthusiastic as her mother about another interview. She sat down across from Tom warily, and when her mother mentioned the connection between him and Mrs. Carbone, she said, "I know that. You run the shack, right?"

He nodded. All the kids in Chilton had been buying Slurpees and hot chocolate from him for years, but not all of them paid attention to who was behind the counter. "And I do some investigating on the side," he added.

Barbara Grove said, "That's right. I've seen your ad in the paper," and this confirmation seemed to loosen the suspicion in her daughter's eyes. Tom adopted as easy a manner as he could, in an effort to warm the teenager up to him. "I promise not to take too much of your time," he told her, flipping open his notebook.

"Do you mind if I take some notes, too?" Without waiting for an answer, the girl's mother went into the kitchen and returned with her own notebook. Though he wanted to ask why, Tom recognized it wasn't any of his business and reminded himself that he was here to talk to the girl.

"Maybe you could just tell me the whole story, starting with when you got to the pond?"

"What do you mean, 'story'?" Harper pulled back in her seat.

"Nothing. I meant can you tell me what happened." But he recognized what was in her face—fear—and made a note of it without writing anything. "No big deal," he assured her. "Just—however you want to say it."

Harper inhaled and then let the breath out with what sounded like a sigh of resignation. "I went to the pond that day because I thought Joy might be in trouble. I don't know what I thought I could do about it—it was stupid of me—but I didn't like the idea of her going to see Delaney alone."

"How did you know they were going to the pond?"

"Facebook. I saw some messages."

"And what kind of trouble would Joy be in?"

"Well, she got arrested, you probably already know that."

"Right. But why in trouble with this *Delaney*, in particular?"

"I don't know. They were fighting."

"And you don't know what about?"

The girl shrugged, which didn't answer the question. "But then Joy yelled at me, so I left, and went up to the shack to use the pay phone. To call my brother to come pick me up."

"Did you see anyone going in or out of the shack?"

The girl shook her head.

"See anyone outside it?"

The girl shifted in her chair and looked at her mother, who said, "Go ahead, honey."

"Well, there was that guy who works for you, the stoner. And then there was a black guy sitting in his car. It looked like he was watching what was going on at the pond." She gazed at a spot beyond Tom's shoulder. "He was wearing a mask."

"And what kind of mask was it?" Tom kept his voice as casual as he could, looking not at Harper but down at his notes.

"I already *told* them this." She took another loud breath in impatience. "A ski mask."

"But you didn't actually see him come out of the shack, right?"

"Right. He was already in his car."

"And he was wearing the ski mask in his car?"

"Yeah."

"What was he doing? Just sitting there, wearing the mask?"

"Well, he made a phone call first, I guess. On his cell."

"You guess?" Tom looked up, letting his pen rest on the page.

"No, not *guess*. That's not what I meant." The girl's knees were trembling across from Tom's own. "Yes, he made a phone call."

"With the mask on? Was the mask over his ears?"

Harper just stared at him. Then she said, "You can still hear through a ski mask."

"How cold was it that day?"

"How should *I* know?"

"Honey," her mother said, "calm down. And be polite."

"I know, Mom, but—"

"Never mind," Tom interrupted. "It doesn't matter. Look, I can see you're upset. Just one more question, okay? Then I'll leave you alone, I promise." He'd said *I promise* multiple times since ringing the doorbell, he realized. He would have to tone it down.

Harper looked at him with eyes that might or might not have been about to brim over; he couldn't quite tell. Why? Was it only the stress of being asked questions about the death of her best friend? It felt to him like something else, something more.

"Go ahead," Harper said, though she sounded as if she wanted him to do anything but.

"Well, it's just that I'm wondering: if he had the mask on, how could you tell who it was? When Chief Armstrong showed you the picture. If you didn't see him come out of the shack, and he was already in the car with the mask on, how were you able to identify him?"

Her eyes slid fast into squinted slits. "That's not what I said. Or if I said it that way, I said it wrong. I saw him come out of the shack, and then he got in the car and put the mask on."

"Okay, got it. Sorry." Tom gave an apologetic nod, as if acknowledging that he'd been the one to make a mistake.

"Were you working there that day?" she asked, appearing emboldened by his apology. "If you were there, you would have seen him."

"I was there." He'd swung by to check on the new guy, whom he'd only hired because he felt sorry for him being such a loser. "And yeah, I did see a black man."

"Then what are you asking me for?"

Tom put a hand up to signal further his wish for peace. "It's just about the mask," he told her. "I didn't see him with the mask." He slapped the notebook shut, watching the girl slump with relief.

He was about to say he was sorry he'd had to intrude on them when the mother stood and held her shoulders in an exaggeratedly erect posture, as if to compensate for her daughter's sudden slouch. "There's a lot of suspicious things going on in this town," she declared. "What happened to Joy, that goes without saying. But those ATM robberies, too. And right before Joy vanished, somebody walked right into our house and robbed us, in broad daylight."

Her daughter winced. The mother didn't seem to notice, but Tom did. "What did they take?" he asked.

"Well, that's not important."

"Did you report it?"

"Well, no. But it happened. I'm just saying, there are some suspicious things."

He knew it was time to leave, before she could get any further into her rant. He'd already gotten what he'd come for. She escorted him to the door and he turned to thank the daughter, but she'd slipped out of the room while he wasn't looking.

Before

Thursday, May 14, 2009

Today, the last order of business for the academic year: the competition for the Lewison Award. I wasn't going to stick around after our last classes this week, because Grandee's so sick and I should get back to Rochester, but Violet convinced me I'd be crazy not to put up my work; the winner of the award receives a waiver of second-year tuition and a meeting with the owners from the Mirage Gallery in New York. "There's nothing for you to do here," she told me, on the phone from the hospital. "She'll still be here tomorrow. Go win your prize—that's what she wants."

Grandee is in no condition to want anything anymore, but I let it go and told Violet I'd see them both first thing in the morning. Then I won the prize, but that wasn't the most important thing that happened. *Don't skip the details.*

Twenty-six of us put up our entries in the sweltering Massey Hall (so hot the plastics people joked that their entries might melt). I entered the series I finished only last week, eight still lifes I call *American Commonplace*. My favorite is the one of Grandee's sewing table, *Pins and Needles*, because when I look at it I can hear in my memory the metallic whir of the machine, see her hands guiding the fabric through the presser foot as she hums along with the radio. The other subjects include the blue creamer and sugar bowl, both chipped; her jewelry box with a tangle of necklaces spilling out; the hand-shaped ashtray my own father made in school as a child, and which Grandee used to hold safety pins; and her winter coat hanging in the front-hall closet, orange scarf draped over the neck. She never looked good in orange (it showed up ancient acne scars on her face), but she never cared. The fact that she didn't care was what made me love the scarf, love *her*, and after finding an exact match to the orange, I laid the paint on thick, raising the scarf's folds to three dimensions, allowing it to reflect light in a way a single dimension could not.

Susanne was recused from reviewing my work because I'm her teaching assistant. The other two jurors—a black ceramics sculptor named Jonatha Hurley, and Bart Richlieu, a white color fieldist we all call Baby Mark because he basically just rips off Rothko—leaned forward to get a better look at the individual canvases, then stepped back to take in the series as a whole.

"Beautiful," Jonatha said, pausing to focus intently on *Winter Wear*. "The impasto on that scarf—ninety-nine out of a hundred people wouldn't think to do that. Ninety-nine and a *half*. I love it." It seemed that she might have uttered the last phrase to herself, not meaning for me to hear it. I tried not to show that I had.

"Ah, yes. Impressive," Bart said, tapping his beard in the habit all the students liked to imitate. "You're the hyperrealist. Interesting. Although—" He stopped himself, appeared to reconsider, then went ahead. "I don't really see how this speaks to the black experience."

I did my best to hide the sudden stiffness I felt in my forearms, my back, and my neck. Next to Bart, Jonatha took in a breath, and I waited for her to come to my rescue.

But she let the breath out and looked me in the eye. Though she remained silent, we communicated. *You*, the look told me.

She could have no way of knowing the paralysis I normally feel in a moment like this. Violet always scolds me for not standing up for myself—"for all of us," as she says. *Any time one of us gets disrespected, it means the rest of us do, too.*

I understand her point but do not agree. Beyond that, it is not in my nature to "stand up"—I prefer to hang back and observe, to live my own life behind the scenes. "Militant is not who I am," I told Violet once, and she said, "Oh, for God's sake. You sound like a woman who doesn't want to be called *feminist*.

"Nobody's asking you to be Malcolm X," she added. "Or Gloria Steinem. Just speak up once in a while, when you don't like what somebody says."

She meant a moment like today, when I didn't like Bart Richlieu questioning how the painting of my grandmother's coat speaks to the black experience. Along with the encouragement I saw in Jonatha Hurley's eyes, I could almost feel Violet kicking me in the seat.

"Well, *I'm* black." I could have left it there, but being brave for a change felt good, so I did not. "And it speaks to *my* experience."

I couldn't tell if Jonatha approved of my answer or found it lacking. Probably somewhere in the middle, which is what I myself think of it, now that I've had time to reflect.

When the award was announced and I had won, Susanne gave me a hug as any mentor would, but there was more in it than that. At first I thought I was mistaken, wishful, but then she got wine-tipsy at the reception afterward and began flirting with me. Though I knew better, I offered her a ride home in her own car because we both knew she shouldn't be driving. When I asked for directions to her house, she said, "Never mind. Show me your apartment," and when I said, "Really?" she laughed and reached across the seat to touch my shoulder, then my thigh, and I sucked in my breath without wanting her to hear it.

An hour later in bed, after we made love (my fingers tremble, just writing those words), Susanne said, "I can't believe we just did this. It's so wrong, in so many ways."

She was right and I knew it, but at that moment I did not want to admit the truth. "It doesn't feel wrong to me," I said, cupping my hand over the bone of her hip to hide the fact that I was lying. That I could touch her at all still struck me with a rush I didn't recognize from anything before in my life. I am feeling it still.

"I'm married," she reminded me. "I'm so much older than you. You're a *student*," and she gave the last word an emphasis suggesting it was the worst thing I could be.

I ignored that part, along with the part about her being married, and said there wasn't all that much difference in our ages. "You're what, thirty-seven? Thirty-eight?" I knew she was actually forty-two; I looked it up online after she did my admissions interview last year.

I didn't expect her to correct me—Grandee always shaved ten years off what she told people, even doctors, who knew better— but Susanne did, seeming to think I might recoil when I heard her actual age. Instead I told her she didn't look it, which is the truth, and said I was twenty-eight. This was adding four years, but I justified it by reminding myself it was to make her feel better about the gap.

She looked relieved. "You don't mind sleeping with a woman with saggy boobs?" She tapped one with her fingertip.

I kissed it and said, "Not if you don't mind sleeping with a chubby black man."

She remained still for a moment, then pulled back to look at me. "Black has nothing to do with it."

"Oh, but *chubby* does?" Teasing her was the only way I could think to change a subject I kicked myself for bringing up. I knew she probably believed herself, but black always has something to do with it.

She didn't smile. "One of the things I noticed, when we met," she said, snuggling closer, "was that I didn't get the sense you didn't trust me, or didn't like me, because I'm white. Sometimes I do get that sense, when I meet a black person. Is that awful of me?"

All I could think was that the weight of her head, lying on my arm, felt perfect. But that wouldn't be what she wanted to hear. I said I didn't think it was awful, though this wasn't precisely the truth. It also occurred to me to ask how often she met a black person in Chilton, but I didn't do that, either. I knew she'd lived in New York before she came here.

"And if I do sense it," she went on, "then *I* feel defensive. Even though I understand that I could be wrong. I mean, how would I know? I just met them. I could totally be projecting onto them something that isn't there. But what if it is?" I knew she didn't really expect an answer; as earnest as I knew she was, she was also somewhat drunk, and I was listening to a monologue in search of its own point. "Like I've always kind of felt that way with Jonatha. We're perfectly friendly, but there's this wall. I could be just as responsible for it as she is, but I only feel it from her."

Even though I did not want to talk about it, I felt I had no choice but to murmur, "And she could be feeling it only from you."

"I know!" The faint scent of chardonnay filled the air when she exhaled. "But I didn't feel that way when *we* met." She waved a hand in the space between us. "That's what I'm trying to say. When you came for your interview. I think it was because you talked about Basquiat, so we kind of got it out of the way."

I considered telling her about what happened in the sauna this morning after my swim. As I arranged my towel and sat down, the white man who'd been in there got up to go out. I closed my eyes to relax, but thirty seconds later he opened the

door again, letting in a blast of cool air, and said, "I didn't want
you to think I got out because you came in." He held his towel
together in front of his chest with a fist the way women do, and
it was obvious he wanted to be absolved.

"I didn't think that," I told him, feeling weary though it was
not even eight in the morning. "I just assumed you were done."
The man apologized, waited a moment hoping I would say it
was okay, then apologized again and retreated when I didn't.
On my way out of the building I stopped to talk to the security guard, Percy, who's the only other black person I ever
see on campus besides Jonatha Hurley and a metal sculpturist,
Lizzy, whom I met when I went to some Students for Obama
meetings.

I'm not sure if I feel a bond with Percy because we're both
black or because we've both worked security jobs, but it's probably both. He calls me Pablo because, he says, Picasso is the only
artist he ever knew anything about, before me. I repeated my
conversation with the man in the sauna, and he shook his head
and said *White guys* as if I'd know exactly what he meant, which,
in a way, I did. Still, I felt a little bad about the encounter. The
man in the sauna was awkward, but at least he thought about
things. So did Susanne. So did I. But at the moment, I wasn't
in the mood for those things. I held her close and, my mouth
moving in her hair, whispered that I hoped she wasn't going to
be sorry about what we'd just done.

"If I am, it won't be your fault," she said. "It'll be out of my
own guilt."

"I don't want you to feel guilty."

"It won't just be a feeling. I *am* guilty."

There was nothing I could say to this. She is married, she
broke her vows. With me. So I'm guilty, too.

"What's your husband like?" Why did I ask this, and at that
moment? To remind us both further that he existed, I guess.

"Gil?" She was only buying time, of course; what other husband could I mean? "Well, he has his own business, called Odd Men Out. He has a few guys who work for him; they go around and fix things in people's houses. That and little contracting jobs." The importance to her sentence of the word *little* was not lost on me.

Then she seemed to realize she hadn't answered my question. She told me he was a good man, but that they were different in a lot of ways. "Just this morning," she said, "he was reading to me from a magazine about some—I don't know, some *star*, and I wanted to say to him, 'For both our sakes, you should be telling this to somebody else.'"

I listened, afraid to recognize the hope I felt generated by her words. Was she saying that *she* wanted to be with somebody other than her husband?

Then she told me what he'd done with the inheritance she received from her parents, blowing it all on a scheme he thought would get them out from under. Of course, it didn't. "It was a *scheme*, for God's sake." She kicked the covers away as if with that motion she could fling off the anger accompanying her words. "We had a nest egg, we had the money for Joy to go to Decker, if she gets in. And to pay for a nursing home for Gil's mother. Now who knows what will happen with that? And they might take our house."

"They won't take your house," I said. I meant it as reassurance, but it only seemed to make her madder.

"How do you know? They're taking people's houses left and right."

Not ready to let her go, I pulled her back to me. "Well, if they do, you can live here."

She smiled, and stayed close, but the evening was over; we both understood that I'd ruined it by bringing up Gil. And the last thing she'd told me about him threatened to tarnish the pleasure I felt in the time we'd just spent together. Was it possible that she'd slept with me—an act I admit I had imagined, but would never have initiated myself—to get back at him for what he'd done?

To keep from wondering (and to prolong her presence in my bed), I told her I had a star story for her. I told her that on the door of my grandmother's room at the hospital in Rochester, there's a sign that looks as if some little kid drew it, yellow stars in a black sky. *Falling stars*, it says. At first Violet and I thought it was just a decoration, maybe from an art workshop on the children's cancer ward. Then the nurse told us it was actually a signal to any medical person assigned to Grandee. It means she's at risk of falling if she tries to get out of bed by herself.

"Oh," Susanne said, putting a hand to her chest. "I love that. They could have just written *FALL RISK* on her door. But that's so depressing and blunt. How much better is it that they put up a picture instead? Using art as a kind of code."

I'd thought so, too, at the time. I didn't tell Susanne what Violet had said when the sign was explained to us: *What is this, a hospital or a nursery school?*

"That's a *good* star story," Susanne murmured. "That's one I *wanted* to hear." Her voice came out drowsy, and she flung an arm over my waist as she nuzzled closer.

She warned me not to let her sleep, but I couldn't help it. A few minutes later when she woke up, she scrambled to put her clothes back on, and I worried she would tell me it had been a mistake. But she didn't, and even kissed me (the cheek, though) before hurrying out the door.

There was no way I'd be able to sleep myself, so I stayed up and finally made a few notes about *Souls on Board*, which I should have already started by now. I don't know what's been holding me back—am I afraid of failing at the project I've planned for so long, the vision that kept me going after my father died, and ever since?—but this day and night have given me new inspiration.

Artist's Statement DRAFT

Souls on Board is inspired by the loss of an airplane that crashed in a thunderstorm off the coast of North Carolina on April 30, 1997. The crash killed 149 people, including my father. Passengers are portrayed in individual panels, assembled in grids laid out to simulate an aircraft cabin: six horizontal rows and six vertical, with a dividing space down the middle to designate the aisle. The panels are separate, self-contained portraits of people who recognize that they are entering the last seconds of their lives.

The concept for this piece comes from Jacob Lawrence's series *The Migration of the Negro* (although those panels tell a progressive story, whereas mine represent multiple experiences of a simultaneous moment). For style, I am influenced by the work of hyperrealist painters, particularly Chuck Close and Alyssa Monks. Medium: oil on linen.

What I hope to evoke in the viewer is

I've been sitting here trying to complete that last sentence for half an hour. But I'll have to put the book aside without finishing, at least for—everything that's happened today has finally caught up to me.

Monday, September 7

S usanne invited me over for a Labor Day barbecue along with members of Gil's crew—some he's had to lay off, and the few still working for him. We haven't seen each other since the night we slept together, which seems like longer ago than four months. I called her after Grandee died, and she called back to say she was sorry, but after that she told me we'd better "let things go" for the summer, she'd see me back here when school started again.

I did not want to "let things go," but I recognized that I had no choice in it. When she asked me to the barbecue, I felt both thrilled and anxious. I considered declining, or at least pretended to consider it, knowing that in the end I wouldn't resist the chance to see her as soon as I could, especially in her own home.

She gave me the same hug as when I'd won the Lewison Award back in May, only a few hours before she came to my house (and my bed). This time her husband was right there next to her, and he shook my hand as I felt my heart batter against my chest. They introduced me to Joy, who was not what I expected; from everything Susanne had told me about her last spring, I'd pictured a lighthearted girl. This one appeared somber, uneasy, although I thought I saw a light in her eyes when she heard my name. Feeling a tension among the three of them, not wanting to wonder about its source, I excused myself to join a group of men from Gil's crew.

But I felt just as awkward with them, not knowing what to talk about and sensing that they felt the awkwardness, too. I believed it was because of me, and not because I'm an artist instead of a contractor or handyman. One tried to talk to me about basketball, and I had to confess that I don't follow the Knicks or anyone else. Another asked me where I'm from, and when I said Rochester, he started to say something else but stopped himself. (*I mean originally*, I guessed were the words; it's happened before.) A third, who smelled like pot, appeared to feel as uncomfortable as I did, and he let me know in an undertone that this was the case—"I'm one of the shitcans, not enough work to go around. Last thing I wanted to do today was come eat hot dogs and suck up, but whatever, he said he's gonna try to bring me back on. Like I buy that. But I figure I don't have a choice, right?"

At first, I wasn't even sure if it was me he was muttering to or not, because he was looking across the room at his former coworkers, who'd edged themselves away. I excused myself to the bathroom, and after feigning the use of it I lingered in the hallway to look at the pictures hanging on the wall. I thought maybe I'd see something of Susanne's, but instead I found a series of framed crayon drawings with the signature *JOY*, in block print letters, occupying the bottom right corners. The later pieces were done in a mixture of crayon and paint—crayon outlines filled in with watercolor, creating an effect that was at once primitive and sophisticated. The work had a distinctive, deliberate style, and I could tell that Joy had a gift, maybe even more so (although I would never have told her this) than Susanne herself.

Joy came up behind me and said, "Don't look at those." But her tone was more embarrassed than commanding. "Those are all old. I don't do that stuff anymore."

I told her they were beautiful.

"Well, you're nice to say so. To hear that from you—I'm flattered." She averted her eyes, and I remembered Susanne telling me she was shy. Yet she showed more energy and animation now than when we'd met a few minutes earlier. "My mother took me to see *American Commonplace* last spring. I loved it."

"She did?" I was surprised Susanne hadn't told me this.

"It was amazing." The fervency in her voice told me the praise was real. "Can I show you my more recent stuff? It's in here." She led me into her bedroom, where a series of impressionist pencil drawings hung on the far wall. I peered closely at each one, exhilarated by the skill I saw.

"You use such minimal detail," I said. "It's the exact opposite of what I do. But the effect is just as powerful—we just go about it in different ways." She asked me how I would define hyperrealism, and I said I thought of it as not only the effort to reproduce life on the canvas but to render it as more real than it actually is.

"How can something be *more* real?" she asked. I said I thought it was a matter of how you looked at things, which was the whole point of art, and not wanting to get us mired down in that particular quicksand, I gestured again at her sketches and said, "I see a lot of Monet in these." The one I liked best was a group of children jointly examining an object in front of them that could not be identified—a ball? An apple? "And van Gogh, too." At the end of the row was a variation on van Gogh's *Hands in Repose*, and I recognized immediately that Joy had used her mother as a model, though of course I could not say so because I could not give away my intimate knowledge of her mother's hands. Instead I told her that though I'd never tried charcoal myself, I'd been struck in reading about it to learn that so much of that medium is erasing: the artist covers the page with black and then creates an image by deciding how much to take away, instead of adding.

Joy nodded. "'I saw the angel in the marble and carved until I set him free.'" She blushed, seeming embarrassed to have the Michelangelo quote so readily at hand.

"You've been talking to your mother." Anyone who knew Susanne would have recognized one of her favorite lines. "Are you going on for a degree?" Then I wanted to kick myself, remembering too late what Susanne had told me: they'd saved enough money for Joy to attend the Decker Institute in New York, but her husband lost everything on that bad investment.

So when Joy nodded and said, "Decker," I tried to hide my surprise.

"Really?"

"You must have thought about applying there," she added. Every art student thinks about applying to Decker.

"I couldn't afford it," I told her. I didn't feel like saying the other part of the truth, which is that I'd been afraid to be rejected. "They don't give any aid." Surely she knows this, I thought. But it wasn't my place to deflate her fantasies of attending the premier art school in the country. Instead I wished her luck and made as if to leave the room, but she caught my arm and said, "Wait. What are you working on now?"

I sensed something in her that I often feel in myself: the impulse to be distracted from the subject at hand. Yet she also appeared genuinely interested in my answer. I found myself eager to describe *Souls on Board* to her, though at school I tend not to talk about it. Why? I get along fine with the other graduate students, but I haven't found anyone I particularly want to confide in, besides Susanne. Joy is different.

I began by describing the plane crash that killed my father

and the phone conversation we'd had the night before it, when he called from Atlanta and I waited for him to describe the meeting he'd had with Linda Martin. How anxious I was to hear what she'd said when he raised to my mother the prospect of meeting me, or at least getting to know me through letters and on the phone.

But instead he told me he wanted to wait until he could speak to me in person about how the visit had gone. That was when I knew he'd never even contacted Linda—that he'd no doubt done the same thing he always did when faced with anything that made him anxious: chickened out. Instead of arranging beforehand to meet with her, he must have booked the plane trip believing that once he got that far, the investment he'd made and the trouble he'd gone to would spur him on to completing the mission. I imagined the scene: he arrives at the airport, checks into some crappy hotel room intending to take a cab to the address he's somehow found for her, but then looks in the mirror and loses his nerve.

What was he afraid of? That she'd close the door in his face? That he'd see the white husband and white children and be reminded of how wrong he'd been to love her, or how wrong for her to love him? *It's not a big deal*, I pictured him trying to convince himself. But of course he would have known that it was a very big deal, him stepping back into her life after she'd explicitly asked him not to. So he got cold feet and boarded the flight headed for home.

Even through the chaos of what followed the news of the crash—having to endure and manage Grandee's grief, as well as my own—I realized I was waiting for Linda Martin to show up. I expected to see her at the funeral. Wouldn't the list of people on the downed plane be printed in the newspaper? Wouldn't she have seen James Willett's name, realized it was my father, made an effort to learn about the arrangements, and decided that she owed him the courtesy of paying her final respects? Not to mention meet the son she'd given up at birth twelve years earlier?

But this was a fantasy, of course—as was every other thing I'd ever hoped for with regard to my mother. Even if she'd seen the name, which was not a given, she might have decided it was another James Willett; she'd have no reason to think he'd have left upstate New York. More to the point, there'd be no reward for her in believing it was her old lover. It was in her best interest to leave the two of us, him and me, tucked together in some corner of her mind as a piece of unpleasantness from her past she'd taken care of, no need to think about it anymore.

I told all of this to Joy even as I realized how irrelevant it was to the question she'd asked me about my work. But instead of directing the subject back to art, she said, "I'm close to my grandmother, too," and asked what happened after my father died. I found myself wanting to continue my story. Now that Grandee is gone, there's no one else who knows it all; even with Violet and Susanne I've held things back, afraid to say everything in case it overwhelms me, afraid to seem too vulnerable.

But somehow, this afternoon, I didn't worry about that with Joy. I told her that after the plane crash I went to live with my grandmother, staying with her as a commuter student during college and for a year after I graduated, when I worked as a guard at the Memorial Art Gallery. I told Joy that in the same way I'd been obsessed before the crash by the idea that my white mother living in the South would come back and ask me to be in her life, I replaced that obsession afterward by imagining what it had been like for everyone on the plane during those last few seconds as the storm pitched them toward the water. That was the plan for my project, I said—to depict those passengers at the moment they realized their lives were about to end.

Almost imperceptibly (but I saw it), Joy frowned. "What?"

I asked, feeling warier than if she'd been one of my professors. When she mumbled *Nothing* and shook her head, I pressed her on it.

"Well," she said, "who am I to tell you what you should do?" She seemed chagrined by her own audacity, but it didn't keep her from continuing. "I was thinking that if you capture them when they *know* what's happening, it's really a portrait of the fear they're feeling, instead of the people themselves. Right?" But she didn't wait for me to answer. "I was just thinking it might be more—haunting, or whatever—if you painted them right *before* they knew. Wouldn't that make it all the more poignant, somehow? All the more sad? Then, if I'm standing in front of the painting and I know what happens in the next instant, I'm thinking, *That could be me. Or any of us.*"

I recognized immediately that she was right, yet for some reason I felt embarrassed to let her know this, and played down my reaction as I made a point of appearing to consider her words. She asked if I'd started any of the portraits yet, and I told her *Not really*. When she asked why, I admitted I was afraid I wouldn't be able to pull it off.

"Well, for sure you won't if you never get started." Joy's answer came so readily, and made so much sense, that I laughed. In the next moment, I knew she'd just told me something more valuable than anything I'd heard from an art professor during the past year, including Susanne.

Joy asked how many panels I planned. When I told her three dozen, she whistled and said, "So it's not a diptych, and it's not a triptych—"

I smiled back. "Right. It's a thirty-six-tych."

"And where did you get the title? '*Souls on Board*'?"

It was an old nautical term, I told her, from when ships carried corpses and needed a way to distinguish between live passengers and dead ones in caskets, in case the ship went down

and all that could be recovered were bodies in the water. (I decided not to mention another origin of the phrase, which had to
do with slave ships and the fact that souls were attributed only
to the white people on them.)

"It gives me the creeps," Joy murmured, shivering as she
wrapped her arms around herself. "But I bet it'll be amazing
when you're done."

Her saying this made us both blush, and I hoped Joy didn't
also have her mother's talent for being able to see this in me.
Then, from the kitchen, we heard Susanne calling Joy's name
before she appeared in the doorway. It took her a moment to
register that I was also in the room, and what passed over her
face then was a smile expressing not only pleasure but posses-
siveness as well, which she tried but failed to redirect toward
Joy alone. Joy, I could tell, saw that I was included in it, too.
Registering this, I hurried toward the door as Joy held her hand
open to indicate that I should precede her out of the bedroom
and back to the party. Something had changed between us, and
in the way she looked at me. I didn't speak to her alone again
during the cookout, except when I was leaving, when I added a
Good luck to my good-bye.

"You, too," she said. I waited for the smile she'd shown me so
frequently during our earlier conversation. But she had already
turned her face away, and the connection was lost.

First Friend

The day before their test on *The Odyssey*, Joy came over to help Harper study, but instead she was helping her set up a Facebook page. She hadn't done it before now because Harper's mother was afraid some lunatic might track her down and kill her.

"Your mother doesn't have to know everything," Joy said, her fingers hovering above the mouse as she paused before the section reserved for a profile description. "Mine doesn't. Here, I'm putting that you have a cat who plays the piano and you're an awesome baker."

"'Pastry chef.' And could that *be* any more boring?"

"Not the part about the piano-playing cat." Joy smiled, and Harper couldn't help smiling back. As if he knew they were talking about him, Chip lifted his head from the bedspread and blinked. "If you want to sound interesting, you could always tell the truth, that you have a mother who's written fourteen unpublished novels and refuses to drive."

"It's not fourteen," Harper said. But she had lost count by now; it might have been fourteen. "And it's not really *refusing*. She would just prefer not to." She hoped Joy would smile at the reference to *Bartleby*, which they'd read the first week of the semester, but Joy seemed to have missed it in her intense focus on creating Harper's page.

"Where are your pictures?" she asked, picking up one of the protein pumpkin bars Harper had made especially for her; too much sugar could make Joy sick. She scrolled around on Harper's computer until she found the file, then clicked through images. "Here's a good one," she said. "It's of both of us, but I can crop it so it's just you."

"Really, let's just forget it. Who am I kidding? I'll end up with, like, three Friends. Can't we just forget Facebook and study for the test?"

"But it's all done! Look, there you are." Joy made a flourishing motion with her hands to display Harper's profile. For a moment Harper flinched, but it was more in expectation of what she might see than what was actually on the screen. In fact, Joy had uploaded one of the few photographs Harper liked of herself, which Joy's mother had taken at Elbow Pond the summer before their junior year. The girls had just come out of the water and wrapped an old Little Mermaid towel around themselves, Joy's sun-blond hair tangled with Harper's shorter brown at the spot where their shoulders joined. The shot made Harper appear almost pretty; someone who didn't know better might mistake her for a popular girl.

There hadn't been any trips to the pond together this summer, which meant that Harper didn't go at all. Part of the reason was that Joy spent so many hours at her nursing home job, but there was another part of it that Harper was afraid to ask about. All she knew was that she'd missed their old routine, and Joy, more than she was willing to admit, even to herself. When Joy suggested this study session, Harper felt bad for wondering why, and tried to convince herself that Joy missed these times, too. It almost worked.

"I'm Friending you right now," Joy said. "I want to be your

first Friend." She gave the keyboard a few clicks, then put the computer to sleep.

You already are my first friend, Harper wanted to tell her. *You know that, right?* But she knew Joy knew. She rubbed Chip under the chin and asked, "Can we look at those questions now?" She was afraid Joy would have to go home before she could help Harper understand anything about the book they were supposed to have read.

But there was plenty of time. Joy explained it all to her, and when she got to the part about the dog recognizing his old master after ten years, even though Odysseus was in disguise and his best friend didn't know who he was, Harper rubbed the soft hair of Chip's head and felt herself wanting to cry. She turned away to try to hide it, but Joy said, "It's okay, Harp. That part's *supposed* to be sad."

To deflect her embarrassment, Harper gestured at the book and said, "I don't see how you get any of this. All that language. How can you tell what the story is?"

Joy shrugged and said, "I'm just really, really smart," and even though she meant it as a joke, they both knew it was true. To subtract from the truth of it (which she did so often around Harper), she went over to the window seat to pick up Harper's only American Girl doll—Addy, the black one, which her hippie Aunt Heidi (everyone in the family called her this, as if "hippie" were part of her name) had sent for Christmas one year—and pulled the doll's head off. Harper's brother had pulled the head off straight out of the box, and they'd never been able to fit it back on properly; whenever Joy came over, she liked to remove Addy's head and play with it like a ball. Harper had never been able to tell Joy this made her nervous, even though she understood that Addy was plastic and couldn't feel anything.

She looked away as Joy rolled the doll's head between her

hands. "We're lucky we got Carbone for English," Joy said. "Don't you think? I mean, she's nice, right?"

Harper shrugged. "I guess." She didn't trust her own judgment enough to say that she sometimes thought there was something off about their teacher. She wouldn't have been able to define it any further beyond "off," and anyway, what did she know? Most people seemed to love Mrs. C. "What are those kids doing in her classroom sometimes during lunch?" she asked. "What's up with that?"

"I think she helps them," Joy said. "Not with schoolwork—more like stuff at home. You know her mother was a drunk once, right? She likes to help kids whose parents are messed up. Like, Keith Nance is in there all the time."

Harper refrained from responding. She didn't want to be forced to feel any sympathy for Keith Nance.

"Speaking of *what's up with that*," Joy added, "what about Tru?" She'd passed him on her way up to Harper's bedroom and said *Hey*, but he hadn't answered. "Why is he so obsessed with solitaire?"

Harper was about to give an answer—she believed it was her brother's superstitious way of trying to ensure that everything would be all right—when her mother rapped at the door and told them it was time for dinner, which meant that it was time for Harper to make dinner.

"Crap. What time is it?" Joy woke up the computer to check the clock. "My mother was supposed to be here by now."

"Your mother's never late." It was one of the many things Harper admired and appreciated about Mrs. Enright: she could be counted on to do what she was supposed to.

"Yeah, well. That was before she started having an affair." Joy began chewing on her thumb.

"What? *What?* She is not." Harper practically shouted it, and Chip jumped off the bed to express disapproval at the noise.

"Yes, she is. This black guy from her school, her teaching assistant." Joy gave Addy's head one last toss, this one almost to the ceiling, before cramming it back onto its body. "He came over for a cookout with some of my father's guys. We talked about art and stuff. He was completely awesome." For a few moments her focus left the room as she appeared to remember the conversation. Then she snapped back. "At least I thought he was awesome, but now, since I figured it out, I hate him. I mean, I hate her worse. But I hate him, too."

"I don't believe it," Harper said.

"I didn't either, at first."

"But why?"

Joy shrugged to indicate either *Who knows?* or *Who cares?*; Harper couldn't tell which. Then Joy lowered her head and murmured, almost as if she didn't intend Harper to hear, "I can't tell you what it's done to me, Harp. Everything I thought I knew about how the world works, or who people are—my faith in my own judgment—it's gone straight to hell."

"Don't say that." Harper felt a chill.

"Okay." But the smile Joy gave did not reassure her. Then Joy jammed her books into her backpack and added, "Of course, if I had a cell phone, I could just *call* my mother. But no." She gave the zipper a furious tug. "My father says I don't need a cell phone. How would he know?"

Harper didn't answer. Not having cell phones because their parents wouldn't let them was something they had in common, so although she sympathized with Joy, she didn't want to lose that bond between them because it felt like one of the last. "He doesn't even know my mother's sleeping with this guy," Joy continued.

"How do you know he doesn't know? Did you ask him?"

Anybody else would have said *Duh*, but Harper knew she could count on her best friend not to do so. "Because he's completely clueless" was all Joy said. She'd shrunk into herself since uttering the word *affair*, and the sight made Harper want to shake her back to her original form. But before she could think how to do so, Joy reached for Harper's computer. "Let's see how many Friends you got."

"Just you, right?" Harper panicked. She hadn't realized Joy would be inviting anyone else to her page.

"Hey, look, you already got five requests."

With trepidation, Harper leaned toward the screen. Eric Feinbloom, that was okay; they'd been real friends ever since Home Ec (you were supposed to say Family and Consumer Sciences now, but nobody ever did) in seventh grade. Eric knew almost as much about cooking as Harper knew about baking, and they planned to open a restaurant together after college. Joy showed her how to accept Eric's request. There was another one from Sandra Sherman. "Who's that?" Joy asked, but Harper pretended she didn't know, rather than admit it was a lady from her mother's therapy group, whom Harper had met a few times when her mother dragged her along. Her mother said she did this so that her problems wouldn't be such a mystery to Harper, and Harper could never bring herself to say she was fine with the mystery, she had no desire to sit in that circle and listen to adults talk about how frightened they were by the world.

The other three requests came from girls in their class— Delaney, Tessa, and Lin. Joy paused when she saw the names. Harper said, "That's a joke, right?"

"It could be." Harper loved her friend all over again for saying it this way, when it was obvious that those girls were just mocking her. "Whatever you do, don't accept them. They'd probably post things on your Wall you wouldn't care about." What Joy meant, Harper knew, was that they would post mean things, cruel things, for other people as well as Harper to see.

She was on the verge of asking Joy to close the account

altogether when Harper's mother returned to tell them that Joy's mother had pulled up in front of the house.

"Just don't do anything else here until I can show you, okay?" Joy gestured at the computer and lifted her pack over her shoulder. There were so many books in it—she took mostly advanced classes—that the weight made Harper feel weary just to look at. She nodded and followed her friend downstairs, sorry as always to see Joy go.

Secure Choice

On her way to pick up Joy at Harper's house, Susanne stopped to buy a pizza. Standing at the counter at Adriano's she ran into Rachel Feinbloom, who laughed when she saw Susanne and said, "Great minds, huh? Glad I'm not the only one who gives her kids pizza for dinner."

"Brain food," Susanne said, and Rachel laughed again as if she'd said something funny. "Eric not cooking tonight?"

"He had the nerve to stay after for SAT prep." Rachel opened the cooler and pulled out three Sprites. "He's kind of freaked out about it—he didn't do great the first time; he gets spacey on standardized tests. Mark and I keep telling him don't worry about it, you want to be a chef, not a brain surgeon, but he still wants to improve his score." She shrugged. "I think it's a matter of pride. The kids are always comparing."

Susanne made a *hmm* sound of agreement, hoping (though she knew she should be ashamed of it) that Rachel would ask about Joy's scores. Probably suspecting this, Rachel met her halfway. "Joy taking them again, too?"

"No," Susanne said, which would have been enough, but then she couldn't resist adding "She doesn't have to." She knew this was obnoxious, but at least it was better than coming right out and saying that Joy had received perfect scores.

"She is so smart." Rachel shook her head, as if contemplating some marvel she just couldn't get over. "Hey, did you hear Delaney Stowell got an *almost* perfect score?"

"Really?" Susanne knew she should try to hide her reaction, but it was too late. "Delaney—you're sure?" she asked, as if Rachel might have uttered the wrong name by mistake. If it was true, she was glad she'd heard this news from Rachel and not Lynette Stowell, who would have been insufferable in delivering it.

"I know. I was surprised, too. Maybe she's more than we give her credit for." Rachel paid for her pizzas, picked up the bag of sodas, and turned to leave, but then a thought appeared to stop her and she put the items back down on the counter. "Look, Susanne, I know this isn't my place," she said, lowering her voice to such a degree that Susanne dreaded whatever was coming next. "I don't mean to intrude, but—well, I'll just say this: I hope everything's okay."

"Of course it is," Susanne said, so shocked by the inquiry that she answered without fully registering how inappropriate it was. They left the pizza shop together and she gave a wave as Rachel pulled away first, then had to sit in the car and concentrate on controlling her breath.

Rachel's question wasn't really about "everything" in that vague, undefined way you say it to people intending to wish them well. It was about Mark Feinbloom's job at Chilton Secure Choice, where Gil and Susanne held their mortgage, and where Gil had taken out an equity line on his odd-job business, after the bottom fell out of everything and after the fiasco with the "sure thing" he'd believed would earn them back their original investment and enough on top of that to maintain his mother at Belle Meadow. It was about the bank sending Gil statements about how far behind he was, and how much time he would be allowed to catch up before the bank took action. It was about Mark Feinbloom telling his wife things he should have kept confidential, goddammit. And it wasn't exactly the kind of thing Susanne could call him on without drawing more attention to the facts.

She knew she hadn't succeeded in appearing to brush off Rachel's question as if it didn't concern her. Why hadn't she had the presence of mind to change the subject—to ask, for instance, if Mark knew anything about the string of ATM robberies throughout the county during the past few months? Now Rachel would go home and tell Mark who she'd run into while picking up pizza, and they'd share a moment of smug sympathy as they shook their heads over the Enrights' foolishness or ineptitude.

Outside Harper Grove's house Susanne beeped, knowing it was rude, but she justified it by reminding herself that if she went to the door, she risked being forced into conversation with Harper's mother. Susanne had avoided her whenever possible since the girls were in second grade, when Barbara Grove drove Joy home from the mall one day and Joy carried in a cardboard case saying, "Mrs. Grove got us matching kittens for Christmas!" and then opened the box to let Salsa step cautiously into the room and, so, into their family. What kind of mother just let someone else's kid bring a cat home without checking first? Not to mention that a few years ago Barbara had just stopped driving, leaving the carpool in the lurch. The last thing Susanne needed today was to get stuck talking to that woman.

It took a second set of beeps before Joy came out, buds lodged in her ears as she studied her iPod and barely nodded in response to Susanne's greeting.

At home they listened to a message from Gil saying he'd be late because of a stove install—the kind of job he would never have taken, before last year—and Joy reached into the pizza box as soon as Susanne set it down. "Could you feed her first?" Susanne said, gesturing at Salsa who nuzzled around Joy's legs, demanding her own dinner.

"No, I really can't. I'm too weak from hunger." In the old days Joy would have smiled saying such a thing, but she hardly ever smiled anymore. Still, Susanne appreciated the attempt at lightness, because there wasn't much of that in the house these days. They each ate a slice without speaking, and reaching to find something to fill the silence, Susanne mentioned that she'd just run into Eric Feinbloom's mother. Had Joy heard anything about Delaney Stowell getting almost perfect scores on the SAT?

Joy made an elaborate show of needing to swallow before she answered. "Of course I haven't heard that. Because it can't possibly be true."

"I don't know. She seemed pretty sure." When Joy didn't respond she continued, "I can't tell you how proud it makes me—how well *you* did. Dad, too. Gotta love those recessive genes." They'd been making the recessive genes joke since Joy was in middle school, when she showed them her math homework one day and Susanne and Gil just looked at each other and laughed.

She'd thought Joy would appreciate being told her parents were proud of her, but instead she looked down at her lap. "What?" Susanne asked, but Joy shook her head. Susanne still felt a lurch when this happened, though she knew she should be used to it by now. Joy had begun retreating from them over the summer, and especially since school started, though Gil and Susanne didn't know why. They saw less and less of her, partly because she took on as many hours as they would give her at the nursing home and partly because when she wasn't working, she spent more time in her bedroom than with her parents. "Tell me, honey. What's wrong?"

But even she could tell from her voice that the invitation was false; she did not really want to hear an answer.

"Listen, I *know*," Joy told her. "Did you think I wouldn't find out?"

"Find out what?" But Susanne stood to begin clearing the plates as she spoke, trying not to understand that Joy must have overheard her and Gil discussing their money problems. Was it possible she also knew there was no way she'd be able to go to Decker, the dream of hers they'd supported for years, promising they'd do everything they could to make it happen? They'd been careful, but maybe they'd let something slip. "We're going to be fine. It's just temporary. Let Dad and me handle it—it's not for you to worry."

Joy made a noise. Standing at the sink, Susanne could not see her daughter's face, so she couldn't be sure what Joy was expressing. She turned to watch Joy leave the room followed by loyal Salsa, who lifted her tail at Susanne as if in reproach.

Not Dominant

The sun wouldn't be up for another half hour, but at seven o'clock they were already waiting for Tom, pacing with hands pocketed, doing the addict's impatient two-step outside the shack's front doors. Above them, the sign that said Elbow Room (or *E bo oom*, where it had been stuck for weeks because he kept forgetting to call the electrician) was still dark, the letters waiting to erupt in orange neon at his flick of the switch that lit the place to a hum. Tom recognized both men as he pulled up and got out without even looking at the pond or at the white mist rising over the orange and red tops of trees. That's what came from always being around something beautiful; you didn't even notice it anymore.

He let them in and waited for their selections. A case of Genesee Cream Ale for the first in line and a pack of Camels for the second guy, Chilton's longest-standing burnout, who'd been a few years ahead of Tom in high school. Both of them looked embarrassed, needing these fixes before breakfast, and Tom felt like telling them but didn't not to worry; his own father—who'd opened this place up back in the Sixties—used to keep a pint of schnapps in his night table and a pack of Luckies under his pillow. To get him up on the right side, he used to say through his hack.

The guy buying the Genny said, "I got a full house coming" as he gestured to the row of blue labels he'd hoisted onto the counter.

Tom went along with it, because the guy needed him to. "Have fun," he said, slapping a PAID sticker on the case.

The Camels buyer was named Cliff something, but in high school he'd been known as Pothead Pete. Tom had been too far behind to be in any of the same classes, but he used to hear his older sister and her friends talk about the kid whose father drove a regular truck route to New York City for two jobs: the legitimate one, picking up stock for Wegmans, and his own weed business on the side. Everybody knew Pete had been sprinkling pot on his Lucky Charms since sixth grade. He was also famous for never looking anybody straight in the eye, which made people nervous. He'd come into the shack to buy cigarettes and munchies for years, but Tom never really spoke to him before this past February, when a turboprop coming in from Plattsburgh went down during an ice storm and first responders from six counties rushed to the scene. Pete showed up and tried to join in—this was when they still thought there might be some survivors—but when he started running toward the fireball in the field before the trucks even arrived, Tom had to tackle him to hold him back. Pete told him to fuck off and said he'd heard the call on the radio, he was there to help. He was a volunteer, he said. "That doesn't mean you just show up," Tom told him, managing to hold back the word *moron*. "You have to go through the training and join a crew." The next time he looked, Pete had disappeared. And when he came into the shack for cigarettes a few mornings later, he didn't seem to recognize Tom from the burning field.

Pete yanked a snack pack of Doritos off the impulse display rack and dropped it next to the Camels, then counted out change and clattered it on the counter instead of handing it over, which usually pissed Tom off. But he let it go. The guy was miserable, you could tell just by looking at him, and Tom both hated and felt sorry for him because he reminded him of his father. There was just a loser type, and this guy was it. "They ever going to come back?" he asked Pete, jerking his head in the direction of the condo construction along the reservoir. *Lakeview Arms*. Really it should have been "Pondview," but "Lakeview" sounded better. They were described as luxury units, but everything had stalled a month or two after the meltdown, and the project had been on hold for a year.

"Is who going to come back?" Pothead Pete looked at the deli slicer as he ripped open the Doritos with his teeth.

Duh, Tom wanted to say, but didn't. "The condos."

"Fuck if I know." Pete was busy rummaging in his pockets.

"But you worked there, right?" Tom tossed him a book of matches.

Pete caught it without thanking him and said, "Before I got shit-canned I did." He wanted to light up right there in the store, Tom could tell, but instead he cupped the cigarette and asked, "Hey, you hiring?"

Tom started to shake his head, then caught himself. What skin would it be off him to throw a few shifts to this guy, especially with the holidays coming? He still felt kind of guilty about the way he'd tossed him out of the crash site that night, and it would give him a chance to be home more, try to figure out how to repair things with Alison. Ignoring the dismay he felt at remembering that his marriage needed repair, he gave Pete—Cliff—an application and a pen, told him that if everything checked out, he could start on Sunday morning. Cliff seemed to stifle a groan, but he muttered *Thanks* before slouching to the door and saying he'd bring the application back the next time he came in.

The shack empty of customers, Tom called Alison. "I can't talk," she said, by way of answering. "I'm late already."

"Are you sure you don't want me to go with you later?"

A pause, during which he dared to hope she had changed her mind. Then she said, "I just really feel like going alone this time. I know it's stupid, but I keep thinking that if we do things differently, the results will be different. You know?"

He did know; he was tempted to believe in this superstition himself. "Okay. But will you call me as soon as you find out?"

"No. I'll tell you in person, whatever it is."

"It'll be good news, I promise."

"We don't know that," she said. "Don't get your hopes up." It sounded more like an order than a wish for his well-being.

"See you around four thirty, then. I can't wait."

She said, "Don't go yet," and he kept the phone to his ear, gratified to think that she needed another moment of his moral support. Instead she told him, "My parents are coming for dinner."

Trying to keep his voice neutral, he asked, "Tonight? Why?"

"I thought it would be nice, if we have something to celebrate."

"But like you said, we might not." The bell over the shack's door rang, announcing the entrance of three high school girls. Because his father had trained him to expect teenagers to try to lift something, Tom kept his eye on them as they shuffled toward the candy aisle. "Either way, wouldn't it be better if it was just us? I mean—either way?"

"I gotta go," Alison said, putting the phone down. The girls brought their selections up to the counter—Jolly Ranchers, Sky Bars, Reese's Peanut Butter Cups. One, with a streak of pink in her bangs, stood back as the other two paid.

Tom refrained from asking if they had Mrs. Carbone for English. They looked about the right age. "This your breakfast?" he said instead. "Nice."

He actually meant it, as in *I wish I could eat a candy bar for breakfast*, but the girls took his comment as sarcasm. "Whatever," the pink-haired one said, as she grabbed the bag from him and strode out leading the other two. He caught what she said under her breath to make the other girls giggle: *Perv.*

He was angry, but only for a moment. Then he saw how funny, in fact, it was. Tom Carbone, once Chilton Regional High's pass-yards record holder and homecoming king, reduced to working a crappy job running his father's old crappy convenience store.

And was *funny* the right word? Probably not, but he was damned if he knew what was. He'd never been a student, one to pay attention in English or any other class. That had been Alison's thing—one of the things he'd ruined.

For the thousandth time he remembered that he didn't deserve her. But watching the high school girls climb laughing into a Volvo worth three of his trucks, he resolved again to do whatever it took to become a husband who did. He'd turn things around somehow; he just wasn't sure how yet.

His father-in-law's Buick was already sitting behind Alison's car on their side of the duplex when Tom pulled up, not even four thirty. He breathed out a curse and parked on the street. On the seat beside him was a bag containing two cartons of ice cream, to give Alison a choice. He'd driven too fast on the way home from the Stewart's store, wanting to hear whatever the news was and not wanting the ice cream to melt.

He knew she'd appreciate his thoughts behind bringing the ice cream: either they would celebrate and pretend she was already pregnant enough to have cravings, or they would eat their way through the disappointment—again—via Philly Vanilla and Heavenly Hash. These were the only two situations in which she allowed sugar in the house. Otherwise, there was nothing except what was contained in fruit and whatever the manufacturers put in Diet Coke, which Alison bought by the case. She called it her "secret vice," which made no sense to Tom because she was not secretive about it at all; one whole fridge door was filled with cans so she could be sure there was always a cold one waiting.

Alison met him at the door. Seeing the red in her eyes, he drew her against him and said, "Okay." He'd been expecting this, and not. He felt more angry than sad, which surprised him. "It's okay. Next time."

Mutely, she nodded against his chest, then pulled away as her parents entered the kitchen from the living room, where they must have all been sitting when he drove in. How long had they been there, and how long had they known? No matter how many times he tried to convince Alison that he should hear such news first, she always said she didn't see why it mattered, they were all family, her parents deserved to know whether they were finally going to have a grandchild or not.

Helen put an arm around her daughter. Doug shook Tom's hand and said, "Sorry, guy." But his blue eyes held the usual accusation Tom saw there.

He never liked looking into those eyes, even though they were so much like Alison's. So blue, so light, they startled people. Drew comments. On Alison they were pretty, the first thing people noticed, the thing she was most proud of about her looks even though of course she'd had nothing to do with it.

Doug Armstrong's eyes were a different story. On him, Tom thought, the blue was a sinister disguise, designed to tell people *Trust me, I'm harmless.* Not dominant; Tom remembered that from biology in tenth grade. He couldn't remember the word for what blue was, beaten out by the darker what—pigments? All he knew was that if he and Alison had a kid, it would have brown eyes. All the Carbones did. It was in the genes, like athletic ability or an ear for music. *Or being a drunk*—but Tom shut down that notion as soon as it entered his mind.

"Tom, so sorry." His mother-in-law made the greeting sound like a condolence, coming toward him with outstretched arms. However cold Doug's eyes made him feel, Helen's false warmth was worse. Though she'd gotten sober ten years ago, when he and Alison were sophomores, it was clear she white-knuckled it all the way; she'd always seemed fragile to Tom, freeze-dried, as if missing the one element—alcohol—that would restore her to her normal state. Against his will, he let himself be taken into a hug. "I told Alison already, this is just a setback, not a defeat. You'll keep trying, it'll take. You're both young and healthy. You've just had some bad luck so far."

Bad luck was not what the doctor called it—he said it had to do with that first fall, and how the doctor in charge of the miscarriage, back then, had handled things. Tom came away from that appointment convinced he and Alison would never have children of their own, a conviction the second miscarriage, a year later, seemed to confirm. He understood you weren't supposed to think of it that way—that you could adopt a child and it would still be your "own"—but he knew what he meant by it, and he knew everyone else did, too. For better or worse, he and Alison still wanted a kid with a mix of their two bloods running through its veins. A kid that looked like them. He or she might inherit Helen's craggy voice, or Alison's shortness, or Tom's father's apparent wish to destroy himself. But it didn't matter. That was what they wanted. Tom hoped for a girl for the first one; Alison, a boy. At least, that's how they'd started out thinking about it. Now they just wanted a baby that would make it to the second trimester.

"I got some stuff," Alison told them all now, gesturing toward the kitchen table, where she had set out tubs of prepared food from the supermarket. "If it had been better news, I would have cooked something. But—you know." She rubbed a hand across her forehead. Helen said *Poor baby* and began putting the food back in the fridge.

"Nobody's hungry, anyway. Right?" she said. Tom knew he couldn't say that in fact he *was* hungry, not having eaten anything since the two full-size Snickers bars he'd pulled off the candy shelf as soon as the pink-haired girl and her friends left the store laughing at him.

He told Alison he'd put the food away, and sent her and her parents into the living room. He took a spoon and ladled potato salad, egg salad, and coleslaw into his mouth without using a plate or napkin. When he sensed he was staying away from the others too long, he put the tubs back in the fridge, checked his teeth in the powder-room mirror, and went in to gauge the mood in the living room.

They were all sitting around looking at the space in front of them; no one spoke.

"Everything's going to change around here," Tom said, feeling that in this moment, in his own house, he had to assert something or lose what little power he had. He was referring to all of it: Alison and a successful pregnancy; their being able to move from this crappy duplex into a house of their own; his finding the money somewhere to upgrade the shack, adding the diner counter his father had always dreamed of installing; the state of his and Alison's union. Doug and Helen nodded, raising their glasses (beer for him, seltzer with lemon for her). "I got ice cream," Tom said, remembering the cartons only then, but Alison shook her head and told them all she was going to bed; it hadn't been the best day.

Trust

A few days after her encounter with Rachel Feinbloom at the pizza shop, Susanne came home from dropping Joy off for her shift at the nursing home and found Gil going through a sheaf of bank papers at the kitchen table.

"Suse," he said. He was staring at a statement as if it contained words in a language he could not comprehend. "You didn't put money in for me, did you? Into the business account?"

She laughed with a degree of bitterness she had not quite realized she felt. "I'm serious," he told her. "Seventeen hundred dollars. I didn't do that. It wasn't you?"

"Of course it wasn't," she told him. "One, I don't have any extra money, remember?" A dig referring to the folly he had shown by investing the trust Susanne's parents had left her, along with his own savings, in a venture he'd been told was a sure thing but that turned out to be a hoax from which they couldn't recover what he'd put in.

Folly was a generous word for it. A betrayal is what it was, they both knew, and Susanne had allowed herself to consider it justification for the betrayal she'd committed herself against him, with Martin, though Gil didn't know about that yet.

"And two," she went on, "even if I *did* have it, I would have just given it to you." She moved toward the table and held her hand out for the statement. He showed her. "You should check with the bank," she said. "Check with Mark Feinbloom. He seems pretty interested in our financial affairs."

When Gil asked what she meant, she remembered she'd decided not to tell him about Rachel's solicitous inquiry—*I hope everything's okay*—when they'd run into each other at Adriano's. "I just mean he could probably trace that deposit," she said. "If you wanted to know."

What was it that had made her add that last line? It went without saying, so why did she propose that there might be an "if"?

When Gil didn't respond, she knew he was considering the same question. If it was a bank mistake, wasn't it up to the bank to fix? If neither of them had deposited the money, it had to be a mistake, and inquiring about it would only result in that amount being subtracted from an account already too low.

"I'm not the kind of guy who doesn't ask about stuff like this," he murmured, as if reminding himself. Susanne remained silent. "But it's not that much money. It's not that big a deal. We'll see." He tossed the bank statement to the other end of the table and rubbed his hand over the top of his head, where the hair had begun thinning in earnest during the past year.

Last May, just before he'd confessed to her about the money, he'd looked so pale and sick that she feared he was going to say he had a terminal disease. So when she understood what it was he was telling her instead, it took a few moments to sink in because she experienced those moments of relief first, before actually hearing him say that he'd taken the bulk of her inheritance out of their joint account, fully assured that he would be restoring the original investment within a few months along with the first of many returns. Had she yelled? She didn't think so. More likely, she couldn't find her voice. "I can't believe you did that," she kept saying, when it came back to her. "Do you realize what you did?"

Now, watching him wear away his hair, she felt the same sick feeling he must have felt that day before asking her to sit down. She'd known she was going to tell Gil about Martin; she just hadn't decided when, and she didn't think it would be so soon after she'd broken things off with him after resuming the affair (despite her intentions) when classes began again in September. Did she choose this moment to keep herself from being tempted again—to reinforce, in her own mind, the fact that it was over? Or was it because Gil looked so forlorn already, trying to make sense of his accounts, that she figured his spirits didn't have that much farther to fall?

She was wrong. After she told him (and what words had she used? She couldn't quite remember, even a few minutes after she'd said them. "I had an affair"? "I slept with someone"? She'd come up with different options in her vision for this scene but forgot them all when it came time), he just sat there looking at her with an unchanged expression, as if he were still waiting to hear what she had to say.

Was it possible she had only imagined telling him? "Did you hear me?" she asked.

He shot out a bullet of a guffaw. "What kind of question is that? I'm sitting right here. You just told me you slept with somebody. How could I not *hear* you?"

She sat back, feeling chastened. When he didn't continue, she thought for a moment that the anxiety in the silence between them might smother her. "Don't you want to know who it was?"

"It doesn't really matter, does it? It was somebody besides me. That's all that counts." Then, both of them understanding that he was just biting the bullet to get through what was inevitable, he sighed and said, "Okay, go ahead."

She told him *Martin*. He'd been bracing himself, but at hearing the name he furrowed his brow and said, "*Who?*"

She reminded him: Gil had met him only once, during the barbecue they'd hosted on Labor Day. Susanne had never talked much about him before that, first because she was afraid that telling the truth about Martin's talent—how exceptional he was—would threaten Gil somehow (though later she recognized this as only a wish of her own she felt ashamed of; she'd always wanted her husband to aspire to more, though he was perfectly content fixing things and restoring them to function. He was a craftsman, he'd always said, not an artist. There was a difference. *If you need to be with an artist*, he told her, shortly before he proposed, *we should break up now, because it's not me*, and at the time she told him *Don't be silly, it doesn't matter, you do work you're proud of and that's what counts*) and later, after sleeping with Martin, of course she did not bring up his name.

When he understood who she was talking about, Gil frowned further. "But he's—"

"I know."

"I mean—"

"That doesn't really matter, though, does it? I mean, what difference does it make that he's black?"

"Black? That's not what I was going to say."

"What, then?" Of course he'd been going to say *black*. But she let it slide because she was in no position not to.

Gil sat back in his chair. "I was going to say he's a grad student, right? I mean, how old is he?"

She shrugged, not because she wasn't sure, but to buy time. "Late twenties. I don't know, exactly." Both lies; he was twenty-four, which he'd confessed to her the second time they were in bed together.

"Jeez, Suse." Gil took his glasses off and rubbed his eyes. She'd always found endearing about him the fact that when he cursed, he did it so mildly—not out of prudishness but because he considered lavish swearing a lack of personal control. Between the massaging he'd done of his hair and face since they'd started talking, it looked almost as if he'd erased an entire dimension of his features, using the force of his shock and dismay to flatten himself. "That makes him closer to Joy's age than ours."

"I know." She'd done the calculating.

"And that means"—he looked up at the ceiling, counting to himself—"we were in high school, Joy's age, when he was *born*."

That one she hadn't thought about. He said, "That's technically a whole generation."

"Well. Let's not get carried away."

"No, really. It's *more* than a generation. *Fifteen* years is what they consider a generation." From the italics she heard in his words, she could tell it was important to him to make this point, so she let it go.

"I drank too much at a reception," she said, "and let myself do something I shouldn't have." Blaming it on the wine. She remembered blabbing on and on to Martin about black people, white people; what was it she had said? Something she'd never have said sober, no doubt. But he'd seemed to forgive her. "It was only that one time." Another lie; it had been six times—the night of the Lewison competition last spring, and then once a week since school had started, until now. She persuaded herself, as she was speaking, that to tell Gil the details would only add insult to injury. The important thing was that she was confessing, wasn't it? It didn't matter whether it was one time or six—the first time was the one that changed things, wasn't it? The fact that the line had been crossed was the important thing—not how many times.

He gathered the papers from the table slowly, drawing them into a pile in an order that might have made sense or might not; she couldn't tell. She could see that as he performed the task, he was forming his thoughts. "I can't believe you did that," he said finally, placing his palm on the papers as if afraid they might fly away. "I never thought you were the kind of person who would do this to me."

Her first impulse was to say *I'm not*. Then she realized how absurd that would sound, on the face of it. "Neither did I," she said instead. A defense had been brewing at some depth of herself, she realized, and now it rose to the surface. "So now we've both done things the other wouldn't have imagined."

A movement of his mouth caused a few drops of spit to fall on the pages of his accounts, and he wiped them with the back of his hand. "You're going to compare them? You're going to compare what I did, here"—he gestured at the bank documents—"to an affair?"

"Why not? They're both betrayals."

"Not the same kind."

"Are you serious? You took my parents' money and just gave it away, without even telling me! What would *you* call it?"

He was quiet for a moment before murmuring, "I didn't give it away. I mean, I didn't think of it like that." But there was concession in his tone.

"It doesn't matter how you thought of it. That's what happened. And it wasn't just me you betrayed. It was Joy, too." How she wished she could hang on to the feeling of righteous anger that accompanied these words. But it was gone as soon as she named it, to herself, for what it was.

Gil was still looking down at the papers, though she knew he was not actually seeing the numbers there. "When I did what I did," he said, in an even smaller voice, "I did it because I was afraid to tell you. And I honestly thought it would have a good outcome—that you'd forgive me once you saw how much we made on the initial investment. I see how stupid I was to think that, now. But stupid isn't the same as—what you did." What word had he been planning to use? *Deceitful? Treacherous?* She was grateful to him for switching tracks at the last minute.

But then he must have decided he didn't want to let her off the hook. "I mean, what I felt was fear. When you slept with him, what did *you* feel?"

She hesitated. "I felt pissed off. And I wanted to hurt you."

"Okay." Though she could see that it did hurt him, he also seemed to appreciate what she told him and to accept it as the full truth. "Thank you for that."

It was partly true; it had been true the first time, the night of the Lewison Award, her drinking too much wine, acknowledging to herself her attraction to Martin (and his to her), and allowing herself to act on it after thinking the words *Fuck it*, meaning her marriage to Gil. But after that, it wasn't about Gil anymore. It was about the excitement she felt at being so intimate with an artist of Martin's talent. Not because she was certain he would be famous—celebrated, even—in a very short time, although she *was* certain of this. She was pretty sure she wasn't a "star-fucker"—a term she'd heard on campus when students clamored to be invited to after-parties with visiting artists.

No, it had more to do with the kind of person she believed Martin to be when she saw what he could do with a brush, what he could render on the canvas. He used color in a way she'd never seen before, and she knew she wasn't the only one who had such a visceral response to his work; it was as if he had access to a more refined, more nuanced palette than the rest of them could see. To be able to make her feel what he did with his art, he had to have a mind that worked in a way that was different from most of the others and, she admitted to herself, from hers. He had to see the world in a way she only wished she could. Was it a kind of wisdom? It seemed so, to her. Especially in someone so young. Being close to such brilliance made her feel elevated, in a way she'd never experienced before. It was heady, exhilarating, a thrill.

But this was not something she could explain to Gil, as she had not explained it to Martin, or even to herself before now. Across the table from her, her husband slumped, as if the conversation had taken all the wind out of him. Eventually he got up and mumbled that he'd be spending the night at the Odd Men Out office, and she let him go. When she picked Joy up at Belle Meadow, she told her that her father had been called away to a faucet emergency in Rochester (a *faucet emergency!* Where had *that* come from?) and that he would likely spend the night in a hotel there when he was done. "Whatever," Joy said, and shrugged. It was her favorite word these days, and her favorite gesture, at least in conversation with Susanne.

The next day when Gil called to say he needed to stay away awhile longer, Susanne told him she'd been doing some thinking and that she understood their marriage would be different now, but did *different* have to mean *worse?* Maybe it would end up being a good thing, she suggested. A blessing in disguise. Yes, they'd betrayed and hurt each other, but it was out in the open now, right? They could move on from there. He was silent on the phone for so long that she wondered if he'd hung up.

Neither of them had any way of knowing how different their marriage would be within a few weeks, and why. For the moment, their crisis was over. They would never think of it as a crisis again, because in light of what came so soon after, it didn't even compare.

After

Wednesday, December 9

They were supposed to transfer me to the county jail yesterday, but there's been some kind of holdup. Ramona's looking into it. This morning I planned to ask her what she could do to force them to let me take a shower, which I haven't done since before my arrest, but that went out of my head as soon as she arrived to say that her investigators had located Linda Martin outside Atlanta. And without too much trouble, to Ramona's surprise. Her name is Linda Martin-Forsyth now. To forestall hearing more, I asked how I was supposed to pay for the investigators who'd done the legwork. Ramona told me not to worry, but the look on her face signaled that something remained to be said.

"What?" I asked, steeling myself.

"She put up the bail money. We stressed to her that this is a case of an innocent person being falsely accused." *An innocent person.* I could have been anybody—they'd decided that it was safer to appeal to Linda Martin's general sense of morality than to her instincts as a mother to defend her child.

"And?" I could tell there was still more; I wanted to get it over with.

But Ramona fiddled with the collar of her white blouse and said, "There's no 'and.' She posted your bail. That's it."

"She didn't ask any questions? About me?" Ramona shrugged and said she guessed not. "Then forget it. I don't want her money." Though I recognized it as ridiculous, I wanted to cry.

Ramona said quietly, "Don't be silly. You need to accept this. And it's not like a permanent gift—she'll get it back after the trial." When still I remained silent, she went on to acknowledge that she understood this was hard. "It's not fair when someone who says he's innocent has to go through all of this."

The nuance of her remark was not lost on me. Not *someone who's innocent* but *someone who says he's innocent.*

"So you think there'll be a trial?"

The question seemed to surprise her. "Yes. I think they have enough to indict."

"Even though it's circumstantial?"

"It's not unusual that that's all a prosecutor has. A grand jury only has to decide whether there's enough evidence of any kind to go forward with the case—the standard is different from the one for a jury in a trial." I must have reacted to this, because she snapped her fingers and said, "Come on. This is not the time to be hanging your head. Tell me what I need to know to help you, then we'll get you out of here."

She asked me to describe my relationship with Susanne, beginning with the day we met a year and a half ago. I told her the basics—just an outline, really—but as I spoke, an alternative memory (the one containing all the details) ran on a parallel track beside the stripped-down version I offered to Ramona. In the memory, I sat across from Susanne in her office at the Genesee Valley Academy of Fine Arts, my application file open on the desk between us. I was nervous, because I was such an admirer of her *Show of Hands* (one of the first exhibits of sculpture I ever saw "in person": sculptures of hands in various poses portraying emotion—clasped in hope, fisted in frustration, fingers twined in the child's steeple game to evoke whimsy), though I was too shy to bring it up. I also didn't know how my own work would compare to that of the other applicants.

"Why do you want to come here?" Susanne asked, the first question in the interview. Later, after we began sleeping together, she told me that she'd left out the sentence she assumed I would understand preceded her question: "You could go anywhere."

But I had *not* understood this. Instead I believed she was challenging me, because I had no recommendations from any real artists, though I'd studied art in the sense that the security job I'd held at the gallery in Rochester, since graduating from college, allowed me to look at and learn from paintings all day.

I shifted in my chair. "I'm pretty much self-taught, so I figure I might have some bad habits I should correct before it's too late. Also, I have this project I want to work on, something I've been planning for years, and I figured it would be useful to—have some help." I faltered at the end because, yes, I was interested to see what professors could teach me, but it was as much for the connections to the official art world, and guidance through those ranks, that I sought admission to the school.

Susanne was smiling a little. "It's okay," she said. "I wasn't asking you to justify your application." She had a little overbite, I saw, and the misalignment made me feel a flash of tenderness toward her. "If you can paint like this with 'bad habits,' I'm not the only one who wants to see what you'd do with good ones." Then she straightened up, closed her lips over her teeth, and adjusted herself back into the role of interviewer. "A number of us looked at your submission—more than the ones who had to. What you do with color is just incredible. You already have fans here among the faculty, including me." She began flipping again through my portfolio pages—photographs of paintings I made in an early effort to imitate the Old Masters, using people from my own neighborhood as models. For my *Birth of*

Venus, I painted a girl in my class, who had hair so long she could sit on it, holding the hair over her crotch with one hand and the other hand covering her breasts, although instead of being nude as in the original, she wore cut-offs and a tee-shirt that said EXISTENCE CAN BE REARRANGED. For *An Old Woman Reading*, I painted Grandee holding open her favorite book, *The Price of the Ticket*.

Susanne asked which painters I was particularly fond of. I went on for longer than I should have about my admiration for Chuck Close, even quoting him about his desire to "knock people's socks off" with his work. Then I mentioned discovering Jacob Lawrence's *The Migration of the Negro* for a project in my ninth-grade history class and how ever since then I'd been fascinated by the idea of painting multiple grids.

"Are you blushing?" she asked, when I paused after saying the word "Negro." I was impressed; most white people can't tell when a black person blushes, and at that moment I wished it was true of her.

"It's just that a lot of people expect me to be Basquiat. But my art isn't political—it's personal. I mean, if something political comes out of it, fine, but that isn't where I start from." I coughed a little to make myself shut up, thinking it was already too late.

"Well, no one would expect you to be Basquiat here. All of our students are pretty good at being themselves, for better or worse." Those teeth sticking out in a smile again. She flipped down her reading glasses to look at her watch, then told me she was sorry but she had another appointment, and stood to say good-bye. Her hand was warm when I shook it, and though I was sure I only imagined it, I thought her eyes lingered on my face.

Of course, I didn't elaborate upon any of this in speaking to Ramona, beyond acknowledging that yes, I had been Susanne's teaching assistant, and yes, we'd had an affair, which began with a single night last May. I'd thought that would be it—that was my understanding—but then we'd ended up sleeping together again after classes started in September. Not long before Joy died, Susanne broke it off. I told Ramona I'd texted her, but Susanne didn't respond. Right after that was the first time (of only two times, before the day of Joy's disappearance) that I drove to her house.

"They have people who can testify to seeing you parked in her neighborhood." Ramona read to me from her notes. "More than once."

"It was two times," I repeated. I knew she must be referring to the frowzy woman from the house a few doors down from Susanne's, who'd come out and, smelling of tangerine as she leaned toward my car, asked *Can I help you?* when I sensed that what she really wanted to say was *What are you doing here?* but realized she could not. "I kept thinking I'd work up the courage to ask her to come out and talk to me," I told Ramona. "That's not a crime, is it?" But I knew how it sounded.

Ramona shrugged. I didn't take it as a good sign that my lawyer was shrugging when I asked if I'd committed a crime. But then she said, "I wouldn't say so, because it requires the assumption that Susanne herself—Mrs. Enright—felt threatened somehow by your actions, and that doesn't appear to be the case. It doesn't appear that she even knew about it—they haven't presented any indication of that." She rolled up her white sleeves. "Did you ever go to her house as an invited guest?"

I nodded, and she asked, *When?* I told her about the barbecue on Labor Day. Had I met Joy then? Yes. Had we had a conversation? Yes. Ramona asked what we'd talked about.

"Art," I said. "Drawing and painting, mine and hers. She's— she was an impressionist. She was good."

Ramona scribbled a note to herself. "Did you ever have occasion to talk to her privately, besides that day?"

I told her no, then panicked. My instincts warned me against mentioning the visit Joy had made to my house on Halloween, but why? There'd been nothing wrong in it, but would Ramona—and other people—believe that? I knew I should correct myself and tell Ramona I'd just remembered a second encounter, but I couldn't make myself speak the words.

Instead I said, "They're going to indict me, aren't they," a statement instead of a question.

She sighed. "I'll say it again: it's more likely than not. But I'm still trying to see if I can talk to the people who said they saw you with the mask—the guy who was working at the convenience store and the teenager, a friend of Joy's, outside. Maybe I can find out something we haven't already been told."

"There *was* a girl at the pay phone." I hadn't remembered before, but now I recalled seeing her nearly in tears as she spoke into the receiver. Her face had reminded me of Rodin's *Crying Woman*. "Why she'd say I had a mask on, though, I have no idea." As in the courtroom when I stood before the judge, I was aware of reining in the anger I felt as I said it. "The cashier I'd met before, at Susanne's house. He worked for her husband, then was laid off. He seemed kind of—well, I'm not sure how much of an impression he'll make on a jury. He struck me as not too clear." Remembering how he rambled on at the barbecue, I'd been going to say "not too bright," then figured Ramona probably wasn't interested in my assessment of the witness's intelligence. And of course, I might have been mistaken. "But the store owner would remember me, I think. He kind of went out of his way to strike up a conversation. I can't think of a reason for him to have anything against me."

"I'll see if I can meet with the teenager first," Ramona said. "But don't get your hopes up—she isn't required to talk to me." She rapped her pen against the pad, considering. "I'm also thinking we might want to ask Susanne. She can testify that she asked you to go after Joy."

"Don't use the phrase 'go after,' " I said, but she didn't seem to realize that I was mimicking her own words back to her, from our first meeting. I added, "Absolutely not. With what she's going through?"

"What she's going through isn't your fault." I felt a streak of relief at realizing Ramona must now believe in my innocence, even if she hadn't started that way. "And I'm sure she wouldn't want to see you on trial for a crime you didn't commit."

She was right in this, I knew. But the idea of making Susanne sit in front of strangers, and discuss our affair on top of her daughter's murder, triggered the gag reflex in the back of my throat. "What about me? Should I testify?" It was not something I was eager to do, but she'd told me it was an option.

"Let's hold off on deciding that for now. It opens you up to be cross-examined, and I don't want to take that risk." Standing, she gave my hand a half shake, half squeeze I understood was meant to transmit encouragement. "You can go home now," she said, and told me to sit tight while she went to sign the papers.

When I got my belongings back, my cell phone had just enough power left to show me the multiple calls I had missed from Susanne. My instinct was to dial back right away, but then reason got the better of me and I showed the notifications to Ramona, who told me not to return the calls under any circumstances, even going so far as to say that if I did, she'd consider dropping the case. Reluctantly I agreed, but I stopped short of deleting the number from my list of recent incoming calls.

Violet came to pick me up and drive me home. "Do you think she believes I didn't do it?" I asked, knowing I didn't have to refer to Ramona by name.

"I think so," Violet said. "She's white, though, so who

knows." It was a variation on something she said often: *With white people, you never can tell.* Sometimes I tried to argue with her, saying that with plenty of black people you can't tell, either, but she waved the comment off as not worthy of a response.

I was surprised and glad to see that there were no reporters outside the jail when she pulled up to let me in. But once we approached my street, I saw that they were clotted in front of the house, alerted to my arrival. On either side of the press throng stood a group of what appeared to be protestors, but until we drew closer I couldn't tell what they were protesting—me, or my arrest?

Moving closer, I recognized two classmates from school, Lizzy and Stuart, both members of Students for Obama, which I joined last year during the campaign. Lizzy lifted a handmade sign that said INNOCENT UNTIL PROVEN GUILTY. She was a talented painter, but the words—on a ripped-out piece of notebook paper taped to a ruler—seemed to have been scribbled in haste. I couldn't help wishing she'd taken a little more care. More prominent signs, lifted on the other side of the reporters, said JUSTICE FOR JOY NOW! and DON'T LET A KILLER WALK. Those sentiments, presumably not executed by artists, displayed themselves more elegantly on durable poster board.

"Fuckers," Violet said, braking. "Do you want to go somewhere else? How about back down to your grandmother's house? I don't think they've seen us yet."

For a moment I considered it, not relishing the idea of facing all the questions. Then I realized I didn't want to be a coward, and told Violet she could let me out down the block and drive off.

"You sure?" She looked dubious, but I could tell she was relieved. I leaned to kiss her, aiming for her cheek, but she moved her face at the last minute and met my lips with her own. Before I could think about it, I pulled away; I hadn't kissed anyone since Susanne, and though she'd been the one to break up with me, it felt unfaithful. "Wow, okay," Violet said, and I could tell

I'd insulted her. "It was just for luck." She drove away without looking back to see how I fared before all the cameras.

Ramona had told me how to handle the media swarm. "I don't like 'No comment,'" she said. "I think people read that as guilt. You don't have to smile, but you don't have to look completely grim, either. Sometimes, giving them a little something leaves them less room to speculate in their stories. It's up to you. Keep it simple, and get inside as soon as you can without having it look like you're trying to escape."

I paid attention to her words, but everything she told me fled my head as I walked toward them. A snowbank blocked my way to the sidewalk, and I debated climbing over it—picturing myself slipping, having it caught on camera—*Accused murderer stumbles on way home from jail!*—before deciding instead to walk around to the driveway, even though this meant it would take me longer to reach the house. From her downstairs window I could see Cass watching; she raised her hand in what could have been an attempt at a fist, though I couldn't tell; she might have just been waving. Regardless, I wondered if she knew how much I appreciated the gesture. I may have hurt her feelings last fall when I declined to stay home and watch the election returns with her, opting instead to accept the invitation to join Obama supporters in the Campus Center, but when it came right down to it, there was only a handful of black people in this town, and I knew that the fist or the wave, whichever it was, meant we would stick together. A microphone from a Rochester TV station was thrust in front of my face and a reporter shouted, "Did you kill Joy Enright?"

Though I'd been warned to anticipate the question, hearing it almost forced me to my knees. My legs wanted to buckle, but I knew how this might look, so I willed myself to stay upright. "Of course I didn't," I mumbled, and the microphone came closer, so close I could smell the cold aluminum.

"Then what were you doing with a mask?" someone yelled from the back.

I kept my mouth shut and eyes straight ahead as I walked up to the stoop, seeing that Cass had left the window. The words *Get in, get in* coursed urgently through my mind, but I made sure not to go too fast, as Ramona had instructed.

"Is it true you slept with the victim's mother? Did you ever meet her—the girl?" I could tell there was more they wanted to know, but thank God I had reached the door. Once I got inside and shut it behind me, I could no longer hear what they asked.

Last Chance Rescue

L et's not," Harper begged her mother, but it was too late. They'd already entered the mall, where they were carried along in the tide of exuberant children and their wincing, mission-mouthed moms.

Harper couldn't remember the last time her mother had ventured out in person for presents, instead of ordering them online. But today, when she'd come home from school, her mother announced that she hoped Harper would keep her company when she went Christmas shopping at Madison Ridge. On the drive over, Harper understood for the first time the meaning of the phrase *Be careful what you wish for*. As much as she'd wanted her mother to start driving again and be normal, she felt flooded by trepidation as she sat in the passenger seat searching for parking spots while her mother drove slowly down each row. She tried to identify the source: Was it merely a dread of the shopping hordes? Anxiety at the thought of being seen with her mother, when other kids at school had not been to the mall with their own parents in years? As they made their way through the Macy's entrance, she realized that while these reasons might be part of it, her main apprehension lay in the memories she knew would be triggered by the approach to Santa's Village. Of course they weren't going to join the line to give Santa their wish lists, but just seeing the excitement of the children waiting their turn pierced Harper so deeply that she felt herself gasp.

"I know," her mother whispered, and now the stab Harper felt was one of gratitude at realizing that she didn't have to explain herself, and that her mother felt the same way.

The perimeter of the village consisted of charities seeking holiday donations. The noisiest and most popular was the Last Chance Rescue Coalition, where kids swarmed the cages containing abandoned cats and dogs. Despite having steeled herself against thinking about the old days, Harper couldn't help smiling and asking her mother "Remember?" knowing she didn't have to elaborate. The day she and Joy had found their kittens at this same pet adoption fair, the December they were in second grade. Harper's mother had taken them first to see Santa, even though (they discovered later) each of them already suspected that such a magical person didn't exist. Then the plan was to visit the mall's tiny indoor rink, followed by hot chocolate, but the girls said they'd rather skip the skating and visit the kittens instead.

"Okay, but we're not getting a cat," Harper's mother said, and Joy and Harper looked at each other and smiled. "I *mean* it," she added, rushing to keep up with them as they ran ahead to the labyrinth of cages and crates. They picked out their favorites—a brother and sister lying with their paws curled over each other. The handler told them that usually there was only one runt to a litter, but these two appeared to be twin runts. "Twin runts!" Harper and Joy repeated in unison, without planning it, delighted by the phrase, and Harper's mother seemed intrigued by it, too. She told Joy to call her mother from the pay phone outside Penney's, and if her mother agreed, she'd let them adopt the kittens.

When Joy hung up and announced that her mother had

said yes, the girls leapt and high-fived each other. On the drive home, the two cardboard carriers sitting between them on the backseat, they brainstormed matching names. "Poop and Pee! Burp and Fart! Barf and Puke!" they shouted, screaming with laughter until Harper's mother insisted they settle down. Eventually Harper suggested a food theme, and by the time they pulled up in front of Joy's house, Chip and Salsa had names as well as homes.

Harper wanted to peek into the cages at this year's litters, but her mother had gravitated toward the table occupied by the police chief's wife, who had so startled Harper's mother by stepping off the curb in front of her as she practiced driving, the day they went to the Inside Scoop. Harper was surprised to see her mother approaching Helen Armstrong, because she'd seemed so intimidated by all the "do-gooder" things the other woman had accomplished. She'd have expected her mother to avoid Mrs. Armstrong entirely, but instead she went toward her wearing a firm expression of purpose.

Spread across the table were pamphlets for a halfway house called One Day at a Time, and Helen Armstrong held one out when she saw them coming. Harper's mother took it without looking at it. The chief's wife told them that all contributions were tax-deductible, not to mention that they would be entitled to place their names in a drawing for two dinners at Rubio's if they donated today.

"This is my daughter, Harper Grove," her mother said, which of course was a non sequitur. Helen Armstrong held out her hand and told Harper she had a pretty name. Harper said thank you, not meeting her in the eye. "She'll be testifying in the Joy Enright case. Your husband came to talk to her, a couple of times."

"Oh. Well, hello, Harper. I'm sorry you have to be involved in something so—awful." Mrs. Armstrong tapped her fingers against the brochures on the table, as if unsure what to do with them. "But I really shouldn't talk about an active investigation. That's my husband's work, and this is mine. I'm on the board here. We have a terrible problem with addiction in this county, and we need more beds, but ODAT is a start." *Odat?* Harper almost laughed at the sound of it until she realized it was an acronym. "People get down on their luck, we try to help them back up. You probably know I battled addiction myself, though it seems like a long time ago now. Everybody needs a little help now and then, right? There's no shame in it."

It should have been a rhetorical question, but it sounded to Harper as if she might really be seeking an answer. Harper had none, but her mother said, "Of course there's no shame," as if it were the most natural thing in the world for her to switch places with the police chief's wife and assume a position of authority. In the old days, she would have fumbled in her purse and handed over a folded bill, then kept her face averted as she rushed Harper through the crowds and back toward the exit. But this was her new mother, who understood that in Harper she possessed a currency previously unavailable to her—that of importance to the town, and to the most important thing that had happened in the town in years. Instead of retreating she wrote a check, tearing it off with a sound so loud it made Harper wince, and when Helen Armstrong thanked her, she stood up a little straighter and told Harper it was time to get a move on— they had things to do.

Affectionate Interest

They disagreed about whether to tell Gil's mother what had happened to Joy. Susanne saw no point in it. "Why would we go out of our way to make her understand something like this?" she asked him, on their way to the nursing home. When they'd gotten up that morning, neither of them had plans to leave the house (knowing how much it would take for them to get through the funeral the next day), but by eleven o'clock they were driving themselves and each other crazy and Gil suggested they go to see Emilia. He surprised Susanne a few minutes later by saying he thought they should "fill her in" on what had happened to her granddaughter. They hadn't told her when Joy went missing, so Susanne couldn't understand her husband's sudden decision to inform his mother about the murder. "I'd give *anything* to be oblivious right now," she said. "I mean, how many upsides are there to having dementia? This is one of them. Why not save her the grief?"

Gil told her he'd agree if he thought his mother would actually comprehend the news. As it was, he believed she would hear the words but that they wouldn't mean anything to her. "Then why?" Susanne asked again, catching herself before adding *What's wrong with you?*

"It just doesn't feel right to keep it from her," he murmured, and she could tell that he understood it made no sense. By the time they got to Belle Meadow, he'd changed his mind.

When they found Emilia in the Solarium, she was having her nails done by one of the aides. "I thought you were never coming," Emilia said, when Gil bent to kiss her. "I thought I was never going home." In the wheelchair next to her, Mr. Trujillo began making a hissing sound; at first Susanne thought it was directed at her and Gil, but then she realized that he was attempting to communicate with the resident cat, Harry (or maybe it was Hairy; Susanne had no idea which), who'd jumped down from the top of the TV. Like other pets Susanne had seen in news stories on TV, this one was famous for its sensitivity in identifying people who were about to die.

"He's looking, he's sniffing, he's rubbing legs," Mr. Trujillo reported to the room at large, like a sports announcer giving the play-by-play. "Look at him! Duck and cover, people. You don't want to be the lap he lands in."

Susanne felt the cat's nose graze the back of her heels. She kicked it away, feeling her stomach turn, and the cat moved from her shoes to nuzzle Gil's. "And we have a winner," Mr. Trujillo said. "Two winners, in fact. I'm glad it's not me. Someday, but not today. It's not my time."

"Shut up," Emilia told him. "That's my son and his girlfriend. You'll be a pile of dust fifty years before they even think about going. That cat knows squat."

"Wife, Mom," Gil said under his breath, so low Susanne was sure his mother hadn't heard it. "Susanne's not my girlfriend. She's my *wife*."

Susanne understood that her husband's look of distress had less to do with the cat smelling death on them (which she knew he didn't believe) than the fact that his mother didn't seem to know the difference between *wife* and *girlfriend*. She'd tried to reassure him about this on more than one occasion—Emilia often couldn't find the right word to describe her relationship to someone, but the word she did pick always belonged to the right gender. "That's supposed to make me feel better?" Gil asked. "That my mother refers to me as her brother instead of her son?" Susanne had stopped pointing out how things could be worse, because it was clear that all Gil would ever compare it to was the way it had been once and the way he wished it were still.

Mirabelle, the aide assigned to Emilia that day, had appeared nervous when she saw them approach. They were used to this by now; ever since the night of Joy's disappearance, people they encountered outside the house seemed at a loss for what to say. *Bring it up, or not?* they seemed to be thinking. Susanne found she had no use for the ones who decided against mentioning it. For the rest of her life, she would know because she had learned in the hardest way possible that nobody wants other people to ignore it when the worst has happened.

She and Gil took seats across the table from where Emilia was having her manicure. For perhaps the hundredth time, Susanne's gaze rested on the plaque proclaiming that renovations to the Solarium had been made possible by a gift from the Donato family, whose mother, Yvette, had been a resident at Belle Meadow and in whose memory her children donated money with "affectionate interest."

It was a phrase that had intrigued Susanne since she'd read the plaque the first time. Did it apply to her relationship with Gil? Or more aptly to Martin? Affectionate interest was present for both men, but what she felt for each of them, beyond that, was so different that she'd never put words to it in either case.

Mirabelle lifted Emilia's hand out of the bowl of warm water and waved two colors in front of her. "Malibu Peach or Jamaica Me Crazy?" she asked, and when Emilia indicated the second, Mirabelle laughed and teased, "Jamaica me crazy, all right."

Susanne asked how things had been at the nursing home lately, and Mirabelle said, "Oh, fine," cautiously and as if she couldn't be sure it was just a polite question.

"I mean since the drug arrests," Susanne said, ignoring the warning Gil sent from the seat beside her.

"This is too purple." Emilia held up her newly painted orange fingernail, and Mirabelle sighed as she dipped a tissue in polish remover, then rubbed it off.

"I mean," Susanne continued, "it must have been kind of disruptive, finding out one of the staff was stealing drugs." *Diversion of controlled substances* was what they'd actually charged Jason Lee with, but "stealing" gave Susanne more satisfaction to say.

And what was she trying to accomplish, by pressing the matter with Mirabelle in this way? Was it a perverse wish to revive every possible memory of Joy, including one she could more reasonably be expected to prefer remain buried? Did she think it would make her feel better to inflict discomfort upon someone else? She couldn't be positive, although the desperation in her voice was, she was sure, obvious to them all.

Mirabelle made a *Hmm* noise looking over at the Solarium entrance, and following her eyes, Susanne saw Jason wheeling in the medication cart. "What the *hell*," Susanne exclaimed, rising, and Emilia barked at her to sit back down.

Jason had seen them and tried to escape the room, but Gil caught up and cornered him in the hall, Susanne close behind. "I can't believe what I'm seeing," Gil said. "You get arrested for selling drugs in a nursing home—*stealing* them, then selling them—and you end up back in the same job? How did you manage that?" Susanne marveled at the fact that though she knew her husband must feel enraged, he sounded merely curious.

Jason mumbled that they'd have to talk to his supervisor, and slipped back through the locked door of the nurses' station. Without returning to check on his mother, Gil stomped up the stairs to the first floor, and again Susanne followed. The supervisor, a heavy-breasted woman named Celeste Knox who always carried a clipboard in front of her chest, met them in the doorway of her office; Susanne realized that someone must have alerted her from the Solarium downstairs. Ushering them in, she offered them seats, but Gil said it wouldn't take that long. "What is Jason Lee still doing here? Or doing here again?" He took a step closer to Celeste, who clutched the clipboard tighter and told them she was not at liberty to discuss matters pertaining to human resources.

"How about matters pertaining to crimes committed in your facility?" Gil kept the same even, unflustered voice, which seemed to throw Celeste off all the more. "How do you expect me to keep my mother in a place where drug deals are going down?"

Susanne winced without showing it. Surely nobody actually referred to drug deals "going down" anymore.

But of course it was Gil's implied threat to pull his mother out of Belle Meadow that Celeste paid more attention to. Under her breath she said, "The charges against him didn't stick. The police could prove the narcotics log was falsified, but not who did it. We felt it was only fair to bring him back. He was going to sue for wrongful termination, otherwise."

" 'Didn't stick'?" Susanne had vowed to let Gil handle it because he obviously felt he needed to, but she couldn't help reacting. The charges against Joy hadn't stuck, either, but that didn't mean she hadn't done what she was accused of. "But he's the one who got our daughter involved in this whole thing. She ends up dead, and he ends up back in his job scot-free?"

Celeste Knox lowered the clipboard between them, as if she understood that a gesture of sympathy—woman to woman, and perhaps mother to mother—was in order. But her expression was one of puzzlement. "They have someone in jail for that. Who has nothing to do with this facility or, if I understand it correctly"—now did she narrow her eyes at Susanne; was she thinking there might be more to see than she'd at first discerned?—"with the sale of illegal drugs." Then she excused herself, getting almost all the way through *Have a great day* before catching herself and finishing with *I'm sorry.*

On their way back down to the Solarium, Gil asked, "You know Joy didn't die because of drugs, right?" She could tell what he wanted to add: *She died because of your friend there. The one in jail. The one they arrested.*

Why didn't he say it? Not because he was willing to entertain an alternative, Susanne knew. It was because they had the funeral to get through. After that, what would happen to their marriage was anyone's guess, and at the moment she couldn't have cared less. Or at least that's what she told herself as they returned to her mother-in-law, who flashed ten fingers of different colors before asking them why her sister never came to see her anymore.

Viable

Alison's next checkup was scheduled for the day before the funeral. She told Tom she wanted to put it off to the following week—too much sadness, too much stress—but he persuaded her to keep the original time. "We need something good right now," he told her. She'd made it beyond four months, the longest she'd ever lasted, though because she'd taken to wearing baggy dresses and sweaters (afraid to jinx things if anyone guessed too soon), you couldn't tell by looking.

The night before the appointment, they went over to Doug and Helen's for dinner. The news was on the TV in a corner of the kitchen, and Tom saw the crawl POLICE SEEK LEADS IN LATEST ATM GRAB. A still photograph from the surveillance video showed a figure in a bulky jacket, probably a man, holding up a flip-flop-wearing woman in a bank kiosk at night. Images from the robberies had been too indistinct for police to make out anything useful except what looked like a Rochester Red Wings cap, which had led to newscasters dubbing him the Triple A Bandit. "You'll get him," Tom said to Doug, though the Chilton cops had failed to get anywhere in identifying the thief. "That hat should help, right?"

"Yeah. Douchebag's so stupid he not only uses the same dis-

guise every time, he can't even *cheer* for a major league team."
Doug pulled the tab on a Genny. "He's either dumb as a stump
or he wants to get caught. My vote is stump."

"What a douche." Tom was relieved to realize that Doug
was inviting him to join in his derision of someone else, for
a change. Since Martin Willett's arrest, he hadn't detected any
lingering hostility on Doug's part about the information Tom
had initially withheld from him. Doug appeared satisfied now
that the case was going the way he wanted, and this seemed to
be all that counted: he would get a conviction in the teenager's
murder, and Mark Feinbloom would have no choice but to cast
his swing vote on the Town Board to appoint Doug permanent
chief.

The relief felt good. Later, Tom would wonder why he
couldn't have left it at that. But he knew the answer was a simple
one: if Martin Willett hadn't killed that girl, it wasn't fair that he
be punished for it. A further question: What reasonable person
would think he *should*? Though of course no one had assigned
Tom the job of serving as the agent of justice, he didn't see anyone else stepping up to the role.

At dinner, Helen did her best to direct the conversation to
something other than the case, trying to engage them in a
debate about baby names. But Doug wasn't ready to give up
fuming about the fact that Martin Willett had been released.
"Do you believe they let that guy walk?"

"They didn't 'let him walk,'" Tom said, when the women
remained quiet because they knew Doug wasn't asking the question to hear a response. "He made bail."

"And how the hell did he do that, anyway?" Doug waved his
fork so forcefully that a strand of spaghetti fell off. "How did
somebody like that raise that kind of cash?"

Helen wanted to bend down to retrieve the piece of pasta,
Tom saw, but instead she held herself rigid in her seat. Nobody

asked Doug what he meant by *somebody like that*. Doug set the fork on his plate with a clatter and announced he was too pissed to eat. "We got one black judge up here, and that's who this asshole pulls?"

"Don't be racist, Dad." Alison spoke in the same tone she always used to tease her father, but of course Doug didn't take it that way.

"It's not racist, it's reality," he said. "If he went in front of either of the other two, bang, he'd be locked up so fast he didn't know what hit him. We're talking a murder charge here, not shoplifting. Not goddam crossing against the light." The veins in his neck throbbed as he listened to his own words. "*When he did this thing*. That's what gets me—he killed that girl, and already the system is giving him a break."

Tom said carefully, "I thought it was all circumstantial."

Doug looked as if he couldn't be more pleased that Tom had brought this up.

"Let me tell you about circumstantial. People have this idea that circumstantial isn't real evidence. But it is. You got the right circumstances, you got a guilty guy, you got a conviction. What do we know about this prick?" He held up his hand to tick the points off on his raised fingers. Alison and Helen had already put their utensils down and sat back to listen, so Tom did the same even though he wasn't finished eating. "One, he stalked the mother. Two, he knew the girl. Three, he had a sketch of her, and four, not only did you see him at the shack"—he jabbed a finger in Tom's direction—"there was a mask at his house identical to the one we got a witness saying she saw this guy wearing a few *minutes* before the girl disappeared." He opened his hands then in a gesture that asked them, What more could you want?

Tom imagined what Doug's reaction would be if he told him what he had so far kept to himself: that Martin Willett had not only been in the shack, he'd been in there looking for a teenage girl.

"I thought it was two witnesses who saw him with the mask," Alison said.

"Well, it was. Originally. But one of them disappeared—that Pothead Pete guy." Doug stabbed at his meat, and Tom thought his father-in-law probably blamed him for the fact that Cliff Ott had just not shown up for his shift at the shack one day, quitting without notice. When Doug went to check out the address Cliff had put on the job application, he found it was a fake. "But we have this teenager who IDs Willett *and* puts him in the mask," Doug added, rebounding as he chewed noisily, with satisfaction. "One hundred percent."

Of course there was no way Tom could mention that he'd spoken to Harper Grove himself, only the day before, at the clandestine request of the dead girl's mother. And that he came away distrusting what Harper had said. But although he could feel Alison's gaze piercing him with a warning, he felt compelled (by what, though? Stubbornness? Belief in the black guy's innocence? A desire to stick a pin in the balloon of his father-in-law's pompous certainty?) to press the question. "That does sound tight. But still, none of that actually proves anything. The police have no actual proof." At the last moment, he decided to say "the police" instead of "you," hoping to take some of the sting out of his challenge.

"What are you trying to say?" Barely perceptibly, Doug leaned an inch closer toward Tom's face.

Tom leaned an inch back and next to him Alison put a hand on her baby stomach, a reflexive gesture that had become familiar to him in the past couple of weeks. He welcomed it; it meant the baby was real enough to her that she felt it needed protection.

"I'm not sure Willett did it," he said, declining to look his father-in-law in the eye.

"No?" The heat of Doug's hatred rose and gathered like the stink over garbage; Tom could feel and smell it. "Then let me ask you something. If he didn't do it, who did?"

"I don't know." It took a moment for the absurdity of the question to sink in. "How would *I* know?"

Doug gave an elaborate shrug. "It's just that you seem to have such a handle on the whole thing. When nobody else does." The sarcasm in his tone was obvious to them all. "Maybe we should bring you in as a special consultant, you think? Since the *police* can't seem to make any headway."

Tom knew better than to respond. He kept his eyes down, knowing he would not want to see the looks exchanged among the other three at the table. He could only imagine what they'd think if they knew where he was headed in the morning—before Alison's OB/GYN appointment—instead of covering Cliff Ott's abandoned shift at the shack.

Willett's attorney set up the meeting. When Tom put the call in to Ramona Frye and told her he had information he was sure she'd want to hear, she sounded suspicious, but when he mentioned that he was the police chief's son-in-law, she was intrigued enough by the fact that Tom had contacted her instead of Doug or the prosecutor that she told him to meet her and Martin first thing the next day.

Willett remembered him right away, Tom could tell, from their brief exchange at the shack the day Joy disappeared. Ramona said she wanted to record the meeting, and asked if Tom minded. He was taken aback but realized he should have expected it. If his voice was on tape, that was it—there would be no chance of telling Doug, later, that there'd been some mistake or misunderstanding. He took a deep breath, hoping it would contain the courage he needed, then went ahead and said he thought there was something wrong with the police case.

"You're damn right there is," Willett said, but his voice sounded more weary than rancorous. Ramona held her hand up to indicate that he should let her do the talking, at least at first.

"Tell us why we should listen to you," she said to Tom. "Tell us why you're here."

He hesitated, not sure where to start. Then he remembered how sick he was of people not saying what the truth was, or hiding part of the truth. He began by describing Susanne Enright's call asking for his help in locating Joy, and (he looked away from Willett) his discovery of the affair between Susanne and her teaching assistant. When Joy was found murdered, he'd given that information to his father-in-law, including the name of the man Susanne's colleague said she was sleeping with. At the time, he'd thought it was the right thing to do, but seeing Doug's eyes light up at the tip had put Tom on edge.

"On edge? Why?" Ramona was taking notes as well as recording the conversation. Willett leaned forward in his seat.

Tom could not go so far as to reveal how much Doug Armstrong wanted to be named permanent chief and how certain he was that Doug believed securing a conviction in this case would clinch it for him. Even more, he could not say that his father-in-law was a racist who barely hid the fact and at times even seemed proud of it.

Instead he said, "Because having an affair doesn't mean you're a murderer. And I know he—you"—he nodded at Willett—"were there that day, I saw you, but the mask thing just doesn't make sense."

"It wasn't my mask!" Willett seemed surprised by the vehemence of his own words. "Somebody planted that in my kitchen. Those officers brought it in with them, the chief stuck it in the drawer when he went in there alone, and then he 'discovered' it."

It was hard to imagine Doug would have gone that far. But Tom would not have bet the house on it. "You can't be sure of that though, right?" he asked. "I mean, you probably didn't look in that drawer before the police came. Someone could have broken in at some other point and put it there. Including whoever killed Joy."

It appeared that Willett had not thought of this. "Possible, I suppose. But I doubt it."

"What about the witnesses? Who said they saw you putting the mask on in your car outside the shack?"

Ramona answered him. "One, the guy who worked for you, wasn't exactly what you'd call solid—he was basically homeless and, you must have known this, completely baked." Despite the circumstances, Tom suppressed a smile at the prim-looking lawyer's description of his former employee. "And now, of course, we can't find him. But the teenager is standing her ground."

"You've talked to her?"

Ramona shook her head. "I tried, but the DA must have gotten to her first."

"Well, she talked to me," Tom said. Hearing this, Ramona peered at him more intently, and he detected a flash of excitement in her eyes. "There's something wrong there, too. I don't believe her."

Willett slapped the table lightly in front of him as if to say *There you go!* Ramona put up her hand again, a cautionary gesture. "Why not?"

"She messed up her story. She didn't look me in the eye. When you put that on top of the other witness pulling out . . ." He knew he didn't have to complete the sentence for them.

"But she didn't admit she was lying, right?"

"Of course not. And I didn't accuse her of anything, either. I'm not sure she thinks I suspect."

Ramona squinted at the page in front of her, which was filled with scribbling. "Would you be willing to testify, if I could get the grand jury to request it?"

Again Tom hesitated. "I wasn't planning to go that far. I just wanted to give you the information."

"But there's nothing I can do with it if she won't talk to me. I don't want to take that chance."

He could feel Willett's plea across the table and realized he had no choice. "Promise me you'll try everything else first," he said. "But if that doesn't work, then okay, you can put me on your list."

Willett let out a breath it seemed he'd been holding the whole time they'd been in the room, and Ramona clicked off the recorder. When they all stood up, Willett covered Tom's hand in both of his own and thanked him, and through the trepidation Tom felt in recognizing that there was no turning back, he knew that if he had the decision to make again, he wouldn't do anything else.

After leaving them, he had half an hour to get to the doctor's office. Though he arrived early, Alison was waiting for him. "I thought you might have gotten the new guy to open up for you," she said. If he hadn't felt guilty, he might have said *There is no new guy anymore, remember?* As it was, he mumbled an apology, but it turned out that there was no hurry, because the doctor was delayed.

In the obstetrician's waiting room, they watched the muted news on TV. Hardly anything was being reported aside from Joy Enright's murder and the arrest of Martin Willett. "I think Dad's right," Alison said, nodding at the footage of Willett returning home after posting bail. "My money's on him."

The facts reported by the media did seem to point to Willett's guilt. And yet. The lack of a motive niggled at Tom; just because you were pissed at someone for breaking up with you, it didn't mean you went out and strangled her kid. Then there was Harper Grove's less-than-convincing ID. On top of everything else were the entries from the journal Tom had read in the evidence room after they arrested Willett. The guy was smart, and he had plans to go somewhere with his life. There was nothing in those pages (which Willett had every reason to believe would never be seen) to indicate rage or anything else that would make a reasonable person think he'd risk losing everything he possessed over a relationship that had lasted only a few months. In fact, he'd been friends with Joy Enright, if you could trust what he'd written in his fancy book. He just didn't strike Tom as a killer, especially after meeting with Willett and his lawyer.

"Maybe he did do it," he said to keep the peace, gesturing at the image of Willett on TV. Alison didn't respond as she tilted her head up at the photos arranged on the opposite wall, a collage of babies born to the obstetrician's practice. "But to be honest, I wouldn't be surprised if it ends up being somebody else."

"Like who?" Again she wasn't really paying attention, he could tell; she was imagining her own baby's picture up there with the others. A live, full-term baby this time, wearing a onesie and biting a fist.

"Maybe one of those girls she was with that day," Tom said. "Maybe Delaney."

Alison laughed briefly and said, "Yeah, right." Then she saw that he was serious. "Of course it wasn't Delaney."

"Why not? We know she's a criminal. You're the one who had suspicions about her in the first place."

She made a *Don't be silly* gesture with the hand not covering her belly. "She's not really a criminal, just more of a spoiled little brat. You said she had a key to the condo, right? So technically she had permission to go in."

"Not necessarily. It depends on how she got it—the key."

Alison picked up a copy of *Pregnancy & Newborn* and started leafing through photos of sonograms. As her pregnancy had advanced, Tom told himself not to look at the pictures in the books, but he couldn't help it. Alison had bought them the first time around, and she'd been the one to point out the progression of the fetus in ultrasound images, though they'd never made it to the stage they were at now: the baby could supposedly yawn, swallow, and suck its thumb. It was still a couple of months before it would form fat layers and taste buds—before it would become viable, able to live on its own. They'd agreed not to find out the gender, because Tom was convinced that doing so would make a potential loss more difficult. Alison wasn't so sure—she said she didn't think it would be any less hard, not knowing—but she'd given in when he asked if they could let it be a surprise.

"And what about the arrest at school that day?" he asked, not even sure she was still listening. "Delaney's boyfriend?"

Without looking up from the page she said, "I told you, he had a prescription." Then she set the magazine aside and added, "You're imagining things. Aren't you the one who's always saying the most obvious answer is usually right?"

He had said that, in the past. It was conventional wisdom. And yet.

"Delaney Stowell didn't kill anybody," Alison insisted. "Dad's right, it'll be the black guy. Just wait."

"Okay," Tom said, because there was no use arguing when he didn't know any better. But in this case, his gut told him that the answer was not as obvious as it seemed.

Before

Thursday, October 22

Am I more sad, or angry? And does it mean there's something wrong with me if I can't tell?

But I can tell, all too well. It's sad.

In bed last Thursday, before we had to return to campus, I sensed something was wrong. Susanne wasn't her usual self, but when I asked her about it, she just shook her head. Then she said (almost as if she hadn't decided whether to speak the words or not), "I was thinking about asking you to paint Joy."

I raised myself on an elbow to look down at her. "I'd love to paint Joy."

"It's just that she might bite my head off if I suggest it. We fight over everything lately." She sighed so hard that the force of it blew stray hairs away from her face. "But I know how much she'd love having—a portrait by you. I thought it might be a way to bring her back to us." Then she blushed, no doubt because the *us* did not include me.

I remained silent, and waited; it's something I've loved about her from the beginning, the way she keeps talking until she finds what she wants to say. Sometimes, when it happens in class, the other students exchange looks and I know they're thinking *There she goes again*. But I never have trouble following the path her mind takes to its destination, which is often worthy of my jotting down to record in my book later. *You have to be in love with your subject. If you don't care about what it is you're painting, nobody else will, either.*

"I could be the one to bring it up with her, if you want," I said.

"That's okay."

"It's because I'm black, isn't it." Despite her mood she smiled, though I sensed she thought that the joke was becoming stale. Trying to guess what might be bothering her, I asked, "She doesn't suspect, does she?" as I gestured at our thighs touching each other.

"Of course not. How could she?" Susanne shuddered. Seeming agitated, she started to get out of the bed. I pulled her back and she fell beside me, giving little resistance. I asked for just five more minutes, trying to hide the plea in my voice, and she fake-sulked down next to me. Looking out the window, I saw the top of a tree unlike any I had ever seen before. How was that possible? It could have been a tree on another planet, for how unfamiliar it seemed.

"When we break up," I said, closing my eyes as the autumn sun came in to warm the seam joining our skin, "this is going to be what I miss most. I don't mean just the sex. But the lying here. The way we talk about things."

She reached without looking at me to put her hand on mine. "Martin—"

"Okay. You're right, let's get up." I swung my feet over the side of the bed. As if understanding that I couldn't hear what she had to say yet, she did the same. We dressed in a morose silence, which continued through the time it took to eat a lunch of ham slices and wrinkled cherry tomatoes as we stood at my kitchen counter, and during the drive back to school.

As usual, she let me out at the foot of campus before heading up the hill to the faculty lot. I waited for her to send her usual guilty, happy, surreptitious wave. But instead she kept going up the hill, and I knew she couldn't see my fingers closing tighter around my portfolio handle, squeezing until it hurt.

I waited six days, skipping both sessions of the sculpture studio I only signed up for because Susanne was teaching it. The whole time I imagined—imagined too much, imagined all the time, even when I was in my attic painting, which I resented because that's always been my inviolate psychic space—calling her. Then, last night, I thought better of it and sent her a text instead: "Joy?" Though I know she's too smart for it, I fooled myself into thinking she might believe I'm only following up on the idea of having me paint a portrait of her daughter. She is not a fluid or comfortable texter, but I know she checks her phone all the time in case Joy has been trying to contact her, so when she didn't respond, I knew what the answer would be. Impulsively, I deleted that text and all the others we've ever exchanged, which I'd kept in a single thread since September, scrolling through it multiple times each day.

I regretted the erasures immediately, then reminded myself that it was for my own good as I went out to Cass's garage to test whether Grandee's ancient Plymouth Fury, which Cass let me store there and which Susanne had never seen, would start after all this time. When it did, I was sorry about that, too, because I knew where I was going to drive it. If the car had only refused me, I wouldn't have had a choice.

I knew that I was taking a chance, driving my grandmother's old clunker up the hill to Susanne's house when she didn't text me back, but I was foolish enough not to care. I went down her block slowly, waiting for good sense to stop me, to wake me up, all the while planning what I would say to her when I called from the car in front of her house. *Come out and see me. I want*

to talk. Please? Just for a minute. I can't stand this. What can I do
to change your mind?

But when I got closer and parked a few houses away from
hers, I lost my nerve and idled for a time before shutting off
the engine and slumping down in my seat. Her garage door
was closed, and I assumed her car was inside. The Odd Men
Out van was not in the driveway, so I figured I'd probably be
safe in calling her.

Yet something kept me from dialing. The last thing I wanted
was for her to think of me as a nuisance. A stalker, even. And
that's what she would think, wouldn't she?

I didn't drive away immediately, as I knew I should. Why?
Did I think I might catch a glimpse of her, walking in front of a
window or rolling the trash can to the curb? From having been
at the barbecue that day in September, I could tell that the only
light on in the house was the one in the kitchen. Was she in
there, washing dishes? Eating a late dinner, alone?

As I was reconsidering my decision not to call, I saw a car
coming in the opposite direction, and instinctively I ducked
behind the steering wheel before realizing that they were the
headlights from Susanne's Mazda shining through my windshield. The ducking down was a reflection of how ashamed I
felt, not to mention a reflection of the fact that I was a black
man in that neighborhood.

I stayed low in the seat until I could tell from listening that
she'd gotten out of her car and entered the house. As I straightened, more lights went on inside. A tap at the window made me
jump, and I turned to see a bushy-haired woman standing there,
peering in as she pulled a big sweater around herself. When I
opened the window, she asked if she could help me, and when
I told her no, I was leaving, she said, "Okay, then," and stared a
moment longer before returning to the house a few doors down
from Susanne's.

I started the car and began trying to pull away from the curb before even shifting into drive. Once around the corner I glided back down the hill in chagrin, feeling (despite my best efforts not to) that I was headed back to where I belonged, from where I most definitely did not.

The Most Distant Object

Almost as soon as they'd been seated at the restaurant table, Susanne saw the text message come through: "Joy?" Her phone was sitting next to her plate, and when it lit up, they both looked toward the screen.

"Joy?" Gil said, forking into his spaghetti, and Susanne started, thinking he had been able to read the message—and who'd sent it—across the table and upside-down. Then she realized he was only asking if it was Joy getting in touch, borrowing one of her friends' phones to send the message. Susanne shook her head, trying to hide the quick breath she knew he'd recognize as a nervous one.

"No. Somebody from work. Joy's got a ride home already."

"With who?"

"One of those kids she's been hanging out with. Delaney Stowell."

"I remember her. Her father's the shrink, right?"

"I don't think shrinks like that word."

"But that's what he is."

"Yes."

"And she's an okay kid, Delaney? She always struck me as kind of wild."

"Yeah, I think she's okay." She did not mention the snake tattoo she'd noticed winding its way along Delaney's shoulder when she'd run into Lynette Stowell and her daughter at Price Chopper during the summer. The snake had gray-green skin, but the eyes stood out for their striking shade of blue. Azure, Susanne guessed, her artist's appraisal automatically kicking in. Or maybe cornflower. Whatever it was called, it complemented the streak of pink in Delaney's hair. Delaney was wearing a tank top, and the store's air-conditioning had raised goose bumps that looked like scales on the snake's skin.

Across from her husband in the restaurant Susanne kneaded her temples, trying to calm herself. Gil had been sleeping at his office ever since she'd told him about Martin, until she called and said she wanted to talk. When she asked him to meet her at Rubio's, their favorite place, he agreed and before they hung up he asked, "How will I know you?" Her heart surged at the old joke between them—at the fact that he was willing to make a joke at all. Their first date had come after an exchange of phone calls when she was looking for someone to put up a temporary wall in the Astoria apartment she shared with a roommate, to divide her own room into a sleeping space and separate studio. The landlord nixed the idea and when Susanne called Gil to tell him so, he asked if she wanted to get coffee anyway. After they arranged a time and place, she said, "How will I know you?" and he said, "I'll be the one who looks like me." She'd laughed on the phone and then worried a little because he hadn't given her any clues, but when she stepped into the coffee shop that day and saw him sitting at a back table, she identified him right away. As he had seemed to know she would.

But if there had been any buoyancy in his mood as he approached this conversation, she couldn't detect it now. She worried about what would come of it, and though she did not

want to admit it to Gil because she was sure it was her fault,
she worried about Joy. All she could think was that they'd been
too smug, congratulating themselves on the fact that she'd never
given them any trouble, pretending even privately that they
chalked it up to luck and didn't feel proud of escaping what
other parents had had to endure. But starting in September,
when something happened to turn both Joy and the mood in
the house grim, it had been their turn. Since Gil's departure
after finding out about Martin, Joy had not mentioned her father's absence, and she hardly spoke to Susanne at all. By then
Susanne was sure it was because she and Gil had refrained from
telling her about their financial troubles, and in addition to fret-
ting about how they would afford to send her to art school,
Joy felt excluded. "Did you think I wouldn't find out?" Joy had
asked her mother even before Gil had left. Now Susanne saw
that it had been a mistake to try to persuade her that things were
all right. Yet she couldn't bring herself to tell Gil now that Joy
was aware of the pressure they were under, because it would only
reinforce the shame he felt in fearing that his daughter considered him a loser.

So all she said was, "You know she wants her own phone."

"Of course I know that. But we talked about this."

"Most of her friends have them."

"All the more reason. If she needs to call us, she can use
theirs." He sopped up sauce with a piece of bread as big as
his fist.

She thought he was being unreasonable, but held it back. She
was hardly justified in accusing him of anything.

"How has she seemed?" Gil asked.

Susanne shook her head, letting him interpret it however she
wanted. Then she said, "You saw her at Belle Meadow this week,
right?"

"Yes, but she didn't seem too happy about it. It's my fault, though. That damn cat jumped into her lap, and I said, 'I guess that means you're next.'"

"So? It was a joke." Foolishly Susanne tried to smile, feeling the stiffness in her mouth. "She needs to lighten up." Immediately she regretted this disloyalty toward her daughter.

Gil snorted. "I guess she's not feeling light about much these days."

"I know." She took a breath; now that she'd taken the step of ending things with Martin, she was eager to continue the momentum toward repairing her marriage. As much as she would have liked to let them lie, certain things needed to be discussed. "What did Mark Feinbloom say? About that deposit?"

"Oh." Gil looked down. "I didn't ask him."

"You didn't?" She watched him flinch at her surprise. "Really? I never would have thought you could let something like that go." She tried to temper the disappointment in her tone, because not only did she understand why he'd neglected to mention the inflated account sum to Mark, she was glad about it; they stood to gain, if only a little, from the bank's failure to identify its mistake.

"Desperate times," Gil mumbled, but she could tell he felt ashamed.

Though she figured his answer would be the same as it always was, she ventured, "Maybe we should take a look at one of those Medicare places for Emilia. No commitment—just take a look."

He shook his head so violently she thought he might hurt himself. "No. I'm asking you not to say that to me again." Then he softened his expression, his tone. "Listen, Suse, it's not going to be that much longer. That we have to pay for my mother. I mean—you know what I'm saying." As long as she'd been married to him, he hadn't been able to utter any variation of the word "death" without choking a little.

What she knew was that he was deluding himself. They'd used the proceeds from her mother-in-law's house for the advance to Belle Meadow when Emilia was admitted in April, but that deposit would run out soon and they'd have to come up with the monthly charges. Emilia was at risk of being booted, if she lived that long. But maybe Gil had allowed himself to forget this.

"I could see if that job's still available, with Rob," Susanne said. "Or maybe he has something else."

Gil closed his fist around his napkin. "If I wanted to work for your brother, I would have done it last year."

"I know." She also knew she didn't need to accuse him of being selfish; he was all too aware of how she felt.

"Business is going to pick up," he said, pushing his plate back. "It has to." He was always asserting things as if the forcefulness of his wishes could make them come true. "I'll be able to hire guys back. Listen, things can't get any worse than they were last year."

Listen. How many times, during their life together, had she heard him direct those words to her? *Listen to this, listen to me.* More often than not followed by something that did not particularly interest her, though usually she pretended it did. The morning of the day she slept with Martin for the first time, she'd been skimming through papers her students had written for her undergrad art history class. Across from her, Gil lowered the magazine he'd been reading and said, "Listen to this."

She didn't have the time to listen—she had to return the papers when the class met at ten—but she could tell from his face that he was eager to share whatever it was with her. She gave a tight smile he took as invitation, wondering how it was possible, after all these years, that he did not notice the tightness, or understand she was in a rush.

"So scientists detected light from a star that exploded more than seven billion years ago." He ran a finger under the lines in the page he was squinting at. "It was the most distant object ever visible to the naked eye. Can you believe that—seven billion years? A gamma-ray burst, it's called." He laid the magazine on the table, and she caught a hint of the expression she'd found so appealing (so irresistible, really) twenty years earlier: his eyes bright and his mouth slightly open with excitement at discovering something that fascinated him. When she met him, he was in the first year of an architecture design program; he wanted to plan additions to people's homes, or maybe even the homes themselves. She remembered the drawings he showed her, and the excitement in his voice when he pointed out details of cornice molding and gambrels, transoms and newel posts.

But after that year, he left the program because, he said, there were too many architects out there; he'd been advised that jobs were scarce. "You're going to quit without even trying?" Susanne asked, knowing she had not managed to hide her dismay. By that time they were engaged. Gil shrugged and said maybe he'd go back someday, but in the meantime, since he had to have a guaranteed income, he'd start hiring himself out to do the handiwork he was so good at, and small contracting jobs. Even then the word "small" bothered her, but it meant she could teach on an adjunct basis and still have time for her sculpture, so she stopped encouraging him to return to school.

Back then, she believed he was selling himself short because he didn't have enough self-confidence. It took her years to understand that he wasn't settling; he genuinely enjoyed building and fixing things for people who couldn't do it themselves. He liked setting his own hours, hiring his own people, and keeping his own accounts. He came up with the name Odd Men Out for his business, and Odd Men Out it remained for the next twenty years. During that time he took on workers, at one time overseeing a crew of a dozen. Now he was down to himself and two others, and the time had passed when Susanne might have applied for a tenure position.

At the breakfast table the morning she began her affair, Gil had picked up the magazine to look again at the story about the gamma-ray burst and told her, "That's before the earth formed. Before the sun, even."

Behind them, their daughter walked into the room saying, "What happened seven billion years ago?"

"Oh, my God!" Susanne dropped her toast, a blob of jelly streaking a student's sentence. "Why aren't you at school?" She rubbed at the essay words with a napkin, though they weren't worth cleaning: *The difference between the two Davids is, Donatello's looks more like a girl then the one by Micheal Angelo.*

Behind her, Joy reached into the cupboard for cereal. "Teacher in-service. I told you that last night."

"Look at this," Gil said, handing Joy the magazine as she sat down. She let her muesli go soggy in the bowl as she read the story about the star.

"Totally cool, Dad," she said, and Gil looked at Susanne as if to say *See?*

Susanne stood. For most of their life as a family, they'd referred to themselves, all three of them, as *Team Us*. But in that moment, it felt as if the other two had teamed up against her. She pretended not to notice as she packed the mostly bad essays into her bag, and told them she'd be late because of the reception for the Lewison Award.

Now, over their pasta at Rubio's, Gil put down his napkin and stood. "We're done, right?"

"I don't know. Are we?" For a moment she wasn't sure what he meant by *done*. The idea that he might have been referring to the marriage gave her a punch to the gut.

"Listen, I'll move back in. As long as you promise me it's over." *It;* this took her a moment to decipher, too. Then she understood he meant Martin. As with *death*, Gil could not bring himself to say the word. "Every time I think of him touching you, and you touching him—" She knew better than to try to assuage his discomfort, and he seemed to appreciate this. He left her with the check, which she took as a gesture of punishment. *I deserve it*, she thought, as she reached to pay.

At home, turning into the driveway, she noticed the big boat of a car—a Plymouth Fury—parked across the street and down a few houses, in front of the Hahnemanns'. One of Betsy Hahnemann's aromatherapy clients, no doubt. Momentarily it struck her as odd that a person who was into aromatherapy would drive such a shitbox—what Gil would have called a beater—from the sixties, no less, but she didn't pause to dwell on it. When she got inside she was tempted to respond to Martin's text message, if only because she knew how he'd feel if she didn't. But she persuaded herself that it was better for both of them if she managed to resist.

Gil returned an hour later, having gone back to the office to collect the clothes and other things he'd brought with him on his "hiatus." They slept in their bed together, though they each seemed intent on avoiding the other's limbs. The next morning Susanne suffered a guilt hangover, remembering their conversation in the restaurant. *Him touching you. You touching him.* After school she took Joy to buy a cell phone, adding it to her own plan instead of Gil's business one. She hoped it would make her feel better to see Joy's excitement, and it did, for a few minutes. But that excitement seemed to recede when Susanne said, "Just don't tell Dad yet, okay?"

Joy was in the middle of opening the box to admire her new possession. She paused, and a look of mischief combined with something else came into her face. "Did I mention I'd like a pair of UGGS, too?" It was a strained joke between them because she mentioned it every few days, along with the fact that Christmas was coming. Though she knew Gil would disapprove if he found out, Susanne had bought a pair for Joy and hidden it in the closet to save as their big gift to her. She was tempted to give her the boots sooner, because Joy was wearing a pair of cheap knockoffs from two years earlier, which leaked.

But no, she would have to wait until the occasion called for it. Joy said, "Buy me some UGGS and I'll keep any secret you want."

"What?"

"Never mind. I was just kidding." Joy put the phone back in its box and the box in its bag as she looked out the window. People had begun putting up Halloween decorations, and ghosts billowed through the trees.

"It won't be long now," Susanne said. She was referring to Halloween, but she could tell from her daughter's expression that Joy thought she meant something else.

After Gil returned to the house, Susanne awaited for the reconciliation to make a difference in their daughter. It didn't take her long to realize how silly her fantasy had been—that Joy, seeing her parents reunited, would suddenly come around and revert to the sunny, smiling child they had always known. It occurred to her that there must be more to it than Joy worrying about their separation and the family's finances; maybe the stress of entering her last year of high school and the fact that she had to make decisions about her life afterward were as much to blame for Joy's sullenness as anything else. Susanne couldn't help feeling lighter, and literally breathing easier, when she considered that whatever was happening with Joy might not all be her fault. Even with Gil back in the house, Joy spent most of her time in her bedroom, and barely spoke when the three of them were in the same room.

The night after Gil's return she'd dyed her hair black, without announcing her plan; when she emerged from the bathroom with her hair still dripping, both Susanne and Gil exclaimed, and intuitively Susanne knew that Joy had done it less because she wanted to change her hair color than because she wanted to hurt them. This realization was painful in itself, and the hair did hurt Susanne physically to look at—the effort her once-blond and smiling little girl had spent to cover all the brightness that wanted naturally to shine through. As if she might be trying to erase or conceal the best part of herself with that dark, impenetrable dye.

What happened to that child? Once she had twirled around in the backyard shouting *I get to be alive!* Now her own mother barely recognized her.

At least she hadn't gotten a tattoo, like Delaney Stowell. Susanne wondered what Delaney's father, the shrink, made of the azure-eyed serpent curling down his daughter's shoulder. Dye would wash out eventually. She hoped the same would be true of whatever it was her daughter was going through. She couldn't wait for Joy to come out on the other side.

Stand up straight, Susanne was tempted to tell her in the meantime. *And please don't hide your face like that.* They were things her own mother said to her, but she wouldn't remember this until later.

Normally Joy slept until noon on the weekends, so Susanne could tell her husband was as surprised as she when, on the Saturday before Halloween, their daughter got up before eight o'clock—an ungodly weekend hour for her—and asked if she could take the car to "go see Grandma."

When his mother first entered Belle Meadow (which Joy insisted on calling BM no matter how many times her parents asked her not to), Gil had made it a point to visit her every day. He believed that dropping in unannounced, at random times—no set schedule—would result in better care, because the staff would be invested in having her bathed, dressed, and "presentable" (Gil's word) for when her son came by. Susanne originally thought him cynical in this, but one Sunday night when they stopped in after having been away for the weekend, they found Emilia sitting in a corner of the Solarium by herself, facing the wall, wearing a stained sweatshirt and sweatpants that didn't fully cover her goose-bumped legs. When they turned her wheelchair to face them, they saw dribbled chocolate pudding drying on her chin. At the sight of his mother's smeared face, Gil recoiled. Susanne knew what would happen next, and it did. Her quiet-mannered husband went to the nurses' station and let them have it—quietly, but for a long time. She caught the occasional words of explanation from the nurse in charge—*short staffed, chaotic, emergency*—but it was clear that Gil's message got through. There had not been a time since then that Emilia hadn't appeared in pristine condition (and most of the time better dressed than Susanne) when they came to visit. She didn't usually make sense when she spoke to them, but she always looked good.

When Joy took a job at Belle Meadow as lobby receptionist for the summer, then stayed on for a few after-school shifts once summer was over, Gil backed off his schedule of daily visits because Joy said she'd keep an eye on her grandmother. But she could only stand to go down to the memory-care unit for a few minutes at a time, she told her parents. "It's totally depressing. That's what we all have to look forward to?" she said. "No thank you. I'm going to lie down for a nap one day when I'm ninety and die in my sleep without knowing. That's the only way to go."

"We should all be so lucky," Susanne remembered murmuring, not sure whether she wanted her daughter to hear her or not. She and Gil decided not to push her to visit Emilia more often, assuming it would only backfire.

So when Joy got out of bed four hours before she normally would have on a weekend, then asked if she could take the car to visit her grandmother, Susanne could tell that although Gil felt pleased by the question, the pleasure was tinged with suspicion. He told her he'd been planning a visit himself before dinner, after he finished building a retaining wall in the Moultons' garden, and he'd love it (and he was sure her grandmother would, too) if Joy wanted to accompany him.

Joy thanked him, but said she had plans at the mall later and would rather go to BM in the morning. Like, after breakfast. Gil reminded her that the staff didn't usually have Emilia out of bed that early, but Joy just shrugged and said that was okay with her, she'd hang out in the dining room and wait. "You don't have to come with me," she told Gil, but Susanne knew it was a measure of his desire to take advantage of the opportunity to do anything with Joy—especially visit his mother—that he agreed to call the Moultons and rearrange his schedule, to accommodate her request. And it was a measure of Susanne's desire to foster her still-tentative reconnection with Gil that she offered to make the trip to Belle Meadow, too.

"Whatever," Joy said, and Susanne tried to avoid recognizing her daughter's displeasure that they hadn't just let her take the car and go to the nursing home by herself.

They arrived at eight forty-five and were admitted by Mr. Trujillo, who stationed himself in his wheelchair at the entrance every morning and spent the day operating the automatic door by pressing the button with his Hush-Puppied foot. "Good morning," Susanne told him, and pressing the tube in his throat from an old tracheotomy, he rasped (as he did to any remark anyone made to him), "Easy for you to say."

As Gil had expected, Emilia was still in bed. The nurses were surprised to see them so early. "Joy was eager to visit her grandma," Susanne said, recognizing that it sounded like an apology because she was afraid the staff would feel the need to hurry through the complicated process of getting Emilia up and ready for the day. For an instant she felt her daughter glaring at her, but then Joy must have decided (Susanne realized, looking back) to play the role she'd been cast in, and nodded to affirm what her mother had said.

Jason, one of the nursing assistants, came out from behind the desk to let them know that there were doughnuts in the dining room. Susanne waited for Joy to decline; she hadn't eaten a doughnut in years, because of what they did to her stomach. But instead she said, "Awesome. Thanks," and accepted Jason's invitation to show her where the doughnuts were. She smiled, then followed him, as he punched in the code to let them out of the unit without setting off the alarm.

"He's got to be twenty-five at least," Gil muttered, watching Jason walk away with his daughter. "Right?"

"I would think so," Susanne said, trying not to wonder if he was older or younger than Martin. Jason was one of the aides most familiar to them, because he was often on duty when they came to visit Emilia. They were always glad to see his name assigned to her, because he was one of the strongest members of the staff and could perform by himself many of the duties that required two less-sturdy people.

"Is he cute?"

It was the kind of question she loved Gil for—of course he knew the answer, but wanted to hear it from her—and it made her smile. "Yeah. He's cute."

"Is this something we have to worry about, do you think?"

She smiled again as Joy and Jason approached, each holding a half-eaten doughnut. "No. I'm sure it's just a crush."

"Well, I guess we have our answer about why she wanted to visit *now*." Gil gave her a wry smile back. "Even I wasn't naïve enough to think she got up at this hour to see my mother."

And in fact they ended up leaving before Emilia even woke up, because after eating two of the doughnuts, Joy said she didn't feel well and thought she might puke. Susanne could tell that Gil was biting back some version of *You should have known better*. When they got home, Joy shut herself in her room for an hour or two. When she emerged, Gil said he was going back to Belle Meadow and Joy could come if she wanted, but she pretended she didn't hear him and said she was going out.

Error Analysis

These questions do seem kind of bogus," Natalie said. A little more than a week left before she would take the civil service exam, and she'd asked Tom to help her study over a pitcher of Samuel Adams Octoberfest at the Tent Pole.

Tom had been the one to point out to her the lameness of the Life Experience Survey section, which consisted of questions such as *Within the past two years, how many times have you taken a day off because you did not feel like going to work? A) Never; B) Once; C) Twice; D) Three times; E) More than three times.* "I think you should write in '*F, too many to count*'" he said, and Natalie laughed and said, "Yeah, or maybe '*What business is it of yours?*'"

"And check out this Error Analysis," she added, picking up the page in front of her. "'*In assessing why you have answered questions wrong, consider the following: you may have misread the question; you may have lost track of time; you may have had difficulty distinguishing the important and unimportant parts of a complex question; you may have chosen an answer simply because it looks good.*'" She wiped foam from her mouth with the back of her hand. "How about '*Because I'm a doofus*'?" Tom smiled even though that section had caught his interest, making him realize how consistently he relied on *D*: choosing an answer, to any question in his life, just because it looked good.

The question of why he was here in a bar with Natalie instead of home with his wife, for instance. Yes, they were dive partners on the rescue team, and that meant something; you felt an obligation to help each other out. That looked good, as an answer.

But of course he had an obligation to Alison, too—a much higher one. Was he having difficulty distinguishing the important and unimportant parts of a complex question? No. The question was not complex. The answer was easy: he dreaded going home to Alison because she'd told him on the phone that she'd had "an inspiration" about how he could get on her father's good side.

Tom couldn't have cared less about getting on Doug's good side for his own sake, but he'd given up trying to convince Alison that she shouldn't care, either. Every time he brought up the subject of the hold Doug seemed to have over her, she responded with some version of *Look who's talking*. Tom hadn't figured out a way to explain the difference he saw between his efforts to preserve his father's business—attempting to fulfill the vision his father had worked so hard for but failed to achieve—and what struck him as a childish wish on Alison's part to remain her father's Ali Cat, even as she yearned to become a parent herself.

Arriving home from the Tent Pole, he stepped in the door feeling wary. Before he could even greet his wife, she was all over him with her idea about how he could curry favor with her father. "I was thinking that maybe you could find something out, give him some information," she said. "You know, that he could take credit for. That the board will notice, when it comes time."

"Like what?" Tom decided to humor her. If a few hours of his time could make her feel less anxious about the tension between him and her father, it was worth it.

On Alison's face then he saw the expression he'd always found most appealing—a smile both animated and mysterious, containing the promise of something she knew he would like. "Well, Dad and Hal came and tried to arrest this kid in school today, for possession of steroids, but it turned out he had a prescription so they had to let him go. The kid is Delaney Stowell's boyfriend. Her father's a psychiatrist, so she has access to a prescription pad. Anyway, it got me thinking."

Tom waited, not connecting the dots. "Thinking what?"

"Well, what if Delaney's part of that drug ring?"

They'd been hearing about it on the news: a well-oiled and elusive black market for painkillers and anxiety meds, covering multiple counties in upstate New York. The state's narcos had arrested a couple of people for possession with intent to sell, but they'd both clammed up, even when offered a break for cooperating, and the dope cops had failed to trace their source. "No way," Tom said. "Those are pros, not some high school girl."

"But she's the type that would think she could get away with it. Overconfident. Snarky." The opposite of the things Alison herself had been in high school. "She bugs the hell out of me."

"Does Delaney have pink hair?" Tom asked. "And a snake tattoo?"

Alison sat back, surprised. "Yeah. How did you know?"

"I've seen her. She comes into the shack." *Overconfident, snarky*—they were the perfect words for the girl who'd called him a perv. Was it possible she *was* involved in the drug business somehow—a shrink's daughter dealing as a lark? It was the kind of thing rich kids liked to do in this town. Anything to combat boredom, especially with winter coming.

To keep Alison in a good mood, he agreed to check it out. The next day, when Cliff showed up for his first three-thirty–to–midnight shift at the shack, Tom drove to the school and waited for Delaney and two of her friends, who flanked her like bodyguards, to come out. She unlocked a Volvo with a vanity plate (VENOM GRRL) and let the other girls in, then took off from the lot without—as far as Tom could see—even looking the other way. "Jesus Christ," he muttered, and by the time he put the truck in drive and got on the road behind her, there were two cars between them.

He guessed they'd go to the mall, and he congratulated himself when it turned out he was right, even though it was a no-brainer—where else would teenage girls go, with the weather this cold? Inside, he followed them, hardly daring to hope (but hoping anyway) that he'd witness some obvious transaction, maybe even one he could film on his phone to show Doug. When it didn't happen—when the girls just spent the next couple of hours sauntering around, sharing a bag of cookies from Mrs. Fields, flipping through clothes racks but not buying anything, occasionally reaching into their back jeans pockets for their phones and letting their thumbs fly across the screens—he thought to himself, *Douche. What did you expect, they'd stand in front of Aéropostale and hand some dude a bag of Oxys in exchange for a wad of cash?* As far as he could tell, none of them even went into a dressing room. They were in plain sight at all times. And they didn't do anything more sinister than pocket a couple of lip balms from CVS.

The next day, exactly the same routine, and the same the day after that. At dinner each night Alison asked if he'd caught Delaney at anything, and Tom was about to tell her he was giving up when Alison said, "I know you'll find something. That girl's up to no good."

He told her he'd keep trying but made a private resolution to give it only through the weekend. On Friday night, the night before Halloween, he caught a break. Delaney led him in the Volvo to the abandoned condo development (Lakeview Arms was the official name, but ever since the financing had collapsed and construction stopped, people had taken to calling it Broken Arms), where a dozen other kids were already hanging out on the stoop in front of unit 11. Delaney moved ahead of them, their queen, and Tom took out his phone to snap a photo of her breaking into the condos to party.

But Delaney pulled a key out of her pocket to let everyone in. Which meant she might have permission from someone, which would mean it wasn't breaking and entering. Maybe trespass, but that wouldn't score him any points with Doug. Who owned these places? Some of the individual units had been sold before construction began, but there was no way of knowing which ones.

An old Silverado pulled up and five teenage boys got out, three of them carrying cases of Genny. No way they were twenty-one, but Tom sensed there'd be more to the evening than underage drinking or even B&E by a bunch of kids having a party. Was it possible that one of these guys was Delaney's partner? That he'd meet up with her in a corner of the condo and pay her for a prescription pad she'd stolen from her father, or that Delaney, having filled the false scrips herself, would hand over a stash of pills concealed in a Burger King bag?

Despite the fact that he'd only agreed to follow Delaney to appease his wife, Tom felt a stir of exhilaration at the prospect that he might actually be onto something. It was the same feeling he got when he saw some guy who'd applied for workers' comp, saying he'd thrown his back out at his job, torquing down the advanced slopes at Bristol Mountain. Nothing like popping people who thought they were getting away with something.

But there was no way he could go inside the condos and find out what these kids were up to, so he wouldn't catch them in the act unless they came outside to do their business away from the party. The guys who'd toted in the beer came back out to unload a space heater from the truck, which they carried inside and then plugged into a generator on the flatbed via a string of extension cords. Dangerous, but not illegal. Tom watched and waited. The party swelled, including a girl dressed like Marge Simpson and a guy who might or might not have been trying to be the Joker (it was hard to tell). He saw the uncostumed kids snicker and point without bothering to try to hide it. *Jesus*, Tom thought. In his memory, he'd enjoyed high school. But now all the crap and the cruelty (never directed at him, but still painful to witness) came rushing back.

Sitting in the truck bed, he read dive manuals, played poker on his phone, and drank black coffee from the Thermos Alison had sent with him. He heard loud music and at one point a couple of shrieks, but they were happy ones—drunken, exuberant. He saw nothing of the type of activity he was looking for. He left just after midnight, the party still going strong.

"Anything?" Alison called out to him when he came through the door, and he swore to himself; he'd felt sure she'd be asleep by now. He told her it was just a party, that's all, and could she remind him again why it was such a big deal? Why it mattered to her so much what her father thought of him? *They* knew the truth—the two of them—so what difference did it make if Doug thought Tom was a douche?

"You don't understand," she answered him, shaking her head, and he said, "You're right, I don't. You're twenty-six years old, for God's sake. The daddy's-little-girl thing is getting a little tired."

She turned her back on him, freezing him out before falling asleep, and he was just as glad not to have the conversation continue. In the morning they woke up to the news that there'd been a fire overnight at the empty Lakeview Arms condominiums, and forgetting their fight of a few hours before, Alison slapped him excitedly and said, "So who did it? You must have seen something," but Tom shook his head and said they'd kept it all inside.

It was a lie; he'd recorded the license plate of the truck carrying the space heater, and he would have been able to recognize those kids.

But those kids had been him and Alison not so long ago, and though they may have been stupid, they hadn't intended to start a fire. If Tom was going to find anything Doug could "use" the way Alison wanted him to, he decided in that moment that it would have to be something about illegal drug trafficking, and nothing less. He sensed what an effort it was for his wife to contain her disappointment, and even though he knew it was not only a lost cause but a foolish cause to begin with, he told her he'd keep looking for a way to make his father-in-law hate him a little less.

Dark Knight

Despite Joy's help in studying, Harper had gotten only a seventy-nine on the test. *How is Odysseus able to listen safely to the siren's song?* Joy, of course, got a hundred and ten, including extra points for the bonus question (*How does Odysseus cleanse the palace of the scent of blood?*).

That was the last time they'd studied together. It was also the last time she and Joy said anything real to each other. Joy had already started hanging out with Delaney Stowell, whom she'd promised to hate ever since the day in fourth grade when Delaney slapped a Post-it Note saying *Looser* on the back of Harper's gym suit, pretending to congratulate her on a kickball catch. "*She's* the loser," Harper remembered Joy saying, after she peeled the sticky off and folded it in her fist. "She can't even spell it right."

But ever since the beginning of the school year, Joy and Delaney appeared to be best friends—which meant, of course, that Joy had to retreat from Harper. A few days before Halloween as they pulled their jackets out of their lockers, Harper sucked in all the courage she could manage and said, "I heard there's a party on Friday at La-La. Do you think I could come?"

La-La was what Delaney and her friends, including Joy now, had taken to calling the empty condos at Lakeview Arms, because of the ornate *L* and *A* towering over the other letters in what people called the "fancy-ass" Lakeview Arms sign. They routinely trespassed in one of the unfinished corner units to drink beer and smoke pot and whatever else it was they did there. Rumor had it that the development might even be being used for some of those drug deals on the news.

"You don't want to do that," Joy told her, tossing her copy of *Othello* to her locker floor.

She was right, of course, and Harper felt a small flash of comfort: Joy still understood her. "Yes, I do," she lied, before saying something truer. "I want to stop being—the way I am."

Joy's jaw gave a quick pulse the way it always did when she was pained. Then her features readjusted themselves into a deadened, blank expression that chilled Harper and made her unable, in that moment, to recognize her friend. "Come if you want to," Joy said. "It's not up to me."

In the girls' bathroom at the end of the day, Delaney blew perfect smoke rings as she watched Harper exit a stall. "I heard you want to crash our party," she said, dropping ashes into the sink. When she saw that Harper didn't know how to respond, she held up a hand to say *Don't bother*. "Sure, whatever, knock yourself out. Just a warning, though, the costumes are going to be epic. For your own sake, don't come in something lame."

Harper didn't know whether to trust Delaney; her instincts told her not to. And she was afraid to ask Joy, but after she checked with Eric Feinbloom and he said he'd been told the same thing, she tried on a high blue wig, green dress, and red bead necklace she hoped would make it clear she was dressed as Marge Simpson. Standing in front of the mirror, she knew how ridiculous she looked, but she did her best to persuade herself that that was the point. Marge was a ridiculous character, right? And didn't a person have to be confident to wear a costume like this? *Anyone who dresses like that in public is a confident person.* It was inductive or deductive reasoning, she couldn't remember which from her practice SATs. She just hoped people would draw the conclusion and maybe think something different about her, this time, than what they always had.

She gave her brother ten dollars to drop her off at the condos and to participate in the lie she told her mother, which was that she'd be watching a movie and sleeping over at Joy's. They pulled into the Lakeview Arms lot, and she climbed into the backseat to change into the costume. "Oof," Truman said as she got out of the car, shivering in the sleeveless dress. "That's a sub-optimal look for you."

Harper ignored him, or tried to, and said she would borrow someone's phone to call him to pick her up. On the way into the corner unit Joy had described to her—no. 11—she saw two kids from her Euro History class headed to the same door, both wearing regular clothes and no masks or other accessories that Harper could see. Same with three classmates from Chemistry: they had on jeans and jackets and sneakers, and their own familiar faces and hair. For a moment she paused, not wanting to continue. But then she saw Eric, having been dropped off by his mother, approaching with a long purple coat over a green vest, his face grotesque with black raccoon makeup around the eyes and a garish, lipstick-red smile lifting from the corners of his mouth. "Oh, you didn't," Harper whispered to herself, but it was all too apparent that he had. Though he was her friend, she knew she didn't have what it took to tell him he couldn't pull this off. "It's the Joker," Eric told her. "From *Dark Knight*. Heath Ledger. You saw that, right?"

"Yeah," Harper said, and then because she felt she had no choice, she added, "Cool." She did not want to walk in with him, but it seemed she had no choice about that, either.

"Nice Marge," Eric said, nodding at the high stack of blue

hair rising from her head. He steered her out of the way of an extension cord running from the truck parked by the front stoop to inside the condo somewhere, and she mumbled her thanks, hoping he'd be able to hear it; if he hadn't alerted her, she would have tripped.

Before they could enter, Zach Tully demanded ten dollars from each of them. Harper had always felt nervous around him because he was the star of the football team, but now she felt nervous because of what happened in school the week before. Heading toward her locker after Chemistry, she noticed a commotion in the hallway and saw that two police officers—the chief, Mrs. Carbone's father, and a gray-haired guy whose cheek bulged with something he was sucking on—had pinned Zach to the announcements board outside the music room. It took two of them because Zach was so strong, a linebacker who was counting on playing for a Division I team and then going pro, even though nobody from Chilton had ever even come close to such a thing before.

It was like *Law & Order*, Harper thought. She knew that what the cops were doing was shaking Zach Tully down.

Delaney Stowell grabbed the chief's arm and shouted, "You can't do that!" A gasp passed through the collected crowd, even from the kids who never showed a reaction to anything. Delaney had touched a police officer—actually *yanked* at his uniform sleeve. They waited for him to grab her back, place her up against the wall beside her boyfriend, and shake *her* down.

But the chief only tossed her hand off, then wagged a finger in her face. "Away," he said, and though she kept glowering at him, Delaney retreated a step. The candy-sucking cop held Zach's arms in place as the chief went through Zach's pockets. He pulled out a chain of keys, a cell phone, a folded-up piece of paper, and a small ziplock bag containing capsules of some kind, which appeared to be the target of his search. He jiggled the bag and whistled, giving his partner the go-ahead to hand-cuff Zach. "Zachary Tully, we are arresting you for possession of a controlled substance without a prescription." He went on to say the further sentences Harper and everyone else knew from every police show they'd ever seen on TV.

"I *have* a fucking prescription!" Zach twisted his body as if he thought he might be able to wiggle out of the cuffs. He flicked his fingers toward the piece of paper the chief had confiscated along with everything else.

"You mean this?" The chief flapped the piece of paper in front of Zach's face. "You think I believe this is legit, you little prick?" He shook the paper open and squinted at it. With the swiftest of movements he glanced at Delaney, then motioned to the gray-haired officer to take a step back from Zach.

"You sure?" the other cop said, and when the chief nodded, he let go reluctantly of Zach's shoulder but remained close enough that their faces were only a few inches apart.

The chief cleared his throat and held both arms in the air to command everyone's attention. "There's been a mix-up," he announced. "We're sorry for the disruption, you probably all heard about the prescription drug problems we've been having, we got a tip and we were following it up." He handed Zach everything he had taken from his pocket, including the pills. Harper could tell that the other cop didn't understand what was happening but was hesitant to ask in front of everyone. "Thanks for your cooperation," the chief added. "We're not always right, and when we're not, we try to admit it as soon as we can. Thanks, folks. We'll leave you all to your day." When he turned toward the exit, all the machinery he wore (gun, belt, radio) created a weighted, jiggling noise. The other officer followed him out of the building, making ferocious sucking sounds. Harper expected the chief to at least acknowledge his daughter as he passed by, but he didn't even seem to see Mrs. Carbone standing there with the other teachers. His face was red, not with embarrassment but anger.

If Joy had still been her friend, Harper could have asked her what she thought the scene was about. As it was, she remained silent when Joy turned to make her way to the cafeteria, cocooned between Delaney on one side and Tessa and Lin on the other. *I knew he was on roids*, Harper heard a football cheerleader say, and another one snorted: *He can kiss D-One good-bye.*

At the Halloween party, Harper kept her face averted and pretended she didn't recognize Zach as he demanded money for admission. She hadn't known about the fee and she'd given all her money to Truman, so Eric paid for them both and they put on the wristbands Zach handed them in exchange. Staticky music pulsed from the corner. They walked toward the back of the room, where candles flickered above a row of open coolers brimming with cans of beer. *This is a mistake*, Harper thought. *In every way. I shouldn't be here.* Even through the murky light, she could tell that she and Eric were the only ones in costume.

For a moment, she entertained the idea of borrowing someone's phone right then, so she could call Truman to come and get her. But Truman didn't have a cell phone himself, and he wouldn't even be home yet to get the message. There was no way she could ask for a ride from anyone else. *Stuck*, she thought, I'm *stuck*, and she fled toward a closed bedroom door seeking a place to hide.

The room was completely dark. She reached for a switch and found it, but no light came on. "Get out," someone said, and even though the words had been hissed, Harper recognized Joy's voice.

"Sorry, sorry," Harper whispered. Could Joy be hiding, too? But why? She retreated, but not before her eyes had adjusted enough to let her see Joy standing in the corner with a guy whose long hair was tucked halfway into his collar. He looked far older than high school age. He slipped something hurriedly into his pocket, then brushed by Harper saying *Watch yourself* on his way out of the room.

She felt the hair on her arms prickle, a warning sign. "Having fun?" Joy asked, though clearly she was not invested in whatever the answer would be.

"Not really." *This party is sub-optimal*, she wanted to say, but didn't. "Who was that?" She tried to sound casual.

"Nobody. I borrowed some money from that guy once, I was just giving it back." Joy walked out of the bedroom and closed the door behind her. Harper followed her to the beer cooler, where Joy popped open a Genesee Cream Ale and took a long gulp. Joy asked, "You going to stalk me all night?"

Harper could tell that they were both taken aback by the measure of hostility in Joy's voice. Hoping to dilute it, she gestured at herself and said, "Delaney told me this was a costume party."

"Yeah, well." Joy shrugged as if to say *What did you expect?* "You gotta stop believing everything people say." She looked around the room, and Harper tried not to understand that she was seeking somebody to save her.

"Why's it so cold in here?" she asked.

"You wouldn't be cold if you weren't wearing that stupid dress." But then even Joy seemed to be bothered by her own meanness, and in a slightly nicer voice she said, "Nobody lives here, so nobody's paying electric."

"Then how did you guys get in?"

"My father was working here until they went bankrupt. I have a key."

"You mean *he* has a key."

Joy shrugged again. "Same thing."

"Aren't you afraid somebody will find out?"

"No." Joy leaned in to peer at her. "Why? You going to *tattle*?" She spoke the word in a baby voice. "Then you'd be in trouble, too." For a moment, feeling how close Joy stood, Harper was tempted to hope that they might make up. But then Delaney Stowell came over and whistled as she threw her arm around Harper's bare shoulder.

"Don't get me wrong, you look good," she said, "but were they all out of Betty Crocker when you got to the costume store?" She laughed, indicating that Tessa and Lin and Joy should do the same. Tessa and Lin did, but after they walked away with Delaney, Joy reached up and pulled a napkin from behind Harper's dress strap.

"You gotta get a clue, Harp," Joy told her, sounding angry. "I won't always be there to save you from yourself." She tried to crumple the napkin, but Harper demanded to see what Delaney had scrawled on it: *Free to good home*, in the black Sharpie people were using to mark their beer cups.

"What does that even *mean*?" Harper said, relieved it hadn't been crueler and that no one had seen it but Joy. She tried to say thank you, but Joy had already moved away.

Most of the party had gravitated to one corner of the condo's main room. Harper set out toward the group and hoped Joy wouldn't accuse her of stalking again. Drawing closer, she saw people warming their hands in front of a glowing-orange space heater plugged into the extension cord Harper had almost tripped over on the way in. Zach Tully lifted the cord up as Harper approached. "Wanna try again?" he said, and she was prepared to see malice in it but then it occurred to her that he might be joking; she thought she detected instead a glint of apology in his eyes.

Or was that only the beer putting the wish into her head? It wasn't her first time—Truman had introduced her to it years ago, though he only let Harper have a few sips from what he stole out of the fridge, not because he was being protective but because he wanted it for himself—so she wasn't surprised at the bitterness, or the bite at the back of her throat. She kept swallowing, each one coming easier, until she finished the first can and then another, observing the Would You Rather game that grew more and more raucous as the number of cans in the cooler went down. Would you rather have no arms or no legs? Be rich and fugly or poor and hot? Eat a bowl of puke or a bowl of shit? The questions got grosser and grosser with each round.

She was beginning to have fun. Was it fun? Whatever it was, she wasn't as cold as when she'd walked in, and she found herself feeling amused rather than embarrassed by her own getup and by the paint on Eric's face. She could feel him sending her warning signals as he watched her pop open her third beer, but she didn't care; she felt warm, she felt good, she felt as if she had discovered the secret of life.

Behind her a voice asked quietly, "How many of those have you had, anyway?" Harper hadn't realized that Joy had circled back to find her. Her bangs shaded her eyes.

"I don't know, but not enough," Harper said, her own voice buzzing in her ears. "I'm gonna drink my ten bucks' worth."

"Five bucks." Joy held up the fingers on one hand and spread them, as if counting for a retard. "It cost five bucks to get in."

"He told us ten," Harper said, nodding at Zach, who shrugged and said *Whatever* before walking away.

Delaney, overhearing, laughed and made a twirling motion at the side of her head. Harper froze and Delaney added, "Would you rather have a batshit-crazy mother or be batshit crazy yourself?"

Harper's throat clutched. She waited for her old best friend to defend her. Instead, Joy laughed, too.

Harper was so stunned she thought she might have hallucinated. Had Joy really just joined in a joke about her mother? Joy, who'd been the one to listen to Harper for so many years and who'd so many times told her she wished Harper could have a mother like her own? She made a face at Joy to say *How* could *you?* but Joy avoided looking back at her.

Harper said, "At least my mother isn't fucking a black guy," only realizing she had spoken the words once she heard them in the air outside her mouth. She must have spit on *fucking* because a few flecks of saliva fell on her chin and she lifted a hand to wipe them off, hearing wider laughter now at the same time Joy made a noise that sounded like one of their cats when it got stepped on.

"Whoa," Delaney said, raising her fingers to her mouth as if she knew she should cover the smile that leapt to her lips. But she couldn't hide what was obvious to Harper and everyone else who'd paused Would You Rather to listen: she wanted to hear more of what Harper had to say.

Eric put a hand on Harper's shoulder, but it was too late. She turned and puked all over the Joker. Exclamations of disgust followed, and someone yelled "Barf alert!" as Eric stalked off to find something to clean himself with.

Delaney was backing up, holding a hand over her nose. "That is *so* gross."

Even through her remaining nausea, and despite the spinning room, Harper could feel Joy's astonishment in the space between them. And her contempt. Her own stomach curled further. "I can't believe you did that," Joy said. She sounded breathless, as if the wind had been knocked out of her.

Harper groaned. She didn't mean to do it, but another stream of beer seemed to be coming up. She turned and retched, but nothing came out. Her blue wig had fallen off in the violence of the first wave, and she bent with the thought of picking it up, then decided it was too much trouble and wobbled to a stand.

She and Joy were alone together in the corner Harper had defiled. "Why are you like this now?" she asked, her throat feeling abraded more by the question than from throwing up. "What happened to you?" But Joy only turned on the soft heels of her scuffed boots and receded into the dark.

I Am Your Father

Alison tried, he could tell, but she couldn't quite hide her disappointment at finding out that Tom hadn't observed anything at the high school Halloween party to offer to her father by way of proving that he, Tom, wasn't a douche. Of course that's not how she said it, but he knew. Though he hadn't planned to go to the shack on Saturday morning, which was Halloween itself—Estelle was scheduled to be on with the new guy, and Tom trusted her to train him right—he also didn't relish the idea of hanging around the house with Alison and feeling like a failure. So he told her he'd be back around lunchtime and headed out.

He knew it would be wrong to admit, even to himself, that he felt more at home at the shack than in the side of the duplex he shared with his wife. Yet these days, it was true. He'd spent as many hours of his childhood at the Elbow Room as in the house he grew up in, "helping" his father while his mother kept books at the Tent Pole; the shack was really all he had left now of his parents, aside from a notebook he'd never known his mother to keep until after she died (it was filled with descriptions of the people she came across at the bar and the stories she wanted to write about them someday) and a set of beer mugs they'd won on their honeymoon.

Estelle, who'd been hired by Tom's father back in the Jimmy Carter days (Tom recalled his father telling him how she insisted on tying yellow ribbons around everything in the store, including the meat slicer), was alone behind the counter. "Cliff call in?" Tom asked, congratulating himself on remembering to say *Cliff* instead of *Pete*. Based on the guy's work ethic so far, he wasn't surprised when Estelle shook her head and said it didn't matter, she was fine by herself. Tom helped her out through the rush, went into the back room to check some accounts that didn't need checking, and when he said maybe he'd stick around a little longer, Estelle called him on it, teasing, until he confessed things were tense at home. "Make her laugh," Estelle told him. She'd been advising Tom on his relationship with Alison since before their first date. "I can never stay mad at Ronny when he makes me laugh."

So he picked up a Darth Vader mask out of the impulse bin by the register and, driving back home, imagined what he would find: Alison sitting in front of the TV with a stack of student papers on the couch beside her. She'd read a paragraph, scribble something in the margins, watch a few minutes of her movie, then turn back to the paper. When she first started teaching, she sat at the desk he'd built her, in a corner of the living room, and asked him to mute the TV while she graded essays. Though he acted put out, secretly he was proud to be married to a teacher. Tom Carbone, the dumb jock, married to a teacher.

He used to love seeing the neat pile she made of the essays when she finished. She placed them on the desk (instead of tucking them away in a folder or the fancy leather messenger bag her parents gave her when she got hired) where she left them to remind herself of the good job she'd done—the time she'd spent evaluating her students' literary skills. Back then, the papers had been covered with her notes in all different colors of ink; she used a variety of pens to make it more fun for herself and, she believed, for the students. *Good point!* she might write with her orange felt-tip, followed by *Example, please?* in green. These days, when Tom looked through her sloppy stacks while she was taking a shower or in bed before him, he saw that the few comments she made with a stark black ballpoint, while watching the Lifetime channel, were not even readable. It was as if she hadn't been able to summon the energy to think or write something that might be comprehended.

He worried that she was depressed. Well, why shouldn't she be? How many miscarriages or false alarms could they expect her to bounce back from?

It was too much to ask, he saw suddenly (and why was it sudden? Why hadn't it occurred to him before?). He was so accustomed to Alison's strength—her energy in pursuing everything she wanted, including a child—that he'd been blinded to the decline in that energy, to the possibility that she could be set back, discouraged. She'd always been the cheerful one when things went wrong; she was the one who picked *him* back up. Not to mention what she did for "her" kids. How had he not seen this before now? It was up to him to be the strong one for a change. To lift his wife's spirits. Or, if they couldn't be lifted at the moment, to at least keep her company in the low ground where they lay.

His vision: Alison would look up from her papers when he came in, see him wearing the Darth Vader mask, and smile. It might be only a small smile, but since a smile was what he was after, he'd consider it a victory. "Luke, I am your father," he'd say, and maybe he could get her to put the papers down and join him in the bedroom for some Star Wars sex.

The idea of "Star Wars sex," and whatever that might mean, made *him* smile as he turned onto his street. A further vision: he'd propose that they drive over to Lake Ontario for dinner that night. It wouldn't be like making the trip in the summer, when you could sit outside and watch the boats go by. But they had a favorite restaurant with a fireplace and wood beams, where he'd taken her after the last miscarriage. Well, maybe that wouldn't be the best idea, then. But somewhere.

Halfway down the street, he saw that Alison's car was gone. Inside, he found the stack of student papers—unmarked—on the coffee table. He called her cell, but she didn't answer. "Come home," he said to the voicemail. "I have a surprise." After hanging up, he worried that his idea of going out to dinner wasn't enough—that she'd come into the house expecting more.

When his own phone rang a half hour later, he picked it up and said, "Where are you?" regretting the harshness in his tone even as the words came out.

His mother-in-law was on the other end, though he didn't know her voice right away, and for a moment when she said, "Come to Mercy, Tom," he thought it was some wacko trying to drum up a religious donation. But then she added, "There's been an accident," and as he understood, his blood went cold.

"Is she okay?" She told him yes but repeated that he needed to come, now, so he bolted out to the truck and made it to the hospital, which was twenty minutes across town, in less than ten.

Both of her parents were with her, in a curtained-off part of a room outside Emergency. Alison sat with her legs hanging over the side of a gurney, her head hanging like a little girl who knows she's in trouble. For a moment, as he approached, Tom sensed Doug and Helen forcing themselves to squelch their shared instinct to close in around their daughter, as if to protect her from him. He tried to ignore the rage this lit in his chest; it was all he could do to keep his voice from shaking with it.

"What happened?"

"I fucked up," Alison said. She never used the word "fuck." Hearing it made Tom flinch.

"Darling." Helen shook her head and raised a hand to Alison's forehead, where blood soaked through a bandage. "You need to rest."

Doug told him, "Come with me," and walked away from the women without turning to see if Tom would follow. *That's because he knows I will,* Tom thought. He wished he had the balls to refuse and say he would remain with his wife, but he and Doug both knew he didn't.

Before Doug could fill him in, Hal Beemon came over to mutter something to Doug around the perpetual hard candy stuck inside his cheek. "What is it with you and those fucking lemon drops?" Tom asked irritably.

"Blocked salivary gland," Hal said, and Tom heard the word he wanted to add but didn't: *Asshole.*

Doug clapped Hal on the back and said, "Never mind him. Good job." When he turned his face to Tom again, it was considerably brighter than it had been. "We're okay," he said. "There's need for some discretion here. But we should be okay."

"What?" Tom had never felt a stronger urge to strike his father-in-law. *Never mind him.* His voice came out louder than he intended, but he'd be damned if he'd obey Doug's hand motion to keep the volume down. "Discretion about what?"

Doug pulled him over to a corner. "I mean it," he hissed. "You keep it together or I swear, I'll—"

"You'll what?" Tom shook himself out of Doug's grasp, but managed to lower the question to a whisper. It was the only way, he saw, that he was going to find out what was going on.

Doug kneaded his forehead with two fingertips, as if trying to rub away the truth of what he had no choice but to say. "Ali went off the road. Into a guardrail, that bad curve on Reservoir. The hairpin? You know the one I mean."

"What was she doing out there?" It was on the other side of Elbow Pond, on the way out of town.

Doug sighed. "We're still trying to piece it together. But it seems like she was helping one of her students, Hugh Nance's kid, he's in her group there, you know, whose parents are—" Though he didn't say it, they both heard him finish the sentence with the word "drunks." Before Tom could respond, Doug rushed to get the rest out, like someone wanting to vomit and get it over with. "The tricky part, the part that may surprise you, it surprised us, it seems like she might have had a little something to drink herself." He did not meet Tom's eyes, covering his own as he rubbed his forehead again.

"Alison? Had something to drink?" Even as he asked the question, he perceived the answer with a clarity he had not experienced for some time before now—how long, he couldn't have said. But *too* long.

"She'll be all right," Doug added. "The doctor checked her out, everything's superficial, she's okay. So's the Nance kid. The baby, too, thank God."

"What baby?" His thoughts had trouble catching up to the words he heard. The image of an infant strapped inside its carrier, in the other car, streaked before his mind's eye.

Doug squinted at him. "What do you mean, what baby?"

This second dawning felt like a description Tom had heard once of the pain that comes when you have frostbite and try to warm up too fast: it's during the thawing that damage occurs. "Jesus," he said, actually feeling himself sway on his feet. Doug put out a hand to steady him, but Tom waved it off and backed up against the wall. "*Baby?* That means..." It meant she'd lied when she came home from the doctor the week before, with all of them waiting, and said the pregnancy hadn't taken—again. But at some point in the meantime, she'd told her parents something else—that the doctor had been wrong, maybe. Or that she'd mistaken what he said, the first time, with Tom the only one she'd neglected to inform.

"Sorry, guy," Doug said, the same words he'd uttered at the

house that day when they were all so disappointed, except for Alison, who only pretended to be. The difference was that this time, he didn't really sound sorry at all. If he felt chagrined that his own daughter, the Mother Teresa of Chilton Regional High, could do such a thing—put her husband though such grief again, and make him think she was suffering with it, too—it didn't show.

This was what whiplash must feel like, Tom thought. He was barely aware of saying to Doug, "You probably think I had this coming."

"I have no idea what you're talking about." Doug held up a hand as if to say *Stop right there, if you know what's good for you.*

"You always thought I was the one to blame the first time. But you're wrong." Tom refrained from describing, as he'd always wanted to, Alison's drunken fall down the stairs a few weeks into their marriage. She'd hidden from Tom the fact that she was drinking, of course; she was pregnant, and on top of that, how many times had she told him she didn't want to be like her own mother, who spent Alison's childhood in a vodka and cranberry-juice haze? The night she fell, he found her stash of nips in the canister labeled FLOUR. When he brought her home from the hospital and confronted her with it, she promised she'd never drink again. That fall had kept her abstinent ever since then—or so Tom had thought.

Neither of them had ever told Doug and Helen why they lost that first baby. Tom wasn't sure why he felt loyal to Alison now, when she'd deceived him again, but he did. He wouldn't mention the cause of the first miscarriage. Did it even matter, now?

Doug's eyes narrowed further, so much that Tom almost couldn't see the blue. "Don't tell me what I think," he warned Tom. "Or thought." He was already moving in the direction of where they'd left Alison and her mother. "We have to get back.

And you won't let her know we've been talking about this." It was more a directive than a request.

"What's she going to think, you dragged me off so you could have company while you took a piss?" Tom knew that every word he said now added to his risk. But he'd withstood too many hits today to care about that. He'd deal with the fallout later.

"Whatever it takes." His father-in-law put a hand on his shoulder, the same gesture he'd made to Hal Beemon when Hal promised to erase Alison's arrest. Tom shrugged it off as they approached Helen and Alison, who was getting instructions from the doctor for her release. The doctor used the phrases "vaginal pain," "heavy spotting," and "obstetrician," and Alison's eyes darted toward Tom for an instant before she returned her glance to the floor. Her face was red, her body bloated with more than the life he now knew was inside it, and he thought, *What happened to her? What happened to* us? It wasn't the first time he'd asked this of himself. But this time it felt like more of a call to action than a helpless wish for the truth to be something other than what it was.

Doug offered to drive them home, and Alison appeared eager to accept, but Tom refused and said he was perfectly capable of taking care of his own wife. "Of course you are," Helen told him, leaning in to kiss his cheek, and the false faith of her words was obvious to them all.

Tom helped Alison up into the truck, where she sat staring ahead of her as he climbed into the driver's seat beside her. He would have liked to have the conversation right there, but Doug and Helen were watching, so he started up and drove out of the hospital lot, away from their sight, before pulling over.

"Stop," he heard Alison say, her voice sounding both tight and tired.

"I am stopping."

"Don't, I said. *Don't* stop."

But he ignored her; there was no way he could keep going. He had been going and going, without stopping, for far too long, a fact he recognized only now. "What the hell, Al." If he'd had more time to think about it, he could have come up with something better than that. Or maybe not: *What the hell* kind of said it all.

"I was going to tell you."

"You were? About what? Which part?"

She shot him a sharp look, then must have realized that she had no right, as her eyes settled into remorseful slits. "The baby. I was going to tell you today," she said, placing a hand on her own belly; he couldn't tell if it was a gesture of tenderness or regret. Or maybe there was a pain there she wanted to press so she'd feel it more. "Tonight. I was going to make a special dinner. Right after you left this morning, I went out and got things for shrimp scampi." He made a sound she mistook for doubt. "Go home and look if you don't believe me—it's all in the fridge! Tarragon was the only ingredient I couldn't find."

"It's not that I don't believe you." But they could both hear in his voice that this wasn't true, and he twisted in his seat to look at her straight on. "But really, Al—why *should* I? You lied that day after you saw the doctor—to all of us. How could you do that? It's been more than a week. How could you keep that from me?" Without even identifying the fear that fueled the words, he said, "What, were you going to have an abortion?"

Her face went so white he thought she might be on the verge of passing out. "I can't believe you just said that to me." She turned away from him to look ahead through the windshield. "You don't know me better than that?"

"I thought I did," he said, wishing he could retract the accusation; he didn't actually think she would have gotten rid of their baby, let alone without telling him. But now that it was in the air between him, there was no calling it back.

"I was afraid," she murmured. "I was afraid if I told you, it would happen again. I wanted to wait until the first trimester was over." Her face crumpled, and she brought her hands up to cover her eyes. "It's so close, now. I wanted to celebrate." With a sudden motion, she punched the dashboard in front of her.

"Al." He reached out instinctively to grab her hand back so she wouldn't hurt herself. "They said you were drunk."

She winced at the sound of it. "I *wasn't* drunk."

"And you had one of your students in the car."

She nodded. "Keith. His father went after him."

"Tell me what happened." *The truth*, he would have added, but at the last minute he refrained from accusing her again.

She closed her eyes, as if replaying the scene inside her head. "Okay. After I bought the groceries, I went into the liquor store to buy some champagne so we could have a little toast tonight. I thought one little glass wouldn't hurt. I mean, look at my mother." She gestured out the window as if Helen might be waving from the side of the road. "She drank the whole time she was pregnant with me, and I was fine! Right? The chances that anything bad would happen, now, are pretty small." She wrung her hands together. "I brought everything home, and I don't know what got into me, but instead of waiting until tonight, I opened the bottle and poured a little glass for myself. Tiny— Thomas, I promise." The first words of her wedding vows, which had always made both of them smile until now. "It was kind of a private celebration. I thought, I'm *doing* it, it's finally going to happen, I'm going to be a mom." The word "mom" seemed to choke her. "Anyway, it hit me right away—I guess I don't have any tolerance anymore."

"So then what?" Tom closed his eyes, knowing it was his own fault that he had no choice but to hear the rest.

"So then Keith called."

"You give those kids your number?"

"Well, not all of them. Only a few. Two, really. Keith's one of them, his father's out of control sometimes, he never knows what's going to happen."

"So he asks you to come save him? And you rush right out?" When she didn't correct him, which was essentially his answer, he said, "You know what could have happened here, right? You could have killed yourself, or him. Or lost the baby, or your job. If your father wasn't looking out for you. If he wasn't the chief."

"He was in trouble," she said tonelessly, as if reciting lines from a script. "Keith."

"I don't give a shit about Keith!" It was all he could manage not to shake her, to make her understand. "*You're* in trouble. *We're* in trouble. How are you not seeing that?" When again she didn't respond, he reached to turn her face toward his and saw that she was staring at something beyond him, which he guessed didn't actually exist except in her own mind.

She mumbled, "I would never drive when I was drinking. I'd never drink with a baby in me."

He did his best not to shiver as another chill buzzed through his blood. "Alison. *What?* You just did both of those things." The measure of shock in her face as she registered his words exceeded any he'd ever seen there before. It was only then that he comprehended how far gone she was—how incapable, in that moment, of anything resembling a reasonable exchange. "It's okay," he told her, drawing her close even as the word that kept repeating in his mind was "betrayal." Of course it was anything but okay, but he didn't know what else to say.

"Mom said she would take me to a meeting," she whispered, her voice muffled against his coat.

Tom made a face before he could stop himself. Before too long (although now was not the time), he would have to tell Alison what had happened back in July, the night after Helen accepted a medallion for her tenth year of sobriety. They'd all gone to the meeting, clapped for her, shared the anniversary cake.

Not twenty-four hours later, at Doug and Helen's house for their usual Wednesday-night dinner, he walked into the kitchen and saw Helen drinking wine straight out of the bottle. He was so stunned at the sight that he stopped short, then must have made a noise he wasn't aware of, because Helen slung the bottle back down on the counter with a glass thump and turned toward him, wine snaking down her mouth's edge and onto her blouse collar.

"Tom," she said, drawing out the pronunciation of his name to such an extent that he assumed she was trying to buy time. But what could she say? "This is not what you think."

But of course, it was. It was *exactly* what he thought. He realized right away that he wished he hadn't caught her. What was he supposed to do now? She begged him to keep it a secret between them: it wouldn't do anybody any good, she said, if he told.

In the truck, to avoid responding to the notion of Helen leading her daughter to the sober flock, Tom eased Alison back against her own seat and went to start the engine again. But she put a hand on his arm and said, "What was Daddy saying to you, when he took you away in there?"

"Nothing. He just told me what happened."

"He wasn't mad?"

"He's never mad at you."

"Not *me*. Mad at *you*."

"Well, of course he was. He's always mad at me." He said this instead of asking Alison what she suspected he might have done, this time, to inspire her father's anger. "What else is new?" Then he was amazed to feel a wet heat crowding behind his eyelids. "I've tried everything I know," he told her, blinking the tears back before she could see them. "I joined the rescue team, I learned how to dive. I'm turning my family's business around.

But all he sees is the douchebag he thinks kicked his daughter down the stairs."

"It doesn't matter what he thinks," Alison said. This was so obviously inaccurate that Tom almost laughed. He wouldn't bother arguing with her; he was grateful *she* hadn't laughed when he referred to the shack as his family's business, as if his father had owned a real company instead of a shithole that sold mostly cigarettes and beer.

At home, Tom eased the truck into the driveway, then helped her into the house. Despite the injuries Alison had inflicted on herself, he couldn't help feeling hopeful; maybe today had been the wake-up call she needed, what Helen would have referred to as a blessing in disguise. And maybe it would bring them all closer—the disaster that might have happened but hadn't, the shared anticipation of a new life among them, one they'd all been waiting to welcome for a long time. He settled her into bed, surprised to find that despite the deception she'd committed against him, he didn't have to fake tenderness in his touch as he pulled the covers over her, confiscating her cell phone while he was at it so that at least for a few hours, her parents wouldn't be able to get to her.

In the kitchen, he looked for the champagne bottle she told him she'd opened for a taste before she received her student's call. He checked the fridge, the cupboard, the recycling bin, and the trash bag—nothing. Had she poured it out, then discarded the bottle on the way to pick up Keith? That was the only explanation. He'd ask her about it when she woke up. For now he just wanted to sit down and think about the other surprise of the day, which he hadn't had a chance to focus on until now: he had another shot at being a father. The pleasure of it, the profound exhilaration, carried him into a sleep as sound as if he'd spent the day climbing a mountain, which (it occurred to him the next morning), in a way, he had.

As Needed for Anxiety

On Halloween—the day after the disastrous party at the condos—Harper was so sure that her connection to Joy had been completely severed that she was shocked almost to the point of exclaiming when Joy stopped by. Truman answered the door and let her in on his way out, calling "Hey" into the kitchen, where Harper, feeling the remnants of her first hangover, finished making the seven-layer bars she owed him. Not having any information about what awaited her, she stepped into the living room with some apprehension. Seeing Joy standing there with her hands thrust deep into the pocket of her hoodie, she said, "I'm sorry I said that about your mom," regretting the words immediately when she realized how stupid it was to remind Joy of how she'd betrayed her. But she was waiting for Joy to apologize, too—for starting the whole thing by laughing at Delaney's joke about Harper's own mom being mental.

Joy shrugged, which seemed to be her default gesture these days. "Why? It's not your fault, it's my mother's. You didn't say anything that wasn't true." She put her hand on the banister post and ran her finger over the wood. "Can we go up?"

"We don't need to. There's nobody here."

"Even your mom?"

"It's her group time. My father took her."

"Oh." Joy nodded. She was the only person Harper had ever told about her mother's being a member of a therapy group. "I forgot."

This meant something. For going on three years now, Harper's mother had spent two hours every Saturday afternoon—between one and three o'clock—in group therapy at the community health center. Until Joy and Harper stopped going to the mall together over the summer, Joy had often been in the car when Harper's father or, more recently, Truman dropped her mother off or picked her up from the session. The fact that Joy could forget something so primary to Harper's life felt like the closing of a door Harper had been trying to hold open, by herself, against a wind that would inevitably blow it shut.

"I'd still rather go up to your room," Joy said. "It's easier to talk there."

"Well, okay." Only then did Harper realize that she was wearing her apron, which said IF CUPCAKES ARE WRONG, I DON'T WANT TO BE RIGHT across the front. Joy had seen her in the apron numerous times, but feeling vulnerable today, Harper removed it in a hurry as she followed Joy up the stairs. Without taking her hoodie off, Joy headed for the window seat and began tossing Addy's plastic doll-head from side to side.

"I wish you wouldn't do that," Harper told her. "That's always bothered me."

"It has?" But Joy appeared more amused by this than perturbed. She twisted Addy's head back on and folded her hands in her lap, an exaggerated show of manners. "You actually did me a favor," she said. "My mother doesn't deserve me keeping her secret. Maybe now my father will find out, and she'll get what's coming to her."

"Why don't you just tell him?"

"I thought about it." Joy stood abruptly, seeming agitated at the turn of the conversation. "But she'd just deny it, and then he wouldn't believe me. Why put myself through that?" When Harper didn't answer right away, Joy asked if there was anything to eat and said she had to go to the bathroom.

"I don't have anything without sugar," Harper said, but Joy shrugged and said sugar was fine, she was through caring about it anymore.

Harper went down to the kitchen and put three of Truman's seven-layer bars on a plate. When she returned, closing her parents' bedroom door on the way back to her own (her mother never left it open, wanting to keep her refuge sealed; her father must have forgotten, which meant he must have been distracted because he knew what a big deal it was), Joy was standing at the window looking out. "It's shitty out there," she said.

"Really?" Harper put the plate down. She could see sun lighting the houses up the hill, where Joy lived. "I thought it was kind of nice out today."

"I don't mean the weather." Joy murmured it as if to herself, and Harper waited for her to elaborate. When she didn't, she held the plate of bars out, but Joy shook her head. "I have to go," she said, looking not at Harper but beyond her. She flipped her hood up around her face and jogged down the stairs toward the door without another word, and Harper tried but failed to avoid recognizing that Joy had not only left her, but escaped.

That night she stood at the stove stirring a blueberry compote when she heard her mother cry out from her bedroom. Rushing to the stairs, she called up, "What? What?" expecting her mother to call and say *Come help me, I need you.*

Instead, her mother came downstairs and waved an empty pill bottle in Harper's face. "Did you take these?" she demanded, showing her the label. CLONAZEPAM. 1 MG. AS NEEDED FOR

ANXIETY. She waved the bottle again to emphasize the absence of sound, the fact that no pills were inside.

"Of course not," Harper said, feeling her face grow warm. She was angry herself; didn't her mother know her better than that? Never mind that Harper had often been tempted, over the years, to try one of the little yellow pills, especially when she felt, well, anxious. Wasn't that what they were for?

But she had never done so, partly for just this reason: she wouldn't have wanted her mother to find out. Not because she thought her mother would feel deprived, but because she knew how much her mother would worry to think that Harper might be like her, susceptible to what she called the screaming meemies. Now, though, it seemed that this worry was secondary (if it existed at all; Harper couldn't tell) to her mother's dismay at finding an empty stash.

"I wouldn't do that," she added, understanding only as she defended herself who had stolen the drugs. She remembered coming upstairs with the snack Joy asked for, and her parents' open door. Her father had not left it ajar by accident. Joy had gone into Harper's parents' bathroom, opened the medicine cabinet, extracted the bottle of meds, and shaken them out somewhere—probably into her pocket. She hadn't had much time before Harper arrived with the treats. And almost as soon as Harper came back with them, Joy had taken off.

But she couldn't let her mother know what had really happened; she still felt enough leftover love and loyalty not to do that to Joy.

Her mother tossed the bottle aside. "And why would somebody just steal the pills themselves instead of taking that, too?"

"So nobody would be able to tell where they came from," Harper said. Probably, she realized, Joy had also reasoned that leaving the bottle might mean the theft wouldn't be noticed so soon.

And what would Joy have done with the pills? Not swallowed them herself; Harper was sure of that. No, Delaney Stowell must have recruited Joy to contribute to her business of selling drugs out of the condo—that's what Harper had witnessed the night before, coming upon Joy and the long-haired stranger performing a transaction in the closed-off bedroom. Maybe the next step was some kind of initiation test, a hazing ritual designed by Delaney and Tessa and Lin: *Now you have to come up with your own merchandise.* If this had been the challenge, of course Joy would think immediately of Harper's mother as a source. Had she even hesitated? Harper wondered. Then it occurred to her what probably happened: Delaney told Joy what she had to do, but she held off because she didn't want to take advantage of Harper that way.

But after Harper told Delaney and everyone else at the Halloween party about Joy's mother and the black guy, all bets were off, and Joy felt entitled to do whatever she pleased. Understanding this, Harper felt a chill in her blood. She herself was responsible for the fact that her mother's meds were gone.

Without wanting to—doing her best to resist it—she remembered suddenly the day Joy had offered (insisted, really, now that Harper thought about it) to come over and help her study for the test on *The Odyssey*. Was she hoping to sneak into the medicine cabinet even then? Had she had a change of heart while explaining the loyalty of the old dog Argos, or was it just that no opportunity had presented itself, that day, for access to Harper's parents' room?

But this was too much to contemplate, and to feel, so she forced herself to stop doing both as she took the phone handset up to her room. She sat with it on the bed and looked across at the doll on her window seat, imagining that Addy was accusing her with her eyes: *How come you always let that girl take my head off?* The thought made Harper smile. Then she remembered that "that girl" was Joy, and took a deep breath as she dialed.

When the woman on the other end answered with a tired, mechanical-sounding greeting including the information that the line was recorded, she almost hung up. But at the last minute she caught Addy's eyes again, which gave her courage to continue with the call. "I want to—I'm not sure how to say it. I think I might know something about the drug stuff that's going on."

"Drug stuff?" The woman must have heard that she was speaking to a teenager, and a scared one, because her voice became warmer, less mechanical. "Can you be more specific, honey?"

"People selling prescriptions. I think I know who's in charge, or at least where it's happening. Some of it." She told the woman about Lakeview Arms and the Halloween party. How she'd "heard" that pills and money had been exchanged there. The woman asked her to identify herself. She asked if Harper could give her any names, promising it would be confidential.

Do it, Addy told Harper with those commanding eyes. "Delaney Stowell," Harper whispered into the phone, then hung up as if suddenly it had gotten too hot.

Delaney Stowell was the reason Joy had changed so much this year. Delaney was the one who'd corrupted Joy, getting her to sell drugs and do who knew what else. It was really Delaney's fault—wasn't it?—that Joy had come into Harper's house and stolen medication from her mother.

Lying awake that night, she did her best to convince herself that it was for Joy's own good, and not because she was angry at her friend's betrayal, that she gave Delaney's name to the police. If Delaney got caught and stopped what she was doing, Joy might see things for what they were and come back to her first friend. It was a long shot, but worth it. She fell asleep trying not to acknowledge that this was only a wish and not what would actually happen, but it was too late; the time for that kind of pretending had slipped away from her, and there was no getting it back.

Saturday, October 31

When Violet called and said she wanted to see me, I assumed she chose tonight because she's hated Halloween since childhood, when her brother flew out of a closet wearing a Freddy Krueger mask and attacked her with a fake razor-glove that didn't, of course, look fake to her at all. She let me suggest the restaurant and I chose Rubio's, perversely, because I know it is Susanne's favorite. "You're leaving, aren't you," I said, before the witch-costumed waitress could bring us our complimentary zombies.

Violet didn't answer right away, and like a child I thought that maybe she wouldn't, if I just didn't look at her. When I finally did work up the courage to meet her eyes, I saw immediately that I was right.

"You had to know this was coming," she said. "We talked about it."

"No, we didn't."

"Well, not about this, exactly. But you know what I mean."

Of course I understood what she was referring to. After Grandee died, it didn't take long for Violet and me to see that what had been holding us together, when we *were* together, was the joint project of taking care of her. We went so far as to convince Grandee that we'd gotten married at City Hall, so she wouldn't object to our sharing a room and a bed. For the first year, we *felt* married, and I almost proposed for real. But something held me back, and toward the end of Grandee's life I was glad we'd only had a pretend wedding. I sensed Violet felt that way, too. We worked as a threesome—Violet staying home during the day to do the job we hired her for originally (taking Grandee to her appointments, giving her insulin shots, and cooking her low-glycemic meals), while I worked as a security guard at the Memorial Art Gallery—but we didn't work as a couple. Violet moved out two weeks after the funeral, and I was afraid she'd return to New York right away, but when she took another home-nursing assignment in Rochester, I allowed myself to hope (because I feel safer with her than anyone) that she might stay on upstate.

I've been letting her live rent-free in Grandee's house while I'm up here at school; that way she has a place to live while she saves money to move to New York, and the house gets looked after. But I've also been holding my breath, waiting for her to tell me she's leaving, and tonight was the night.

"You could come, too," she told me. "I mean, not to live together. But I know a lot of people down there. You'd have a connection, if you wanted to—you know. Start over. Start a new life."

"I have something here," I said quietly. I knew she'd think I was referring to my studies, so I wasn't surprised when she reminded me that there are art schools in New York, too. Ones besides Decker, ones that might offer aid. Maybe even ones that have classes as good as those at Genesee Valley Academy of Fine Arts.

I ignored her sarcasm, which has always made me cringe, and repeated that this is where my life is. I have no right to wish she would stay; I understand that. She is ignorant of Susanne, of the fact that I took up with my art teacher, and that although Susanne broke things off with me and reconciled with her husband, I still harbor what I know is the impossible idea of our ending up together.

Grandee would have been appalled by all of it; Violet would just get mad. I felt sad for myself but sadder for Grandee, even though I knew this was ridiculous. Grandee loved Violet. She loved Violet and me together. One of the last things she said, in the hospital, was that she wished she could live to see our children.

"This might be the last time, then," Violet said tonight after I walked her to her car, and I left her feeling flattened, thinking I would just go home to bed. But on the drive from the restaurant I decided instead that I would work for a few hours, to take my mind off the fact that she is leaving and that in addition to losing her friendship here, I will have to figure out what to do with Grandee's house. Before she died, she told me she didn't expect me to hang on to it forever. I know she didn't want me to feel that burden. Sell it and take up a new life somewhere, she said, and I suppose that at some point, I will. But in the meantime, at least until I graduate with my degree, I try to avoid thinking about it—losing the place where I grew up, where Grandee made a home first for my father and then for me.

In my apartment at Cass's house after saying good-bye to Violet, I took out my sketch pad and looked at what I'd done recently. Not much. It's taken me almost two months to heed Joy's advice and start the first portrait for *Souls on Board*: my father. Since Susanne ended things between us, I'm more grateful than ever for the distraction of new work, even though it's been slow going. At my easel I've propped up one of my earliest sketches from back when I was twelve, just a few months before the plane crash. On a Saturday morning, my father brought me to work with him so I could "help" him tune a Steinway for a concert that night. I wasn't particularly keen on accompanying him, because I knew his ulterior motive was to try to convince me that I should become a piano technician myself someday, and even though I hadn't discovered art yet, I knew that his occupation wasn't for me. I just hadn't figured out how to tell him this, because he seemed so intent on the idea of handing his own father's tuning hammer down to his son.

In the piano hall I fidgeted—I was twelve, I didn't want to be there, and the sound of him playing the same key over and over, as he turned the hammer on the pin, made my teeth grind. Finally, I offered to go out and buy him some coffee, because I knew he wouldn't refuse. I didn't mean to sneak up on him when I reentered the room, but he was so absorbed in what he was doing—listening for the right tone—that when I said *Dad* behind him he turned fast, startled, and the hammer flew out of his hand, upending the coffee so that it splashed straight up at my chin, scalding the skin. I still have the scar, and I still remember the pain and the shock of it. I still remember him crying because he felt so shaken, even though I kept telling him it was my own fault. That night, after returning from the emergency room where they dressed the burn, I sat in bed and, doing my best to ignore the hot sting under the bandage, sketched what I'd seen in his face as he realized what he had done. Love, guilt, helplessness, confusion. But mostly love. Though the sketch is old now, it's still the closest expression I have to what I want to remember about my father.

So I tried to work in my studio, but I'd forgotten what tonight was. After being interrupted three times by trick-or-treaters ringing the bell, I brought the sketch book downstairs and settled into Grandee's favorite reading chair, the only piece of furniture I moved up here from the house after she died. On the table next to the chair I keep the stack of books she'd read last, including two she borrowed from the Monroe County

Library. The overdue notices had been among the mail that piled up while she was in the hospital. I'd planned to write to the library, tell them I lost the books, and pay them back. But I haven't done it yet, mainly because I know Grandee would frown on such behavior.

She always did the house up for Halloween (jack-o'-lanterns, fake cobwebs, spiders and skeletons suspended over the door) and she liked to answer the bell dressed as Glinda from *The Wizard of Oz*. Of course, despite the wavy red-blond wig, high tiara, and billowy pink dress with angel wings sprouting from its shoulders, none of the trick-or-treaters ever guessed who she was. "What's wrong with these kids?" she'd say. "I look just like her!" I never had the heart to point out to her that my friends didn't recognize her as Glinda because Glinda was white. I did ask her once why she'd chosen the costume, and she told me she'd always liked the idea of a good witch; who didn't?

It took me until the age of thirteen to realize that whenever I thought of the mother I'd never met, I imagined her as Glinda. Not with the pink dress and the wings, but with the same face and smile—a benevolent, wish-granting fairy. No doubt this has contributed to my fantasies about the open arms she'll greet me with, if our paths ever cross either by accident or on purpose.

Putting the bowl of peanut butter cups by the door so I wouldn't be tempted myself, I sat in Grandee's chair and looked at my Artist's Statement draft, but I didn't get very far. At nine twenty I stood, stretched, ate the remaining candy (what did it matter if I was chubby now?), and was about to shut off the stoop light when I saw a hooded figure walking toward the door.

"Oh, sorry," I said, hoping to forestall whoever it was, "I just gave out the last of it."

"That's okay." It wasn't a trick-or-treater, I saw as she stepped toward me, but a teenager. A young woman. When she stepped into the light and pulled her hood off, I saw that it was Joy.

"Oh," I said, at the same time she was asking "Do you remember me?" When I said *Of course I do, how could I not?* the answer seemed to make her falter. When she didn't say anything else, I asked if she wanted to come in, even though I felt nervous about it. She thanked me without a smile, her expression suggesting that she was fighting her own instinct to show friendliness or warmth.

In less than two months since Labor Day, her face has changed. She looks tougher, harder, more on guard—but still I recognized the person I spoke to that day, when she discussed her own art shyly and, when we began talking, showed so much interest and animation in hearing about mine.

No animation was evident in her eyes now. I waited, sensing that it was important to her to direct whatever would pass between us.

She sat, crossing her legs and arms as she settled into Grandee's chair. I took the couch, leaning forward so as not to give the impression that I assumed her visit was a social one, when it obviously was not. Despite trying to match her serious demeanor, I was not prepared for what she said—what she demanded. "I came to ask you: you're sleeping with my mother, right?" Though she'd made a point of meeting my eyes just before speaking, hearing herself say the words seemed to cause her to look away.

I made a noise—involuntary, indistinct. Not a word, just a noise. I knew that the right thing to do was to say she should be talking about this to her mother, not me, but I could tell how difficult it had been for her to ask the question, and I wanted to show respect for that. "No," I said, realizing that the literal answer was only a temporary salvation. "I'm not."

"But you *were*. Right?"

Now it was I who looked away from her as I nodded.

Sinking back in the chair and seeming to shrink, as if my response had touched her physically, she said, "I knew it."

"Then why did you ask?" I didn't mean to challenge her, though I could see she took it that way. Why put herself through this—confronting me—if she really did know the truth?

"I don't know." She lifted her hoodie around her head, putting her features in shadow. "I guess I thought maybe I was wrong. That there was a chance, somehow. I knew you'd tell me the truth." A grudging acknowledgment of our brief, past connection, and the fact that she'd felt it, too.

Now that this exchange was over—the crucial information in the air—she let her guard down and began talking as if we knew each other far better than we actually did. Since I'd expected her to be angry after my admission, the fact that she spoke as if I were a friend took me aback, and I felt more awkward than if she'd sworn at me and stomped out of the house. Her parents were fighting all the time, she said. Her mother was so tense Joy could see the veins popping in her neck. Though they hadn't come out and told her so, she knew they were in danger of losing their house, because her father's business was going down the tubes and because of a stupid mistake he had made. An investment gone wrong with someone he'd trusted, whom he shouldn't have. Of course I didn't let on that I'd heard the same story, though Joy might already have guessed.

I cleared my throat, because I was afraid she'd just keep talking if I didn't interrupt somehow, and end up telling me things she would regret, if she hadn't already. She sat up a little straighter as if to take hold of herself, then apologized and added, "It's just that on top of everything else, there's no one to talk to. It sucks." I didn't tell her that her mother had mentioned the distance Joy had put between herself and the people she used to be close to—her family, her best friend. "Leave it to me to just start babbling to some random black guy," she said in a tone of self-hatred, and then, when she saw my face, hurried to add, "I mean, black has nothing to do with it. But—you know what I mean. I don't even really know you." Though her saying "black" startled me, it did not sting as much as "random," because I'd felt a true affinity with her during that conversation about our work. Trying to hide that I felt hurt, I told her that if there was any way I could help, she should feel free to ask.

"Well," she said, standing up from the chair and pulling the hoodie more tightly around her, "at least you stopped—you know. With my mother." What had she been going to say? *Sleeping with*, again? *Having sex?* It was hard for me to believe she would have used the term "fucking." She let the phrase slide, whatever it was. "That's something."

There was no point in letting her know that this had been her mother's idea, not mine. That if I'd had my way, we would *not* have stopped.

I was about to close the door behind her when she asked, "Where do you work?" as if it had suddenly occurred to her. She turned on the threshold to look back into the apartment. "Didn't you tell me you had a studio here somewhere?"

"In the attic," I told her, recognizing immediately that I had made a mistake. But when she asked if she could see, I felt I had no choice but to say *Sure* and lead her up.

Immediately she walked over to the canvas containing the first few strokes, the hesitant beginning of my father's face. I couldn't deny the pleasure I took in the exclamation Joy made when she saw it. "That's *awesome*," she said, as if she'd forgotten entirely (if only for that moment) the reason she had come. I know it's the word all teenagers use (like "sucks"), but in her exhalation of it now I heard more than just politeness or habit.

But I was feeling nervous; what if someone had seen her enter my house? It was one thing for Cass to look the other way, do her best to hide her disapproval when she saw Susanne with me. A white teenage girl was another matter entirely. I was on the verge of saying that she could come over another time, if she wanted (though I already knew I would discourage this if she took me up on it), when Joy stepped toward the window and peered into the round pencil holder containing the bouquet of bookmarks Grandee had made. "What are these?" she asked, picking one up.

I described the tradition to her, how each year my grandmother would take some leftover fabric from a piece of clothing she'd sewn for herself and stitch it around cardboard to make me a bookmark. I only ever used two at a time—one for my commonplace book and one for whatever book I was reading—but I rotated them and kept the others in this container and another in my bedroom. "These colors are unbelievable," Joy breathed, picking up the orange one Grandee had fashioned out of the scarf I'd painted for *American Commonplace*.

"You can have it, if you want," I told her, though as soon as she was gone I knew I would regret having given the keepsake away. But my slight trepidation had swelled to a near panic as I imagined Cass watching and waiting for the white girl to emerge, or a group of mothers from down the street escorting their children up to my stoop for candy and encountering Joy on her way out.

Joy thanked me and stuck the bookmark in the pocket of her hoodie, then allowed me to usher her back downstairs. At the door she thanked me again, told me she was sorry for being a jerk when she first got there, and tripped lightly into the night. Looking out after her, I saw with relief that my stretch of the street was empty.

Back in Grandee's chair, I reached for the pad I'd set aside before Joy's appearance, turned to a new page, and began sketching quickly, trying to remember all the details I'd noted as we spoke. All the expressions she had exhibited during the half hour of her visit: dread when she asked about my affair with her mother, resignation when I confirmed that she was right, admiration when she saw the results of my first brushstrokes, pleasure when I gave her the bookmark to take home. Dark spaces occluded her eyes, but the face I drew was bright, intelligent, alert. I knew from Susanne that it was a face Joy had kept hidden from her mother for quite some time now, and I knew it was the face Susanne would want most to preserve.

When I finished, I sat back and remembered with a short stab that Susanne would not be following through on her request for me to paint Joy's portrait. For a moment I thought about crumpling the sketch up and tossing it in the trash. But in the end I ripped the page out and stuck it in the drawer I reserve for things I probably won't ever need again, but don't want to get rid of, just in case.

Diversion

Though they knew that everyone at Belle Meadow—the nurses, the aides, and as many residents as could follow the action—would be watching the Yankees try to win the World Series on the big screen in the Solarium that first Wednesday in November, Susanne and Gil decided to go ahead and throw the party they'd planned for Emilia's eighty-sixth birthday. They assumed Joy would want to stay home and watch Derek Jeter while she worked on her *Othello* paper, so they were pleased when she volunteered instead to come and help with the party, serving cake and ice cream on paper plates to Emilia and the other Belle Meadow residents after dinner. Emilia reached up to take off her bib (the staff delicately referred to it as a "clothing protector," especially when family was around, but they all knew a bib was what it was), and when Mirabelle asked, "Don't you want to eat some of your own nice cake? It's your birthday, you know," Emilia ripped the bib off and flung it to the floor, and Susanne saw that it was all Gil could do not to applaud.

When the police entered the room, Susanne saw them before Gil did, and instinctively she understood that whatever had brought them to Belle Meadow meant her family was in trouble.

The older officer, with blue eyes that made her think of Paul Newman though this man's face was not as symmetrical or handsome, approached and asked, "Mr. and Mrs. Enright?" Next to him Joy stood staring down at the floor, and it was this more than anything—her inability or unwillingness to look her mother in the eye—that signaled to Susanne how serious it was. "We're arresting your daughter, I'm sorry to say."

Susanne breathed "What?" at the same time Gil demanded, "What for?"

"Possession of a controlled substance without a prescription." Gil opened his mouth to say something else, but Doug Armstrong held a hand up to indicate *Don't interrupt.* "Criminal sale of a prescription for a controlled substance. Illegal sale of prescription drugs."

"That's horse pucky." Gil actually laughed, and for a moment Susanne was tempted to, too, but for the wrong reason: most people would have said "bullshit" to what the cop told them, but Gil stuck to his old-fashioned profanity even in a situation like this. Joy had been standing to one side of the officers, but when she heard why they'd come, she moved away, not meeting her mother's eyes. The impulse toward laughter left Susanne, who abruptly felt sick to her stomach.

"We don't understand what you're saying," she told Armstrong. "I mean, we do, but it can't have anything to do with our daughter. Joy doesn't do drugs."

"You may be right about that." He nodded to concede her claim, which made Susanne feel absurdly gratified. "We're not charging her with *taking* them. As in ingesting." He pantomimed the tossing of pills into his own mouth, and Susanne had to look away. "Just the possession, and the selling. But that's bad enough. Worse, in some ways, when we're talking about the law."

Gil said, "You've got the wrong girl. You must have. And

anyway, what are you doing *here*? This is a nursing home, for God's sake. We're celebrating my mother's birthday."

"I'm sorry to crash the party," Doug Armstrong said. "I mean that sincerely." Susanne tried not to show her irritation at his words; in her experience, anyone who went out of his way to say he meant something "sincerely" didn't mean it at all. "But we can't help where a crime takes place."

"You're saying a crime happened *here*?" Now she couldn't keep her own voice from scaling.

"Well, not in this room precisely. But the facility itself, yes. It originated at that development out by the lake—I think you were working on that some, weren't you?" Armstrong nodded at Gil. *How much else does he know about us?* Susanne thought. *About everyone in this town?* "We've been following your daughter and one of the employees here," Armstrong added. "We wanted to make sure of it before we moved in."

One of the employees here—it had to be Jason, of course. Joy's crush. Although Armstrong was suggesting that it wasn't because of a crush, or because she wanted doughnuts, that Joy had allowed Jason to lure her away from her parents that day; she'd followed him so that they could trade drugs and cash. If someone wanted a source for drugs to sell, wasn't a nursing home the perfect front? Staff handed out Ativan and Norco like candy here, to keep the residents docile if not asleep. And who would ever expect a sedate, respectable place like Belle Meadow to be tied up in illegal drug trafficking?

Armstrong told them, "We apprehended a customer who purchased drugs from your daughter. Xanax. Hydrocodone. Klonopin. Plus a blank prescription from a psychiatrist, the father of one of your daughter's friends."

"Delaney Stowell," Susanne told Gil, but she could tell he'd already guessed.

"Also, we just confiscated these from her jacket." Armstrong held up a cellophane bag filled with small yellow pills. "They look like benzos to me."

"Why are you looking here in the first place?" Gil asked. Then he repeated, "This is a *nursing* home." Her husband seemed literally stunned, Susanne thought. As if from a blow to the brain.

Armstrong answered, "We've been keeping an eye on one of the aides here." Yes, Jason—of course, Susanne thought again. "We knew he was part of the whole thing. There were cell calls back and forth between him and your daughter; one call wouldn't have meant much, but there were enough to where we were pretty sure we had something."

"Then you've absolutely made a mistake." Gil wore an expression Susanne didn't see in him often: triumph in anticipation of proving the other person wrong. Ordinarily, he was not that kind of man, but she knew that when it came to somebody accusing his daughter, what kind of man he was might change. "Joy doesn't even *have* a cell phone."

Armstrong raised his eyebrows. He looked at Susanne, and when she didn't back Gil up, her husband raised his eyebrows, too.

"I was going to tell you," she told Gil. "There just hasn't been a right time." The truth was that she'd been afraid to announce another betrayal when the truce between them, and Gil's return home, was still so fresh. Joy seemed to have understood that she should keep the phone hidden. Even Susanne hadn't seen her use it after the first week since they'd made the trip together to purchase it.

Though she could tell Gil was cringing inside, he would not show this to the police. "What happens now?" he asked.

"We'll need to take her down to the station for processing, but then it's up to a judge. Those blank scrips can go for a hundred and fifty a pop, and the pills are worth a lot, too. What she did is a felony"—Armstrong paused at the sound of Susanne's gasp—"but I wouldn't let that scare me too much right now, if I were you. They're a lot easier on youthful offenders. She'll probably get off with diversion and counseling."

"A felony," Susanne whispered.

"I know this is hard. A shock," Armstrong said. "You know I have a daughter myself." Only then did Susanne remember that this was the father of Joy's English teacher.

Over Joy's protests that she had been set up and that it was all a mistake, the officers took her to the station, completed their procedures, then released her to Gil and Susanne, telling them they'd have to bring Joy to the courthouse for arraignment the next day. Susanne dreaded other people finding out about it, but it turned out that Joy's name was not released to the media because of her age.

And they hadn't been home more than a half hour—Joy still insisting that she didn't know what had happened, or how the drugs had gotten into her pocket ("Jason must have slipped them in there for some reason, but I don't have a clue why he would do something like that")—when a police clerk named Natalie called to tell them the charges were being dropped. Susanne answered the phone, and when she asked "Why?" Natalie said she wasn't sure, she didn't have all the details, but probably they were after *bigger fish* and that prosecuting Joy would just be a distraction. When Susanne asked if that meant they considered Joy innocent, Natalie said that she had no more information than what she'd been told to convey. The police chief himself, Natalie added, wanted to express his apologies for any inconvenience.

"That doesn't sound right," Gil said with a frown, when Susanne repeated the conversation to him. "That doesn't make sense."

"Well, I know. But maybe she *is* telling the truth, and Jason did set her up? It would benefit him if he could throw the blame somewhere else, wouldn't it?"

"I guess." She could tell he was trying to convince himself, as she was.

"I mean, we're not going to argue with it, are we?"

"No, of course we're not."

They went to Joy's room, where they found her curled on her bed around Salsa. When they told her about the call, she smiled and said, "See?" as if she'd proven a point. "I told you."

"It's not that simple, Joy." Gil looked pained. Susanne herself felt almost euphoric about the charges being dropped, but she didn't want to show it in front of her husband; if Joy had been guilty of anything (and wasn't it likely that she at least knew about Jason's stealing and dealing drugs, even if she hadn't participated in it herself?), she didn't want him to think she was celebrating Joy's having gotten away with something she shouldn't have. "We still want to understand what was going on."

"*Nothing* was going on. They just told you that, didn't they?"

"No. They told us they weren't pursuing charges against you. They didn't say they made a mistake." Gil lowered his voice, and Susanne knew it was an effort to mitigate the sting of his next words. "You're still guilty of what they arrested you for: you had those drugs in your possession."

"Because he planted them on me!"

"Why would he do that?"

"I don't know. I don't know." She was sputtering. "How would I know what's in some random guy's head?"

"Okay. We can hear you." Gil held up a hand against the heightened volume of her denial.

"But you don't believe me."

"I didn't say that."

"You didn't *have* to say it." Joy reached beyond Salsa for the earbuds on her nightstand and put them on.

"This isn't over," Gil told her, and Susanne could tell that their daughter was only pretending she hadn't heard him. Outside Joy's closed door, he repeated himself to Susanne. *This isn't over.* She nodded to show solidarity, even though secretly she hoped he was wrong.

After

Friday, December 11

I knew that attending the funeral was out of the question, a fact I accepted though it frustrates and angers me. But this morning I did call to arrange for flowers to be delivered to the church. The florist enumerated the various options—bouquets and wreaths and sprays with names like *Greater Glory*, *Remembrance*, *Display of Affection*. When I hesitated to choose any of those, she said, "How about *Uplifting Thoughts*? A beautiful collection of bright gerberas," and I said, *Fine, that sounds good*, not because it did sound good but because I could tell she was wearying of reading the list to me. She asked what the card should say, and I hesitated before responding. "'Thinking of you in this time of loss'?" she suggested, and I repeated, *That sounds good*. How did I want the signature to read? This I had considered before making the call, and I told her, *No name or anything, just "Love."*

The florist's tone and manner were friendly and solicitous, a practiced art. But when I proceeded to give her my credit card information, there was a silence on the other end after she confirmed the spelling of my name. "Is this some kind of a sick joke?" she asked, her voice hardening and distant, as if she were holding the phone away from her ear in anticipation of hanging up. I told her it was not. "I can't help you," she said, the last words barely audible before she went ahead and killed the connection.

The reporters were still stalking me, camped on the street outside Cass's house. I haven't been able to work since my arrest on Monday, though I tried after returning home when the bail was posted, thinking (hoping) that sitting in front of the easel with my palette would transport me, the way it always has, to the state of suspension I only ever achieve when I'm painting and that I need more desperately, now, than ever before. Of course, it didn't work. What's happening to me now—what's happening to all of us—defies transcendence.

After the florist rejected me, I called Violet and told her I was going crazy, alone in my apartment. "You have to get out of there," she said. We've been speaking twice a day and it's the only thing that's saved me, along with the time I spend talking to Ramona about my case. The small bit of hope my lawyer's given me, suggesting that I might survive this—be acquitted—has kept me sane.

If you can call it sane. Yesterday, when I went up to the attic and tried to work on the portrait of my father, I ended up dipping my thickest brush in alizarin crimson and, making a sustained sound in my throat I'd never heard or felt before (it scared me, even as it brought relief)—a sound I was sure the reporters would have called "savage" if they had heard it— I began streaking the windowpane, not stopping until the glass was completely covered. The attic was high enough that they wouldn't see, but in some ways, I wished they could. I wanted witnesses to my torment. I wanted—I *want*—to be believed.

"Get out of there," Violet told me again, when I went silent on the phone.

"That's easy for you to say. How? Where?" I moved the curtain an inch to see that only two news trucks remained; the funeral itself, I realized, must be the day's bigger story.

"Go to school. It's private property, right? Go for a swim or something. Get security to throw them out, if they harass you there."

It had not occurred to me. She was right; Percy would have my back, if I could just make it to campus. And that shouldn't be so hard, right? Within the jurisdiction stipulated by the judge, I am allowed to come and go as I please. I am still innocent, at least in the eyes of the law. They can bother me only so much before they become guilty themselves.

There might be other people there, too, who'd be glad to see me. I tried to convince myself of this as I dressed, taking care to choose nicer clothes than I would normally wear for a day at school. Stuart and Lizzy, from Students for Obama—they'd understand I was being framed. Wouldn't they? And the sign they'd lifted in support after my release—INNOCENT UNTIL PROVEN GUILTY—may have been crudely scrawled, but the two of them had shown up and defended me. If they were on campus today, I'd seek them out.

Doing my best to breathe normally, I picked up my gym bag and my portfolio and, deciding to face the reporters because my victory would be that much greater, walked through the front door instead of the back.

They jumped when they saw me, scrambling, looking surprised. I took a few steps in the direction of the bus stop, out of habit, then doubled back and kept my gaze straight ahead until I reached the Fury parked in the driveway and backed out. The news trucks followed me through town and up the hill toward campus. Because there were fewer classes on Fridays, I found a spot right away. But so did they, and when I got out of the car, there they were in my face again.

Just get to Percy, I thought, repeating the mantra to myself as I walked more quickly than usual.

"Have you spoken with Susanne Enright?" one of the

reporters asked. "Are you aware she's burying her daughter today?"

No, I imagined saying. *Really? I haven't been paying any attention.* What would they think if they knew how much time I'd spent trying to figure out what Susanne must be feeling, about Joy's death and about my arrest? Dying to talk to her, but knowing I had to obey my lawyer's instructions about not returning her calls?

I began sweating from the fast pace I was setting, hoping it didn't show. Finally I reached the doors of the athletic building. The newspeople followed me inside. Behind the desk, Percy set aside his paperback and rose, coming toward us all. I felt the relief of a kid whose big brother has come to the rescue.

"Thanks," I whispered, when Percy closed his big hand around my bicep. I waited for him to tell the rest of them that they had to leave.

But instead Percy whispered back, "Sorry, Pablo" and began moving me toward the door I'd just entered.

"What are you doing?" I didn't bother to keep my own voice down, and Percy told me, "I got orders. It's not up to me." As the cameras whirred, recording it all, he picked his radio up from his waist and made a call. When I tried to shake his hand off, saying *Okay, I got it, I'm leaving*, Percy told me that wasn't an option—I had to be escorted off campus by security.

That was the final straw. Which is how I thought of it later, looking back: of all the surreal offenses and the indignities that had been piled on me that week, beginning with the officers ringing my doorbell five days earlier and then carting me away, this was the one I could not, finally, abide.

"You can't do this!" The words actually hurt my throat as they came out, I yelled them so loud. "I'm a student here! I haven't done anything, I did *not* commit this crime, you'd better fucking let me go!" I don't say "fuck" often—there's something in me that believes Grandee might hear me—but when I do, another part of me feels a rage that would be delicious if I didn't know from experience that what always follows isn't worth it.

"Hold on," Percy told me, still in an undertone. "For your own good, for God's sake, shut up and calm the hell down."

It was too late for that, I knew. Too late to do anything for my own good. The scene had already been captured on camera; it would lead the news, with my expletive censored: SUSPECT ERUPTS IN OUTBURST AS VICTIM IS LAID TO REST.

Are you happy now? I told Violet in some corner of my mind, as three more guards arrived and joined Percy in pulling me out of the building (I have bruises up and down both arms now). *I stood up for myself like you said I should, and see where it got me?*

Even the reporters seemed unsettled by the scene unfolding before them. "Careful, dude," one of the cameramen urged, as I nearly tripped over the camera cord despite being held up on both sides by guards. They shoved me into the Fury, and Percy tossed my bags in after me.

"Better not come back," he told me. "If you know what's good for you."

That phrase again. I sat behind the steering wheel, feeling more separate from myself—and the world I'd thought I inhabited—than I ever could have imagined. Then I started the car and drove home without being aware of it, only barely registering the distant sound of a church bell as it tolled in re-membrance of Joy.

The Departed Child

The night before the funeral, they lay next to each other without sleeping, as if waiting for someone to come and shoot them in the head. Each apologized if a limb or hip brushed the other, the way strangers apologize for touching by accident.

Once, Susanne had accompanied Joy and her class as a chaperone on a field trip to a Shaker village. What Susanne remembered most from the visit were the adult-sized cradles designed for "soothing bedridden patients." At the time she'd felt revulsion at the idea of spending her days in bed, but now she found herself imagining the comfort of being rocked to sleep in a cradle big enough to contain her, and maybe to double as a coffin if she never made it out.

As a young woman before she met Gil, and then after she married him and before they conceived Joy, Susanne had resented the need for sleep because she imagined it was making her miss all kinds of things she could have been doing with that time. When she was pregnant and felt sick so often, not only in the first three months and not only in the mornings, sleep became both blessing and torture—a blessing at night when she managed to shed consciousness, a torture when she woke up to the dread nausea pounding in her gut. Once Joy was born, of course, sleep was more precious, so she craved it and coveted it and stole it whenever she could. Then for a few years she almost returned to the attitude and stamina of her youth, working late hours in the tiny extra bedroom that served as her studio and still rising rested with the sun. That was when she was making the sculptures for *Show of Hands*, and she remembered feeling, for a brief time, that somehow she'd managed to do what the magazines told you was impossible: have it all. Of course the feeling didn't last, as she knew it could not. She knew no one could have it all, except through those momentary delusions. Still, she was happier back then than she could ever remember being. Her mother had always told her, *Put your good feelings in the bank to draw on when the bad ones come.* It made sense to Susanne at the time. Only later—only now—did she understand what a naïve concept it was.

The clock on her nightstand read 2:07. She put the clock in the drawer to hide the neon numerals, but still she lay awake.

After her mother-in-law had entered Belle Meadow, Susanne's sleep became disturbed again. She lay in horizontal, stationary free fall, her heart thudding when she thought of all the residents (she couldn't help thinking of them as inmates) in wheelchairs, some needing to be fed, all needing help at the toilet, their pleasure now consisting only of as much freedom from pain or discomfort as the nurses and aides and medication could offer. After she began the affair with Martin, it occurred to her that maybe part of the reason she'd deviated from her marriage had been to alleviate the existential panic she felt at night: now it was guilt that gave her insomnia, rather than despair. At least the guilt was focused. She could perseverate on what a bad person she was, and how horrible she felt about betraying Gil, instead of the misty, inchoate notion that someday she too (if she was lucky! That was the hell of it!) would be committed to the care of others—would be, essentially, someone other than herself. Waiting to die. In her vision, Gil had either died already or was still able to live at home; though she didn't understand why, she'd never pictured them together at the end, one at the other's bedside. When she imagined herself in a place like Belle Meadow, she thought about Joy coming to visit, with her own husband and maybe a little girl, Susanne's granddaughter, who would chase the resident pet cat and provide tiny pockets of joy to Susanne and the other inmates with her cute voice, her funny questions, her outsized smile. She'd remind them of their own ancient innocence, of being able to govern their own movements and especially of what it had been like to look ahead with hope.

But now that could never happen. No grown-up Joy, no granddaughter. The idea that her daughter had *died*, had experienced this most profound mystery before she did, was beyond fathoming. The doctor had prescribed sleeping pills, but no matter how long before going to bed she took them, they didn't take effect right away after she lay down. It was the same feeling she'd had while pregnant: that she might vomit at any moment, and that to do so would be a relief, but she wasn't sure she could endure what she would have to, to reach that point. And then on the other side of sleep, if it did come, was waking up and remembering. Gil slept a few hours most nights, but he was always awake in the morning next to her, looking up at the ceiling. Most days they had to grab each other, arms or hands or shoulders, before they got out of bed. Making sure to touch something alive and solid. Coming apart after that contact was its own little grief, on top of the insurmountable one that threatened to knock them over (the wave they saw coming but couldn't avoid) as soon as they stood up.

She was not going to sleep this night. Beside her, Gil had begun snoring—a troubled, tortured sound she'd never heard from him before. Moving lightly, she got out of bed and went into the bathroom. She closed the door and turned the light on, without looking in the mirror.

All Joy's life, Susanne had imagined the worst things possible when it came to her daughter. She forced herself to persist in conjuring these scenarios, rather than setting them aside, because superstitiously she believed this would keep them from happening. The scariest and most vivid vision came the summer they rented a cottage on Cape Cod from friends of Susanne's parents. Joy was eleven and newly lovely, her face a combination of the trusting, outgoing child she had always been and the wiser but still winsome woman Susanne and Gil saw emerging, to their shared delight (when they weren't feeling nostalgic for the child she'd so recently been), as their daughter grew taller than her mother and began both making and understanding adult remarks. One morning Gil had gone out for an early swim at the beach and Joy wanted to sleep in, so Susanne left her alone in the house while she walked to the bakery in town and back, a quarter mile each way. When she returned half an hour later, Joy told her that a man had come by to check on the furnace in the cottage's basement. "You let him in?" Susanne asked, trying not to let out the gasp she felt, and Joy shrugged and said, *Yeah*. As it turned out, the stranger's visit had been legitimate; the homeowners had arranged the plumber's visit but forgotten to mention it to their guests. "Next time, honey, just ask him to come back when your parents are here," Susanne said as casually as she could manage. It was no big deal, Joy told her. Susanne said, *I know*. But that day and for weeks afterward, all she could think about was what might have happened if some pervert had been watching the house, seen a beautiful young girl staying there, waited for the parents to leave, and then pounced. She never told Gil about it, because she knew he'd say she shouldn't have left Joy alone like that, and he would have been right.

In all of her disaster fantasies, Susanne was guilty in some way—mostly for allowing her attention to wander elsewhere than with her child. She'd always recognized this, and always tried to dismiss it as the natural but unfounded fear of not being a good-enough mother.

But now that it had actually happened, she saw she'd been right all along. She'd let her fight with Joy escalate to such an extent that Joy felt the need to flee. What kind of mother did that? And she'd taken Joy's phone away—or let Gil take it—despite having a bad feeling about it, despite believing that they should have come up with a different punishment. If Joy had had her phone, wouldn't she have been able to call for help?

At the moment she died, Joy would no longer have been angry at her mother; she'd be more afraid than she'd ever thought possible, wanting her mother there to save her, or at least to hold her as she slipped out of the world. Susanne had not been there. She would never be there, except in the dreams she'd have for the rest of her life, in which she said to Joy, after Joy yelled at her *You are such a hypocrite*, "Let's just stop this, honey, okay?" She allowed herself to believe that Joy would have relented—would have wanted to make up, too.

In the bathroom she opened the cabinet and took out the bottle of pills. In a few hours she would have to sit in a pew near the box containing her daughter, then lay her baby to rest. *Lay her to rest*: an impossible task. There was no way, she understood in that moment, that she could do what she was expected to do. Required to do. And yet there was no avoiding it. She shook out a handful of the pills and swallowed them with water she caught in her cupped hand under the faucet. As soon as they were down, she lifted the toilet seat and retched, and when she was finished she slumped against the sink and made sounds she did not recognize as they came from her own body, scalding as they emerged.

Gil was at the door within seconds, seeing the pills in the water before she could flush. Immediately she identified the look on his face as a mix of fear and fury. "You would do *that* to me, too?" he yelled, taking her first by the wrists, then hugging her so close that she had to fight for breath.

"What difference does it make?"

He didn't bother to respond to this. "Did you get rid of them all?" She nodded. He yelled, "Are you sure?" Then they were both crying as he led her back to the bed.

"I didn't want to die. That wasn't it," she told him, when she could speak again. "It's just—"

But there was no way to identify what it *just* was.

"I know." His voice had drained of anger, and in some ways this was worse. "Listen, we just need to get through today. Then we can figure something out." Susanne knew they both understood that there was nothing to figure out and that getting through the day would make nothing better, but they both pretended he was right, for their own sakes and for each other's.

Some hours later, having dressed and made their way to the funeral home without remembering doing so, they held each other up as they walked down the aisle toward the front pew. As at their wedding, Susanne did not actually see the faces of the people turned toward her, so intent was she on reaching her destination. As they were about to take their seats in the front row, her knees buckled, and Gil barely managed to catch her before she would have sunk to the floor. For a moment she resented him: *Just let me go, I don't care, it's better down here, it's safer.* Why the word "safe" occurred to her, she did not know; she did not expect to feel safe again for the rest of her life.

It was the second Friday of December, six days since Joy's body had been found in the woods that should have been searched more thoroughly but were not, because everyone thought she was submerged in the frozen pond. Five days since they'd determined it was not an accident but murder. Anybody who wanted to attend Joy's service could miss school without being marked absent. When she'd first learned this, Susanne thought vaguely (all of her thoughts were vague, these days) that she appreciated it; turning to watch all those kids come into the church, though, it occurred to her that maybe she shouldn't trust the swelling of her heart at the sight, because wasn't it possible that some of them were just taking the free pass from classes?

Then again, maybe not. It wasn't as if they'd been excused to go skiing or snowboarding, something fun. Probably a lot of those she was seeing, tugging at their ties or wobbling on heels more suited to a wedding or a job interview, would have preferred sitting in those hard chairs at those hard desks, learning hard things, to crowding into a church pew with the closed coffin of a dead schoolmate in full view. She decided to assume everyone had come for the right reason, the real reason: to honor Joy's life. To tell her parents they were sorry. And to show, by turning out in such numbers, that her presence among them had meant something they would not soon forget.

The smell of flowers was overwhelming, and yet she welcomed it as something to focus on. Dozens of arrangements—hundreds of flowers—circled the casket and decorated the steps to the altar. *Do you want flowers?* the funeral director had asked, when he helped them write the obituary. *Or do you want to do an "in lieu of" and donations instead?*

Gil suggested that people might send money to the art school in Joy's name. Maybe they could start a scholarship, he said.

No, Susanne told them, surprised that she possessed enough energy for such a strong opinion. *I want the flowers.* In the end they decided on both.

And there they were, the flowers, in every color imaginable except black. If she squinted, their shapes became blurry and indistinct, like one of Joy's drawings. She kept squinting, until Gil asked her to stop.

The minister, a blond and uninspiring man named Donald Putnam who looked unhealthily skinny even under his clerical robe, had visited them briefly to plan the service, even though after he left, neither Susanne nor Gil could remember what any of them had said. He was new to the congregation since they'd last gone to church, back when Joy was in sixth grade. She'd attended Sunday School here and sung in the children's choir, but after that year she announced she didn't want to go anymore, and her parents agreed that she was old enough to make this choice for herself. Secretly, each was relieved; neither of them enjoyed attending services, or got much out of them aside from the social aspect and the feeling that it couldn't hurt to have their daughter taught some of the things they themselves had learned in Sunday School. "Also it'll help if she ever goes on Jeopardy," Gil had said. "There's a fair number of Bible-related questions on there." Susanne laughed at the time, but she felt guilty about it now. What if she had only worked harder to have faith, like developing an underused muscle? Wouldn't it be paying off for her now?

After a time she stopped turning in her seat to watch people come in. Her neck hurt from craning, and her eyes hurt not from crying but from puking up the pills, which had broken blood vessels in her skin. Without telling Gil, she'd downed two of the different kind the doctor had prescribed—not the ones for sleeping, but the ones to make her feel calm—after patting foundation onto the fine red lines around her eyes. Next to her on the velour seat, Gil thrummed his fingers on his thighs. She'd offered him a pill, but he refused, and now she felt guilty about this, too. Taking something artificial to blunt whatever she would feel at her daughter's funeral. Shouldn't she have remained exposed to whatever presented itself to her, during this

hour and the ones to follow, at the meal in the function room at
Coleman's Inn? Defenseless, that was the word: that's what she
should have been, sitting there a few feet away from her daughter's casket. The idea that she *could* defend herself against what
would rise up inside her was ridiculous. And yet she'd taken the
pills and felt obscenely grateful when they kicked in, removing
her just a tiny, crucial distance from the words and movements
around the bubble that contained her and Gil.

The children's choir sang "Ode to Joy," accompanied on the
violin and piano by two members of the high school orchestra.
Susanne didn't know either of them, and she had to look away
from the violinist, a long-necked girl with a single braid pulled
forward over the shoulder not holding the violin, tears streaking
her cheeks as she drew the bow. When the song was over, she
didn't wipe her face or use a tissue to blow her nose but closed
the score with a regretful, lingering motion that left Susanne
wondering whether it was the occasion or the music that caused
her to cry.

Then Donald Putnam took the pulpit and said, "We're here
today to celebrate Joy. It's no coincidence that her name is the
same as the emotion many of you felt in knowing her. I did not
have that pleasure, but in meeting with her parents, looking at
the photos they showed me and hearing about her life, I have no
doubt she was a very special young woman whose precious time
on this earth was taken from her too soon. Only God can judge
whoever did this. Police think they have the man. In praying for
the soul of the departed child, we pray for his soul, too."

Susanne felt Gil moving beside her, and reached a hand out.
He wanted to jump up, she saw, and put a stop to it—any talk
of the murderer and the circumstances under which Joy died.
They had discussed this with the minister, she remembered now,
and he'd agreed. Now he was ignoring what they had asked.

"Wait," she whispered so only Gil could hear, thinking of

how embarrassed Joy would be if her father made a scene. It took everything her husband could muster, she knew, to force himself to sit back against the pew beside her, his rage seething out in a single, extended sigh only she could read.

The minister moved on, calling Joy's friends up to give readings or reminiscences. Gil relaxed, and Susanne knew he was glad she'd prevented him from acting on his impulse. One by one, teenagers she'd known since they were Joy's earliest classmates came forward, most of them nervous in the pulpit, many of their voices too hushed to be heard. But it didn't matter; what mattered was the number of them, the stricken expressions on their faces, the way they couldn't seem to help looking at the casket when they were speaking, as if they believed that from inside it, Joy might be able to hear. Susanne thought, with a sadness she could barely acknowledge, about how surprised Joy would have been, and how moved. Every time it seemed the tributes might be finished, another classmate stood and walked to the front. Most read something, heads bent over paper—a poem or a psalm. This made sense to Susanne; it was easier to recite from what was already written than to say something without a script.

At some point, it occurred to her that she hadn't seen Harper. She almost turned to look, but caught herself when she realized that she couldn't be sure of what her own expression would convey to all those eyes aimed at her. A drawback to the pills she'd taken; along with muting her emotions, they diminished her ability to modulate what she showed in her face.

But then there she was, Joy's oldest friend, slumping her way up the steps toward the altar, a bra strap showing near her collarbone (only Harper, Susanne thought, hating herself for it; only Harper would have a bra strap showing in winter, under a sweater) as she gripped the edges of the lectern and forced herself—the effort was almost palpable in the atmosphere around her—to look up and out at the people in the pews. *Good girl*, Susanne thought, as Harper pulled a piece of paper from her pocket and smoothed it on the lectern. In a soft and halting voice, she credited her selection to Wordsworth and read, "'She lived unknown, and few could know, when Lucy ceased to be. But she is in her grave, and, oh, the difference to me!'" She kept staring at the paper after she was finished, and Susanne heard a murmur pass among the pews. *Come down now*, she told Harper in her mind, and Harper seemed to hear it, because finally she moved to fold the paper back up. "Only Joy, not Lucy," she said as she descended the altar steps, an afterthought in case someone might not realize. "And there's an exclamation point at the end."

Her heart clutching, Susanne reached to touch the girl's arm as she went by, but she was obstructed by Delaney Stowell, who bumped into Harper on the way up to speak her turn. Delaney stood straight-backed and confident in the place Harper had just vacated and said, in a voice no one had trouble hearing, "Joy and I knew each other since preschool. But we didn't really become close until this year. I'm glad we got that chance before she—before what happened."

Susanne looked sideways at Gil. Were they finally going to find out why Joy had been hanging out with Delaney these past few months? He didn't return her glance, but she could tell he was listening as intently as she was.

"She was *so* smart," Delaney said. "Well, you all know that. She helped me study for the SATs, and I did much better than I ever would have done on my own."

"I didn't know they studied together," Susanne said under her breath and Gil shook his head, but she didn't know whether it was in agreement or by way of asking her to shut up.

"I saw her that last day," Delaney went on, casting her eyes downward in a dramatic sweep. "I saw her right before she died.

We went to the pond to go skating, like we did when we were kids."

"That's not true," Susanne whispered to Gil. "Joy didn't take her skates."

Across the aisle Keith Nance said, "Holy shit, can we be done here already?" He may have intended to mutter it under his breath, but it was loud enough for almost everyone to hear, including Delaney, who ended her remarks without a conclusion and returned imperiously to her seat.

It appeared that Keith had, in fact, fulfilled his own wish. Susanne waited for Donald Putnam to dispense—from his position of an authority and insight none of the rest of them had access to—a benediction that would somehow include a divine understanding of who Joy had been, who she might have become, and the meaning of her death. Instead, he assured everyone that they'd been forgiven and dismissed them without even mentioning her daughter's name. Susanne had not realized, until it didn't come, what she'd been hoping for at the end of the service, which was (let's face it, she thought, following Gil numbly back down the aisle, a trip she both did and did not want to make) the end of Joy.

A limo waited outside to take them to Coleman's, but first she needed a few minutes to herself. There was a line outside the ladies' restroom, but when people saw who moved to join them, they reached out to guide Susanne forward to the front, the guest of honor of this event and so entitled to pee before anyone else, the only thing they could offer. In the stall she sat on the closed lid and stared down at her hands, grotesquely fascinated by the fact that she was unable to remember the word "fingers." Finally she put them to her face, and the contact of her own skin against skin gave her whatever it was she needed (was it as simple as the need to feel something? Anything?) to stand again and exit. In the hallway she moved toward raised voices as Harper cried out to Delaney, "Everything you said up there was a lie. *You* weren't her friend. She didn't help *you* study."

Seeing Susanne approach, Barbara Grove tried to shush Harper, who ignored her. "You're the one who killed her," she shrieked, and a gasp passed through the line as Delaney flattened herself against the wall, as if Harper's words had shoved her. "This is your fault—she never would have done those things, if it weren't for you."

"Freak," Delaney whispered, but Susanne saw that her characteristic poise had been shaken. Lynette Stowell grabbed her daughter out of the line, gesturing at her husband across the room. Geoffrey Stowell strode up to take his daughter by the arm. She shook off his grip but he grabbed her more firmly, yanked, and whispered something fiercely in her ear that none of the rest of them could hear.

"Let go of me," she hissed back, but she followed him toward the door leading out to the parking lot. *HED DOC*, Susanne thought, remembering the license plate known to everyone in Chilton. *Yeah, right. Why don't you start with your own kid?*

But talking to Geoffrey Stowell in her mind was only a way of delaying the questions triggered by what Harper had shouted. *She never would have done those things, if it weren't for you.* Which things? Was it possible that Delaney (and not Jason the nursing aide) was the one responsible for Joy's selling drugs? Why would Delaney need Joy, if she had direct access to her father's prescription sheets?

Of course, Susanne thought then, recalling where Joy had been arrested, putting it together. In wanting to expand her business, Delaney would have enlisted Joy's help to steal meds from Belle Meadow, knowing she had a contact at the nursing home with a key to the cabinet containing painkillers and sedatives.

She went to find Gil and, in the limo on the short drive to

Coleman's, whispered to him what had happened. For a moment when she finished, she wasn't sure he'd heard her, or paid attention. But when he reached down to grasp and then squeeze her hand, she understood his message—*It doesn't matter now*—and, realizing he was right, she turned to watch through the tinted window the dark day go thudding by.

Girl on a Swing

After the service, Tom left Alison in the pew with her mother and slipped through the back of the church after his father-in-law. There'd been some altercation between Delaney Stowell and her father, and Doug had followed them out. In the church parking lot, Geoffrey Stowell spoke close to his daughter's face—angry, spit-out words, Tom could tell even from a distance. Had Doug pursued them because he sensed there might be trouble—a domestic dispute of some kind? The girl turned away from her father. Tom waited for Doug to issue a warning to the pair, a rebuke for the scene they were creating. Instead, after a short exchange, the three of them parted when Lynette Stowell came out of the church and the family got into a Beamer and drove away, presumably to Coleman's for the reception.

Tom considered retreating before his father-in-law could see him, but decided to stand his ground; something about the scene—the interaction among the doctor, his daughter, and the chief of police—didn't seem right to him. Didn't make sense, especially on top of the encounter he'd witnessed between them a few weeks earlier, at the town's annual 5K road race to raise money for the sober halfway house where Helen served on the Board of Trustees.

Tom had committed to running, even though he would have loved to sleep in on a Saturday, because the race was Helen's baby; she'd organized the first one years earlier, when she became president of the Police Auxiliary. At the time she'd just received her first-year sobriety medallion, which—though technically it was supposed to be anonymous—she'd made a big public deal about. Doug hadn't wanted her to ("Why does everybody have to know our business?" he'd said, and Tom understood that he felt embarrassed, not wanting to acknowledge any vulnerability in himself or his family), but Helen herself invoked the name and example of Betty Ford more than once.

Alison had entered every year since that inaugural race, but this time Tom begged her not to, for the sake of the pregnancy. She agreed, as long as he promised to run in her place. By seven thirty that day they were handing out free coffee and racing bibs to the runners, whose route would take them on the perimeter road around Elbow Pond.

When Helen blew the whistle to signal the start, Tom took off among the hundred others in the pack. He got through the three-plus miles, hating every minute, and when he crossed at the end he bent over to rub the stitch in his side. Moving away from the other finishers in case he was going to puke, he caught sight of Doug and another man talking intensely, hands waving, behind a stand of pines. Neither of them had run the race (Doug had won it the first five years, then declined to enter after he'd been beaten in the sixth year by an elite cross-country star—female—from Canandaigua). Had they tried to conceal themselves for this conversation? That could hardly be it; anyone glancing in that direction would have seen them. Yet Tom felt he'd stumbled on something clandestine, witnessing the men's exchange. He moved slightly, surreptitiously, to put himself in better position to identify the other guy. He looked

familiar, though he couldn't quite place him. Then he realized it
was Delaney Stowell's father, the shrink.

When he'd stepped on a twig that cracked under his sneaker,
both Doug and the doctor looked up, and Doug called him over
with a half-assed wave. "You know Geoff here, don't you?" Tom
shook the shrink's hand. "Best son-in-law I ever had," Doug
said, clapping Tom on the shoulder, and Tom delivered his
scripted line: "*Only* son-in-law, too." Stowell laughed—a forced
heartiness if Tom ever heard one—and said he had to get going.

"Us, too," Doug said, as the shrink beeped open a BMW with
his remote.

"What's his deal?" Tom asked, after Stowell peeled out and up
toward the hill's summit, the location of Chilton's most expen-
sive homes. Just before it turned, Tom caught the vanity plate:
HED DOC.

"Nothing." His father-in-law shrugged, and Tom thought for
a moment that the look Doug gave him was a nervous one, but
then he figured he'd misread it. What did Doug have to be nervous about, especially when it came to Tom? It was the other
way around. Always had been, always would be. "Just never
hurts to be nice to a guy with a Beamer. Right?"

Tom had agreed, though he tended to hate Beamers and
the people who drove them. Now, standing in front of the
church after Joy Enright's funeral, watching Geoffrey Stowell
peel out with his wife and daughter, Tom hated him. When
Doug turned to come back to the church and saw Tom watching, a wrinkle of something—fear?—passed through his father-
in-law; Tom could see it in the sudden, slight jerk of his breath,
which no one else except Alison and Doug's own wife would
have recognized.

Tom asked, "What's the deal with her?" referring to the psychiatrist's daughter, who'd obviously been upset by something
following the funeral service. At the last minute he caught

himself from using his and Alison's nickname for Delaney, Snake Girl.

Doug shook his head. "No idea. The father testifies for us sometimes, is how I know him. Headshrinker stuff." He moved his index finger in a circle at the side of his head. "He's supposedly one of the best."

"One of the best with a fucked-up daughter," Tom said, and Doug shrugged to concede the point before people started flowing out of the church. Alison and Helen came over, hooked to each other by the coat arms. Alison had cried through the entire service; her mother kept handing her new tissues and tucking the used ones in her purse.

At Coleman's, the function room grew crowded as people milled around the platters of lunch food. It had the atmosphere of a party, though the noise was subdued. Joy's parents sat together at a table in the corner, not eating despite the fact that they had been brought many plates piled high with salads and sliced meat and desserts.

Tom found seats for Alison and her mother, then moved toward the food table to take a place in line, scanning the room for Snake Girl. Doug was in the hallway shooting the shit with Hal Beemon, and Tom assumed they were congratulating themselves on the quick arrest of Martin Willett, which Tom knew Doug would take credit for without mentioning that his original information had been handed to him by his son-in-law.

He was wondering if Geoffrey Stowell had dropped his daughter off at home, rather than bringing her to the reception, when he glanced out the window and saw Delaney sitting by herself on a rickety swing set at the edge of Coleman's back lot. One of the swings had fallen apart, but the other held together enough for a teenage girl to sit in as she smoked and stared at the frozen ground beneath her. The sight reminded Tom of paintings he'd seen on school field trips to museums, portraits of young women gazing into the distance.

Girl, on a Swing, with Cigarette, he thought, checking to make sure Doug and Hal were still engrossed in their conversation, then slipping out the back door to approach her.

"Hey," he said, and Delaney looked up warily, clearly displeased by having her solitude interrupted. "You get put in a time out?" He was surprised when he recognized that she was tamping down a smile—something he hadn't seen the day she came into the shack to buy candy for breakfast and called him a perv, or any of the times he followed her and her friends to the mall or the abandoned condos.

She held up a new cigarette for him to light, and when he told her he didn't smoke she said, "Lame excuse. You should carry one anyway, for situations like this." But she produced a Bic from her coat pocket and lit it herself, then dragged deep and exhaled a plume of smoke and breath they both watched dissolve in the cold, hard air.

He told her his name and she said, "I know who you are. You're Carbone's husband, you run the shack, and you dive for dead bodies. Kind of a Renaissance man."

He wanted to think she wasn't making fun of him but couldn't quite persuade himself. "More like a jack of all trades," he said.

"That's what I hate about living in a Podunk town like this. Everything overlaps with everything else. Every*body* overlaps." She waved the cigarette for emphasis. "There's no mystery."

"Well. Except this." He made his own gesture toward the gathering inside, referring to her dead classmate and the questions still surrounding what had happened to her.

"Yeah. Okay, you got me." She stamped the half-smoked cigarette out under her UGG. He'd thought she might stand up from the swing when he joined her, but she remained seated and gripped the swing's rusty chains.

"So what was going on with you two?" He tried to keep his voice casual, though he could tell she wasn't about to be fooled. "You and Joy. Before she took off that day?"

"Nothing. What do you mean?" Delaney shrugged as if she didn't know what he was talking about, but it wasn't convincing.

"I know about the parties." He took a quick look behind him to make sure no one else had come outside and could overhear. "I know about the scrips."

Registering no reaction to his words, Delaney began pumping in a gentle swing. "So is your old lady preg, or what?"

She'd paused slightly before the word "preg," and he sensed immediately that she'd been going to say *knocked up* but thought better of it at the last moment. Even so, her question, and the sudden shift in topic, took him aback. Alison hadn't planned to tell anyone at school until she began showing. But maybe she was beginning to show and she didn't realize, and he didn't realize either because he was a guy and didn't know how to look for such things.

"I thought so." The measure of self-satisfaction already evident in Delaney's face went up a degree or two.

"How could you tell?"

"Truth?"

"Yeah." He said it even though he wasn't sure.

"Well, she always has a bottle of Diet Coke with her, right? During class."

"So?" Alison had been a Diet Coke fiend even before they'd started going out in tenth grade.

"So I always thought maybe it wasn't just Diet Coke. Partly because of the way she acted, partly because she was always popping mints at the end of every class. One day I swiped the bottle when she wasn't looking, and I was right. I mean, there was Diet

Coke in there all right, but it was totally spiked. Seagram's. Trust me, I know." She allowed her voice to display a tinge of pride before she seemed to understand that this was nothing to take pride in. "But right after Halloween—right before Joy died—she started bringing straight ginger ale. I figured, preg."

Her last words barely registered through the roar in his ears. *Spiked, Seagram's*—those were the ones he heard. He turned away from Delaney, afraid for a moment that he might keel over into the snow.

It explained everything: the way Alison had pulled away from him. Her distraction, her weeping for no reason. Why her eyes were red so often (her contacts, she always said) and why she was asleep sometimes when he worked an early shift and got home shortly after the school day ended.

What was wrong with him? Could he have been a bigger *douche*? Every impulse told him to turn around, stalk back into the building, and accuse his wife. But his higher consciousness understood that now was not the time. He set the information aside in his mind—just out of reach—and with a degree of control he would not have expected of himself, he said to Delaney, "If she has anything to say about that, I'm sure she will."

She smirked, but he could tell it had an impact; it might take a while, he thought, but even Snake Girl could be put in her place. She got off the swing abruptly, letting the seat clatter behind her, and changed the subject. "So the chief asshole is your father-in-law."

He was tempted to laugh at the way she said it: *chief asshole*. The biggest, most powerful asshole. Doug Strong Arm. But again, he couldn't affirm what the girl said because it might get back to Alison. "The chief's my father-in-law, yeah."

"And what, he's making you do his dirty work, asking about Joy?"

"No. I'm doing it on my own." *What the hell*, he thought.

One on one, she didn't seem like a bad kid; she had more on the ball than he'd expected. Would it be worth appealing to her sense of justice? "The thing is, I'm pretty sure they got the wrong guy."

Her head jerked up, and he saw a light in her eyes that hadn't been there before. "The black one? I'm with you on that. What would he have to gain by killing Joy, right?"

"Well," Tom said carefully, wanting to capitalize on this new source of agreement between them, "even if I had an answer to that, I couldn't tell you. But people do things sometimes for reasons that don't make sense to anyone else."

"Like I don't know that. Come on—don't patronize me."

"Sorry." *Go easy*, he told himself. "Look, if you know something, you should tell me. Or the police." He paused, weighing the wisdom of his next words before deciding to say them. "But I'd rather you tell me."

"I can't tell the police. That's the point." Now she did stand, letting the swing seat squeak up behind her, and leaned close enough that he could smell her breath. Did the rancidness come only from the Marlboro, or was fear mixed in there, too? She spoke quickly, as if wanting to avoid hearing her own words. "She was blackmailing the police. Specifically, the asshole."

"Who was?"

"Joy."

It took him a moment to make sense of the two people she was talking about: Doug and the dead girl. The dead girl had been blackmailing Doug. "What are you talking about?" Recognizing that he was entering territory from which there was no turning back, he felt both alarmed and excited, and thought he detected a bit of the same combination coming from Delaney.

She said, "When they busted Joy at the nursing home and brought her down to the station—isn't that what they always say on TV, 'down to the station'?—she heard two women in the bathroom talking about how he, the asshole, covered up Mrs. Carbone's DUI. They didn't know she was in there, the women." She coughed, then shoved the pack of cigarettes back into her pocket. "They cops? We have any women cops in this town?"

"They were probably clerks," Tom said, not wanting to inflame or derail her by giving a direct no. Natalie would have been one of the women, he knew. The other was probably Jean Stryker, whose name he and Natalie laughed at although they knew they shouldn't, because she was the domestic abuse specialist the police hardly ever had to call in. Jean sometimes spent hours hanging out with Natalie at the dispatch desk.

"Of course there aren't any women cops. Big surprise." Delaney let out a cheerless laugh. "Anyway, so Joy got in touch with the asshole and let him know what she knew, and said she'd make it public unless he dropped the charges against her. So— poof! Charges gone, the very same night." Delaney gave a sharp snap of her fingers.

Tom forced himself to stand as still as he could, a difficult task in light of what was going through his mind. He felt both shocked and not at all surprised that Doug would behave in the way Delaney described, and the crash of conflicting inclinations caused his head to ache. "Are you sure?" he asked.

"Damn sure." Delaney dropped her voice. "Look, think about it. Why do you think I stuck around to talk to you when you came out here—for fun? I'm telling you this because I don't want somebody put away for something he didn't do. The black guy. I may be a lot of things, but I'm not that much of an asshole." *Like your father-in-law*, she didn't have to add. "And I don't want someone who *is* guilty getting away with it."

It took Tom a few seconds to register her implication. "You think he could have—you're saying you think he, the chief, might have—" but to finish the sentence would have been a blasphemy he'd never be forgiven.

"Well, you have to wonder, right? Why he's got such a hard-on to pin it on the black guy. To pin it on *anyone*, if the evidence isn't there."

"But it is there. Circumstantial, anyway."

She made a dismissive *pfft* noise. "So what was he doing that day? The asshole. Did you check?"

Tom did his best not to show that her suggestion dug into his gut. "You should stop talking like this."

"Why?" She looked directly at him, seeming to understand that he wouldn't have an answer either of them would be satisfied with. "Something more important to you than the truth?"

"Hey. I'm the grown-up here." It felt like a lie even as he said it, but he hoped it made some impression on her. "You don't get to talk to me that way."

She apologized, though he wasn't sure she meant it. "How did you know she was blackmailing him?" he asked. "Did she tell you?"

Delaney shrugged. "Kind of."

"What does that mean?"

"Well, it was her specialty. Blackmail. I mean, she didn't call it that or anything. But that's what it was."

"If you don't start spelling things out—" He started to turn away, but she raised her hand to call him back and said, "Okay. She was blackmailing me, too."

"Joy was? What for?"

Delaney hesitated, a move that appeared unfamiliar to her. "This is confidential, right?"

He nodded, even though he had no authority to assure her of what she asked.

"Okay." Delaney closed her eyes as if the confession didn't

count if she couldn't see it. "I *was* giving Joy scrips. She was right back there, at the church, when she called me out."

"*Who* was right?" He knew who she meant but needed her to say it.

"Sorry—Harper. Harper Grove. Sounds like a place to live, right? In Florida or something." "Florida" caused specks of spit to settle on her chin, and she wiped them away with an embarrassed swipe. "Anyway, so yeah, I gave Joy blank sheets, from my father's office. But it wasn't my idea. I didn't make her do anything—she made *me*."

"She made you do it? How?"

When Delaney hesitated again he said, "I can always report you for what went on at the condos. I know who started that fire."

"Oh, stop." Wearily, she retrieved the Marlboro pack and shook out another cigarette. "I'm giving you what you want." This time, after lighting, she inhaled deeply. When she exhaled a plume of disgust, Tom couldn't tell whether it was directed at the sensation in her lungs, herself, or him. "Like you said, people do all kinds of crazy shit, right? Ask my father."

Her words summoned for him the image of Geoffrey Stowell and Doug conferring in quiet voices after the ODAT fundraising race. Then the sight of them in the parking lot at the funeral home today, less than an hour ago. "Did the police find out?" Tom asked her. "About the scrip sheets?"

Warily, Delaney nodded.

"Then why didn't they arrest you? Or your father?"

She held the cigarette down at her side, seeming to forget it was there. "This is what I meant before about living in Podunk," she said. "Everybody's business all tied up with everybody else's. You sure you want to hear?"

He nodded, though the question sliced inside him a quick furrow of doubt.

"My father's seeing your mother-in-law." Then, noting Tom's confusion at the word "seeing," she clarified: "As a patient. She's a drunk, too, right? He's been trying to help her get sober again. Not that it's doing any good."

If he hadn't witnessed Helen sneaking wine in the kitchen right after her supposed sober anniversary, this would have been all Tom needed to conclude that everything Delaney was telling him was a lie, concocted just to fuck with him or to cause someone else—her own father?—some grief. As it was, he believed she was telling the truth about this and, so, about all of it. "You're saying Doug's covering for you and your father, to keep the news about Helen falling off the wagon from coming out."

"Right. Just like he did for your old lady with the DUI." She made a false laughing noise. "He only has that temporary chief's job because of three people, right? The Town Board. And I heard he's not their favorite person."

She watched, her eyes narrowed, as he caught up to all the new information processing itself inside his brain. "Wait a minute," he said. "If the police found out about you giving Joy the scrip sheets, then what would she still have to blackmail you with?"

This question Delaney swatted away as if it were a gnat. "Look, I've told you enough already, haven't I? I've told you everything you need to know to help get that Willett guy off."

"But that part doesn't make sense to me. And if she was blackmailing you, why shouldn't *you* be a suspect as much as the asshole should?"

Now the laugh Delaney gave was a real one. "Are you shitting me?"

"No, I mean it. What should stop me from thinking you're telling me all this about the police chief to deflect suspicion from yourself? I read the report. Hell, I was *there*. You were one of the last ones to see her that day."

"Holy shit." She sighed, as if she could barely believe what a complete drag he was, and—probably—what a mistake it had been to talk to him, even given what he threatened her with. "I wasn't the last one. Whoever *killed* her was the last one." Now they heard groups of people leaving Coleman's, a sign that the reception was breaking up. As she turned to leave the swing set before they could get caught together, Delaney added, "I've done a lot of things I shouldn't have, I admit it. But choking somebody to death isn't one of them." She headed back toward the building.

Tom let his own breath out, not having realized he was holding it. The directive from his diving instructor came back to him: *Stop, think, and breathe.* The right thing to do, he knew, was to tell somebody connected to the force—maybe Natalie?— what the girl had said, and let Natalie persuade him why it was ridiculous.

But instead he went back inside and found Alison. Her eyes were red today, he knew, because of crying and nothing else. "Where were you? I needed you," she said, leaning into his side as he put his arm around her. From across the room, Delaney Stowell let her eyes settle on them as if watching strangers. Tom turned his back and allowed himself to feel temporary comfort in consoling his wife, even as he foresaw plainly the pain ahead for them both.

Classic Signs

When they arrived home after the funeral and reception, Gil pulled into the garage and they sat there without making a move to get out of the car, neither wanting to go into the house. Recognizing this, he left the motor running to keep the heat on. Between them on the console lay the garage-door remote, and when his fingers made a barely perceptible move in its direction, Susanne intuited instantly what he was thinking: *All I have to do is push a button, the door will close, we'll go to sleep, it will be over.* The same feeling she'd had in the dead of morning, impulsively swallowing the sleeping pills. Gently, she picked the remote up and moved it to the other side of her seat. She knew he would misconstrue her action; he would interpret it as some version of *We have to keep going, we owe it to her, she wouldn't want us to do that.* All their married life they had been having conversations like this, saying one thing (with words or not) but communicating another. At least, this was how it seemed to Susanne. She didn't think Gil felt the same way. It had bothered her, once, but after all these years she'd grown accustomed to it, and now—especially with their daughter dead—it didn't matter. She still considered it a foreign language they spoke to each other, but she had adjusted, and she understood it well enough to translate what she needed to know.

She also understood now that she couldn't allow herself an escape; it was too easy, when really what she deserved was to be punished. For so many things, some of which she probably had no idea. But others made up a running list in her head, beginning with *I shouldn't have slept with Martin* and continuing with *We should have paid more attention when she started staying in her room so much, when she dyed her hair, when she didn't seem to care about anything. When she was arrested for drugs!* Weren't they the classic signs? What was wrong with them, as parents, that they hadn't recognized the signs for what they were? The most practical offense—*We should have let her keep her cell phone*—gave her a punch to the gut, imagining her daughter's desperation in those final moments, the futility of calling for help. Had Joy cried out for her mother at the end, the way dying soldiers were said to? "We have to go in," she said to Gil, shutting the car door on a vision that was too much. He remained motionless for a moment, then followed her into the house with a broken sigh.

Usually she placed her purse on the counter, but today it could go on the floor. What did it matter? Salsa came to greet them—she'd always been like a dog that way—but slunk back as she got closer, as if they gave off a smell to be avoided. Susanne stood in the middle of the kitchen, then had to turn suddenly to grab the countertop for support. Gil didn't notice, because he was busy collecting his toolbox from the mudroom. He began taking the faucet apart. When Susanne asked him what he was doing, he reminded her that for years she'd been asking him for a two-handled faucet instead of the single-handled one. "I'm going to replace the cartridge with a ceramic disc," he said.

She laughed, a dead sound to both of them. "I don't even know what that means."

Without planning to, she took steps toward the hallway and down to where the bedrooms were. Joy's door was open. "Hey!" she shouted at Gil. After going through Joy's room looking for something to bury her with, they'd closed the door and agreed not to open it again until—well, they hadn't decided on the *until*. "You weren't supposed to do that."

"Do what," Gil said without interest, his voice muffled from under the sink.

When she reached to pull the doorknob toward her to shut it again, she thought for a moment that she was imagining what she saw: the rumpled comforter and, on the wall along the bed and extending to the closet, the hooks that had secured Joy's artwork in her private gallery—the gallery she'd invited Martin into on the day of the barbecue. Susanne recalled coming upon them when she'd been looking for Joy, recalled worrying that she'd shown too much surprised pleasure when she realized that Martin was also in the room. She remembered the flash of confusion in Joy's face when she saw her mother's expression, and the detachment that replaced it a moment later.

The memory took only an instant, and to shake it off she entered the room slowly, perceiving only dimly that in the face of the intrusion she witnessed, she should be afraid. At the same time, she sensed within her a bizarre excitement: *She's here! She's here!* even as she knew that of course the room's disruption could not be attributed to Joy. Six hooks hung empty of the charcoal pieces Joy had considered her best, including children competing over a toy and the reproduction of a van Gogh modeled on Susanne's hands.

She called for Gil again, his name catching in her throat. "What," he said from the doorway, a wrench hanging from his hands.

When he saw what she did, he rushed in to grab her and pulled her out to the hall. Raising the wrench now as a weapon, he went into the room, first bending to peer under the bed and then approaching the closet to yank the door open, his breath as he did so coming out in a cry she was sure he hadn't intended.

She watched him step back with anticipation of being run at, attacked, but no such thing happened. The closet's interior was just as Joy had left it: her sweaters and corduroys hanging tidily, summer clothes folded in vacuum-sealed bags on the top shelf. Her shoes and boots—except for the fake UGGs she'd been wearing the day she left—sat on a two-tiered floor rack, next to the hamper containing the worn clothes Susanne had not been able to bring herself to wash.

Her whole life, she would never stop regretting her decision to hold off until Christmas to give her daughter the boots she'd bought her. Or the fact that Joy died wearing the fake ones.

"Son of a bitch," Gil said. He darted out to check the rest of the house, then returned to sit on the defiled bed. Salsa had come to watch from the doorway, slinking around Susanne's ankles in fascinated fear. "Somebody came in here. While we were at her *funeral*." He laid the wrench across his lap, and Susanne recognized his impulse to avoid soiling his daughter's comforter with the tool.

"We don't know that, do we?" she asked. "*When* it happened? I haven't been in here since—in a long time."

"I have." He could have said it as an accusation, but instead his voice was a spike of loneliness that lanced her. "I come in here every day."

"But who would—who would—"

"That's what they do. People. They read the funeral announcements, they know nobody will be home." He sounded more sad than disgusted.

"How did they get in?"

"I don't think I locked the door." He blinked, as if he had just recovered the concept of trying to protect against intruders. "I don't think I've been doing that."

She knew he expected her to criticize him for it. But she could not. "And why would they take the—why would they take her—" She waved at the wall that had been stripped of their daughter's art, understanding for the first time why people who had not been assaulted physically often felt, when robbed of valuables, that they had. "Do you think they thought they were worth something?"

Gil stood and laid the wrench gently on Joy's bureau, next to the Derek Jeter Bobblehead. "It was probably just some crime junkie, looking for a souvenir. Listen, help me with this."

Through a daze, she joined him in straightening the comforter across the bed. "Should we take the hooks out?" she asked, gesturing again at the wall, and he told her no, maybe they would get the drawings back someday. Immediately she recognized this as wishful thinking, as she knew he must, too. But neither of them would name it for what it was.

Once the comforter had been smoothed out, Salsa jumped up on it, assuming her favorite spot near the wall. Susanne and Gil left the door open and returned to the hall.

"Thanks for trying to save me," she told him, remembering his rushing to remove her from what might have been harm's way.

"What?" He had forgotten. "Oh, that." His face was vacant, and his arm went slack as if the wrench he'd carried out suddenly became too much for him to handle. "Don't thank me— I didn't even think."

Before

Colossal Joy

Two weeks into November—Friday the 13th—Susanne was on the verge of a nap, her head still pulsing despite the aspirins she took after dragging herself home from sculpture studio, when she heard Joy come in from school. A few minutes later there was a meek tap at her door and her daughter said, "Mom. You awake?" Her voice was much softer than the one she'd used to eject her parents from her bedroom after her release from the police station the week before.

Susanne considered not answering, then raised herself on an elbow and told Joy to come in. She'd barely slept since Joy's arrest, but she knew it would be wrong to ignore an opportunity to hear whatever her daughter might have to say.

Joy went over to her mother's dresser, where Susanne kept one of her earliest hand sculptures: the tiny set of baby hands, fingers curled in fists so that only the barest sliver of nail on each was exposed to the viewer's eye. The hands were miniatures, smaller than any real baby's could ever be. She'd named the piece *Colossal Joy*.

Joy lifted it carefully, with both of her now-woman-sized hands, the way she was taught as a child to handle all of her mother's work. Susanne said, "Your first modeling gig," and they both smiled.

"First and only." Joy replaced the piece as tenderly as she'd picked it up. "I don't think I ever told you how much I love your stuff. Have I?"

Had she? Susanne didn't know. She couldn't remember Joy ever mentioning her work before, except for the day in seventh grade when she came home from school to say that her art teacher had asked if Joy's mother might be willing to come in as a guest speaker sometime, to show them what she did. The teacher passed around photos from the Rochester newspaper of Susanne's exhibit, and Keith Nance asked Joy if her mother liked doing "hand jobs."

Susanne blushed and felt a pang remembering Joy's struggle to tell her this story, which she saved until Gil had left the supper table. When Joy confessed that she didn't know what a hand job was—that she could only tell because of the way Keith said it, and the giggles he'd gotten, that it was something dirty—she had to explain it to her daughter.

"I appreciate that," she said, hoping Joy was not recalling the same event.

"Why did you stop?" Joy asked.

The question caught Susanne up short. It had been a few years since she'd sculpted anything, or wanted to, but neither Joy nor Gil had commented on this before now. Martin had been the last person to ask about her work. They'd been lying in bed one Thursday at the beginning of October when he said, "Why hands?" pulling one of hers toward him and kissing it.

Because of Rodin, she told him. It was from Rodin that she learned she did not need to sculpt anything other than hands, if she didn't want to—his own figures of disparate body parts (fingers, legs, heads, torsos) had taught her this. A piece of something could be as beautiful as its whole, he maintained. She'd quoted him in her Artist's Statement: "Where can one find more perfect harmony than in this fragment?"

Then she told Martin about the months she spent hosteling

through Europe with her boyfriend from college, and how moved she'd felt when she saw *The Creation of Adam* on the ceiling of the Sistine Chapel. "At first I thought their hands were touching. But then Danny said to look closer—the hands don't actually meet. They just miss, he said. For some reason I couldn't get over that image, them wanting to reach each other and *almost* making it, but not quite. Danny and I broke up right after that." She paused, returning Martin's sympathetic squeeze. "It makes me sad every time I see it."

He tightened his grasp. "*We* reach each other," he'd told her, and this lifted her sadness for a moment.

It was shortly after this conversation that she knew she had to put a stop to it, whatever they were doing. Only on that Thursday did she understand what it meant to him—their affair, their communion; between themselves, they had not given it a name. And though it did not mean any less to her, she knew as she always had that it was temporary, whereas (she saw in his eyes that day, and heard in his voice) Martin seemed to be thinking it might lead to more.

In the bedroom now, when Joy asked her why she'd stopped sculpting, Susanne thought about telling her the truth: that it didn't feel *necessary* anymore. There'd been a period of years when she would not have known what to do with herself, or who she was, if she hadn't been thinking about art, or planning it, or doing her best to make it. She didn't know why that feeling of urgency had left her—only that it had.

But she hesitated, not wanting her answer to suggest to Joy that she herself might lose interest in her own artwork someday. Joy seemed to sense she shouldn't press the question. Instead, as Suzanne stood up from the bed, she told her mother, "I'm glad I'll have this."

"You'll have it?" It took Susanne another beat to understand what Joy was saying. "You mean after I die?"

Now it was Joy who blushed. "I didn't mean—"

"It's okay. You don't have to wait until then." An impulse she couldn't tell right away if she regretted. "You can take that to Brockport with you." She gestured at *Colossal Joy*, only realizing, as she did so, her mistake. She did not want the piece sitting on a desk in some dorm room. Was that wrong of her? Selfish?

She was saved from having to dwell on it when Joy said, "What if I don't go?"

"Go where? You mean to college?"

"No. Brockport."

"Joy, we talked about this. Even with a scholarship, Decker's too—"

"Never mind. Got it." Joy waved as if to say *Don't waste your breath*.

Not wanting to get into a fight, Susanne picked up the piece on the dresser and said, "I'm glad you asked about this." *Glad you think you'll want to remember me*, she might have added, *especially after the week we've just been through*.

How could she bring it up now—the questions that persisted, between her and Gil, about why Joy had allowed herself to become involved with Jason and his criminal enterprise? (Which was how Susanne preferred to think of it—didn't that at least sound better than "drug ring"?) It could wait, couldn't it? The last thing she wanted was to spoil what she felt, unexpectedly and with a blind rush of gratitude, between herself and her daughter—a closeness she'd been missing for months. She hadn't allowed herself to realize the loss she'd been living with until this moment, when that acute absence was replaced with the particular surge of love she'd only ever felt for this particular person in the world, the one who had made her a mother.

She went into the kitchen and Joy trailed, declining her mother's offer of tea.

Susanne could always tell when her daughter fretted; her two top teeth bit into her lower lip. "Listen, I know I'm grounded," Joy said, and Susanne waited for whatever request was sure to follow. "But can I borrow your car just this once, just for like an hour, to drive out to the pond?"

"Why?" A moot question—Susanne and Gil had forbidden her to go anywhere without one or both of them.

"I want to go skating." Joy appeared to be stifling her excitement; didn't her mother's question imply that Susanne was considering giving permission? "Like the old days."

Like the old days. A phrase intended, no doubt, to appeal to Susanne's memories of that time—to her nostalgia not only for the summer afternoons they spent together on that lazy, sunny shore, sharing the big scratchy blanket held down at the corners by their flip-flops and bottles of sunscreen and the cooler Susanne packed with sandwiches and juice boxes and chips, but also for the winter afternoons when parents, mostly mothers, brought their kids to the same shore to skate while they ducked in and out of the Elbow Room to stay warm, some surreptitiously (or not so surreptitiously) lacing cups of the shack's hot chocolate with Baileys or Kahlúa or even red wine (Lynette Stowell introduced this one into the mix, cheerfully referring to the concoction as "Couch Coma"). The shore's hard ground led onto a long rectangle of silver ice, which turned a corner about three hundred yards out as it bent into the "elbow" bordering the woods. Sometimes kids raced each other on their skates as far out as the elbow, but mostly their parents prohibited them from going farther because they couldn't be seen beyond the turn.

Bringing up "the old days" was a miscalculation on Joy's part. If Susanne had been inclined to waver in the ban she and Gil had placed on their daughter, her resolve reasserted itself when she realized Joy was trying to manipulate her. Feeling a psychic nudge from Gil, she told her daughter, "You know I can't let you do that."

"Even though the charges were dropped?"

"Yes. You're still grounded. You had those drugs on you."

"Jesus Christ." Joy muttered the words as if she'd been doing so all her life, although Susanne had never heard the oath from her daughter before.

"Joy. I know you're upset, but please, let's be civil." Though she hadn't thought of it in years, she remembered suddenly the tenets of a book someone (Rachel Feinbloom?) had lent her when their kids were in preschool together. PET—Parent Effectiveness Training. The idea was that you didn't punish your kid, you didn't reward her, and you didn't pull any version of the "Because I said so" authority that would lead her to rebel. Instead, when she did something you wished she hadn't, you were supposed to tell her how her behavior affected you.

"I feel like you're pushing me away," Susanne said, flailing, not knowing whether she was doing it right. This was probably a line she'd heard once on TV. "When all I'm trying to do is get closer."

"Oh, that is such *bullshit*!" Joy raised her voice to a level she'd never used inside the house before. She was edging toward the back door and the garage, though only later would Susanne register that her daughter had already decided to take the car whether Susanne gave permission or not. They'd been wrong, she thought grimly. She and Gil had automatically given Joy her own set of keys when she got her license; it wouldn't have occurred to them that they couldn't trust her.

"What did you just say?" Susanne didn't really need to have the words repeated; her question followed the blow of hearing them all too clearly.

"You are such a hypocrite! You expect *me* to 'behave myself'"—Joy drew elaborate air quotes around the words—"when what *you* did was so much worse."

"What *I* did?" Later, Susanne would recognize that she had

hurried to accuse in an effort to avoid the more precarious position of having to defend. "*I* haven't broken any laws. *I* haven't been arrested."

"Well, guess what. Adultery is, too, a crime—I looked it up. A misdemeanor, but it's still illegal in this state."

Standing in the doorway, Susanne felt her arms wrapping themselves around her torso more from shock at her daughter's words than from the cold outside. *Adultery*. For a moment, she thought she might have heard Joy wrong. A moment later she thought, *Of course she knows. How did I think we could keep it from her?* "Be quiet, Joy. People will hear you. And come inside—it's freezing out here."

"You just had to relive your hippie-dippie college days, shake up your boring suburban life. You think you're cool because you slept with some black guy?" Joy yanked open the Mazda's door. "I can't believe you would do that to Daddy. I'm going to tell him, when he gets home tonight."

"Joy." How had she let her life come to this? Though Susanne was quite sure her next words should be some kind of reprimand, instead she said, "He already knows."

For a moment, Joy appeared stricken. Then her defiance reasserted itself. "Like hell he does. He wouldn't stay with someone who cuckolded him."

Cuckolded—was that one of the vocabulary words she'd learned for the SAT? In another circumstance, Susanne might have smiled. But now Joy was getting into the car, and although Susanne called after her that if she did this she'd be sorry, they both knew there wasn't a thing she could do to stop what was happening.

She waited and watched, thinking (though she knew better) that Joy might come to her senses before she reached the corner, reverse direction, and slink toward home. When she didn't, Susanne turned back toward the house, trying to figure out what to do when she got inside. Call Gil? But if she did, she'd feel compelled to tell him what their daughter had said. He'd have to know about it sometime, but she didn't feel ready to report to him, yet, how wrong they'd both been—how deluded they were (she saw now) to allow themselves to believe they'd managed to keep Susanne's affair a secret.

Behind her came the sound of her own name, in a voice so soft that at first she wasn't sure she'd heard correctly. When it repeated, she hadn't even turned yet to see Martin before he added, "I don't want to scare you" as he held a hand up in apology.

She was both surprised and not; she hadn't spoken to him outside of class since that last lunchtime they'd slept together, several weeks before. And even in class, their exchanges were perfunctory, formal. Yet it felt right that he should be the next person she saw after the quarrel with Joy, not only because he was the subject of Joy's accusation but because he was precisely who she needed at that moment. How could he have known?

Later, she realized that of course he had *not* known; he could only have intuited, or come to her house for some reason of his own. She pitched forward, but he misinterpreted, or perhaps it was she who did: was she approaching him for a hug? At the last second she stopped herself short, understanding with chagrin that it was not because she didn't want to touch him, but because she worried that Betsy Hahnemann might be watching through the window.

"She took my car," she told him as she gestured after Joy, though of course he would have seen this himself. "I can't let her get away with this. *Goddammit.*" Knowing that Betsy Hahnemann would lend her her Camry (and knowing too that there'd be a price to pay in terms of gossip, later), she started toward her neighbor's house, but Martin pulled her back.

"Wait. I have one."

"What, a car? You do?"

He gestured at an old, big boat of a Plymouth that looked vaguely familiar to her. "But are you sure you want to follow her?" he asked. "I mean, think it through. What are you going to do when you do find her, *if* you do? Drag her away and pull her into the car, like a little kid having a tantrum?"

She envisioned the scene; he was right. But if Joy would go so far as to take the Mazda without permission (Susanne would not allow herself to think the word "steal"; maybe she had "diverted" the car?), who knew what she might do next?

"Did she say where she was going?" Martin asked.

"She said to the pond, to go skating. But then she just stomped out, without her skates. I can't believe what she says anymore." Then another thought occurred to her, replacing anger with fear. "She got arrested last week. You probably heard that, right? The charges were dropped, and she says she didn't do anything—that she was set up. We didn't know what to believe." She remembered the looks she'd observed Joy exchanging with Jason at the nursing home. The looks contained more than flirtation, she realized now; "collusion" would be a better word. "What if she *was* dealing drugs?" she said to Martin, because it was easier to phrase the question than state the conclusion she'd already come to. "What if she was doing it, and she still is?" She started toward the Plymouth urging him to follow, and when he didn't, she turned to find out why.

"It might be better if it's not you." Martin spoke the words slowly to make sure they would sink in. "Why don't you let me go? She won't recognize my car, and I'll keep a distance. I won't do anything unless I think she's in trouble."

Susanne felt herself falter. Of course, she thought, Joy might flip out all the more if she did see Martin, given what she'd just yelled at her mother about her sleeping with "some black guy."

But he went on to say, "We're friends, from the barbecue.

Trust me," and he got into the Fury and turned the key before she could think of a way to stop him. In the next moment, she was glad she hadn't been able to. He was right; someone needed to keep an eye on Joy, but if Susanne chased her, they'd only be shifting the venue of their confrontation. Making it public instead of confining it to the house.

"Make sure she's okay, okay?" she called over the high noise of the engine, and Martin waved in—affirmation? Reassurance? Both, or neither? She couldn't be sure—before he pulled away.

Test Yourself Now!

Everyone knew that Joy had been arrested, and then everyone knew that the charges had been dropped. But no one was quite sure, if you listened to the whispering in the hallways, how the police had known to investigate her, or why she'd been let off the hook.

Harper was surprised along with everyone else when it was announced on the news that police weren't going to press charges against "the Chilton schoolgirl," but she understood along with everyone else that it didn't mean they couldn't have. *You can do the crime without doing the time*, she'd overheard in the cafeteria.

Someone—God knew who, or when—had scribbled *Jennie Cruz likes pussy* on Harper's desk, and every day when she sat down for English, she put her notebook over the words so she wouldn't have to read them again. But just knowing they were there set her head grinding, which made it hard for her to concentrate on what went on in class.

When she was young, her mother had read her "The Owl and the Pussycat" every night before bed. Harper could still remember (the memory warming her like the Powerpuff Girls flannel sheets she slept in back then) the loving lilt of her voice as she bent close to Harper's hair and practically sang, "O lovely Pussy! O Pussy, my love, what a beautiful Pussy you are, you are, you are! What a beautiful Pussy you are!" It killed Harper that growing up meant she had to learn a new meaning of "pussy," which spoiled the word for her, and the memory, forever.

At the beginning of the semester she'd tried, secretly before class once, to rub out the comment about Jennie Cruz (who had probably graduated years ago), using wet wipes she brought from home, but it turned out she wasn't secret enough, because Delaney Stowell noticed and announced, "Betty Crocker has OCD, just like her brother." Automatically, Joy said, "She does not," and Harper sent her old best friend a hug with her eyes across the aisle, though Joy didn't see it because she was looking down, which was all she ever seemed to do anymore.

Of course, the wet wipes didn't work. A week later she brought in a Sharpie and ran it over the message about Jennie Cruz (though covering it up was not as satisfying as removing it would have been), and Mrs. Carbone sent her to detention, which provided Delaney and her friends with a new thing to mock Harper for.

It was Friday the 13th and cold outside, but Mrs. Carbone shoved open the classroom windows from the top and before she returned to her desk, she leaned her face out to breathe in a couple of lungfuls of the bright, chilly air. Kids exchanged furtive glances. There was a rumor she'd been arrested for DUI and that it involved Keith Nance somehow, but it couldn't be true because she wouldn't still be here teaching, would she? And how messed up would it be for the person who tried to help her students affected by their parents' drinking to be a drunk herself?

Joy sat next to Harper in class because the seating was assigned, but they avoided meeting each other's eyes. They hadn't spoken in almost two weeks, since the day after the Halloween party, when Joy showed up at Harper's house and (Harper was sure) stole her mother's pills. She'd considered telling Joy she was on to the theft, to let her know she hadn't gotten away with it, but she hadn't done so (and probably wouldn't) because there didn't seem to be any point: Joy was beyond retrieving as a friend.

After class she went to the library, where she worked for a few minutes on her *Othello* paper at one of the computers, then logged onto Facebook, something she did multiple times a day because Sandra Sherman, her mother's friend, tended to post links to Harper's wall like "Are You Phobic? Test Yourself Now!" and Harper always rushed to hide them as soon as she could. But there'd been no action on her page since the last time she checked, so she logged into Joy's account using the password SALSA (her own, of course, was CHIP). She'd gotten in the habit of using this method to see what Joy was up to, since they'd grown further apart. Under the message notifications, she found a thread between Joy and Delaney Stowell, exchanged the night before.

Condo at 3:30 today, Joy had written. *Last time, I swear.*

Dude, Delaney messaged back, *you gotta get your fone back so we can text. And you said last time LAST TIME. Not meeting you at La-La or anyplace else.*

3:30 or I confess was Joy's response.

Confess what? Harper wondered.

Why should I believe you its the last time? Delaney had written, to which Joy replied, *Don't need you anymore, other source of $$ came thru.*

Then y you harrassing me?

Cuz I can. Also it's spelled harass. Joy had inserted a smiley face next to the comment, which unsettled Harper almost as much as the messages themselves.

Beeeeyatch, Delaney had written back, and Harper couldn't

tell if it was a teasing remark in return or a genuine insult. But no smiley face accompanied the word. *Ok, but not La-La, its burnt out gives me the creeps! 3:30 at pond, last time for real or else.* The messages ended there.

At home, her mother's curtains were drawn, the signal that she didn't want to be disturbed. Harper told Truman she wanted to go to the pond. "Why?" he said, though she could tell he didn't really have any interest in the answer.

It was a fair question—one she would be asking herself for years to come. She'd told herself she wanted to go for Joy's own good—to help Joy, if she needed it.

But who was she kidding? Even if Joy *wanted* her help, Delaney would have Tessa and Lin with her. Three against two. Or three against one and a half was more like it, Harper thought.

It would take her years to be able to acknowledge the idea that her real reason had to do with wanting to watch Joy get punished. For her to be able to understand how angry she was at Joy's betrayal in stealing her mother's pills.

"I'll make you moon pies," she told Truman.

"Double batch," he stipulated, and when she agreed, he picked up his keys.

As they approached the pond, they saw a group of people gathered on the shore's edge around the benches you could sit on to change in and out of your skates. Mothers helped their little kids stay upright on their double-runners, escorting them to the ice. "That was us once," Harper said. Truman said, "That's *still* you," and she slapped his parka arm with her mitten.

To one side of the benches, Joy stood amid a small huddle. Before Harper could get out of the car, her brother squinted ahead through the windshield and added, "Hey, isn't that your friend the drug dealer?" He pointed at Joy, who stamped her fake UGGS on the ice and hugged herself to stay warm.

"She's not a drug dealer." But, of course, Joy was. The words had emerged automatically, as Harper noticed so many of her words did now.

"Whatever," Truman said again. "Get yourself a ride home." They both knew this wasn't going to happen and he would be making the return trip, but he still said it every time.

He sped off, leaving exhaust to blacken the ice beneath his tires. The noise made everyone at the pond look up as Harper approached, hugging herself in an effort to keep warm. Delaney said, "You weren't invited." She looked at Joy to confirm that her claim was right, and Joy shook her head slightly: *No, I didn't ask her.*

"You don't have to be invited to come to the pond." Harper had no idea where she found the nerve to say such a thing— and to Delaney Stowell, no less. "What's going on?" Her heart knocked at the audacity of her own question.

"Exercise," Tessa said, earning laughter from the others. Then, just as quickly as they had sought to banish Harper, they all seemed to forget she was there.

"Come on," Joy said to Delaney. Harper wondered whether she was the only one who could tell that beneath her cold look and the harshness in her voice, Joy was shaking. "Just give it to me already."

Delaney reached into her pocket and pulled out an envelope. She seemed to be considering whether she had any option other than meeting Joy's demand. When it appeared that nothing occurred to her, she held the envelope out and Joy grabbed it (moving fast to hide the shaking?) before Delaney could change her mind.

"I meant what I said, though. That's it." Delaney leaned close to Joy, and Harper watched their ribbons of exhaled breath mingle in the air between them. "Try again, you'll be sorry." Her vehemence came out with drops of spit.

The mothers on the ice, appearing to sense trouble, moved

their kids away from the teenagers. A little boy looked at Harper, and she saw fear in the child's face. It was a moment she would always remember, though every time she tried to describe it to herself, in years to come, the right words failed her.

"Joy," she said urgently, "let's go. I'll call Truman to come and get us."

"Shut up," Joy said, not turning to look at her.

"Joy—"

"I said *shut up!*" Now she did turn, and Harper didn't even recognize her friend's face, so grotesque was it in its fury. Delaney and the other girls smirked, Lin shooing her away. Her eyes stinging, Harper backed up, watching them watch her as she retreated from the circle they'd denied her access to. Once she reached the shore, she turned to face the shack and started toward the pay phone at the side of the building, her legs feeling weak from the futility of her trip here—the mission she hadn't even been able to identify to herself.

She slid a quarter into the phone with trembling fingers as a guy who worked in the shack, the one who creeped her out and smelled like pot, stood in front of the door and tried to light a cigarette in the breeze. Then a black man came out, practically running right into the creep. Before getting into his car the black man smiled at Harper, but she blushed and looked at the ground. What if that was the guy Joy's mother was having sex with? Immediately she felt ashamed of the thought—wasn't that the same as believing all black people looked alike?

In the car he made a short phone call on his cell phone, then drove away. As she waited for Truman to answer, Harper cast a look around at the bleak sky without really seeing it. Out on the pond, she saw Joy break free from the other three girls and start sliding across the ice toward the crook in the elbow. *Run!* Harper felt like calling after her. She had no idea where the impulse to warn Joy came from, and Delaney and Tessa and Lin obviously couldn't have cared less—they had no inclination to chase or follow, now that whatever transaction they'd come for was complete. Nevertheless: *Go, go!* she urged her friend silently, feeling vicarious victory in Joy's escape.

Friday, November 13

What happened to Joy? And did I have a part in it? I must have—we all did. But what, exactly, was mine?

On the eleven o'clock news just now they said that Joy is presumed drowned, but they haven't retrieved her body. I had to turn the sound down when Susanne came on, her husband behind her, and said she didn't believe her daughter was under the ice, and could anyone who knew anything please, please contact the police, so they could bring their baby home and put her to bed.

Watching her, I realized I had never seen her cry before. I'd never seen her face twisted in anything like what I just saw. It was nothing like the way I saw her face move in pleasure when we were in bed. Before now I would have made the mistake of thinking the expressions were similar—the features contorting in ecstasy like the ones contorting in grief. I'm ashamed to say that somewhere, my mind was registering this to remember in front of the easel someday.

Is there anything I could have done to prevent it?

Of course, it had occurred to me to tell Susanne about Joy's visit on Halloween. I knew she would want to know that Joy had shown up at my house and demanded confirmation of our affair. But after that initial inclination, I decided it was really up to Joy to tell her mother; there was no need for me to get involved in the business between mother and daughter. If Susanne and I had still been in touch, of course I would have. But she'd made it clear she didn't want any contact. I decided to obey another of Grandee's favorite sayings, and let it lie.

But all this week the grapevine at school's been buzzing with the news that Susanne Enright's daughter had been arrested for drug possession, and I realized that Joy was in deeper trouble than I'd understood. After considering, I worked up the nerve yesterday to approach Susanne toward the end of her scheduled office hours, as I used to on the Thursdays we slept together. It amazed me, the difference between how I felt on those days and how I felt now—from absolute pleasure to absolute dread.

After all that, she wasn't there, and somebody said she'd taken a personal day. Which made sense in light of the arrest.

I knew that if I left a phone message or texted that I wanted to talk to her about Joy, she would respond finally. But I allowed myself to believe that the message would be better delivered in person, so that I'd have an excuse to speak to her face-to-face. My plan was to linger after sculpture studio today, but she told us she had a "killer headache" and left the room before we'd even put away our materials. I couldn't have caught up with her without drawing attention I knew neither of us would want.

So I drove to her house as I had twice before, in Grandee's car, both times losing heart before texting or calling to say that I was outside and wondered if she would come sit and talk with me for a minute. My plan today was simple: if the Odd Men Out truck was in the driveway, I would leave.

But as it turned out, only the Mazda was parked there, and the garage door was open so I saw that her husband wasn't home. This time, to alter the pattern that hadn't worked before, I put my phone away and simply began walking toward the house. Approaching, I heard voices shouting at each other: Susanne and Joy. "That is such *bullshit!*" Joy screamed at her mother. They were arguing in the kitchen, and hearing them through the garage, I stopped short on the walkway, knowing I was beyond their sight. At first, I couldn't make out the actual words. But then I heard Joy say "some black guy," and felt myself flinch physically, as if someone had kicked me in the gut. A few moments later, when Joy got into the Mazda and backed out with a screech, I found myself tempted to hide behind a bush so Susanne wouldn't see me.

But I didn't need Violet's voice in my head to tell me I had no reason to feel guilty, and instead I moved toward Susanne, doing my best not to startle her. She put a hand to her heart when she saw me and for a moment I was afraid she'd scream again, but instead she looked relieved when she realized it was me—grateful, even. Just remembering the expression on her face, now, makes me want to linger on how good it felt, and I wish I could stop there. Especially because all that came after it, in its speed and chaos, is more of an outline than details I can trust myself to fill in.

It must have taken less than a minute for us to decide together that I should be the one to follow Joy, alone instead of with Susanne, to make sure Joy didn't get into more trouble than she already was. I drove toward Elbow Pond hoping she hadn't lied to Susanne about where she was going, because she had too much of a head start for me to actually follow. I was relieved when I arrived at the lot in front of the Elbow Room (which I know the kids call "the shack") and saw the Mazda parked haphazardly in the corner, and I pulled the Fury into a space on the opposite side.

On the pond, a few younger children were wobbling on their skates near the shore, their mothers standing around watching and chatting as they sipped from cups and Thermoses. I saw no sign of Joy, so I assumed she was in the shack. After a moment considering what I might say when I encountered her (I decided to pretend it was a coincidence, then take it from there, depending on her reaction), I turned off the engine and headed inside.

There were a lot of cars in the lot, but I realized when I saw no other customers in the place that they must have belonged to the mothers out on the pond. The clerk behind the counter looked up but not at me when I entered, and I did a double take, remembering him from the barbecue at Susanne's house. I raised my hand in a half wave, but he just scowled in response, and I figured he didn't remember our brief conversation that day. He continued to watch me after I headed down the first aisle, feeling compelled to act like a customer even though I felt the urgency to find Joy.

Being watched in a store was, of course, nothing new; it's happened all my life. I remember going to the Vinyl Village in college, to browse and sometimes buy old records to play on the hi-fi my father said my mother had left behind. I made them suspicious there my first few times, because although I could tell they expected me to head for the racks featuring Sam Cooke, Billie Holiday, and Otis Redding, I passed these by and stopped instead before the bins containing Shostakovich, Berlioz, and Chopin. When I took the LPs into the listening room, the clerks at the counter pretended not to keep an eye on me, but I knew they did. Once they got to know me—which happened during my third visit to the store, when I came out of the room with the cover to Debussy's *La Mer* by Leonard Bernstein and the New York Philharmonic, asking if they could find me the better recording by Boulez and the Cleveland Orchestra— they relaxed, then began greeting me by name every time I came in. I could tell they were pleased with themselves for having a black friend. I know this kind of thing is supposed to bother me; I know that other people, especially black people, would say it should. I sometimes feel disappointed when I recognize the limitations of a relationship because of how others show themselves to be, but I can't go so far as to say it bothers me.

Why do white people think their tests for you are the only ones that matter? It's as if everyone on both sides understands that all you have to do is pass those tests, and then things can be fine. I'm pretty sure it's never occurred to these people that I have tests for them, too. The difference, of course, is that they can't imagine any repercussions that might matter to them of failing my test. But it matters to *me*. That's not always enough, but it's better than nothing.

At the end of the aisle, I picked up an item at random—a package of index cards, I think—and brought it up to the counter. "Find everything you were looking for?" the clerk said, and I couldn't tell whether he was mocking my purchase or genuinely wondering if he could help me locate something else from my list. I held my breath because the mix of smells coming off him was so strong—stale perspiration and marijuana—and realized that what I had taken to be a scowl could have been purely the nature of what years of pot smoking had done to his face. When I didn't answer right away he added, "What the fuck are *you* staring at?"

As if the word "fuck" were a signal of some kind, the door to the rear office swung open and a man who must have been the boss came out as I was saying to the clerk, "We've met before, remember? I was just trying to place you."

I was doing my best to smooth the moment over, but what I said only made it worse, if it's fair to judge from the way he seemed to receive my words, clattering my change on the counter between us instead of dropping it into my hand.

"Problem?" the boss asked.

"No problem," the clerk said, but he was unable to hide what he thought of me. "Smoke break," he added, and without waiting for permission or dismissal, he headed toward the door.

His boss shrugged at me, and I read it as the apology I believe he intended. He said *Hey*, then asked, "You play?" For a moment I thought he wanted to sell me some lottery tickets. I must have looked confused because he added, "Football. You're just—you look like you could have been a tackle. *I* played, is why I ask."

He got redder and redder the more he talked, and wanting to save him, I shook my head. "My grandmother wouldn't let me." I realized how that sounded but resisted defending it: the truth was that I'd always been glad Grandee wouldn't allow me to go out for football, even if I'd wanted to.

"Smart lady." He laughed. "I'd be better off myself if I hadn't taken all those knocks to the head."

I smiled back, appreciating his effort to make up for the awkwardness in the air. Remembering that Susanne was waiting for a call from me, I decided it couldn't hurt to ask, "Did you see a girl, a teenager, in here? About this big?" I held a hand up to indicate Joy's height.

"There's a few of them out there. See?" He pointed out at the pond, and now I saw a group of girls gathered to one side behind a stand of trees that must have hidden them from me when I first pulled in. There were four of them, including Joy. Relieved to have her in sight, I took a few steps toward the window to see that she and another of the girls were yelling at each other. Gesturing. Fighting the way girls do, without any physical contact.

I told him I saw who I was looking for, and on my way out I almost bumped into Cliff (his name came to me suddenly, though too late), as he flicked his lighter desperately in flameless clicks. He muttered something I couldn't quite decipher, but I didn't ask him to repeat it. Beyond him, at the pay phone, I saw another teenage girl who appeared on the verge of tears. She seemed so miserable that I smiled, but she let her eyes dart down without returning the smile and turned her back to me to look out at the ice, in the direction of the abandoned condo complex and the woods Cass had told me the kids call the Undead Forest.

I am used to this, too: white people looking away when you catch their eye, though I hardly even register it anymore. I got back in the car and turned it on, idling for a moment as I considered my next move. Joy may have been arguing with her friends, but there was no reason to think she was in danger. And I knew it would hardly do for me to head out there and insist that she go back home. *Some black guy*, I remembered her saying to Susanne, and I imagined the looks the other girls would give me—let alone what they'd say to one another, afterward—if I approached them now.

I opened my phone and dialed Susanne, who answered on the first ring. "She's fine," I told her, hearing that she sounded frantic. "They look like they're wrapping it up, whatever it is. I'm sure she'll be home soon."

"Oh, thank God." I could almost feel the warmth of her breath coming through the phone, and the intimacy of it made me wince. I hung up before she could ask me to stay until Joy left, or thank me, or say anything else; it was too painful, and as I put the Fury in gear and pulled out of the lot, I resolved to stop all this foolishness and—how does the phrase go?—move on with my life. Easier said than done, though. Like everything.

At home I sketched for a few hours, then turned on the TV for company as I ate a microwaved meal. That was when I saw the breaking news about a girl believed missing and presumed drowned, and I kept watching (if I could have held my breath the whole time, I would have) until they identified her as Joy. Then Susanne came on the screen, and I had to turn the set off. I reached for my phone, at the same time realizing I could not call her. I could not do anything other than sit here and pick up this book and start writing, though now that I've come to the end of it, I'm no closer to understanding what might have happened than I was when I began.

Zero Visibility

Friday afternoon and Tom was stalling again, not wanting to leave the shack to go home. Alison had invited her parents for dinner, saying she wanted to make it up to all of them—lying about being pregnant, worrying them all with a DUI her father had had to make go away. "How about making it up to me by not having your parents over?" Tom asked, but she pretended to think he was joking.

He was glad to have an excuse to go to the shack in the first place, feeling the need to check up on Cliff, who'd already missed two shifts—without calling in—since he'd been hired. Tom resolved that the third time would be the last; he was inclined to allow a couple of strikes, but he'd be damned if he'd let somebody who worked for him make him look like a chump.

Alison told him he couldn't fire the new guy. "Why not?" Tom asked.

"He's an addict. That's a disability."

Tom snorted. "Bullshit. He just likes getting high."

"Okay, don't listen to me, but it's true." She shrugged and raised a hand as if to say *Go ahead, find out the hard way*. "We had an in-service about this. You have to give him a break."

He was still pissed off about this as he drove to the shack, but as it turned out, going in ended up being a good move, given the tense moments between Cliff and the black guy. Sitting in the back room, he'd heard Cliff say "fuck" and came out to see what was going on, which the customer seemed to appreciate even if Cliff obviously did not. After Cliff left in a huff to smoke outside, Tom made a stupid remark about football and then felt like an idiot, but the guy was generous enough not to seem to resent it. Their brief exchange left Tom feeling good about himself: he was no racist, even if he did have one for a father-in-law.

Cliff returned to his post after his smoke break, but it was only to collect his jacket from under the shelf. "You're on till five," Tom reminded him, but Cliff said, "The hell with that, I got someplace to be" and huddled out again into the cold. With anyone else Tom would have followed him out and told him he was fired, but remembering Alison's warning, he took Cliff's place behind the counter and felt like the guy had done him a favor by giving him a legitimate excuse not to go home yet.

A few minutes before five, Estelle came in for the night shift. She laughed when Tom told her Cliff had taken off early, as if anything else would have surprised her. When Tom dawdled in leaving, she grinned and said, "The Strong Arms coming for dinner again?"

"Busted," he told her, grinning back, and then he had no choice but to head home. Doug and Helen had beaten him there, as usual, and as usual he parked on the street. In the kitchen, Alison and her mother chatted over their glasses of Diet Coke. His wife's cheeks were flushed from opening the oven to check on the meatloaf, and when Tom stepped into the house, he tried to believe it was pleasure instead of surprise he saw on her face. The expression he read there, despite not wanting to recognize it, was the familiar one of *Oh yeah, I forgot you were coming.* If it weren't for the fact that he knew how much her accident had scared her, he might have guessed—from the flush and the briefly confused look in her eyes—that she'd been drinking. He tried to ignore the thought as he went toward the women to deliver a kiss first to his wife, then to his mother-in-law, before cracking a Genny. Alison handed him a glass, telling him that since he was late, he'd have to drink it with dinner.

"Why the rush?" he asked, then remembered. Of course: another meeting. She'd been going every night since the one after the accident—thirty meetings in thirty days was what they advised. Sometimes Helen picked her up, sometimes she went by herself. When she came home, Alison could be quiet or energized, and if he asked, she might tell him things other people had said. In only two weeks, Tom had become familiar with the phrases she and other drunks (for some reason she preferred this word to "alcoholic"; Tom assumed it had something to do with wanting to appear down to earth and not teacherly, as she scarfed down Chips Ahoy! in a church basement trying to satisfy the urge for sugar she wasn't feeding with wine and whiskey) were supposed to say to themselves, to stay sober. *Keep it simple. You're only as sick as your secrets. First things first.*

When Doug's cell phone rang in his pocket five minutes after they'd sat down, they all understood that the meal was most likely over. While his father-in-law stood to answer it, Tom heard his own cell ringing in the kitchen. Seeing that the call was from dispatch, the first thing he thought was *I shouldn't have had a beer.*

But what he heard erased any traces of fuzziness he might have felt: they needed him at the lake. To recover a body. *Leave now.* He and Doug hung up at the same time, meeting back at the table. Alison waved with one hand as Helen told them, "We get it, go." Doug bolted out to the Buick and took off while Tom hauled up his diving gear, which he kept on standby at the back door, threw it in the truck, and peeled out after his father-in-law.

Shit, shit, shit. He didn't feel ready. It was dark out; the dive would be in black water, his first in zero visibility.

If someone had told him in high school that someday he'd find himself groping around in water for something nobody wanted to touch, he'd have laughed and said, *Yeah, that'll happen. Right after I become a Boy Scout.* In his wildest dreams he'd never thought he'd end up a rescue diver. But he took the class, then joined the crew, because he knew it would boost his stock in Doug's eyes (which he cared about only because Alison cared about it), and he wasn't sure how else to do that. To his surprise, he was good at it. Or maybe it wasn't a surprise: maybe he'd guessed, in the part of himself he avoided looking at, that he was destined for this. That he *would* be good at it—steady, his wits in place no matter what happened, unlikely to panic. The same quality that allowed him to withstand and even sometimes enjoy the pressure on the field, being rushed as he sought someone open to a pass (hearing inside the heat of his helmet the whoosh of the words *You got time, you got time*—and the miracle of it was that just by telling it to himself, he *made* the time), kicked in on his first dive and each one after. Jack, the dive instructor, had told them that fourteen to sixteen breaths per minute was what a beginner could expect, but from the start Tom had measured the experienced rate of eight to ten. In the pool, practicing, he managed to avoid the hard, sharp obstacles (chicken wire, rebar) the trainers planted for the newbies so they'd learn to feel in front of them before they moved, and he was the only one of his group who'd located and brought up, every time, the dummy drowning victim named Laureen, after Jack's first ex-wife. Natalie and the others in the class had called Tom "Gills," and he tried not to show how much he liked it.

But before now he'd only gone under to bring up the gun a guy he'd known in high school had used to shoot his wife and her woman lover (another of their classmates, Jennie Cruz), and the broken pedal of a five-speed belonging to a boy abducted by his ex-con junkie father as he rode home from school one day. This would be his first attempt to locate an actual person, and in zero vis, at that. Was anyone ever ready for this? He told himself to calm down; he'd have help out there, lots of people around, he wouldn't be doing it alone.

He pulled up next to the woods, behind Doug's car, and saw the hovercraft waiting at the edge of the water. Doug, having just been briefed, filled him in: teenage girl believed to have fallen through, in the water too long by now, no way she was still alive but they needed to find the body.

Tom remembered seeing them out there only a few hours earlier, and wondered which girl it was that had gone under—Snake Girl or one of the others? The mission was recovery, not rescue, though of course they weren't telling the family that. As Natalie helped him into his suit, he tried not to hear what he knew were the parents' voices, screaming: *Go get her! Go!* The boat sped them out to the hole and he let himself fall in, fall under. He gave a single pull on the tether to let Natalie know he was okay to leave the surface. In many ways, it was a relief: once he was in the water with his mask and his tank, he heard only the sounds of the air moving through his regulator; he'd left the voices, and their panic, behind.

He began sweeping with his gloves in a grid pattern as he tried not to let himself recognize the truth, which was that he did not actually want to find a body down there. He finished working the grid once, then tugged on the tether to signal Natalie that he was starting back without having detected anything. Maybe they're wrong, he thought. The girl didn't go under; something else made the hole. Or maybe she fell through but escaped somehow, then ran away. Or something. They'd find out later.

Then he felt it: a hand on his wrist. Latching on, fingers

around the skin of his dry suit, the grip cold and hard. He shook it off, flipped onto his back, and began kicking his fins with everything he had toward the surface. *What the fuck!* He knew how stupid it was to swear inside his mask, use up the air required to do so, but he couldn't stop himself. (Later that night, going over the entire fiasco in his mind, he corrected himself: Not *couldn't* stop. *Didn't.*)

He began kicking so violently that he barely registered the urgent pull signal from Natalie, asking if he was okay. Before he'd realized he had freed himself from whatever had seized him, he'd done the unthinkable: pulled his mask off and begun battling toward the top. Natalie yanked on the tether—*Trouble?*—but Tom ignored it, giving no signal back. The shock of the cold water hitting his face triggered an almost unbearable impulse to breathe, but at the last moment he remembered his secondary air supply—the bailout bottle—hooked up the regulator, and started to take in breaths that wouldn't kill him. Breaking the surface, he heard the screaming begin from the mother on shore. Though he couldn't make out the words, he knew the scream was some variation of: *Where is she? You have her?* and he knew he had failed.

He got on the boat, threw the mouthpiece aside, and gasped. "Anything?" Natalie said, holding the radio ready. Tom shook his head.

"I got tangled up in some weeds. That's it." His breath came in heaves. "Creepy as shit, but no body." Later, he would try to convince himself that it might have been different if he'd thought there was a chance she was still alive. He also tried telling himself that maybe he'd been wrong, after all; maybe it *had* been only a weed, and not the hand of the dead girl, wrapping itself around his arm.

But he didn't believe any of it. He knew better. Those parents were entitled to an answer; he'd had a job to do, and he hadn't done it. Worse than that, he lied. Given up the body and given up, in all likelihood, any chance he'd ever had of proving to Doug that he wasn't a loser, that he could be trusted.

He watched his father-in-law go over to tell the parents their daughter was still missing, and found himself hoping—praying, if he were to be honest, though he wouldn't have thought he knew how to pray—that his baby was a son, so he'd never have to go through what they were enduring. At the same time, he recognized that nobody in that moment deserved a prayer to be answered less than he.

After

Monday, December 14

I probably should have known this, but I did not: when the grand jury is deciding whether to indict you, you don't get to be in the room. I'd pictured it like a court proceeding in a movie—Ramona and me sitting behind one table, the prosecutor, Nelson Kovak, and his team behind the next. The jury members seated in their box as they listen to all the witnesses, keeping their faces impassive so as not to give anything away to either side.

But when I asked Ramona on the phone yesterday what I should wear, she set me straight. Only if I were testifying would we be allowed in, and I was not going to testify. So I asked her where she would be while they were in session, and she said her office, which means she is not even coming up here from New York for the day. It took me a moment to remember that of course she has other cases, other clients besides me to defend. Though secretly I think my case must be the most important—murder, with implications pertaining to race—I tried to sound as if I wasn't bothered by the idea of having to wait alone by the phone as a bunch of strangers (most likely all white) considered the evidence against me.

But as it turns out, I won't be alone. Violet and Cass are taking me to the movies, a double feature of *The Blind Side* and

Invictus. When Violet suggested it, I wanted to ask if she were insane. That was only in the first few moments, though; as soon as I let the idea settle, I saw how right it was. Without being able to work, or to move through the world unafraid of attracting attention I do not want, what I need is the chance to be absorbed in a drama other than the one of my own life. If I can be in the dark while I do it, friends at my side, all the better.

If need be—if by the end of the second movie I haven't heard a report from Ramona yet—we will stay for a showing of anything other than *The Lovely Bones*, which I chose from the listings purely by title but which Violet quickly assured me I did not want to see.

I will open this book next on the other side, once I know the decision. I've tried to imagine how I will feel if they indict me, and I know I can't, quite—which scares me, because I can sense the rage gathering in my belly, and it feels stronger than any willpower I might be able to muster to keep it down. I don't stand a chance if they send me to trial. Not here, and not being an outsider with black skin.

But stop thinking this way—stop it, stop, until I have to. *Don't close the door till you're out of the room*, Grandee would tell me. It's not open very far, but it's still open. That's something.

You Are Commanded

The Monday following the funeral, the hallways in school felt hushed. It was as if they'd all been punished, Harper thought. There was also a sense of waiting. What for? she wondered. The worst was over; one of them had been murdered and was never coming back. Police had taken a man into custody, but some people doubted he was the killer. On the news every night she saw people protesting Martin Willett's arrest. Then there were the protests against the protests, and it seemed a competition to see who could have the last word. Of all the collective chants, the one that lingered in Harper's mind was *He did it, let him fry!* Was it that this cry was so much louder than the others? Or was it just because she felt so guilty about what she had done?

She was in a hole; it was a phrase she'd learned from Mrs. Carbone in English, about what makes a good story. *When people are in a hole*, she told the class, *other people like to watch them try to get out*. The holes were metaphors, of course. For trouble. Situations they didn't want to be in, that threatened them somehow. Mrs. Carbone said she herself had always been most interested in stories that depicted characters trapped in holes of their own making, but you could also fall in as the result of other people pushing you, or because of fate—circumstances you had no control over.

The man in the Jack London story, who died when snow fell off a branch and put out the fire he'd managed to build: he was in a hole of both kinds. He shouldn't have started his journey in the first place, because the cold was too dangerous, but he couldn't control the snow (although, as Mrs. Carbone pointed out, he should have realized the danger the branch posed and built the fire someplace else). Odysseus fell into a different category: his hole consisted of obstacle after obstacle he had to overcome, in order to get home after the war. Being who he was, he hadn't had a choice about going off to fight, so you couldn't really say he'd gotten himself into the trouble he faced along the way.

The case of Bigger Thomas was more complicated, Mrs. Carbone told them when they read *Native Son*. Or maybe you could say he was in more than one hole at the same time. Yes, he smothered the white girl with the pillow, but he hadn't set out to kill her—he was only afraid that her blind mother would know he was in the room with her daughter, and then he'd really be in for it, because he was black. He chose to use the pillow, but he hadn't chosen being black, which was its own hole. They had a big argument in class that day. Keith Nance said you couldn't have it both ways—either you were responsible for what you did, or you weren't. And being black, or being poor, was no excuse. The only person who had an excuse—*maybe*, Keith said—was the retard in *Of Mice and Men*. (Don't use the word "retard," Mrs. Carbone had told him.) Otherwise, Keith went on (ignoring her), if you were stuck in a hole you'd dug for yourself, that was your own fault and nobody else's.

But sometimes, Joy argued, you don't realize you're digging your own hole until it's too late.

Harper's head had hurt during that class, because she understood both sides—or were there more than two sides?—but she wasn't sure what she would have said if someone asked her opinion. She was glad when the bell rang and she was relieved of having to think about it anymore.

Now she understood only that she was in a hole. She'd been presented with an opportunity that seemed it might lead to two things she wanted: first, her mother started driving again, which was a kind of metaphor for her reentry to the world. She went out to buy groceries instead of ordering them online. She'd rejoined her old book group and skipped a few meetings of Saturday afternoon therapy.

On top of which—the second thing—Harper felt less like a loser at school, maybe because now she mattered. The DA had talked to everyone else from the pond that day, including Delaney and Tessa and Lin, but none of them identified the black man who'd been at the shack right before Joy disappeared. Harper was the only person they'd found to testify that he'd been wearing a mask, once they lost track of the pothead store clerk who'd also been on the witness list.

She'd stepped into the hole without thinking about the consequences. But *why* she was in it didn't really matter, she realized; what mattered was that she didn't know how she was going to get out.

And the hole was this: she did not think Martin Willett was guilty. When she saw him on TV, saying that he would never have done anything to hurt Joy or anyone else, she believed him. Plus, he was an artist, and sometimes she thought that making art must be like baking: you loved putting ingredients together to create something that hadn't existed before. You took care to choose the right color to put on the canvas, the same way you kept tasting your icing to make sure it was just sweet enough. That was not the kind of person who killed someone, was it?

When it came right down to it, would she really be able to say she'd seen him in a ski mask, when she had not? Was such a lie worth what she seemed to have gained by promising it to the prosecution?

Nobody at school was talking about who might have done it. That wasn't as important or as relevant as the mementoes—flowers, stuffed animals—that began piling up outside Joy's locker. The locker itself was covered in photographs kids taped up of themselves with Joy from the time they'd all been in preschool—blindfolded under piñatas at birthday parties, riding scooters, flashing peace signs from horses on the merry-go-round at the county fair. Since Harper's locker was next to Joy's, she couldn't help seeing the photos, though she didn't linger to study them. She did not put up any of her own, though she probably possessed more of these tangible keepsakes of Joy than anyone else.

Nobody talked about the funeral, either, or how weird it had been to see teachers in a church and at the reception, some crying, all looking stricken in a way they did not allow themselves to appear at school. And though Harper had anticipated it with dread, no one mentioned her outburst in the line at the ladies' restroom at the church; even Delaney Stowell herself barely gave her a glance in the hallway on the way to homeroom.

She went to school only for her first-period class, after which her mother planned to pick her up to drive her to the courthouse, where she was scheduled to appear before the grand jury. *Please excuse Harper from school after 8:45 today*, her mother had written in the note, *as she has been subpoenaed*. That word, SUBPOENA, appearing in big letters at the top of the summons she'd received from a court officer who knocked on the door, apologized for the intrusion, and handed over the envelope.

The next day, Martin Willett's lawyer had come to talk to her. Harper felt more comfortable speaking with Ramona than she had answering questions from the police or the prosecutor (whom she found even scarier than the police chief), but still her mother insisted on sitting in as she had during those sessions. For the visits from people interviewing Harper, her mother put on outfits she used to wear to work. She put on makeup. Her eyes were clear and her voice was steady; she'd told her family that she was weaning herself off the medication. Harper could tell that her father and Truman wanted to but didn't dare trust her mother's resolution.

But she herself could not have been more hopeful, even as she tried to defend against it. And this hope was what she tried to focus on, instead of the fear she felt as she repeated to Ramona what she'd told the others already: how she had separated herself from the other girls gathered on the ice that day, after Joy yelled at her, the harsh sound of the words exchanged between them causing Harper's head to start pounding. (This part was all true, but as she anticipated what was coming next and what she would have to say, her temples started to twitch all over again.)

"And did the police show you a photo array and ask you to pick out the man?" Ramona Frye poised her pen over a pad already half-filled with notes.

"No," Harper said, though she was not sure what "array" meant. "They showed me a picture and asked if he was the guy."

Ramona held up a finger. "Wait a minute, wait a minute," she said. "They showed you *a* picture? One?" She sounded excited and agitated at the same time, as she flipped through pages that looked like a police report. "They say here you picked him out of an array. A group of six photos."

Feeling her breath accelerate, Harper tried to tell herself that she wasn't the one in trouble now; the police *had* shown her only a single photograph. If that wasn't the way they were supposed to do it, that wasn't her fault.

"Sorry," she told Ramona. "It was just one."

Ramona had asked a few more questions after that, but

clearly her attention was not on Harper's replies, which made it easier for Harper to repeat the lie about the black man wearing a mask before he drove off. Had there been anything else going on with Joy that Harper wanted to mention, aside from her presumption that Joy had been involved in the selling of drugs? Some way Joy might have acted that seemed out of character for her?

She had not thought of it before in terms of any relevance it might have to Joy's death, but when Ramona put it that way, Harper remembered the day that she'd finally gotten the courage to take the SATs. Most of her class had already done so, but she'd let the first deadline pass without registering. The practice test was one thing—she hadn't timed herself on it, and it didn't really count. She knew her mother had been right in suggesting that Harper take a few of them before the actual test day, to make herself "more comfortable" when she sat down in the room with the pencils and the proctors, but she also knew that no matter how many questions she answered leading up to that point, it wouldn't help. Her brain would freeze, her breath would speed up, and she'd have to put her hand on her chest because it was the only way she could think of to try to calm it down. *Three pints of red dye and two pints of yellow make orange dye, and two pints of blue dye and one pint of yellow make green dye. If you mix equal amounts of green and orange, what percentage of the new mixture is yellow dye?* She would never feel anything other than panicked, let alone "comfortable," trying to answer *that*.

Truman dropped her off at the test center, a high school in Canandaigua, ten minutes before it was scheduled to begin. She'd asked him to get her there in plenty of time, but he refused to wake up when she told him he needed to. "Why are you taking it way the hell out here?" he asked her, but she didn't feel like explaining that she preferred to take the test surrounded by strangers, instead of the kids she saw every day. The people out here didn't know she was a loser, or that her mother was weird. Their not knowing might make her perform better. At least, that's what she hoped.

Late because of Truman's dawdling, she ran into the Canandaigua lobby with her nerves on fire. She was grateful to find that the line for early-alphabet last names was one of the shorter ones, and she made it through quickly after proffering her ID with a shaking hand. Rushing toward the girls' room, she knocked into someone standing in the end-of-the-alphabet line, and muttering *Sorry* with a quick glance backward, she did a double take at seeing that it was Joy.

"What are you doing here?" she asked, forgetting for a moment that she needed to pee, and also forgetting that since school had started, she wasn't sure if she and Joy were friends anymore.

Joy flushed, which Harper could see through her friend's effort to assume an unflustered expression. "Uh, taking SATs," she said, then tried to distract Harper from her confusion by adding (in what would once have been a jokey tone but now sounded at least halfway genuine) "Duh."

"But you already got a perfect score."

Over the speaker came the announcement that it was almost time, so Harper swallowed her next question—why, if Joy *was* taking the test again, she was doing so in Canandaigua instead of at home. Did she have some reason to stay anonymous, this time around? "You're in the wrong place," she said, just noticing then. "You should be in that one." She pointed at the line she'd just left, under the sign that said *A–L*.

"It's okay, they'll take me," Joy said, moving forward with her ID closed inside her fist. "They just want everybody in there now." She flicked her fingers toward the auditorium entrance, as if Harper were a bug she wanted to send that way. "You should go."

Harper joined the herd surging toward the doors, telling herself that needing to go to the bathroom was just mind over matter, she could hold it until they got a break. But when they were instructed to begin and she looked at the first essay prompt—*Is there any value in uncertainty? Plan and write an essay in which you develop your opinion on this issue*—all she could think about was how much she had to pee.

At the break she bolted for the bathroom, already knowing she would get a bad score and feeling hopeless about the remaining sections, including the one she was worst at, math. She considered calling Truman, just cutting her losses on this attempt and taking the test the next time. But he wasn't expecting her to need him for another three hours, so she was here for the duration; she might as well do her best to answer the questions and hope to get lucky.

Joy caught her arm on the way in and ushered her to the side of the auditorium. "Don't tell anyone you saw me here, okay?" Harper felt her heart lift from the touch and from the confiding nature of her tone; maybe Joy did still want to be her friend. "It's just that I didn't really do as well as I said," Joy went on, in a whisper. "The first time. But I couldn't tell people, since I knew I was supposed to get a good score." She gave Harper a smile, but it wasn't a real one; Harper could see the difference right away. Joy's next words sounded wry, self-deprecating ("deprecate" being one of the vocabulary words Harper had put on her flash cards): "I have my reputation to protect."

The thrill of receiving such a confession—the intimacy of it—lasted only a moment, but Harper still felt its warmth as they resumed their seats. Maybe whatever had been bothering Joy, and causing her to gravitate toward Delaney, had run its course; maybe there was still a chance that things would go back to the way they had been. Not long after, Joy offered to come over to Harper's house so they could study *The Odyssey*, and she told Harper about her mother's affair. Then, at the Halloween party, everything had fallen apart.

Ramona Frye took more notes as she listened to the story. "Does it mean anything?" Harper asked her. "I mean, *I* don't think it means anything—that she lied about getting a perfect score. She was only telling people what they expected to hear."

"We'll see," the lawyer said. She seemed to be choosing her words carefully as she began packing her notes away and stood to leave.

Harper's mother asked, "Where will I be sitting during the grand jury? Will I be close enough to hear everything?"

Ramona told her that she wouldn't be allowed in the room at all.

"What are you talking about? Of course I'm going to be there." Her mother looked at Harper as if she thought her daughter might be able to translate for her, as if she had misunderstood.

Ramona explained to them that in the grand jury room it was just the jury itself, the prosecutor, and the stenographer, along with any witnesses, who would enter one at a time.

"But I need to be there. *She* needs me." Her mother cast an imploring look at Harper, asking her to confirm this, and Harper nodded. But when Ramona said that she was sorry, there was nothing she could do about the rules, she felt secretly elated that her mother wouldn't be there when she told the lie again.

On Monday after Euro History, her mother picked her up from school to drive her to the courthouse. When Harper got in the car, she had to move the subpoena off the passenger seat. It was really little more than a letter; IN THE NAME OF THE PEOPLE OF THE STATE OF NEW YORK, it said, followed by

You are commanded to appear before the grand jury in
this district court as a witness in a criminal action against
Martin Willett.

Harper resisted the urge to crumple it and instead laid it on
the backseat. She could hardly remember—as her mother drove
toward the center of town—all those years that her mother refused to drive. She was adept at it now, even aggressive. She
parallel parked with ease in a spot only a block from the courthouse, which was decorated with elaborate wreaths and ribbons
to make up for the fact that the Town Board had voted to dis-
continue allowing the nativity scene that used to be displayed
after every Thanksgiving. Walking into the courthouse, they encountered the tree that had been featured on the news the whole
weekend because the board president had referred to it as a "holiday tree" instead of a "Christmas tree," setting off a controversy
that knocked the murder of Joy Enright down to second-head-
line status each night.

"If that isn't a Christmas tree, then I'm Hillary Clinton,"
Harper's mother said to the guard who greeted them and
checked their IDs before they could proceed. The guard looked
as if he wasn't sure how to respond, and Harper didn't blame
him. Her mother had been out of practice talking to strangers
for so long that she was rusty; when she did it now, her comments often came out making only skewed sense, or no sense at
all. For a moment Harper wanted her old, timid mother back,
then felt guilty about the impulse and focused instead on the
task before her, which she had avoided thinking about because
she did not know how to get herself out of the hole she was in.

Her mother gave her a kiss for luck outside the grand jury
room when the prosecutor came to get her. "Remember
everything so you can tell me later," she said, and Harper knew
she meant *for the book*.

She nodded mutely, wriggling to put distance between them. She was wearing a skirt her mother had bought her for the occasion, and it made her waist itch, but her mother had told her not to scratch. The prosecutor came up to them and clapped his hands together, as if preparing to dig into a good meal. "Are we ready?" he asked, and Harper nodded again as her mother told him, "Absolutely we are." Her mother asked him if there might not be some special allowance for her to accompany her daughter into the courtroom, "considering her age and what's being asked of her." *Say no*, Harper willed him, and when he did, making sure to sound apologetic as if he'd like nothing better, too, she muttered thanks as she followed him into the room.

When he'd come to interview her with his assistant, a woman who used a pink pen with a feather on the end, Mr. Kovak had worn black jeans and a sweater vest as he asked her the same questions, more or less, as the police and then Martin Willett's attorney. He was a man who might have been her father's age. He had less hair than her father, but his features moved in his face more, and she had no trouble hearing his voice, whereas she usually had to ask her father to repeat whatever he said. Today she saw that Mr. Kovak also seemed comfortable wearing a jacket and tie; the only time she'd ever seen her father in a jacket was at her grandmother's funeral.

"Nothing to worry about. Honey," Mr. Kovak whispered, the clumsy endearment an apparent afterthought. "It's natural to feel nervous, but you'll be fine." The jurors were already seated, and she sensed them looking at her. "We'll get started in a few minutes. I'll say your name, you'll come up, and we'll establish who you are. Then just answer my questions. Tell me the same things you told me when we talked at your house, and you'll be done in no time."

Walking up to the stand, her legs trembled and she put a hand out to the railing to help herself into the seat. But Mr. Kovak asked her to stand to get sworn in. She had thought she'd need to put her hand on a Bible, so she felt momentary relief when all they wanted her to do was hold her hand up and say yes. A few feet away from her, the court reporter clicked quietly as Mr. Kovak asked Harper her name, her age, and a few questions about her friendship with Joy. There were more people in the jury box than Harper expected. A few of them took notes, but most merely stared at her.

Counting silently as a way of letting her mind do something other than recognize the impossible situation she was in, she felt a tightness in her chest and hoped she might be having a heart attack. If she went ahead and did what Mr. Kovak had said—answered his questions as she had when she was not under oath—she'd be helping to send to trial a man she believed had not been the one to kill Joy. (She'd thought this from the beginning, remembering how Martin Willett had smiled at her as she hung on the pay phone waiting for Truman to pick up. But then she convinced herself that it was stupid to think somebody might not murder somebody else, just because he had smiled at you. Who was she to say whether he was guilty or innocent? That was for a jury to decide.

But then she remembered that if she hadn't agreed to say she'd seen him wearing a mask, he might not even have been arrested. But then she thought, *Maybe they have other evidence I don't know about. Maybe he really did do it, and I should play my part in punishing the man who killed my friend.* This was the way her mind had been battling itself for weeks.)

Now here she was, *a witness in a criminal action against Martin Willett.* Beyond helping to ruin an innocent man's life if she repeated the lie, she'd be setting herself up for perjury charges, which (she'd looked up online) meant they could send her to jail for three years.

If she *didn't* give the answers they were expecting, the district attorney's office would be mad at her. But that wasn't the worst of it: the worst would be disappointing her mother. And she didn't even want to think about what people would say at school.

"Let's talk about the day Joy disappeared," the prosecutor was saying suddenly, and she snapped back to attention. "I know it's not easy, but we need you to describe what happened after you left Joy and the other girls on the ice and went up to the shack."

She could do this without compromising herself. Almost eagerly she leaned forward and said, "I needed to use the phone. To call my brother."

"Right. Okay. So you call him to come get you, and then what?" As he spoke he opened his hands in front of him, as if spreading the pages of a big book. The jurors who'd been taking notes stopped writing to look up in anticipation of her response.

Harper paused, manufacturing a lump of phlegm in her throat. "Could I get a drink of water?"

"Sure." Mr. Kovak was doing his best not to appear annoyed, she could tell, though he didn't succeed entirely. His assistant rummaged loudly in a bag at her feet, twisted open a bottle, then came forward to hand it to Harper. She took a long drink, her hands and mouth shaking, and water dripped down her chin.

The prosecutor gave her a tissue, waited for her to wipe her face. "Okay. You were about to tell us what you saw while you were outside the shack waiting for your brother."

"I saw a man come out. He got in his car and made a phone call." Though she knew better, part of her thought that maybe if she said it all fast, nobody would notice what she'd left out.

"Okay. And you were able to identify this man when police interviewed you? The man was Martin Willett?" She nodded. "We need you to say it out loud," he told her.

"Yes. I didn't know his name then, but that's who it was."

"And after he made the phone call while sitting in his car, before he drove away, did he do something else?"

She pictured her mother shifting anxiously on the bench outside the grand jury room, and forgot the question.

"So *what else* did Martin Willett do before he started the car and drove off?" Now the prosecutor seemed less committed to concealing his impatience, as he took a step closer and tried to make eye contact with her.

"I can't," she whispered, looking down and twisting the skirt fabric in her hands. Then she gave up and pulled the waistband aside to dig at the itch with her fingernails. "I can't do it."

"It's okay," he told her, though clearly it was anything but. He made a *calm down* motion with his hands, and she sensed it was directed at himself as much as at her. He turned to the jury and said, "Just give us a minute, this is a hard thing for a child." Then he moved right up to the stand so that only she could hear him. "What's the matter?"

"I can't," she repeated. "I can't say it, about the mask."

"Why not?" The hiss got away from him, and she looked up to see that the jurors had heard.

She took care to keep her own voice to a whisper, a mighty task given what she felt as the words erupted and then emerged. "Because I lied! I didn't see him. I mean, I saw him, but he wasn't wearing a mask. He smiled at me, he got in his car, he made a phone call, and he drove away. I'm sorry, but that's the real truth."

Their eyes were locked now. His nostrils flared, and for a brief, panicked minute, she imagined him lifting a hand to slap her. Instead he only retreated a few steps, took a breath, and turned back to the jurors. "Okay, Miss Grove," he said. "Let's summarize your testimony. We've established that you saw Martin Willett at the scene of your friend Joy's disappearance on November thirteenth. Is that right?"

"Yes." She said it emphatically, an effort to redeem her failure to be the witness he'd counted on.

"Okay." Mr. Kovak made a movement with his mouth that she couldn't read—residual anger, or maybe just resignation. "With our thanks for your appearance today, you are excused."

She left the stand and headed swiftly for the exit that would lead her back to the hall. She had no idea what she would tell her mother now, but she did not want to remain in this room a moment longer than was required.

Before she could reach the door, the clerk who'd admitted her came in and whispered something to Mr. Kovak's assistant, who then stood to beckon the prosecutor over to confer.

Despite her eagerness to leave, Harper paused to watch. Did this have something to do with her? She heard the jurors murmuring, and then Mr. Kovak swore and rubbed at his forehead. He approached the jury box and said, "People, I'm sorry to have to inform you that due to an unforeseen development in this case, we are also excusing you from this proceeding. Sit tight for a moment, if you would. The clerk will let you know whether there's another case for you today, or if you get to go finish your holiday shopping." He tried to smile, but it didn't come off because he was so obviously rattled by whatever he had just heard.

The murmurs were louder this time as the jurors looked at one another and then back at the prosecutor, appearing confused. Mr. Kovak packed his papers up and brushed past Harper into the hall. When she saw her mother rise and head toward him, she rushed toward the restroom in the other direction.

She returned ten minutes later. The hallway was empty except for the guard and her mother; the prosecutor was gone. Harper waited for her mother to say something, and when she didn't, she followed her out to the perfectly parked car, no words passing between them.

They sat beside each other, the keys dangling from the ignition. "Aren't we going to go home?" Harper asked.

Her mother shook her head, but she was not answering the question, Harper knew. "I don't understand," her mother said. "You lied about what you saw? You *didn't* see that man that day?"

"No. I mean, yes. I saw him. The lie was about the mask—I didn't see that. He didn't have one." She looked ahead through the windshield as she spoke. There was more relief to telling the truth than she had imagined.

"But I don't understand." Her mother's hands remained folded in the lap of her coat. "Why would you do something like that?"

Harper shrugged. Was it possible she might get away with acting as if she didn't know the answer herself?

Instead her mother said, "That's not how we raised you. We didn't raise you to be a liar."

The relief and release Harper had felt dissolved in an instant, hot indignation taking their place. "I did it because I saw what it did to *you*!" For a moment, she worried that her words might strike her mother like a physical blow. But her mother only looked puzzled, her hands twitching in her lap. Before she could say again that she didn't understand, Harper rode the force of her own fury and added, "This is the first time we've seen you like this—*normal*—since, I don't know, years. Don't you know I'd do anything I could to make that happen? So would Tru. So would Dad. There just hasn't been a way, until now." It all sped through her so fast, and took so much energy, that she thought she might have to lower her head to her knees.

"Oh. *Oh*," her mother said. They were little expressions of pain, Harper realized.

She asked, "Should I drive?" She wanted nothing more than for the car to start and for them to be moving away from this place.

Her mother shook her head slowly and turned the key. They drove home in silence, except for the exclamation her mother made when the light turned green and someone beeped behind her. Harper was tempted to feel sorry for her, until she remembered being called a liar. What right did her mother have to be mad at *her*?

At the kitchen table, her mother dropped into a seat with her coat still on and cradled her forehead between her fingers. "You don't understand. It's not that easy," she told Harper, who replied, "Yeah, well. Neither is this." Without giving either of them a chance to define "it" or "this," she left the room and, when that wasn't far away enough, left the house. Only when she made it outside did she realize she'd been clenching her stomach from the moment she left her history classroom. She went back in long enough to rip off the itchy skirt and put on something that made it easier to breathe.

Quickening

The day the grand jury was scheduled to get Martin Willett's case, Alison woke up moaning. For a moment, Tom thought that it was just her usual dread of the workweek. But when she sat up clutching her middle, he knew it was more than that, and fumbled frantically for his phone. A few hours later, after the emergency-room doctors had run their tests, he and Alison were told that her pain had nothing to do with the pregnancy. It was just indigestion, the doctor said, or possibly a trace of food poisoning.

"But the baby's okay?" Alison asked, still lying on the exam table. Tom felt pierced by the measure of agitation in her face, and reached to brush a piece of stray hair from her forehead.

"He's fine," the doctor said. "You'll start feeling him move soon, if you haven't already." He left the room brusquely, seeming not to notice the effect of his words. Their regular obstetrician knew they wanted to be surprised by the gender, but in the anxiety of what had brought them to the hospital, they'd forgotten to let this doctor know.

"Quickening," the nurse explained, seeing their expressions. "That's what it's called when the baby moves."

They were halfway home, both stunned by and savoring the news that they were going to have a son, when Alison's cell phone rang, identifying Helen as the caller. Tom felt a presentiment of what was to come—it announced itself in the form of a chill that began in his throat and threatened to choke him, but he managed to cough it away—and the next few moments played out exactly as he expected: Alison telling her mother to slow down, to calm down, to slow down again. Then listening without speaking, before she turned to Tom and held the phone away from her mouth long enough to whisper, "They arrested my father—go, go," and him whispering back, "Where?" because she could have meant either her parents' house or the police station, and she waved with alarmed fury in the direction of the house. He pulled a careful U-turn, pretending not to notice Alison's next motion with her hands telling him to speed it up—now that he knew he was driving not only himself and his wife but the bundle of skin and cells that was growing into their son, it occurred to him as it never had before that every time he drove this truck, he operated a weapon potentially lethal not only to anyone in his path but to him and his passengers, as well.

Even with his caution, they arrived within minutes. Helen rushed out to meet them crying out, "You're too late! They already took him!" and Tom did his best to look as if he had no idea what she might be talking about.

"Who?" Alison asked. "Who came, Mom? Who took him? What did they say?" They led her back into the house, each guiding her by an elbow. Tom had never seen his mother-in-law looking so—what was the word?—*disheveled*, he thought, for a perverse moment imagining that Alison would be proud of his vocabulary if she knew what was in his mind. The Helen he'd always known held things in: her breath and emotions both. Her hair and clothing were always in place, like her words and her actions. Aside from the night last summer when he'd walked in on her swigging wine straight from the bottle, Tom had never seen anything resembling fear in her face.

But there was fear now, beside the anger. "State guys," she said, as Alison put water on for tea with unsteady hands. "Troopers. He'd come home for lunch early, we had the leftover ziti. He must have eaten too much because he lay down on the couch for a little nap, and that's when they came to—arrest him." She stumbled in saying "arrest."

"Did Dad know them?" Alison asked. "Were they guys he knew?" It was a question that didn't make sense to Tom, and he saw Helen puzzling over it, too. Then he realized that she was envisioning the scene, her father accosted in his own home by men who'd entered uninvited, charged by some authority to intrude and then remove him against his will. Did she think it would be better or worse if those men were familiar to her father? Did she allow herself to imagine that, if they'd met before and maybe shared a beer or a laugh or a resentment against a common superior, Doug wouldn't mind so much their carting him off, and might even try to make light of the whole thing? *What a fucking joke*, Tom could hear him saying, doing his best to engage their camaraderie.

Or would it work the other way if they all knew each other, Doug averting his eyes and the troopers also looking elsewhere as they snapped on the cuffs? "Did they use handcuffs?" he asked Helen, before she could respond to Alison's question about whether the men were acquainted.

She looked at him so blankly that for a moment he wondered if he'd only heard the words in his mind, and not spoken them. But just as he was about to repeat himself, she said, "Yes, they used handcuffs. They took him out of here like a criminal."

Alison set down the teacup before her mother, who looked at it but did not move.

"Do something," Alison told him, and of course Tom could not tell her that he already had.

Returning the call Tom had made to the district attorney's office the day before, saying it was urgent, Nelson Kovak asked, "This can't wait? We go to the grand jury tomorrow," and Tom said, "That's why I need to see you tonight."

He thought he'd heard Kovak groan over the phone before saying, "I can't come to you," and Tom told him that was fine, that was better, he'd meet him at the prosecutor's office. After supper he told Alison he had to check on a delivery at the shack and drove to the courthouse office building. Though he knew he was being paranoid, he parked the truck in back so nobody driving by would see it and wonder what Tom Carbone was doing at the criminal division.

He began telling Kovak and his assistant, a woman named Tabitha, what Delaney Stowell had said to him after Joy's funeral. Tabitha took notes with a pink feathered pen while Kovak asked questions. Though both of them were obviously trying not to let on how surprised they were by each new revelation, Tom could sense the growing uneasiness in the room. He understood why: until he'd called them, the prosecutor had been preparing a case against Martin Willett. After he told them about Joy blackmailing Doug, Kovak said, "Wait a minute. Jesus Christ. You found this out Friday? And you're just telling us now?"

Tom looked down at the table, where his fingers were twitching. "I know," he said. "You have to understand, this is my father-in-law."

Kovak made a clucking sound like *So what?* When they were finished, he left the room without shaking Tom's hand. Tabitha told him not to feel bad, her boss was always that way. "And just so you know, but this is between us," she said, placing the pink feather cap back on her pen, "you're not the only one to come in and talk to us about this guy. Armstrong."

Tom started. "Who else? What did they say?" But Tabitha indicated she'd already told him too much, putting a vertical finger against her mouth. *Active investigation*, she said.

"But you're still going through with the grand jury tomorrow? With Willett?"

"Well, that's the plan. It's already lined up, and we don't have anything firm on Armstrong. They want an indictment before the holidays."

"But if he's not the right guy—"

"Trust me," Tabitha said. "Nelson's a lot of things, but he won't prosecute if he doesn't have a case. Or if somebody else ends up looking better for it than Willett. We're just not at that point yet."

Tom headed for the shack instead of home and checked on a delivery that didn't need checking, so he could tell himself he hadn't lied to Alison. He made sure he didn't return until after she was asleep. He didn't sleep at all himself, figuring that Kovak had set things in motion and that the police would be making the move on Doug at any time.

But he'd forgotten about it in the rush to the hospital and then the news about the baby, so when the call came from Helen as they left the doctor's office, he felt almost as blindsided as Alison.

They persuaded Helen to come with them back to the duplex, so the reporters wouldn't be able to track her down right away. Alison offered more tea, but Helen asked, "Do you have any wine?" When Alison laughed, thinking it was a joke, Helen repeated it.

Alison shot Tom a look of confused dismay. He knew what she was thinking: that her mother might be having a stroke, or that her cognitive abilities had been compromised by the trauma of watching her husband arrested in front of her.

"No, we don't have any wine, Mom," Alison said in a light voice, still trying to jolly her mother back to herself. "And even if we did, you don't drink, remember?"

"He could go get me some." Helen jerked a thumb toward Tom, the most indelicate gesture he'd ever seen her make.

Finally Alison seemed to understand that her mother might be serious. Her features collapsed. "I'm not sending him out to get wine for a sober person. Do you think I'd stand here and watch you pour ten years down the drain?"

Helen raised her hand at Tom. "Tell her," she said.

"Tell me what?" Alison made the now-familiar gesture of putting her hand over her abdomen.

"I'm *not* sober." Now Helen made a laughing sound herself, though it was clear she felt anything but amused.

"What are you talking about?"

When Helen didn't answer, Tom went over to put an arm around his wife, but she flung it off and said, "What the hell's going on here?"

He said, "There was this night last summer I walked into the kitchen—"

"Oh, for God's sake. It was way before that." Helen swung her legs onto the couch, lay down, and covered her forehead with the tastefully manicured fingers of her left hand, her engagement and wedding rings clinking against her glasses. When her skirt hitched around her hips and she didn't smooth it down immediately, Tom knew she had given up.

"Do you want me to call Dr. Stowell?" he asked, realizing only after he said it that Alison didn't know about her mother being in treatment with Delaney's father, and that he himself knew it only because it was part of everything Delaney had told him about Doug after the funeral.

"Why would she want you to call *him*?" But it was dawning on Alison even as she asked the question, Tom saw, that

Geoffrey Stowell might be trying to help Helen get sober again. Instead of focusing on this fact, Alison turned to accuse Tom: "How would you know that and I don't?"

"I didn't. It was just a guess," he said lamely, knowing that he would eventually have two choices: either undo this lie and tell her everything (including his role in her father's arrest), or keep the truth to himself and do his best to forget it. In that instant, he recognized that his marriage could not survive either choice, in the first case because Alison would refuse to live with him, and in the second because he would not be able to live with himself.

It struck him like a sucker punch: there was no way out. Later, he would identify this as the moment he knew the marriage was over. But at the time he refused to accept it, thinking instead about how they were all going to get through the next few hours.

"A guess, my ass," Alison muttered, but on the couch her mother was muttering, too—*oh my God, oh my God*—and Alison turned her attention to her.

Tom went into the bedroom and—setting the volume low so that the women wouldn't hear—turned on the TV, where the local station broke into its regular programming to carry the story. State police had arrested the Chilton interim police chief, Douglas Armstrong, for witness tampering and obstruction of justice in the case of Joy Enright's murder.

Further charges, possibly including second-degree murder, were pending.

Holy shit. Hearing the last sentence, Tom sucked in his breath. Before speaking with Delaney, he'd assumed that Doug's pursuit of Martin Willett—the "hard-on" he had for the black man, to use Delaney's word—resulted from his desire to get a conviction in the case, believing it would make him a shoo-in for permanent chief. Delaney had been the one to suggest there might be more to Doug's zealousness, but Tom hadn't been able to swallow the idea that his father-in-law would go as far as killing someone (especially a teenage girl) to get what he wanted. He hadn't mentioned Delaney's suspicions to the DA.

But somehow, they'd found out what Delaney knew, either from the girl herself or through their own legwork.

"Police have not released information about a possible motive for Armstrong's actions," the anchorwoman said, "but a source close to the investigation says it is believed the victim may have threatened to expose the interim chief for deliberately concealing a family member's DUI arrest and then wiping it from the books. Such an act, if discovered, would likely not only have prevented Armstrong from being named permanent chief but led to criminal charges."

The anchor ended the report by saying that grand jury proceedings against the previous suspect in the case, Martin Willett, had been suspended, with charges vacated against him after the police chief's alleged wrongdoings had come to light. Tom turned off the TV, imagining through his own held breath what Willett must be feeling right now. He was glad he'd played a role in exonerating an innocent man, but had it been worth what he'd sacrificed? What about the vow he'd taken, *forsaking all others*? Why couldn't he just be that guy who stood up for his family because they were family, whether they deserved it or not?

But if he'd learned anything by now, it was how pointless it was to pretend to be something you weren't. He left the bedroom. Alison sat with her feet tucked beneath her, across from where her mother still lay on the couch. "Where do you think he is right now?" Helen was saying. "A cell somewhere? Alone, or with other people? You know how he gets in confined spaces. He'll have a heart attack."

Alison murmured sympathetically, "It won't be that long, Mom. He'll be released on his own recognizance."

Tom couldn't tell, after he joined them, whether the women wanted him there or not. His own instinct was to leave them alone, but Alison might accuse him later of abandoning her, so warily he took the chair across from his wife and asked, "Did you tell her the news?"

"News?" From her prone position, Helen turned to look at him and gave a bitter guffaw. "I can't take any more news."

"Mom. We found out we're having a boy." Alison leaned forward, touching the skin on her stomach covering the baby. Tom could tell how much she wanted the information to please her mother, to distract her even momentarily from the disaster of the day.

At first Helen registered no response, as if she hadn't even heard her daughter. Then she said, "God help him," and turned away from them, pressing her face into the couch.

Mary Krismis

"Who was that?" Gil asked. When Susanne hung up the phone and kept her back to him, she could feel him already dreading whatever it was she would turn to say.

And how to say it? The obligation to convey the information was a blessing of sorts, she would realize later, distracting her as it did from the information itself. It was a state trooper from Rochester, she told him, calling to say that they had arrested Douglas Armstrong that morning. The trooper gave her a few details, which she listened to without interrupting, before saying they would be in touch with any further developments.

"They called, instead of coming? At least Armstrong always came to notify us in person." Hearing him say this, Susanne realized that Gil was indulging in his own form of distraction. "At least he had the decency to do that."

"Decency? *Decency?* Are you listening to yourself?"

"What did they arrest *him* for?" They'd just finished a lunch of frozen pizza, which they had not had the patience or interest to cook all the way through, and when he looked at her she saw that Gil had a piece of mozzarella sticking to his chin. She didn't tell him.

"They just said they'd taken him into custody in connection

with the case. Preliminary charges now, but he said there would probably be more. Possibly including murder." She said the word as easily as she said her own name now; she had learned to do it without thinking of Joy at the same time. "And they've dropped the charges against Martin."

"They're saying *Armstrong* killed her?" She wasn't sure he'd even heard the part about Martin. When she shrugged, Gil said, "God, Susanne, didn't you pay attention?"

"I *was* paying attention." She knew he didn't mean to sound as if he were accusing her, but still it took some effort to refrain from snapping back at him. "They said they might add other charges later. And yes, they used the word 'murder.'"

It would not be long before they learned the particulars: faced with the accusation of withholding possible evidence, the second arresting officer, Raul Dominguez, had told the FBI he believed that Doug may have planted the ski mask in the drawer at Martin Willett's home after instructing Dominguez to remain with the suspect in another room while he searched the kitchen. In the cruiser on the way to Willett's house, Dominguez said further, it was possible he'd seen Doug tucking something (black, soft, bulky) into the pocket of his uniform jacket.

Susanne and Gil liked Dominguez; he'd been the one to return the Mazda to them, after Joy disappeared, rather than make them retrieve it from the pond themselves. "I can't see any reason for him to lie about the mask," Susanne said when they learned of his FBI statement, and Gil agreed.

The investigators knew that a teenage girl, the victim's friend, had been scheduled to testify to the grand jury about seeing Willett in a ski mask outside the shack, but they considered her a weak witness, especially in light of the fact that the original person who'd claimed to see the mask—the clerk at the Elbow Room— was essentially a vagrant who couldn't be trusted, even if the police had been able to locate him.

After the trooper's phone call informing them of the chief's arrest, Gil wadded pizza crust between two fingers and said slowly, "I never did like Armstrong—I didn't *trust* him—but what motive would he have to kill her?"

"They said she was blackmailing him." Susanne could not believe she was saying such a thing about her own daughter, but it was the word the trooper had used. "His daughter, the English teacher, got arrested for drunk driving, and Joy found out about it. He was trying to shut her up. At least, that's what they think it might be."

"Blackmailing? No. I don't believe that. That's not the kind of girl she is." Susanne had noticed that they took turns slipping into the present tense. Then he surprised her by adding, "*Goddammit.* I wanted it to be Willett."

"Why?"

"I already hated him. Now I have to hate two people, and probably even feel sorry for—your lover"—she could tell he'd tried but failed to resist using the phrase—"because of what he went through. If he *is* innocent." He tossed the crushed crust back into the box. "You haven't been in touch with him, have you?"

"No." Of course she didn't add that she'd thought about it every day since his arrest, wanting to see and hear Martin tell her what she had almost consistently assumed and now knew for sure, which was that his arrest had been a mistake. (Though was "mistake" the word he would use? she wondered.) "I think I will now, though. Just to—I mean, if it's all right with you."

He blinked at her. "You're coming with me tonight, right?" It took her a moment to recognize that he was not doing what it sounded like—saying that if she accompanied him to the dinner for families of residents at Belle Meadow, he would condone her seeing Martin one last time.

She reached over finally to brush the string of pizza cheese from his chin. "Yes."

He was looking directly at her, and she could tell he was trying to read her the way he might read an electrical emergency or some other problem he'd been called in to fix. Trying to assess how much damage lay underneath what could be seen. She stood and began clearing the table, feeling that whatever was allowing her to function, at that moment, wouldn't survive further scrutiny.

She had no desire to go to the nursing home's Holly-Day Extravaganza, but she knew it wouldn't be fair to send Gil alone. He took the first shower, after which Susanne found her husband standing in front of the bureau mirror, looking agitated as he pressed his damp hair to his head.

"What?" she asked. "You look fine." She was not accustomed to him worrying about his appearance.

"It's not that."

"What, then?"

"I just suddenly realized where my mother lives." He didn't turn to her as he spoke but addressed her in his mirrored reflection. "Don't ever let me end up in a place like that," he said, as he had said so many times since Emilia was admitted. "Really, Suse. I mean it. Shoot me first."

"Okay," she said, as she always did, though of course she did not mean it.

It was a luxury she wished for herself—to think about something other than the fact that their daughter was dead. At Belle Meadow, after they had been admitted by Mr. Trujillo, Harry or Hairy grazed the back of Susanne's heels, and Susanne jumped away with a cry.

"Don't worry," Mr. Trujillo consoled her, "that whole death thing is just a myth, you know," but she'd already started toward the restroom to calm herself, a hand to her heart.

Earlier, after they'd learned of Doug Armstrong's arrest, Susanne asked Gil if he wanted to go get a tree. He looked at her as if she were speaking another language—the language of insanity—before he realized she was serious, shook his head, and said, "The one at BM will be enough." When Joy was alive, he'd scolded her about her nickname for Belle Meadow. But since her death, they both referred to it as nothing but.

The tree in the nursing home lobby stretched to the ceiling, its branches sprayed with white. Every resident's family had been invited to provide an ornament. After being assured that they would get it back, Gil wanted to contribute the one Joy had made in kindergarten—a wreath of green-colored paper with the painstakingly printed words MARY KRISMIS in the center, surrounded by glued-on cranberry beads—but Susanne wouldn't let him.

In the Solarium, they sat with Emilia and the other inmates. When his mother pointed at Gil and said, "Where's your girlfriend?" he did his best to force a smile, gestured at Susanne, and told her, "You mean my wife. She's right there."

"No, not that one. The other girl." Emilia shook her head. "My sister. The one with the black hair but it used to be yellow."

"You mean your granddaughter," Gil said, but his voice broke on the word and they had to leave the meal early, barely making it back home before Gil threw up in the sink. Susanne put him to bed and insisted on taking his temperature, as if what he was sick with was a virus or a germ. The reading was normal, but her husband fell into a sleep so deep it might have been a coma, and she watched him with envy until it occurred to her that this would be the best time for the call she'd been waiting to make.

Identify All Parts

Tom and Alison supported Helen between them, each holding an elbow, at Doug's arraignment. She kept insisting she didn't need them there, but she was wobbly enough (*hungover* enough, Tom thought, though he and Alison had not discussed her mother's breach of sobriety after Helen demanded Tom drive her home the day before, following Doug's arrest) that Tom was afraid to let her stand when, after Doug pleaded "Not guilty" to the charges of obstruction of justice and witness tampering, the judge announced bail and the bailiff began leading Doug out. Tom expected his father-in-law to turn toward them all, the way defendants did on TV, but instead he kept his steely eyes straight ahead. If he noticed the sound of Helen whispering his name from ten yards away, he didn't show it. "Don't worry," Alison pleaded with her mother. "They'll bring him home in a few hours; you can talk to him then."

Alison wanted to stay with her mother until her father's release, but Tom convinced her that they should leave her parents alone. "Who knows what kind of a mood he'll be in," he said. "And anyway, what can we do?"

Doug's run as the top cop in Chilton, and a pillar of the town's foundation, had come to an abrupt and unsavory end.

Even if he managed to get acquitted on covering up Alison's arrest for drunk driving and the DA decided not to prosecute for anything else, his reputation had been damaged beyond repair.

But that wasn't what Tom cared about. Really what he was afraid of was that sooner or later, Doug would find out about Tom's betrayal. Once he learned that Tom had gone to the DA about him, Alison would find out, too. And though Tom would have given anything to believe she'd side with him if it came to that, he was pretty sure he knew better.

At home, he suggested that Alison help him assemble the crib to distract herself from worrying about her parents. Despite the fact that she considered it bad luck to spend too much time preparing a nursery that far ahead, in the end he persuaded her and they laid out all the pieces on the floor of the extra bedroom. They got as far as the first instruction—"Identify all parts"—before Alison, kneeling beside their future baby's bed, bent over and began sobbing into her hands.

"It's okay," Tom told her, going over to rub her back. Of course it was anything but okay, but he had no idea what else to say. "What's the matter?"

There was so much the matter that his own words struck him as absurd.

"Why is everything falling apart, right when I'm trying to pull myself together?" She pulled away from him to slump against the wall. "My mother's drinking again. Fantastic. Every night she went to those meetings with me and said, 'Hi, I'm Helen, I'm an alcoholic.' And held hands with those people and said the prayer. A fraud is what she is. A fucking *liar*."

There was a time he would have taken heart to hear this. But by now he knew it would not last, her anger at her mother. Helen would apologize, and Alison would forgive her, because to do otherwise meant risking more than she knew how to. "And why are these people persecuting my father?" She gestured across the room as if *these people* were standing in the corner. "What did he ever do to them?"

Tom lowered himself next to her, understanding that when he stood up again, he would be a different man. "Al, I have to tell you something. You're not going to like it, but all I'm asking is that you wait till I'm finished before you say anything."

She put her hands over her ears like a child. It was the gestural equivalent of avoiding news broadcasts, which she'd done ever since her father's arrest. "No. Whatever it is, I don't want to hear it. Not now, Tom. Please—I'm begging you."

But now that he'd started, he could not pull it back. And to her credit (he'd always known she was stronger than she herself believed), Alison remained in the room and listened. He began with the day Susanne Enright called to solicit his help in finding Joy and ended with the same story he'd told Nelson Kovak—everything he'd learned from Delaney Stowell after Joy's funeral.

Alison hugged her knees to her chest as she took it in, but he could not tell what effect it was having on her. When he finished, he leaned back against the wall, exhausted. She heaved in a deep breath. "You're saying he did those things first because of my mother and then because of me," she said. "Right? Protecting Delaney's father, for my mother's sake, by not arresting Zach Tully when Delaney stole a scrip for him. And then covering up my arrest." Her voice dropped in shame on the last word.

Well, for his own sake, too, Tom thought, but did not say it. *Looks better for a permanent chief not to have drunks in the family, especially when they've made such a big deal about being sober.*

The night of Joy Enright's funeral, he'd confronted his wife with what Delaney Stowell had told him—that despite Alison's best efforts to fool them all into believing she'd been a teetotaler since the night of her first miscarriage, he knew she'd continued drinking, even at school. That the champagne the day of her accident had not been, as she'd told him, the first sip in years—

a "private celebration" of the successful pregnancy. That he doubted it had even been champagne she was drunk on, when she drove Keith Nance off Reservoir Road; that the next day, when she was too vague in answering his questions about what she'd done with the champagne bottle, he'd thought to look in the flour canister (as in the old days), and there were six plastic nips of vodka lined up in a circle like toy soldiers in a ring. He'd gotten rid of them without mentioning it to Alison, waiting to see if she'd notice their absence and tell him she knew he'd discovered her secret. She never did, which made him believe that she had not looked in the canister again after the day of the accident. He was certain she had not taken another drink; he was on the lookout—as vigilant now as he had been neglectful before—but besides that, he could tell how profoundly it had shaken her to understand the extent to which she had deluded herself as well as the rest of them, and to come so close to losing her baby, the thing she'd always wanted most.

She did not seem surprised that he'd found out. In fact, she said she was relieved. Tom knew it would make more sense for him to feel angry, but instead he was confused. "If you feel relieved," he said, "then why didn't you tell me yourself?"

"I kept thinking I would. I wanted to. But I could never bring myself to follow through."

With trepidation he asked, "*Why* did you do it?" When she knew what drinking like that could do to a person; when she'd seen the consequences in her own home. When she knew what she was risking. Was it him? On the last question he felt something like a sob escape with the words, but he managed to turn it into a cough.

She shook her head, and now it was he who felt the relief. There was no single answer, she said. "It's just these giant waves of dread, and drinking was the only thing that made them smaller, kept them farther away." She wrapped her arms around herself. "I can feel them coming before I actually feel *them*, but there's no way to stop it. It's the scariest thing in the world."

This hurt to hear: she'd told him once, back when they were in high school, that sitting or standing or lying next to Tom was like being sheltered by a big, soft wall. She felt safe there, she said, and he wanted to tuck her into his side as when he pulled the football close on those rare occasions it was clear he was going to take a sack, all those guys rushing at him in an effort to bring him down, trying to slap the ball out of his clutch.

Her saying this (and his remembering it since) was what had convinced him that they were together because of more than a charitable impulse on her part. But what did it mean that the big, soft wall had collapsed in the years since then, and he was the last to know?

"I get his lying for us," Alison said, and Tom sensed she regretted having to admit that her father had lied. "I don't even think that's so bad." He waited for her to ask what *he* thought about it; as it turned out, though, she knew better. "But that other stuff. You can't honestly believe he planted a mask in the black guy's drawer, can you? Why would he do something like that?"

"I think he panicked about how the board's vote would go." Tom knew she could guess this herself but somehow needed him to say it. "And it might not have been his idea to begin with—he might have gotten it from Cliff."

"Who?" She looked annoyed, as if he were puzzling her on purpose.

"Pothead Pete. He didn't like the black guy. So when Joy went missing and the police came to interview him, he said he'd seen Willett wearing a mask. I think maybe Doug just saw his chance and grabbed it." Maybe it would hurt less, Tom reasoned, if he said "Doug" instead of "your father."

But Alison was not capable, it seemed, of hurting less when

it came to her father. "You knew all this. And didn't tell me. Instead, you told the DA." She struggled to lift herself up and he moved to help her, but she waved him away. "Get out."

"I'm not going anywhere."

"Then *I* will. Actually, that's a better idea, anyway." She left the baby's bedroom and went to their own, where she began jerking open drawers. Tom followed and caught her gently by the wrists.

"You can't leave."

"The hell I can't."

"But—I don't want you to." He knew how feeble this sounded, but it was the truth.

"You should have thought of that before you went around accusing my father of terrible things." She barely got the words out before she collapsed on the edge of the bed in fresh sobs.

He sat beside her, feeling encouraged when she didn't push him away. "But he *did* those things. I *had* to tell. You don't see that?"

"All I see is you've always hated my father." She clenched her fists as she sat beside him.

"That's not true. If anything, he's hated *me*."

"And the minute you get a chance," she went on, as if he hadn't spoken, "you stab him in the back."

She'd regret it later when she remembered saying this to him, he knew. Her lip trembled and she took a deep breath that looked as if it hurt her both going in and coming out.

Tom could have pointed out that everything her father was suffering he'd brought upon himself. He could have told her what he'd learned through a text that morning from Natalie—that the state guys had flagged a ten-thousand-dollar cash withdrawal Doug made back in November, the morning after receiving a call from a cell phone registered to Joy Enright, whom he'd arrested at Belle Meadow a few hours before she made the call. Circumstantial, of course. But what was it Doug had said, back when it was Martin Willett's life on the line? *You got the right circumstances, you got a guilty guy.*

He could have said all these things, but he knew Alison wouldn't be able to hear them. Instead, he let her go without a fight.

She remained with her parents for the next two days, without calling him. It was only as he was driving from the shack to meet up with Natalie after her dispatch shift that he heard, on the radio, the news that Doug Armstrong had apparently fled the state with his wife and was being sought as a fugitive.

His heart skidding, he pulled over and called Alison, but she didn't pick up. He drove to Doug and Helen's and found her sitting in front of the TV—not the news, but a rerun of *Buffy the Vampire Slayer*—and eating directly from a pint of Rocky Road. She looked up and said, "You need to knock now." When Tom failed to respond because he was in the process of recognizing that instead of being upset and shocked over her parents' escape, she must have helped them in it, she added, "You need to be invited."

There were four border bridges within a couple of hours of Chilton. But Doug wouldn't be foolish enough to try those, Tom knew. Neither would he risk driving to the eastern part of the state and trying to cross there. More likely he'd head south or west, trading in his car as soon as he thought he could do so without being traced.

It was pointless asking Alison if she knew which direction her parents had gone, but he asked anyway. "I have no idea," she told him, digging into the carton for the last spoonful.

He sat down on the ottoman and picked up the remote, hoping to continue the conversation without the sounds of the television. She reached to take it back from him and turned the volume up so high he couldn't stand it, and this time he had no choice but to leave her.

What Real Could Be

Three days before Christmas, the tree had had it. There were almost more dried brown needles on the floor than on the tree itself, and Harper was unable to keep up with the vacuuming because they fell so fast. "It's a fire hazard, Barbara," her father said at breakfast. "We just timed it wrong this year. But we can't take a chance by leaving it up." He asked if she wanted to get another one to replace it, but Harper's mother shook her head and said, "I think we've all had more than enough Christmas, haven't we?" She refilled her coffee cup and drifted out of the kitchen in her robe, which they all knew she might or might not replace with real clothes at some point before returning to bed that night. Since Harper had discredited herself, there didn't seem to be any way of telling which kind of day it was going to be when they all got up.

"Nice going, Betty," Truman said, throwing down an ace of clubs so hard it flew off the table. He had never before resorted to calling her by the nickname she was taunted with at school. But after Harper and her mother returned from the courthouse that day and her mother went straight to her bedroom, she caught the brunt of her brother's fury.

"What did you want me to do?" she asked him. Their father

had moved to the dining room table, where he sat again seeking pieces to the puzzle he'd been putting together for more than two months. "Commit perjury? They could have locked me up."

"How about not lying in the first place?" Truman said.

"Oh, okay, Mr. Morality. Mr. I-Always-Do-What's-Right."

"I don't give a shit if you lie about other things. That's not what I mean. But you gave her something to look forward to—that was the problem."

"But how mental is that? She looked forward to me being part of the case about my best friend's murder?"

"Not the case, stupid. It was the *book*." Her brother flicked his soda can and it fell off the table, too. "You gave her something to hope for, and then you took it away." She could tell Truman knew he was twisting the knife in her but didn't care. When she didn't respond he added, "How about not being mental yourself?"

He refused to help her undress the tree as he usually did. She began taking the ornaments down and packing them in their boxes. Chip ate tinsel and puked, the sound of it worse than the actual mess. In the dining room, her father exclaimed and Harper rushed in, assuming something was wrong.

"This isn't fair," he said, gesturing, and Harper saw that although he'd finally fitted all the pieces he'd shaken out of the ziplock bag that first day and scattered across the table, the finished picture was missing a dozen or more. "They're not all here."

Harper didn't remind him of what he'd told her before, that he enjoyed just sitting at the table searching for pieces, not caring how the picture turned out. He may have thought it was true at the time, but obviously it wasn't true now.

"Most of it's there. You can still tell what it is," she said instead, pointing. "A house by a river. That beautiful tree. Somebody doing—something." She couldn't actually make out whether the figure on the river's bank was a person, or not. The missing pieces were needed to fill in whatever it was.

"Maybe it's an abstract," she added. She remembered the word from a trip her art class had made to the museum in eighth grade, although if her father had pressed her now to define it, she would have failed. She'd understood it to mean the opposite of real, but Joy explained to her that no, it wasn't the opposite; it referred to the artist's idea of what real could be. There's a spectrum, she'd told Harper. All artists start with reality, and then they add or subtract to create what looks right to them.

"I wasted hours of my life on this," her father muttered, as if he hadn't heard her.

Harper thought it best not to tell him that contrary to what she would have expected, she loved how the puzzle turned out, precisely because she had never expected it to add up to anything, and she enjoyed the surprise of seeing that it did.

She left her father sitting there, wondering if he would sweep it all into the wastebasket or leave the pieces assembled for a few days, to remind himself that he had worked on it in good faith trusting that what would appear beneath his fingers was something he wanted to see. It took her three trips to haul the ornaments up to the attic. The next time she walked by the dining room, the table was empty. She went straight to the kitchen and began to bake, wanting to fill the house with the smell of sweets that were all she knew to offer her family, which she hoped they would not be able to resist.

Tuesday, December 29

I haven't written here since the day the grand jury met, but it isn't because nothing's happened; it's because so much has.

When Ramona called to tell me that the district attorney's office was not going ahead with the indictment because new evidence had caused them to focus their suspicion on someone else, I knew I should want to celebrate as much as Violet and Cass did, when they drove me straight from the Cineplex (we were only halfway through the Morgan Freeman movie when the call came) to a steak house down the road, where they ordered champagne and insisted on multiple toasts along with their treat of a dinner I did not have the stomach to eat. I wanted to feel excited, but I could not. The arrest and the accusations, the questions and the crowd outside my house, the phone hang-ups and being kicked off campus (which hurt more than anything, to be honest) made me feel burned and battered, as if I'd been outside too long in a high wind.

Hearing the revelations about the police chief, I thought it would mean I could move in public again without being looked at with the distrust that had been aimed at me since my arrest. At least there'd be that, I told myself, but instead I found that the stares were longer and harsher now. Instead of causing the people who'd assumed my guilt to feel ashamed that they'd suspected me when there wasn't enough justification, the prosecutor's decision to drop my case seemed to make them conclude that I'd gotten away with something. And not just anything, but murder. While somehow manipulating the system to escape my own charges, I had also managed to get the spotlight thrown on the police chief. It's absurd, and yet they seemed to believe it.

A few days after Armstrong's arrest, I moved out of Cass's and back down to Rochester, back to Grandee's house, taking some time to regroup and decide what to do next. Violet couldn't understand why I didn't pack up the same day I was a free man and leave the state. Or, if not the state, then this disgusting hickville I'd chosen to come to for school, and join her in New York City. I'd be free in a different way there, she told me—free to make whatever art I wanted, and to live a life without having to worry about looking different or about what anyone else thought. "You would blend in," she said, thinking this idea would appeal to me. But I don't want to blend in. I want to stand out—just for the right reasons.

Still, I knew she was right. I had to make a move, and New York was the most logical destination. I called a real estate agent and let her convince me to put Grandee's house on the market, reminding myself that I could always take it off before committing to a deal. I'M GORGEOUS INSIDE, said the sign the realtor posted outside the rusty fence, and when I protested because it wasn't exactly true, she told me to relax: "In my experience, people like it when someone tells them what they should believe."

But she didn't get the chance to find out if she was right. The night after I moved back into the bedroom I'd occupied most of my life, someone set fire to the house. Erupting while I was asleep, the flames would have killed me if Violet hadn't kept the smoke detectors up to date. I jerked awake to the sounds of beeping, felt myself inhaling smoke, grabbed my phone from next to the bed, and ran toward the back bedroom where I'd stored my paints and the unfinished portrait of my father. But the fire had a head start, and I had to turn and pitch myself toward the front door instead. I escaped just in time, with only the phone and the clothes I was wearing.

The fire trucks arrived and I stood on the sidewalk with a gathering crowd of my old neighbors to watch the house being sprayed. The woman who'd been Grandee's best friend for more than fifty years, Nell Walker, put a hand on my shoulder and said that God didn't give people any more than they could handle. Then she made a point of saying it was a good thing my grandmother wasn't around to see what had happened, and I knew she was talking about more than the house being destroyed.

When the firefighters told me they'd been unable to save anything, I felt stunned to the point of muteness. On the other hand, there was a sense of relief I couldn't ignore. What if I'd started the paintings for *Souls on Board* sooner and ended up losing more work than just the first few brushstrokes of my father's portrait? It was almost enough to make me wonder if I'd had some premonition without being able to identify it, though I knew even as the thought crossed my mind that this sounded more like something Grandee would believe, not me.

The next morning the fire chief held a news conference, saying that although he had no actual information so soon after the event, he hoped it would not prove to be the case that my home had been destroyed in an attempt to run me out of town by "some faction of our citizenry dissatisfied by the recent dismissal of the charges against Mr. Willett up in Chilton." But it didn't take long for investigators to determine the fire was arson, despite the pains whoever did it had taken to conceal the intent. Only hours after the grand jury was excused in my case,

I'd been walking through my apartment in Cass's house when someone hurled a brick through the window, this time carrying a note saying *Guilty as charged.* I did not report it to the police. But when the fire occurred at Grandee's, I assumed that whoever had thrown the brick—or that person's brother, or cousin, or son—had carried his hatred to Rochester and was responsible for the arson, too. I wouldn't have been surprised to learn that the arsonist was the same person who'd set fire to the church on my corner the night Obama was elected.

But since there was no surveillance footage of the neighborhood and no one seemed to have filmed it on a cell phone, there was no way to figure out who it might have been. Almost as quickly as they determined the fire was set, they dropped the investigation.

If I hadn't already been convinced it was time to leave, the fire would have clinched it. The day after Christmas (which I spent at Nell Walker's house; I knew Grandee would have wanted me to accept the invitation, but I found myself more comforted to be there than I'd expected), I called Violet and told her I was ready. She said she'd help me find a place, but in the meantime, I could stay with her. "Come now," she said, after I finished giving her the details about the rock, the fire, and the destruction of my work. "Don't even wait till morning. Go out and get a cab to the bus station right now. And don't look back, you hear me?"

I promised, but I knew there was one more thing I had to do. One more thing I *wanted* to do. As soon as my cell phone was repaired, I called the number I'd known by heart since the summer, having composed the message I would leave when it inevitably went to voicemail. Shocked when Susanne picked up, I found myself momentarily unable to speak.

"Is that you?" she asked, and I nodded before remembering she couldn't see it, then rushed to tell her, "Yes, it's me, I'm here."

"Good," she said. "I thought you weren't going to call me

back." Without letting her know I'd never received her message and had called of my own accord, I closed my eyes at the sound of her voice in my ear. Just that one word, "good," and I was ready to change my plans and stay forever, until she said it was time for us to meet in person, so we could say good-bye.

Diminishing Perspective

S he had not seen Martin, except on TV and in the newspaper, since the day almost two months earlier that Joy had
left her, then died. She always thought of it that way, as a leaving: her daughter had left, their last words uglier and more
hateful than any they'd ever exchanged, never to be repaired or
undone except in Susanne's dreams and fantasies, which she
would experience every day for the rest of her life. Occasionally
these visions were as wrenching as the actual rupture had been,
but most of the time they came to her as solace, especially the recurring image she had, both asleep and awake, of Joy sitting
quietly on the edge of Susanne's bed, her hands folded as she
smiled at her mother. She did not speak, but the smile contained
everything—forgiveness, love, and especially a lightness of the
heart that Susanne felt when she awoke or came back to herself,
and that lasted, on her luckiest days, for hours before fading.
Though she understood that the bedside visit was not real—that
she was manufacturing what she needed to see—it still brought
her comfort of a kind she knew Gil would not allow himself,
and she pitied him because of it.

She asked Martin to meet her at the mall; it was twenty miles
outside Chilton, and the most anonymous place she could think

of. It held no memories for them together. She'd thought he would appreciate the suggestion, but instead he insisted on seeing her at school. Susanne had heard what happened the day of Joy's funeral, when he'd been escorted off campus, so she was surprised at first at his request. Then she understood it was his way of reclaiming one of the things that had been stolen from him.

Massey Hall was deserted for the holidays. Arriving before Martin, she chatted with Percy at the security desk, wanting to ask him who'd issued the order directing that Martin be evicted if he showed up, then realizing she *didn't* want to know (she still had to work with these people, and she knew she did not have the courage to confront whomever it had been). Over the years, she and the security guard had built a rapport based on small talk—*how are you, how was your weekend, it's freezing/gorgeous/pouring out there.* Though she knew it was wrong to feel proud of it (some professors didn't acknowledge Percy as they went in or out of the building), she did feel proud. But neither of them had taken the step of moving their conversations from the superficial to anything that mattered, and now it was too late.

Watching Martin approach the building, she imagined how fast his heart must be beating though he walked with deliberate steps, unhurried—trying, she could tell, to feel again that he belonged here. Stepping inside, he paused a moment to let his eyes adjust to the dark lobby. "Percy," he said.

"Pablo," Percy greeted him back, not looking at Martin at first, then raising his eyes and adding, "Sorry, man." Martin nodded again, and Susanne understood she had witnessed something important pass between the two men, even if she couldn't have named precisely what it was.

They walked together to the sculpture studio, keeping a foot of distance between them as if they'd agreed on this beforehand. Once there she took a stool, but he declined and stood by the window, where the weak winter sun revealed details of his face she had not noticed before, even in bed: a pockmark at the top of one cheek, the small scar of a burn on his chin. If they'd been in bed, she would have asked about the scar. As it was, she knew she no longer had the right to do so.

She'd thought she would be the one to start the conversation; it had been her idea to meet today, after all. *I'm sorry* were the only words she could think to say, and she knew how insufficient they were. But before she could find any others, Martin turned and took a step away from the light and back toward her. "I just need to know if you ever thought I was guilty," he said. "We don't have to talk about anything else. But I need to know that."

She nodded, then realized from his expression that he misinterpreted the gesture. "No—no!" she said. "I'm just saying I understand. I get what you're asking." She opened her purse, took out the bookmark she'd been keeping there since she found it in Joy's drawer, and put it on the table between them.

"Oh," he said, exhaling the word.

"You kept these in your bedroom." Her voice wobbled on the word "bed."

He hastened to answer. "Yes, but remember, I also kept some upstairs. In the studio. She came to see me, Susanne." When he spoke her name, she remembered (with a pleasure she couldn't deny, though she tried to) how different he made it sound than anyone else ever had. "On Halloween."

She calculated: that had been a few days before Joy's arrest, and two weeks before she left. "Why?"

He hesitated; if it had lasted another moment, she would have said (guessing that she did not want to hear his answer), *Never mind.* "She came to ask if I was sleeping with you."

She felt the words before she understood them; they hit her in the stomach, a cruel punch. Yet it didn't feel as if Martin had been the one to deliver it. The blow came from inside.

What Martin was telling her meant that Joy had known about her mother's infidelity for more than two weeks before she died. After their confrontation that day—the last conversation they would ever have—Susanne thought to wonder how Joy had found out, but the question became moot when her daughter didn't return home that night. However it had happened, Susanne assumed the discovery was fresh when Joy picked a fight, disobeyed her mother, and sped off to met Delaney Stowell at the pond.

How long had Joy been aware of it? Could it go as far back as September, the day Martin had been in their house for the barbecue?

It was too much to bear recognizing for more than a few agonizing instants. To distract herself, she tried to summon an image of the exchange between her daughter and her lover. Where had each been standing when Joy made her demand, when Martin supplied the answer? "You were in your studio?" she asked. He'd always been protective of the space upstairs. The first time he took Susanne up to see it, he told her that she was the only person he'd ever invited up to the third floor.

"She asked if she could see it. I didn't want to reject her." He emphasized the word "reject." "She was—upset."

"Why didn't you tell me?" *If you had told me, I could have done something about it. I could have talked to her. We wouldn't have had that fight, and she wouldn't have—*

"Right after it happened," he said, "I didn't tell you because she asked me not to. I figured it was between you and her. Then I thought about it and realized, No. It meant something to her, that it was me. So I did try to tell you. That's why I came to see you that day."

That day—Friday the 13th, the last day she saw her daughter alive. The day Martin had appeared after the argument with Joy, then offered to follow her, to make sure she was okay. Susanne had asked that of him herself, using those very words: *Make sure she's okay, okay?*

"You could have called before that," she said. "By then it was too late."

"You weren't answering my calls." She heard no bitterness in his voice, but because she knew him, she knew that bitterness was what he felt.

She could have pursued it: *Why didn't you leave a message? Tell me it was important, that it was about Joy?* But she knew he was right; she'd been the one to cut off the relationship, to reject *him*.

Besides (she had to acknowledge to herself, excruciating as it was), she would have gone out of her way to avoid finding out what he had to tell her. She'd had no way of knowing that Joy's life was at stake.

Martin picked up the bookmark. "You could have given this to the police," he said. "Why didn't you?"

"Because I knew it didn't mean anything. I mean, anything to do with—" But she would not say the words "her death." "I knew it wasn't you."

It hurt to see his relief when she said it, to realize that he'd been living under that shadow along with the one cast by the police, the prosecutor, and the people he lived among.

Outside, a snowplow was scraping right up to the building. If the mound was still there in a few weeks, she knew, her students would hold an informal snow-sculpting competition to usher in the new semester. Bart Richlieu had offered to continue covering her classes for the spring, if she wanted, but she told him she'd be back to teach. She knew she'd need it more than ever from now on, talking about art and watching people try to make it. She'd need it for more than the money now.

She told Martin she'd heard about the fire, and asked if they'd caught who did it. When he shook his head, she asked how much work he'd lost.

"Hardly anything; I'd just started a portrait of my father for the new piece. *American Commonplace* is still here." He gestured down the hall, toward the room in which students were allowed to store their work.

"Thank God. I mean, not about the portrait . . ." But she trailed off, recognizing that her reaction was insufficient, and also understanding that he sensed the limits of her sympathy and would not hold it against her. He had lost a painting (an unfinished one, at that), not a child.

"I'm leaving," he blurted, and at first she thought he meant he'd had enough of this conversation, which she did not understand yet would be their last.

"Okay," she said, picking her purse up. "I'll walk out with you."

"No, I mean really *leaving*. As in moving. To New York."

In that flash of a moment she saw him sitting before an easel by a window, his brush lifted in the light of the sun reflecting the East River as he tilted his head to consider the canvas before him. There was noise on the street below, but he didn't hear it. As he did now, he lived in the same place he worked. But he was not alone in this vision she had of his future, which was more vivid than any she had of her own.

"Well," she said, setting her purse back down. "I probably don't have to say I'll be thinking of you."

This was also insufficient, but he would forgive this, too. She waited for him to make that bad joke again: *It's because I'm black, isn't it?* She waited for him to pick up the bookmark and slip it into his pocket. But he did neither, only nodded before he gave a slight smile, then turned. She watched him recede down the corridor toward Percy's station, his figure becoming smaller with each step.

Diminishing perspective, she thought, then forced herself toward the materials cabinet where she took out a package of clay, not yet knowing what she would make with it. Watching Martin walk away had exposed a fresh layer of the grief she'd felt since Joy's death, or maybe it added a layer; she couldn't tell which.

All she knew was that she felt the old craving—the itch that went back as far as she remembered but that had abandoned her these last few years—to watch something take shape beneath her fingers. It wouldn't replace Joy and it wouldn't replace Martin, or whatever it was that Martin had himself replaced. It wouldn't make her feel like a good person, because it couldn't undo the things she'd done that she would, now, always regret— and suffer.

But it was something, and at the moment, it felt like the only thing she could do. She cut off a block, secured the clay on an armature, and began pressing, making indentations, brushing smooth circles with her fingers. She wanted to feel it all; she did not want to use any tools. "I'm glad I'll have this," Joy had said, in the last few minutes Susanne spent with her daughter. No, Susanne was the one who would always have Joy's hands in *Colossal Joy.* Now she would sculpt her head, her hair, her face, in an effort to always have those, too.

What was the line Martin had quoted to her once? *Art makes the absent present and the dead almost alive?* If in the end what Susanne created now didn't resemble her daughter as much as she hoped, she would not destroy the effort but put it away inside a cupboard, because even a failed facsimile would be better than what she had now.

After (Further)

Friday, April 30, 2010

This morning I met with people from the Mirage Gallery, one of my prizes for winning the Lewison Award last year. I could have had the meeting sooner, and I might have if not for everything that happened in the months afterward, but in the end I'm glad I waited. Before now, I would only have been able to show them the pieces I retained after the fire, the still lifes in *American Commonplace*. And though I like them enough (and there's been some interest in showing them), it's not what I'm doing now.

Originally they asked me to come to the gallery itself, but when I told them about the size of my canvas, they offered to visit my studio, which is also my apartment, instead. I was nervous but excited: since finding this place in January and setting up my work space, I've gotten a good start on the northeast corner of *Souls on Board*. If I can keep that pace up (and I see no reason not to, given that I'm teaching only two studio classes a semester), I should be able to finish within a few years.

My original plan had been to paint individual portraits of passengers faced with the realization that they were about to lose their lives. I'd amended that after talking to Joy at her house that day, when she asked me to describe my work; I liked her suggestion to render the people on the plane *before* they understood what was about to happen. She'd said it would be more poignant—she also used the word "haunting"—and I agreed.

But since the fire at Grandee's house and the loss of the portrait I'd begun of my father, I'd also reconsidered my instinct to paint separate panels, each distinct from the others. Was that really what I was after? Or was it more in keeping with my vision to depict the entire airplane cabin in a single scene, re-creating more accurately what my father and the rest of the victims had actually experienced? They may have been thinking about themselves (wouldn't we all be?) when the first bolt of lightning struck, but they would not have been able to remove themselves or their consciousnesses from the presence and company of the people around them.

So, instead of a "thirty-six-tych," I am creating one huge mural measuring twelve by twelve feet. I like the symmetry of those numbers, and my hope is that the effect on the viewer will be all the more dramatic for the single outsized scene.

The owners of the Mirage agreed. And they all but guaranteed to show it when I'm finished. With that kind of interest, and with the life I've built for myself here (mostly, I admit, I am thinking of Samantha when I say that), it's hard not to spend much of my time feeling euphoric, especially given what I came so close to losing in the last year.

But I try to curb it, the euphoria, because I know how fast things can change.

I want to write about what happened last week before I forget it (though so much of me would like to forget) when I flew down to Atlanta and rented a car to drive to the suburb my mother lives in, thirty miles north of Hartsfield-Jackson. I had taken to thinking of her as my mother, which I resisted for most of my life; she'd always been *Linda* to me, as I tried to protect myself from hoping she would ever be anything more. But once

Ramona located her and Linda offered the bail money, I allowed the fantasies back in. The bail money had been returned to her, and I could have left it there, but I wanted to thank her. (Who was I kidding? It would start with thanking her, but it would end up where I'd always wanted it to: I would have my mother, finally, once and for all.)

I didn't have a plan beyond actually seeing her and somehow finding a way to express my gratitude for putting up the money. She owns a boutique in the same town she lives in, selling local artists' jewelry and handmade gifts. What happened to her dream of becoming a pianist? I wanted to know, but determined I would not ask. I found the boutique easily enough, in the middle of a block on a quaint street in her quaint town. Parking a few doors away from the store, which is called Peachtree Gems, I sat for a few minutes watching people stroll up and down the block: all white, except for a Rasta-looking skateboarder who appeared intent on startling the white people out of his way.

As I stepped inside, a defective-sounding bell gave a faint ring over the entrance, and the woman behind the counter looked up. My mother and I locked eyes, and there was no doubt in my mind that she knew immediately who I was, as I knew her.

She took in a breath. If not for the fact that I understood what shocked her, I would have thought it was because I was a black man entering this kind of store. I watched her in the second moment make the decision not to acknowledge who I was, and the realization triggered in me an equal mix of relief and despair.

"Can I help you?" she asked. I knew she was trying to give the smile she would greet any customer with, but it sputtered and died. I wanted to tell her not to try so hard, but of course I could not.

"J-just looking," I stammered.

"Of course! Well, anything I can do." Then she hustled away from the counter toward the jewelry case, where another middle-aged woman, the only other person in the store, was peering down at the necklaces.

But I had gotten a good look at her. What was it we shared that sealed the knowledge for both of us? The prominent bone ridges above the eye sockets, giving them a slightly lopsided look as our foreheads overwhelmed the lower portion of our faces. Ha! I'd always thought these features came from some African ancestor of my father's, but no, it was my white mother's side. In another circumstance, I would have smiled at the irony.

"Those are Swarovski crystals," I heard Linda say to the necklace browser. Her voice still sounded shaky to me, though of course this could have been how she sounded all the time. "Just look at them shine in the light."

I moved to a shelf containing homemade Christmas ornaments, the kind Samantha loves. Would my mother wonder why I was buying it? I chose a hanging moon, pewter studded with pastel stones. Bringing it up to the counter, I cleared my throat, and Linda came toward me, now looking down at my intended purchase as she spoke. "That's a beautiful one." Then she almost seemed to want to stop herself, but she couldn't help adding, "You have an excellent eye."

I thanked her and pulled out cash rather than my card, to avoid forcing her to look at the name we share. She fumbled to wrap it in tissue, saying "Sorry, sorry" as it tore in her trembling hands. In that moment I heard Violet telling me to *man up*, ask for what I wanted. In spite of my inclination to escape, I said to Linda, "You know who I am?" the words catching in my throat.

She took another breath so big I could tell it surprised us both. "Yes. I think so." Why had she added those last three words? Were they intended to mitigate the way she knew she would then behave—to allow for the possibility that she might, in some fractional measure, be unsure? I had wanted to ask, "Do you recognize me?" but lost my nerve at the last moment, the question suggesting as it did the existence of memory as well as raw awareness.

And the only thing she might remember of me, if she remembered anything at all, was glimpsing the full head of black hair I was born with, before she gave me away.

But there was Violet in my head again, not letting me withdraw as I would have if it were up to me. "I came to thank you," I told Linda, reminding myself not to mumble. "For posting my bail. You didn't need to do that."

I forced myself to meet her eyes as I spoke, but she returned the gaze so steadily that I had to break it and look away. My words had disconnected the pretense of politeness between us, I saw too late.

"You have nothing to thank me for." I watched her consider whether to leave it at that, or speak the words that so obviously came to her next. She couldn't seem to resist, and in an even lower voice she added, "If you're so grateful, I would have expected you to honor what I asked for in return."

"What you asked for?" As much as I hated looking stupid in front of her, I had no idea what she was referring to.

"All I requested when your lawyer called is that if I gave the money, you'd promise not to try to contact me." She set her jaw in a way I recognized from looking in the mirror. It was the expression I make at myself when I am defying something, in myself or in the world. "And now here you are. You and your father, the one thing I ask you for, you can't seem to give."

It pains me to remember, now, that I laughed. I thought she might have been making a joke, or trying to, because it seemed to me she spoke through an odd smile, and her words struck me with the surprise of a punch line. Before I finished laughing, though, I saw that I was wrong.

"What do you mean?" I said it before understanding that I might be heading down a road better left unexplored.

From the eyebrows raised in that high, wide forehead, I saw that it was her turn to be surprised. Was it by my laugher? Or by the suggestion that I really might not know what she was talking about?

I started to tell her that nobody had told me there was any condition on her posting the money through Ramona and her team. Then the rest of what she'd said caught up to me. "Wait. My father?" When she only tightened her lips in response, I said, "Are you saying he *did* talk to you?" I could barely get the words out; the task of comprehending and speaking them at the same time was too great. "Before he—before the crash?"

She made a move as if to turn away from me, but instinctively I reached toward her arm to stop her. Before I could make contact, she pulled the arm away, and it was this gesture—what it did to me, inside—that made me understand, finally, that there would never be anything beyond this moment between us. "You *knew* about that? All this time I thought he came down here and backed out, because I knew if he'd come to see you, you would have told him it was okay for me to call you, and he would have been happy to tell me that on the phone—" I wasn't even forming the sentences in my head, and I didn't recognize my voice in speaking them. "I asked him to come down here for my birthday and talk to you. It was the one thing I asked him for."

"I know that. And he did. How could I know he didn't tell you that?" Her fingers twitched on the counter between us. "Look, he's not the reason you never heard from me—I am." Then, as if she'd rehearsed it many times over the years, she added, "I don't think people who make a mistake, especially when they're young, should have to pay for it the rest of their lives."

A mistake. As if she'd checked the wrong box on a multiple-choice test because she didn't read the question closely enough, and learned as a consequence to pay more attention.

"He's been dead for twelve years!" I recognized that it was a non sequitur, that it didn't make sense after her flimsy offer of a self-defense, but I didn't care. "And all this time I thought—" But I saw that there was no point to it, and shut myself up.

"I know when your birthday is." Hearing herself say this appeared to distress her, and I was glad to see it. She nodded at the ornament I'd pulled out my wallet to purchase. "You can have that," she told me, in an urgent whisper. "That and anything else you want, you can just take."

She could have been speaking to a thief—someone who'd come in to rob the place. She could have been pleading for her life. Take the money and run, she might just as well have said; her tone was that desperate for me to leave.

I pushed the ornament aside gently and shook my head, then walked empty-handed back toward the door and into the insufferable heat. From that moment on, I knew, I would always associate the word "mother" with nausea and the sound of a broken bell.

In the rental car, I opened the window and had to take some deep breaths before feeling sure I would not be sick. The dreadlocked skateboarder came up from behind to shout "Move out, brother!" and thumped the hood as he sped by.

For the rest of my life, I thought, my chest still heaving, I will wonder if this trip was worth making. If I gained from it more than I ever lost.

But I was wrong; I had my answer even before my return flight was over. Yes, it had been the right thing to find Linda, because it meant I knew the truth—about both of my parents. If my father had come home that day and told me (and he would have done it so gently, I knew, feeling a prick to my heart) that my mother thought it best for all of us, including me, for her to remain out of my life, I would never have become an artist, or found the life I have today. After he died I was so angry at him—not so much for dying, but for what I was sure was his failure to talk to Linda about me—that I decided the hell with him and what he'd wanted. I would not follow him in his career as a piano technician (reliable, respectable, but also largely invisible, preparing an instrument for someone else to play); I was going to do what I loved even if it wouldn't earn me a living (his biggest fear for my future), which was to paint.

Yes, this *is you—this,* I heard in my head as we prepared for landing, but it wasn't Violet's voice I heard this time; it was my own.

The plane was on time and the journey smooth, Samantha met me at LaGuardia, and an hour after I arrived home, the people from the Mirage called to arrange today's meeting. Though I've only been here a fraction of a year so far, I can already tell I am home.

Let Down

The first day of May, the rhododendrons outside the hospital in his relocated hometown were in full bloom. *Color*, Tom thought as he passed them on the way in, feeling the shock of discovery. He hadn't been noticing colors. For how long? He had no idea, but he couldn't remember the last time he registered the pleasure of the reds in nature, the purples and the pinks—how just seeing such brilliance in the world could actually cause something to shift inside your chest.

Back in November, whenever he'd thought ahead to the day or night the baby would be born, he'd imagined having to hover in the background behind Doug and Helen, waiting for them to decide to step aside and give him space so that he could move forward, toward his wife (even now she was still his wife, though the papers ending that would come through soon) and their new child in the hospital bed.

But of course back then he was imagining Mercy, in Chilton, not this bigger, newer hospital in the middle of New Hampshire. And he'd worked himself up so much over the vision of being excluded that when the time actually came (not day or night but at the moment between; when he looked it up later, his son's birth had been recorded at the exact moment the sun set), and Alison said she wanted Tom next to her for the delivery, he felt shocked by the absence of anything other than gratitude, complete and simple and untarnished by the rupture of their breakup or the resentment he would always hold toward his parents-in-law.

The fact that neither Doug nor Helen was present in the room felt like a gift he did not deserve, even though he was more responsible for it than he could ever let Alison know. Her parents' disappearance—they'd been gone more than four months now—had taken a toll on her, especially because she could not contact them without risking that they would get caught.

Tom guessed Florida. Doug had always talked about Florida as a retirement destination, even though Tom thought it was more for Helen's benefit than his own. He was pretty sure Doug never intended to retire.

And he hadn't "retired," had he? No—he'd jumped bail like a gutless wonder before the DA could determine whether there was enough evidence to add second-degree murder to the charges already filed. "Gutless wonder" had always been one of Doug's favorite phrases, along with "douchebag," for the cowards he encountered on the job. Would he think of it in terms of himself, now that he was on the run? Tom doubted it. He'd see himself as a victim of persecution, though he'd never have a chance to accuse anyone of doing the persecuting.

At first, Alison had been inconsolable. But within a day or two she settled down, and Tom figured her mother had called or otherwise notified her about how she could reach them, if she needed to. She'd seemed once to almost let slip to Tom where they were, but he managed to detour the conversation without her realizing.

He figured she'd probably confided in Eveline, her AA sponsor. But that was okay: no way the state troopers or the FBI would have any reason to question a middle-aged clerk at the

New Hampshire Small Business Development Center. Eveline was the person Alison and Tom had to thank for pointing out to Alison that she didn't drink *because* of the "giant waves of dread" she'd described once to Tom—that, in fact, the drinking created the dread. Tom would always be grateful to Eveline for being willing to repeat this until Alison both believed and understood it to be true.

There was no way they could remain in Chilton, after what Doug had done, though it took them a month or two to realize it. Alison had started the semester teaching, but right before February break she told Tom she couldn't take it anymore, she was moving, she needed a fresh start. At first he panicked, but after a few days he saw it as an opportunity. The writing was on the wall as far as the shack was concerned; it wasn't going to turn around, no matter how hard Tom tried. So he sold it to Hugh Nance, who planned to raze it for a gas station. Tom knew he'd let his father down, but if he had to choose between his father and his own child, there was no question; the difference between him and Alison in this regard was, as he saw it, the marriage's fatal blow.

It took them a few more days to settle on New Hampshire as a place they could both see living in, and raising their son. Tom signed on to a short-term gig with a security company, and eventually Alison's new school district might need an assistant football coach. Maybe he'd even take some accounting classes at the college in the next town over. He didn't care what kind of jobs he had to work in the meantime, as long as he could keep paying child support. The lawyers had said they could prescribe custody in the divorce papers, but Alison and Tom agreed they would turn to that only as a last resort.

In his bassinet beside Alison's hospital bed, the baby made little puckering noises, and when Tom turned to smile at Alison, he saw that her eyes were wet. From here he would take them back to the side-by-side duplex he'd bought with proceeds from the shack, and Alison would let him carry the baby into her half, the left. He'd go out and bring back something for them to eat, along with a bag of frozen peas the nurse had recommended for Alison's sore and swollen breasts. (So far, though she and the baby had both tried, she had yet to experience what the nurse called "the let-down effect," when hormones released milk toward the nipples. *Don't worry*, the nurse told her, when Alison got frustrated. *It'll happen. And when it does, you won't be able to hear him cry without leaking.*)

After they'd eaten and before she put the baby to sleep, Tom would kiss them both good-bye and go to the duplex's other side. He might or might not call Natalie, who'd forgiven him when he told her he'd rummaged through her desk drawer that day, taking advantage of her trust. Who'd passed the police exam, gone through the academy, and been hired to the Chilton force by Raul Dominguez, the new chief. Who'd convinced Tom that of course what he'd actually felt under the water that night *was* a vine or a weed—he'd let his imagination run away from him, thinking it might have been the hand of the dead girl grabbing his own.

And who might or might not visit the next weekend; she'd told him to wait and see how he felt.

But first, they had to get the baby home. "What are you naming him?" asked the aide who came to wheel Alison out of the hospital. Alison held the baby in her lap as Tom followed with her overnight bag, the kit of hospital freebies he'd been psyched to receive until he saw the contents (nasal aspirator, infant thermometer, a pacifier, and extra-thick sanitary pads), and the bouquet of balloons sent by the superintendent at the school Alison would be joining in the fall.

"What are we naming him?" Alison repeated the aide's question to Tom as they rode the elevator down.

"I thought we picked Matthew."

"That's a nice name," the aide said. "You don't hear it so much anymore."

Alison wrinkled her nose. "I was thinking about it, and I'm not sure. *Matt Carbone*." She herself would be reverting to Armstrong when the divorce was final; even Tom, who'd never been any good at figuring out symbols in English class, recognized the significance of that choice. "It sounds like a car mechanic."

"So? He can be a mechanic if he wants to, right?" As they waited for the elevator doors to open, Tom directed his question at the aide, who seemed to sense that she'd stepped into delicate territory and merely smiled to indicate that she preferred to remain neutral. "Or he could be a teacher. He could be a cop. We decided to let him decide, right?"

"I guess," Alison murmured, sounding unconvinced. But instead of submitting alternatives, she only chirred at Matthew in the backseat during the ride, and when they pulled into the driveway, Tom knew it was safe to think of his son this way. Matthew. Matthew. For the rest of his life, just hearing the name would ignite a fire inside his chest.

When the baby had finished nursing, Tom offered to burp him, and after patting out a couple of deeply gratifying belches, he handed Matthew back to her and got ready to leave.

But Alison asked him to stay a minute. He sat back down and as she stroked the baby's head she murmured, "I want my parents to know about him."

After a moment in which he wasn't sure how she expected him to respond, he said, "Of course you do."

"Do you really think the phone is tapped? I mean, my *cell*?"

He shrugged. "I swear I don't know, Al. All I *do* know is they want him back there. And I'd expect them to pull out every stop in the book."

"You couldn't find out?" But she already knew the answer.

And knew she couldn't take the chance to test it—not with this baby she'd just brought home, not with her own freedom as well as her parents' on the line. "You don't really think he could have done that, do you?" She covered the baby's ears as if to protect him from their conversation.

For a moment Tom thought she was referring to Matthew. Then he understood. "I think he did plant the mask, and I think he got Harper Grove to say she saw Willett in it." He spoke slowly, wondering if the incomplete answer would be enough. When he saw that it wasn't, he added, "I don't think he would have planned to go after Joy and kill her, if that's what you mean. But if they met up and she threatened to expose him—you know, a heat-of-passion kind of thing—well, I don't know." She hadn't looked at him the whole time he was speaking. "What do *you* think?" he asked, but she shook her head and got up to take the baby into the bedroom, where he could hear her laying him down before getting in bed herself.

He waited until they were both asleep, then slipped out the door. This was how it was going to be, for as far ahead as he allowed himself to look, which—these days—wasn't far. It wasn't the way he wanted, and it wasn't the way they'd planned, but once he'd made the decision to find out what happened to Joy Enright, the only way he could have remained with Alison was if she acknowledged the complete truth about her father. When that didn't happen, this other arrangement had to be made, for everyone's sake.

One thing he'd learned from all of this: the road was harder to navigate if you tried to see the whole thing ahead of you at once. If he thought *divorce*, he felt himself slipping. *Divorced father*, even worse. Better to break life down to its pieces and focus on them one by one. The rhodies outside the hospital this morning. The way the nurse smiled, placing Matthew in Alison's lap. The sounds of his son settling into his first infant dreams. And

Natalie on the other end of the phone line, ready to listen—wanting to.

After that, he might sleep. But he guessed it was more likely that during his son's first night home, he would lie awake listening to make sure that on the other side of the wall, all was as well as (in spite of everything) he had faith it still could be. Behind him he shut the door lightly, then opened it a crack so he'd know if he was needed.

License

I need the car tonight," Harper told her father. Truman was skateboarding on the ramp he'd set up in the backyard, and they listened to the sounds of him scraping and banging and swearing as he repeatedly tried and failed to land a kick flip. "Tru is going to ask you, too, but I need it more." Lately, she'd discovered how much she enjoyed declaring things.

After Joy disappeared and Harper told the police the lie they wanted to hear, she began having a recurring dream of being a passenger in a car that was speeding down the highway, no one in the driver's seat. Once she broke down and confessed, just before the grand jury was canceled, the dream went away. Her mother had driven a few times since that brief period in December, but it was her father who took Harper out as much as he could when spring came, forcing her to practice things like merging onto the highway and parallel parking even when she didn't want to. He told her she would thank him later, and he was right: she did. When she passed the road test in March, she expected Truman to be glad that he didn't have to drive her around anymore, but instead it presented a new conflict when they wanted to use the car at the same time.

"You know the rule," her father said now. Whoever needed

the car for work got first dibs, but beyond that, they had to figure it out for themselves. Since Truman had lost his job at the dollar store and Harper's catering service with Eric Feinbloom had taken off, she got the keys more often than her brother and ended up chauffeuring *him*.

It didn't seem to bother Tru all that much. He spent most of his free time on his skateboard now, ever since giving up solitaire at the dining room table. "It doesn't really do anything, does it?" he'd asked Harper out of the blue one day, when she passed through right after he'd lost another game. "I mean, that was kind of mental of me, right? Thinking that if I won, it would make things better." Hardly able to believe that her brother was admitting such a thing to her, she hesitated, not sure how to respond. "It's okay," he told her. "I know it was."

In the living room, the cat jumped up on the piano and skittered across the keys, causing Harper to exclaim because instead of a constellation of random, dissonant sounds, Chip seemed to have set his paws down on an actual chord. What were the chances? The sound and surprise of it filled Harper with a delight that was new to her. She'd thought she'd experienced every feeling she would ever have again, for the rest of her life—that it would all be repetition from now on (and that this was what being an adult meant)—but Chip's accidental music caused her to hope, suddenly, that there might be more. In that moment, she resolved to count on it. And to be on the lookout for those new feelings, even—especially?—when it seemed likely they would never come again.

She hadn't been asked to the prom, but that was okay (really, it was better than okay) because at midnight she was with Eric in the gym—which had been transformed beyond recognition into a combination ballroom/casino/karaoke stage—preparing to serve up food and pastries from the menu they'd been sanctioned to create for the occasion. The kids at Chilton Regional

High's after-prom party would get to sample Eric's famous ravi-
oli and specialty omelets, topped off by Harper's red velvet
cupcakes decorated with tiny chocolate mortarboards and butter cream diploma scrolls.

When the prom-goers entered just after midnight, most having changed into regular clothes, they dispersed in different directions—some to the poker table, where the principal was dealing
out hands; some to the dance corner, where everybody's favorite
gym teacher started a limbo line; some to the pile of Hula-Hoops
and others toward the piñata (the art teacher had sculpted the
school's bulldog mascot out of papier-mâché, which contained
not candy but gift certificates for music downloads, pizza, video
games, and a hot-air balloon ride). Along the back wall, in front
of bleachers collapsed for the occasion, Mrs. Carbone was man-
ning the mocktail bar. She'd moved to New Hampshire at the
beginning of the semester and had her baby only a few weeks
ago, but for some reason she'd asked if she could come back and
chaperone the prom. There was a rumor she'd joined AA and
quit drinking like her mother, though Mrs. Carbone never announced this herself. Harper was still getting used to the fact that
some or most or all of what she'd learned in English last fall had
been taught to her by a drunk person. But she was glad if Mrs.
C. was better now, especially since she had the baby to take care
of. Maybe she'd come back to show her students—and herself—
what she could be like sober. She looked alert and happy, showing pictures of the baby to anyone who asked.

A few girls still in their prom dresses came directly to the
dessert station and started piling into the food. Among them
was Delaney Stowell, who bit into a cupcake and made a sound
of pleasure. Only then did she seem to notice Harper behind
the table. Harper steeled herself, waiting for Delaney to cut
her down.

Delaney seemed to consider it, but then said only, "These

are good," as she placed another cake onto her plate. Then she added "Harper," before turning back to resume gossiping with Tessa and Lin.

Contrary to what she'd expected, nobody had given Harper too much grief when the case against Martin Willett got thrown out, probably because they didn't know she'd confessed on the stand to lying. The grand jury proceedings were confidential, she found out afterward. All the news reports had said was that the evidence was insufficient, especially when police had another potential suspect.

More for Eric's amusement than her own, she'd prepared a Post-it Note ("HAZARDOUS WASTE MATERIAL") to attach to Delaney's shawl, on the pretext of adjusting the chiffon around the snake tattoo on her shoulder. But Delaney's compliment made her change her mind, and she threw the note away.

Since Joy's death, Harper had often thought she felt the presence of her first friend, and now was one of those times. Joy hovered slightly behind her so that she couldn't be seen, but the air she inhabited contained the rich weight of their history together, and the warmth of what they'd felt for each other for so long. This was how Harper learned that at least one of the famous Bible quotations—"Love is stronger than death"—was true. Hearing Delaney Stowell call her by her real name, she allowed herself a half smile she imagined only the Joy in her head would see, but Eric noticed, too.

"What?" he said, smiling back.

She knew she would not be able to explain it. She told him *Nothing*, but he asked again. "Do you ever quit?" she said, and he told her no, he didn't. So she told him the truth: *I feel Joy*, she said, and he seemed to understand immediately.

"Me, too." He stepped a little closer and now Harper felt the two of them, Joy and Eric, one behind each shoulder. Wanting to preserve the moment, she closed her eyes.

They'd be going their separate ways in September, Harper to the Culinary Institute and Eric to the state university up by the border. But they'd only put their restaurant plans on hold; they still intended to open one after Eric graduated and Harper had gained some experience as a bakery and pastry chef. They hadn't gotten as far as determining where it would be located, or how they would raise the start-up money, or the name or menu or décor. Neither had suggested to the other that anything might happen during the next couple of years and that one or both of them might decide to do something else. Harper knew it was as much a comfort to Eric as it was to her, the vision they'd concocted together back in seventh grade, and she knew that he had no more interest than she did in suggesting it was only a childish dream they'd have to reconsider before too long.

Their serving trays had been cleaned out by their classmates coming back for second and third helpings, the cupcakes long gone from their tiered stand. "Well done, partner," Eric said, and Harper blushed in a mix of embarrassment and pleasure as he high-fived her. By the time they packed it all in the trunk of Eric's car, the party was over, and they saw the faint hint of sunrise behind the hill.

Commencement

They had coffee in bed again now, a habit they'd cultivated when they were just married and living together for the first time. Before Joy. Once she was born they hadn't had the time or the luxury to settle back against their pillows with their mugs and watch the early news before making their slow way up and into the day. It had been almost eighteen years since the last time, but on the middle Monday in May, five months after they buried their daughter and two months after his mother died, Gil got up first and went to feed Salsa. Susanne heard him—noted his departure from the bed—and turned over, praying without thought to be allowed to fall back to unconsciousness. But within a few minutes Gil was back, saying "Here." Resentfully, Susanne opened her eyes and turned back toward him, saw the mug he held out, reached for it without having to think. Just that easily they were those newlyweds again, only this time holding between them a grief they could never have imagined back then. She accepted the coffee and they lay propped against their pillows, sipping, as they had all that time ago.

When they'd both finished, she waited for him to say they should get up. He'd always been the one to say it; that had been their routine. When he didn't, she put her mug on the nightstand and reached for his hand. This was a habit from the old days, too, only they'd both forgotten it until now. He turned to look at her, surprised, but did not pull his hand away.

They'd cleared the air between them, or at least most of it— too late, but it was better than leaving it undone. In March, she'd come home from campus one day to find Gil standing inside the door, waiting for her to enter. "What?" she said. She felt a clutch in her gut, at the same time knowing that nothing could ever give her as much pain as she'd suffered already.

"Why did you lie to me?" He'd seemed almost reluctant to let her pass through the threshold and into her own house.

She assumed he'd found out somehow that the affair with Martin had lasted longer than just one night. How he would have learned this, she couldn't guess, as she couldn't guess why this would be important to him now.

"I didn't think it mattered, in the long run," she told him. "It seemed like it would be adding insult to injury."

"'Didn't think it mattered'?" It wasn't sarcasm she heard in his voice; it was a combination of dismay and disbelief. Sarcasm would have been easier. "How could it not matter? How could you let me just sit there and wonder where that money came from?"

Money. She sat down to buy time. "I'm not sure I know what we're talking about."

"I went to see Mark Feinbloom. *You're* the one who said I should. I thought about it and you were right—I'm not the kind of person who lets something like that slide. And I had to go in about Mom's accounts anyway." He sat across from her and rubbed his scalp. "Why would you keep it to yourself, when you knew what he was going to tell me? I really just don't understand, Suse. Just explain it to me."

"No, *I* don't understand. You first."

A shadow crept into his eyes as they narrowed across from

her. "You made that deposit to my account, then told me you didn't. It's not that I don't appreciate your doing it, even though I don't know where the money would have come from. But why lie? Why say you didn't? Why wouldn't you want me to know?"

Her mind raced ahead of itself. "He told you?" Words intended to draw information, without giving the intention away.

"He looked up the deposit slip. Signed by Susanne Enright. Cash."

In a flash she understood, hearing a cry fly from her throat. Gil looked at her with an expression of quizzical concern. The fact that he hadn't figured it out for himself made her feel not angry, as it might have before Joy died, but protective—another emotion she had not experienced since then.

But she didn't want to tell him before she was sure, so instead she said, "Rob gave me the money, to help us out. He gave it outright—he said he didn't need it to be a loan. I knew how you'd feel about that. I figured you wouldn't accept it if you knew."

She watched him take this in; she could tell she'd done a good job of selling it. Then he asked a question she hadn't anticipated, in the fleet concoction of the lie. "You asked your brother for money?"

"No. Not exactly. But he must have guessed the business was in trouble when he offered you that job."

Gil's eyes remained focused on her, as if he were trying to determine whether she might be lying again, or still. The recognition that her marriage had come to this—that her husband now questioned or challenged so many of the things she told him—caused her lips to go dry suddenly, and though she ran her tongue over them, it brought no relief. "Well," he said. "I'm *not* accepting it. As a gift. I'll pay him back, with interest. I want you to tell him that."

She agreed. After he left for a plastering job, she went to the bank and stood at the door of Mark Feinbloom's office, not sure whether to knock or not, because his back was turned to her as he worked at his computer. When she cleared her throat, he glanced over and stood, looking surprised but turning it into the pitying smile she'd become accustomed to from everyone during the past few months.

She told him she'd come because of what Gil had told her about the deposit last fall—that the slip had been signed with her name—but she hadn't been the one to put the money in. The deposit had been made not in this branch, the central and most convenient one, but at a satellite in Canandaigua. When she asked Mark if he would look at surveillance video from that bank's cameras, to find out who had actually added the money to Gil's account, he regarded her in silence for a moment. She could almost feel him thinking what she herself had thought: *What difference does it make now?*

"We just need to know," she told him, and he nodded before saying he'd find out what he could. A few hours later he called to say—as Susanne had known he would—that it was Joy on the video, depositing money to Odd Men Out.

"I'm not sure why, if she wanted to keep it secret, she wouldn't have just used an ATM," he added, but Susanne understood immediately, with a stabbing sensation that made her fold over: because of the robberies at ATMs during the past months, her daughter had gone out of her way to be careful.

She was certain neither she nor Gil had ever referred to the bank's foreclosure threats when Joy could have heard. And yet: how careful had she been? If she hadn't been sleeping with Martin, wouldn't she have picked up on the fact that Joy was worried, and why? And if Joy had trusted her mother—if she hadn't suspected her of cheating on her father, and felt afraid to bring it up—wouldn't she have just come out and asked her parents how much trouble they were in?

It was her own fault—all of it—Susanne saw now, thinking for a moment that she might actually choke on the mass that rose swiftly to her throat. Before this she'd managed, somehow, to keep it down. Now she had no choice but to recognize that though she had not strangled her daughter, she was responsible for Joy's death nonetheless.

The next day she forced herself to tell Gil, knowing how he would feel once he understood that Joy's actions appeared to have been triggered at least in part by his financial failures. But she only managed a single sentence before Gil interrupted her and said, "Wait. Wait. You told me *you* put that money in, from your brother. The *bank* told me it was you."

"Well, that's what they thought. She signed my name to the slip."

"So how do they know it was Joy?"

"I asked Mark to look at the video."

"When?"

"Yesterday."

"And you're only telling me now?"

She hesitated. "I was trying to spare you."

"*Spare* me? From what?"

"I knew how you'd feel if you found out she did all that to help save your business." *All that*—selling drugs, blackmail. No need for her to spell it out; they were both more aware of the details than they wanted to be.

"Why would she think it needed saving?"

"Gil. Come on. Because it does."

He slumped back, the knockout complete, and she was tempted to make the spontaneous decision not to tell him the rest of what she'd planned to: that contrary to what she'd led herself and him to believe at the time, Joy had been aware of the affair between her and Martin.

But of course Gil deserved to know that this, and not only the stress of hearing her parents fight about money, was what caused Joy to distance herself from them in the weeks before she died. She also told him she'd slept with Martin six times, not once. Getting rid of that piece of deception made her feel hollow in a good way, as if she were making room for something she could not have accommodated otherwise.

She forced herself to meet his eyes as she admitted everything, and waited for him to pull away, too. It was what she deserved, and she was prepared for it to hurt all the more because now that they were alone again she felt closer to him than ever, including the earliest days of their marriage.

When instead of retreating he reached for her hand, brought it to his face, and held it there, she convulsed in grief and relief against his arm. He murmured, "I know. I know," over and over, until it grew dark out and she let go of his arm so he could stand and turn on a light.

Now, as they dressed for the graduation ceremony, she said, "I've been wondering something. Would you do it over again, if we had the choice?" When he didn't respond right away, she thought maybe she hadn't been clear. "I mean—try for Joy? Have her?"

The confusion erased itself, replaced by the tender expression she remembered from the times she'd most loved watching her husband and daughter together. "In a heartbeat," Gil said, and the further relief of this—of knowing they felt the same way— brought a hot sting to her eyes. For the first time since they'd lost Joy, she felt something she couldn't call hope yet, but that she wouldn't have called the opposite of hope, either.

The first recipient of the Joy Enright Memorial Scholarship was Felicity Cross, a ceramicist going into her second year of the MFA. During the committee's discussions about how the money should be awarded, Bart Richlieu had worried aloud that it might look funny, to use his word, if they chose the program's only remaining student of color. "Won't it seem like we're over-compensating for what happened to Willett?" he asked.

"No," Jonatha Hurley said. "It'll seem like we're giving an award to the student we think deserves it the most."

"But—"

"Bart," Jonatha told him, "shut up."

After the ceremony, which had been moved to an indoor hall because of rain, Susanne felt exhausted; normal life still exhausted her, though she could at least imagine the time now when this might not be the case. She wanted to go home, but Gil convinced her to stop at the reception under the tent behind the Campus Center. When they stepped outside, she saw that the rain had stopped and the clouds appeared to be moving on. They took seats at a table bordering the wet grass to watch the students play an outsized game of Jenga, using a high stack of two-by-fours they'd painted in primary colors and spent hours setting up in the center of the quad. Some of the students balked at destroying it once they'd con-structed the tower, but others persuaded them after it had been photographed from every conceivable angle to preserve their handiwork for posterity. They took turns cautiously pulling planks from the bottom, nobody wanting to be the one to send the boards tumbling. Each time one had been removed safely, a cheer went up among the crowd.

The students invited their teachers to play and wheedled Susanne into taking a turn. She pulled the board someone pointed to, assuming she would be the one to make the whole structure fall. When it didn't, she gasped and everyone laughed, including her, though the sound of her own laughter was foreign to her.

Watching the new graduates, Susanne murmured, "Martin would have been one of them," testing whether she could speak his name safely. When Gil nodded and reached to cover her hand with his own, she knew she could say this and much more. But for now, she just sat and watched the game, waiting like everyone else for the sun to emerge and finally warm everything, after a winter too long for them all.

During

All Other Cases Are True

Stumbling over a hard vine sticking up from the cold ground, she looked back, but no one was following her. What had she thought—that Delaney Stowell gave enough of a shit to start chasing her through the woods, in her new UGGs and with her long, laser-smooth legs bare between her skirt and boots? What did Delaney care what Joy did with the pad of prescription sheets? She didn't seem afraid of getting caught. She didn't seem afraid of anything, although Joy knew this was partly an act because Delaney had sweated plenty the day of the SATs, until Joy got home and called her to say *No problem, they barely checked the ID.*

But sometimes an act was enough, if you could convince yourself as much as you convinced other people.

She was afraid—had been afraid for months now, ever since Jason took her aside at BM to ask if she could ever use some extra cash, because he'd heard her say she wanted to go to a college her parents couldn't afford—but that would end after today. She knew Delaney meant it when she said this was the last time, but Joy had already decided that for herself. One last set of proceeds (she refused to use words like "score," at least in her own mind, knowing it was ridiculous to think that this meant she was not a real drug dealer but clinging to the delusion anyway) and she'd hang it up. Thirty thousand dollars, Jason had said, this new customer would give her for the whole pad. She'd have to split it with Jason, but it'd still be a big pot. When she added it to what she'd saved already, she'd be able to go to Decker at least for a year or two, if she got in. She'd have to pretend she'd won the big scholarship, but that would be her last piece of deception, and maybe her parents would be able to hire a nurse so that her grandmother could move out of BM and into Joy's own bedroom.

"Don't leave me here," Emilia had begged the last time Joy visited her. She knew her parents believed that her grandmother didn't know what she was saying; that she no longer made sense. And it seemed to be true, when her parents were around. But Emilia was perfectly coherent when she spoke to Joy. "Don't just leave me. I wouldn't do that to you."

As much as she loved her grandmother, as much as she wanted to go to New York to study art, she wouldn't take any more chances after today. This was the last time; her nerves couldn't handle it anymore.

Not to mention the *guilt*, the *guilt*, the *guilt*, which came over her so hard and fast now she felt as if she were drowning. This was what it was like to drown, she knew: you lost sight of the world above your head as it receded farther and farther, even as you reached and grasped and fumbled to seize it back. How had she thought she might avoid this? By justifying everything she'd done, telling herself her parents had betrayed her; by making that random deposit into her father's account? A lame gesture if there ever was one.

Too late, she wished she'd gone back to her mother's car and home, instead of taking this crazy, slippery, freezing jog through the woods. Delaney and Tessa and Lin would have just ignored her and gone on their own way. But she would still have had Harper to deal with, she remembered, swatting at a branch she almost missed as she pitched forward through the thick brush. Harper, whose faithfulness made Joy feel equally sad and guilty.

What was it that had caused Harper to blurt what she did, at the Halloween party, about Joy's mother and her affair? Right before that Delaney had said something and Joy laughed, without even hearing what it was. She laughed because it was easier that way, and because she wanted Delaney to keep providing her with scrips. Whatever it had been, it made Harper mad, but by the next day she was over it. Though this made things easier for Joy (who justified the theft of Mrs. Grove's pills by reminding herself how much Harper hated it when her mother was on them), she found herself wishing that Harper would hold it against her, for once. She didn't deserve for Harper to love her, not now, but when all this was over, she would do whatever it took to earn her best friend back.

She ducked a low-hanging branch at the last minute, just before it would have whacked her in the eye. This place, she knew as she pitched through it, was called the Undead Forest. Of course, most people didn't really believe the story about ghosts rising out of the ground. But she still felt relieved when she came out on the other side.

At the edge of the lot her father had once been excited to call his job, his "big break," she stood for a moment and blinked. Everything looked so ordinary—the gray sky, the curve of the lake at its elbow, the row of half-finished condos with its broken, pathetic sign—and yet she felt, suddenly, like someone she'd never been before now. How had this become her life, running through the woods to escape people she didn't want to spend time with, in search of someone she didn't even know? She couldn't wait to get home and make up with her mother. Tonight she would sit both her parents down and confess everything: the business she let Jason cut her in on, the pills she stole from Harper's mother, taking the SATs as Delaney Stowell.

The idea of telling them felt so good that for a moment she thought about turning around instead of even meeting this guy. But she'd have to return through the same woods, too soon after emerging, and besides that, she'd be giving up all that cash. Okay, then: get it over with. She took a breath and headed toward La-La.

They all look alike. She remembered hearing her father say this to her mother one day when he got home from work. Joy had banged into the kitchen on the force of her indignation and said, "*Who* all looks alike?"

"What do you mean, 'who'?" her father said. "Those condos. They're cookie-cutter. You can't tell them apart."

It had been true once, but the fire the night of the Halloween party had changed all that. The right-side units, including the one she headed toward now, were only black, burnt-out shells of buildings.

How will I know you? The familiar line popped into her head from the story of how her parents met, what they jokingly called their "origin story." When she was younger, she loved playing along when her parents said they'd pick her up from school or Harper's house or art class. "But how will I know you?" they'd ask and, already giggling, she'd give the answer she knew they were waiting for. *I'll be the one who looks like me.*

But the last time her mother had invited her to repeat the routine, during the days her father was living away from the house, Joy let the line lie in the air between them, then (knowing how obnoxious it was, but unable to help herself) announced that the question was obsolete. "Now you'd just send each other selfies. End of story," she said, having to turn away from the hurt look on her mother's face. To steel herself against feeling the same hurt, she dyed her hair a few days later so that finally, there could be no doubt: her parents would not recognize her anymore, as she no longer recognized herself.

"Over here," a man's voice hissed from a corner, and she saw a crack in the door at no. 19. "For crying out loud."

For crying out loud—it was an expression her father might have used. Joy loved this about him, his refusal to swear, his old-fashionedness. If he weren't so gentle all the time, she might not hate her mother so much for what she'd done to him. But as it was, every time she thought of her father's face and imagined him finding out about Martin Willett, she felt like shaking her mother and screaming, *What's wrong with you?*

Well, that's pretty much what she *had* said, before hijacking her mother's car and screeching away from the house. It was another moment of not recognizing herself. Everything would have to come out in their conversation tonight—finally, they would all know the truth. The prospect of such relief made her feel almost dizzy as she stepped through the door of the condo and into the dark room.

How had anyone ever thought these would pass for luxury units, with so few windows? It was supposed to be a big selling point that they fronted on the pond, but what did it matter if you couldn't see the water from where you sat?

She smelled him before she could see anything—pot and BO. Familiar somehow, though she couldn't immediately place it. It took a few seconds for the glare from outside to go away, and when it did she saw the silhouette of a man with a cigarette dangling from his mouth, diving to shove away a tangle of bedding and other junk.

"Shit," he said, peering as he moved closer to where she stood. Her own eyes hadn't adjusted yet. She blinked, barely registering his curse and what it might mean, still unable to make out his face.

"You broke in here?" she asked. "You're a squatter?" She felt affront on her father's behalf, even though he was not the owner. Besides, it was easier to accuse someone other than herself.

He was muttering to himself, more real curses: *goddam, fuck it, son of a bitch*. The next words he aimed directly at her. "I did not break in here." He flicked his ashes toward the mouth of a dented Bud Light can. "I have a key."

A key? Was that what he'd said? She moved a few steps toward him to hear better, but everything was still too dark and she tripped over the sleeping bag, exposing the clothing and other items he'd tried to hide under it as she entered. Getting up from her knees, she watched him kick a Red Wings baseball cap back under the pile, then tried too late to pretend she hadn't seen it, as bile soured in her throat.

"You know who I am," he said. Not asking a question, but accusing *her*.

With an abrupt surge of clarity she had not felt in months, she understood her immediate situation like a conditional case from the logic portion of the SATs. *If he is living here, then he does not have the money to pay for the scrip pad I brought to sell to him.* She remembered the tip from the book of practice tests: Conditionals are false only when the first condition (*if*) is true and the second condition (*then*) is false. All other cases are true.

She hesitated, unsure what to say. Was he asking if she recognized him as one of her father's employees? Or was he trying to tell if she knew that the baseball cap meant he was the ATM robber? Or was he referring to both? In the end she settled on half of the truth. "You're the new guy, the last one my father hired. So you stole the key when he was still working here, right?"

"Well, shit." He rubbed his face, and at first she thought he might be crying. Then she remembered the red eyes running, the way he kept wiping them with his bandanna when he came over for the barbecue on Labor Day. "I wouldn't have had to steal anything if I still had a job, now would I?" His face twitched, and he looked not directly at her but down at the empty chip and candy bar wrappers that lay in a pile beside his feet. "*Was* the new guy. *Was*," he repeated, his voice containing a fresh level of hostility. "Your father shit-canned me."

She'd never heard the term before, and absurdly, through the dismay mounting in her throat, it struck her as funny. *Shit-canned*. She figured out its meaning from the context, something Mrs. Carbone always urged them to do.

"If he did that, he didn't have a choice," she said, thinking of the conversations she'd overhead at the dinner table after being excused to do her homework, when they hadn't known she was listening. Listening was how she learned the meanings of "underwater" and "equity," too. "He was going bankrupt. *Is* going. Didn't you know that? The economy."

"'The economy.'" He repeated her words in a mocking tone. "That's bullshit. People still need their cat doors, don't they?"

"I don't know." She faltered. *No*, she wanted to say. Not cat doors, which was the type of thing her father seemed to be doing—when he did get called—after the condos went belly-up and before the more general meltdown. His work had dried up even before Wall Street went south; after the crash, the burst bubble, the global financial crisis, she heard him say he should have seen it all coming, it was like the rumbles that happen in the farthest underground, before the earthquake hits.

Then she remembered where she'd seen this man since the day of the barbecue. "But you have that job at the shack, right?"

"Jesus, that shithole." Then he began muttering, another thing she remembered from when he was at her house. "Why does this kind of thing always happen to me? All I'm trying to do is make some money to get the hell out of here. Head south, whatever. But then you show up—it had to be you, right? Of course it did—and give me another goddam problem to deal with." He moved closer and she stepped back, reaching behind her for the doorknob. "What do *you* need to be doing this for? You got enough money for those fancy boots." He gestured down at her feet.

"They're fakes," she said, the muscles in her legs growing mossy beneath her. "Really. They're not waterproof, they leak. My feet are so cold they're numb." She yanked at the knob and it came off in her hand.

The man—whose name she remembered now, irrelevantly, was Cliff Ott (not Pete, that was only his nickname)—began to laugh, so hard he had to bend over. "Oh, that's beautiful," he said. "Perfect! Nice job, Gil. Way to be a craftsman." *Craftsman*—it was a word she'd heard her father use over and over to describe the people he most admired and what he aspired to be. From the time she was little and showed him her first drawings, he talked about her craft, and it made her feel she was doing something important, even as she struggled to understand what he meant.

She knew she should fling open the door and run, but her legs had turned from moss to water. *I have got to figure a way out of this,* she thought. Until now she'd imagined that all of it could be undone or at least recovered, maybe even redeemed. Yet the statement *If you have gone too far, then you cannot go back again* had to be true.

Somehow, the busted knob—its failure to perform the function it was designed for—appeared to energize him, and he moved behind her to lean against the door. Blocking the only exit, she realized, unless she were to run into the bedroom, throw open a window, and scramble out, assuming he didn't follow and catch her. It would not be smart, she understood, to attempt such a thing, and anyway, she did not trust her body to do as she commanded.

"You're not going to hurt me or anything, right?" How much she would have given for him to reassure her of this.

"Why would I hurt you?" But it wasn't an answer to her question.

"Because I can leave right now and not say a word to anybody." Her voice trembled, but that could work in her favor, she thought. Nothing wrong with letting him know she was scared, that she understood he had power over her. "I'm already in trouble, there's no reason for me to let them know I was trespassing here."

He sucked so hard on his cigarette that her own lungs hurt, watching. "So you remember me coming to your house?"

"Of course." *Duh*, she might have said in a different circumstance. *How else would I know who you are?* Instead she said, "Why wouldn't I?" wondering how he would respond if she tried to flatter him.

"Well, you spent all your time with that black guy. I figured you must be doing him, all that whispering in the hall. Then you brought him into your bedroom."

Doing him. It took her a few stunned moments to understand what he meant. Then, without planning to, she gave a bitter bleat. "*I* wasn't doing him." Could it possibly be worth appealing to his sympathy? "My mother was."

She was ashamed to feel gratified by the interested flash she saw in his face as he took this in. Regretting her revelation, wanting to move his attention away from it, she added, "He's an artist; we were talking about art. He's working on this big piece, people on a plane right before it goes down. His father died that way. He does this kind of art called hyperreal, trying to show everything realer than it actually is."

Hearing this rush of words come out of her mouth, she thought of the story Mrs. Carbone had taught them about the queen telling tales to the king who intended to kill her, managing to keep him so interested in hearing the next one that he continued to spare her. Talking to keep herself alive.

Babbling, Delaney would have called it. *You're babbling, dude.*

Cliff said, "That's bullshit. 'Realer than it actually is.' Art, fart," he added, making himself laugh. Momentarily distracted by the sight of his rotted teeth, she failed to notice that he'd been gradually pushing her without touching her, directing her with his own movement away from the door and toward the center of the room.

"They'd find you, you know. If something happened to me." *Something has already happened to me.* "They'd figure out I was coming to meet you."

"No, they wouldn't." When he exhaled with impatient certainty, she told herself not to turn her head at the smell of his breath. "The kid at the nursing home, your partner there, doesn't know who I am. And the phone I used to call him is at the bottom of that pond." He gestured out the window, toward the woods and the safety she now craved on the other side. "Everybody thinks I'm so stupid, but they're the ones who haven't figured it out yet, right?" His voice held a tinge of triumph.

"Here," she said, reaching into her jacket and pulling out the blank pad Delaney had given her. "Just make sure you take it across the state line, to Vermont or something, so you don't set off the flag at the pharmacies around here." Though she knew it was a desperate wish, she thought wildly that maybe if she just gave him what he wanted, along with advice that could be useful, he would let her go out of appreciation.

He took it from her, squinted, and recited "Geoffrey Stowell, M.D." "Where'd you get it?"

"This friend of mine. Her father's a shrink."

"So, what, you and the nursing home guy split it with her?"

"No. She owes me." She remembered the Facebook message Delaney sent her when she got her SAT scores: *Almost 2 good, dude. My mother sez they musta sent the wrong ones—jeez tks Mom!* "Well, she doesn't really owe me," Joy amended. If she confessed to being a criminal herself, would he feel a kinship between them? "She paid me for it. But then I kind of blackmailed her."

Blackmail was not how she had thought of it, of course; she just considered it a bonus, on top of what she charged Delaney originally for a job well done. But "blackmail" was the word the police chief had used, when Joy worked up the courage to tell him that she knew what he'd done to cover up Mrs. Carbone's arrest. "Bullshit," Mr. Armstrong had said, after demanding to know how she'd found his private cell number. (She refused to say she'd gotten it from Delaney, who'd taken it off her father's phone when he wasn't looking.) "I already had your charges dropped—that's all you're getting." When she remained quiet at the other end of the line, he swore again and asked what she wanted. She faltered; was she really doing this? Blackmailing a police officer? She sputtered out *ten thousand* and he complied within an hour, but not before calling her a little twat.

How she wished she had her phone now. Her fingers twitched at the thought of it.

Keeping his eyes on the scorched wall behind her, Cliff showed his teeth again, though the sound he made was something other than amusement. "Gil Enright's kid blackmailing somebody. Guy won't pay anyone under the table, even for just moving a fucking fridge. What'd he do when he found out?"

She shook her head and shivered at the image. "He doesn't know." Then, as if it mattered to the man who stood in front of her, barring her escape, she said, "I'm not really the kind of person who does those kinds of things."

Now he did laugh. "Yes, you are. You just told me you did them. That *makes* you that kind of person." He lit a new cigarette, crushing the spent one into the carpet under his boot. "If you aren't 'that kind of person,' then who is?"

"Okay." What was he, some kind of a philosopher all of a sudden? If she weren't so terrified, she would have scoffed. "You're right."

She had said it only to appease him, but a second later she realized it was true. Hadn't she been the kind of person to do this kind of thing as far back as second grade, when she only pretended to call her mother from the mall that day to ask if it would be okay to adopt a cat?

No, she told herself. *That's not fair. I was only a little kid who wanted a kitten.* It was another thing she would confess to her parents tonight.

But Cliff appeared not to be listening. "There were a whole lot of things I always said I'd never be, either. Now I'm pretty much all of them."

Watching him as he spoke, she saw suddenly how she would draw his face if she ever got out of this. A mere sketch of the features themselves, with some shadowed nuance to the rheumy eyes and perpetual scowl. Her pictures were not the kind that would ever help the police catch anyone. That was for realists, like Martin. Hers were portraits of what *she* felt when she looked at someone, or at a scene. If she were to draw Cliff Ott, it would be an attempt to capture her own fear as she stood before him— along with (she realized) his.

She was in a hole she had dug herself, she understood then, remembering what Mrs. Carbone had taught them about the value of literature. *When people get themselves into a hole, other people like to watch them try to get out.*

"I just want to go home," she said, knowing it wouldn't do any good but unable to hold back the wish. *Home*—how fully it hurt saying the word out loud now, as if someone were pulling a jagged rag up her throat and out. In the past few months, she'd thought of *home* as the place her mother had poisoned. She could barely bring herself to remember the suspicion she confirmed, by reading her mother's texts back in September, that she was having sex with her teaching assistant. Joy's disillusionment in Martin had been profound—she'd felt so inspired talking to him about art—but it was nothing compared to the anger she felt toward her mother.

But now it occurred to her, as it had not before, that she herself had been a source of the poison, too. Resolve surged within her: starting tonight, they would reclaim their life as a family. The three of them: Team Us.

Now Cliff looked directly at her, and everything inside her dropped and turned sour. He focused on her face as if it were the first one he'd seen since emerging from a cave he'd been trapped in for years, and she tried but failed to avoid understanding what this might mean. "If you go around blackmailing people," he said, "that means you have money somewhere, right?"

But maybe, instead, this was another chance. Feeling the words rise and spout like a hose gushing, she said, "Yes! I do have money. If you let me go, I'll bring it to you. Sixty thousand, give or take, in cash." Exaggerating the amount so he'd jump at it.

"Where?"

"In my bedroom. Hidden behind my drawings, inside the frames." As soon as the words were out and she read his expression, she understood her mistake. Gasped on the enormity of it. Here she was supposed to be so smart, and she'd just said the stupidest possible thing.

She thought, *I'm not going to see my mother again.*

At the nursing home the cat had jumped into her lap, and instinctively, exclaiming, she shot up to dump him out. But it was too late; she'd already been marked. "I guess that means you're next," her father said, trying to make her laugh.

Cliff stepped closer and whispered, "It would've been better for both of us if you hadn't recognized me. When I asked if you knew who I was. It would've been better if you just lied and said no."

The jagged rag started to strangle her from within. Choking, she cried out, "I won't tell anybody. Nobody has to know," and without planning it, she reached up to touch his face. He yelped as if a snake had bitten him, then lunged to grab at the scarf around her neck. She backed up, but she'd run out of room.

"I *told* you I'm not going to hurt you," he whispered, and in the last moment because it was what they both needed, she let herself believe him.

After—The Last

June 9, 2014

Martin Willett's new installation *Souls on Board* at the Mirage Gallery is a breathtaking visual and visceral experience, but not for the faint of heart. Measuring 144 square feet and occupying an entire wall, the mural depicts passengers on an airliner moments before a lightning strike plunges them all to their deaths.

The piece launches Willett—who made his debut at Mirage in 2010 with the deservedly lauded *American Commonplace* series, and who received a substantial Cusk Foundation grant for emerging artists the following year—firmly into the ranks of the most intriguing high realists working in the country today.

Willett derived his inspiration for *Souls on Board* from the 1997 airliner crash that killed his father and 148 others. "Originally, I conceived of the piece as a grid of panels, each one a self-contained portrait," he says. "But then I realized that these aren't separate stories—they're separate experiences of the *same* story."

It is a considerable challenge to describe what Willett manages to convey. The grim nature of the mural's subject matter is offset in part by his choice of vibrant color, which emphasizes aspects of the passengers' faces even more than the impasto technique he employs with judiciousness and nerve. Only stepping back, considering, does the viewer realize that these colors are far brighter than in "real life."

In the context of the passengers' plight (which we know but they do not, yet), the hyperintensity feels perfectly apt, and true. Approaching the mural, we realize that all we may have taken for granted at first glance bears a closer look, revealing crucial details we didn't originally notice.

A teenage boy wears earbuds and an expression no doubt aiming at nonchalance, but we can tell that in fact he feels moved by whatever he's hearing through that private sound system; his lips, parted in a tremble, give him away. A woman in a severely cut business suit has slipped her socks and shoes under the seat in front of her and seems almost giddy at the sensation of flexing her naughtily naked feet.

The most prominent and compelling portrait is that of the man in a window seat who appears to be reading, but who is in fact holding the book upside-down, his attention obviously elsewhere. The subject of this portrait is Willett's father, James. Though Willett says he has an idea of what may have been distracting his father (who died when the artist was twelve), he declines to discuss it.

The racial distribution among the passengers in the piece reflects that of the actual flight manifest: mostly white, along with a few subjects of African-American, Hispanic or Latino, and Asian ethnicity. Though Willett prefers to avoid addressing the social politics of race in his art, he is no stranger to it in his own life. As a student at

Genesee Valley Academy of Fine Arts in upstate New York five years ago, he was arrested in the murder case of Joy Enright, the teenage daughter of one of Willett's teachers. Originally believed drowned, the girl was later discovered strangled. The charges against Willett were dropped when police focused on another suspect. But in the aftermath of his release, the Rochester home he had inherited from his grandmother, and in which he was raised, burned to the ground in what police believe was arson with racial motivations.

Willett does not speak publicly about that time, except to say that he was friends with Joy Enright, who was a budding artist herself, and that she was instrumental in his conception of *Souls on Board*. With a portion of the Cusk award, he and his wife, abstract painter Samantha Rouen, have established an after-school art program in Joy's name at an elementary school in their Brooklyn neighborhood.

Chuck Close, one of Willett's artistic progenitors, describes his own process of painting large portraits as "incrementing"—he begins with the tiniest details, then adds tone and texture to create ever-larger fragments that eventually cohere in the finished piece. Each painting contains so many minuscule bits of information that if you move too close to the canvas, you can't take it all in.

Willett has borrowed and built on this concept to create his own. Do yourself a favor and catch the exhibit while you can; approach it from different angles, adjust your distance, and allow yourself to linger. We're all souls on board this flight, the artist reminds us. Nothing is too small to matter, and even when we think we have the whole picture, there is still more to see.

Acknowledgments

I'm grateful to my family and friends for their continued and sustaining support of my work, and to Emerson College for the generous leave to write this book. My deep appreciation for their specific contributions and counsel goes to Ondine Bréaud-Holland, Michael Dondiego, Katie Gergel, Molly Treadway Johnson, Elizabeth Kulhanek, Laurie Levenson, Megan Marshall, Yasmin Mathew, Maria Rosa Monsayac, Denise Neary, Lori Ostlund, Lauren Richman, Robert Sabal, Adam Schwartz, Ann Treadway, Michaele Whelan, Monika Woods, Maxine Yalovitz-Blankenship, the Peabody Essex Museum, and Sergeant Blake Gilmore of the Massachusetts State Police.

I know how extremely fortunate I am to have Kimberly Witherspoon as my agent and Deb Futter as my editor. I hope they know that I know.

Always and ever, for all and everything, thanks and love to my husband, Philip Holland, my Beau of Amherst, who reads me better than anyone.

About the Author

Jessica Treadway is the author of *Lacy Eye* and *And Give You Peace*, as well as two story collections, *Absent Without Leave and Other Stories* and *Please Come Back to Me*, which received the Flannery O'Connor Award for Short Fiction. A former reporter for United Press International, she is a professor at Emerson College and lives with her husband outside Boston.